S0-BBB-171

OVERHEAD

Tor books by Jack M. Bickham

Ariel
Day Seven
Miracle Worker
The Regensburg Legacy

Novels in the Brad Smith series

Tiebreaker
Dropshot

OVERHEAD

OVERHEAD

Jack M. Bickham

A Tom Doherty Associates Book
New York

This is a work of fiction. All the characters and events portrayed in this book are fictitious, and any resemblance to real people or events is purely coincidental.

OVERHEAD

A Tor Book
Published by Tom Doherty Associates, Inc.
49 West 24th Street
New York, N.Y. 10010

ISBN: 0-312-85143-X

Library of Congress Cataloging-in-Publication Data

Bickham, Jack M.
Overhead : Jack M. Bickham.
p. cm.
"A Tom Doherty Associates book."
ISBN 0-312-85143-X
I. Title.
PS3552.I3094 1991
813'.54—dc20 91-6578
CIP

Printed in the United States of America

First edition: June 1991

10 9 8 7 6 5 4 3 2 1

OVERHEAD

prologue

Zurich, Switzerland

The small private hospital not far from the Lindenhof on the heights overlooking Old Zurich was shielded from the streets by a high stone wall. Known to a few, and savagely expensive, this long-term rehabilitative facility had no unexpected or unwanted visitors; an electrically operated iron gate, guarded around the clock seven days a week, saw to that.

From his upstairs window, a gaunt, bearded, death-pale patient watched the gate for his first visitor in months. The patient, registered and treated under a fictitious name and fabricated background, had until a few months ago been the KGB's premier agent-assassin at work in the western world. More lately he had almost died.

His code name was Sylvester.

He had not expected this visitor for weeks yet . . . perhaps months.

From his window Sylvester could see a considerable distance between aged yellow-stone buildings beyond the hospital grounds. He could see a narrow band of the Limmat, gleaming today in the thin sunlight, and the towering bulk of the old Grossmunster, where

Zwingli had fought to establish the Reformation here so long ago, and—much farther away, through industrial haze—the new Zurich on the far bank of the river. Sylvester had memorized every facet of his restricted view during the days and nights he had lain in his bed or stood here as now, weighing suicide.

There was a diffident tap on his room door.

"*Entrez,*" Sylvester said.

A white-uniformed male nurse looked in. "Your visitor is here," he said, also in French.

Sylvester nodded acquiescence. The attendant swung the door wide to allow the visitor to enter, then quietly closed the door, leaving the two men alone.

Sylvester's visitor was a man in his fifties, thick-shouldered, of medium height, with a dense mane of grayish hair, a heavy chin, and brilliant dark eyes. He wore a plain dark suit and tie, and had a trenchcoat over his arm. He stared hard.

"Yuri?" he asked uncertainly in English.

"Good morning, Eduard," Sylvester said.

Eduard relaxed markedly and came across the small hospital room to embrace Sylvester. In his gruff gladness, he hugged too vigorously, making daggers of pain lance through Sylvester's chest where so much surgery had been done. Sylvester stiffened slightly and his superior released him immediately, all contrition.

"I am so sorry, Yuri! I forgot your injuries!"

"It is not so bad, Eduard. No harm done."

Eduard held him at arm's length, peering keenly at him in the bright diffused light from the windows. "I would never have recognized you! Only your voice told me your identity! Let me look at you!"

Sylvester stood patiently while his superior looked at him first from one angle, then another.

Finally Eduard was satisfied. His sharp dark eyes, often so angry and cruel, inexplicably filled with sentimental tears. "Ah, Yuri. Yuri! The suffering you have gone through!" He paused, took out a handkerchief to wipe his eyes, and made an obvious effort to get himself back together. "They have done a magnificent job! Your face is totally reconstructed. The old wounds no longer show. And their work . . . let me see closer in this good light . . . yes . . . their work has left only the tiniest hints of sewing. And you have healed beautifully. With that beard no one could ever recognize you. Once you have taken the sun for a few days, you will look a new man entirely!"

"I am still thin," Sylvester told his old comrade. He held out a bare arm on which the flesh hung like wet sheeting.

"And weak?" Eduard asked.

"Still weak. Yes. But I have been exercising as best I can. I am gaining strength rapidly."

"You are eating sufficiently?"

Sylvester allowed himself a thin smile at that. "They complain I eat enough for three men."

"Good. Good."

There was an awkward silence.

Sylvester walked carefully to his bed and sat on the edge. He met his superior's eyes frankly. "Why do you come?"

"An assignment, Yuri—if you are well enough."

"It is important?"

"Of course. Otherwise headquarters would never ask."

Sylvester nodded. A pulse of bitterness welled up in him, but he summoned his professional discipline and squelched it. "I am not the man I was. But each day now I am gaining strength. All surgical work is finished. Tell me the problem."

"You think," his superior asked uncertainly, "it is at all possible?"

Sylvester's nerves were almost as raw as they had been over the last months of agony. His patience snapped. "God damn you, Eduard. Tell me the assignment. You know I will accept if I believe it is at all possible for me."

"Of course, of course," Eduard said with quick apology. He glanced toward the door.

Sylvester rose, walked to the corner table, and turned his radio on to soft music, old-time American-style music from a station that played nothing else. He returned to his supervisor's side. "Speak softly. Now no one can possibly overhear."

Eduard nodded. "You know of the American project in their West which we call Rifle?"

"The research in anti-satellite technology? I know the name, little more."

"Their research in the field is scattered all over the United States. However, Rifle is a small part of the total anti-satellite, anti-ICBM effort. It is in their state of Montana. We have worked for more than three years, infiltrating two agents inside the Air Force laboratory. Now, however, one of them has been found out."

"One of our people? Found out?"

"Taken into custody, Sylvester. Being interrogated at this very hour at an old military fort in the city of Missoula."

Sylvester digested this incredibly bad news. "And?"

Eduard's eyebrows knit with worry. "If their FBI can make our agent talk, our years of effort at the site will be ruined. We will in all likelihood lose our other agent either through another arrest or by being forced to pull him out.

"Sylvester, penetrating that laboratory is of *crucial* importance to our national interest. We were very close to getting out the electronic diagrams at the heart of their research. The new friendship between our countries be damned, this is one area where we have to keep up with them, and our efforts must not be exposed. Our agent *must not* talk. Some one must go there and see to it."

Sylvester thought about it. He knew his superior had no concept of how thin his physical reserves still were. Taking the assignment represented the potential for a killing expenditure of energy—energy that Sylvester was not quite sure he had.

"There is no one else?" he asked softly.

"No one of your skills and background, my friend."

Sylvester took a breath. It made new pains in his chest. "Then," he said, "I accept the assignment."

Eduard heaved a breath of relief mixed with admiration. "You are certain?"

"Of course!"

"You can . . . plan to depart and begin this work . . . when?"

"If you can assist me in cutting through the formalities here at the hospital, today."

Missoula, Montana

Four days later, Sylvester—with another entirely new identity—walked off a Northwest flight out of Minneapolis. Brutally tired, he endured the wait for his luggage, then went through the handsome little airport and found a car rental desk. Within three hours he had met his contact at a downtown motel and had both the necessary information and the keys to a muddy, battered-looking brown Dodge pickup truck with Montana "Big Sky Country" plates, title papers that could never be traced to anyone, and an engine and drive train better than any stock truck that had ever come out of the factory.

Sylvester hurt: his chest, his back, the places in his side where bone had been removed to save his lung, his face and neck where plastic surgeons had cut and mended and cut and rearranged and cut and built him a new face out of the gargoyle wreckage of the old. More than three thousand tiny stitches. In his fatigue, Sylvester could feel every one of them.

No matter.

About forty hours later, late at night, a telephone repair truck pulled up in front of one of the many Twenties-style brick buildings on the grounds of old Fort Missoula. Long closed as a military base, the old frontier bastion now had a few historic sites remaining, but functioned mainly as housing for state, local, and minor federal offices. The building where the telephone truck pulled up had a wood sign in front saying it housed "Special VA Research."

Wearing the coveralls of a telephone workman and carrying a small toolbox, Sylvester limped up the front walk and entered the building. Bright lights shone on old beige plaster walls and gleaming military-green asphalt tile. An army sergeant, discreetly armed, sat behind a reception desk that blocked the front foyer.

The sergeant looked up from his magazine as Sylvester entered. "May I help you, sir?"

"I have a work order for the second floor system," Sylvester told him.

The sergeant frowned and consulted a clipboard. "I have no record of that."

Sylvester put his toolbox on the corner of the desk. "I'll show you the work order."

"Well, sir, it really won't matter, because if I don't have any authorization—"

The sergeant stopped talking right there because Sylvester had opened the toolbox and removed a dark blue Makarov pistol with a stubby silencer screwed on the muzzle. Sylvester leveled the pistol and squeezed the trigger. The weapon made a sharp putting sound and the sergeant's skull exploded.

Pocketing the Makarov, Sylvester pulled his other weapon from the case: a Heckler and Koch MP-5. Slamming the magazine into place and working the action to load the first round, he ran for the stairway.

Danger gave him more strength that he had felt in months. He reached the upstairs door in moments. He threw it open and went through, trusting the floor plan given him by his Missoula contact.

To the lett, an empty corridor that looked like a military hospital, lights dimmed, doors to rooms closed. To the right, another desk—another guard station—two army enlisted men standing beside it. They had perhaps one second to react to Sylvester's presence. In that second he hosed them, ten or twelve rounds, blowing them back against the wall in a crashing of chairs and splatter of blood against the white paint of the partition behind them.

Running to his left, Sylvester saw a door on his target room slam open. An athletic-looking man in a business suit ran out, pulling an automatic from a shoulder holster. Sylvester fired from the hip as he ran. The man looked startled as the holes punched in the middle of his chest. He skidded sideways and sprawled dead.

Sylvester stepped over him and entered the target room.

A small security light glowed in one corner. There was a bed. The woman in the bed sat up, wide-eyed with terror, clutching the sheet to her throat. She said something, but the racket of the MP-5 had turned off Sylvester's ears.

"I have come for you," he told her in Russian.

Her face changed. Intense relief and happiness suffused her features. She swung bare legs out of the bed to get down. Sylvester noticed they were pretty legs. She had a pretty face, too.

Sylvester leveled his weapon and squeezed off another burst, and then the girl in the bed was left with no face at all.

one

It was spring in the Dallas area, a beautiful time of year, and I was sort of enjoying it until the night of the tornado.

I knew the weather was unsettled and potentially dangerous, but I wasn't paying attention. People told me later that local TV weathermen were hysterical, broadcasting warnings on all the channels. Unfortunately, I didn't have my set on. I was reading a magazine with part of my mind and using the rest to stew over the lady in my life, Beth Miles, in faraway California. Then I heard the siren.

At first I thought it was a fire truck or police. Then it began to dawn on me that police and fire sirens didn't rise and fall like that.

I put my magazine down on the arm of the easy chair, looked around the living room of my Richardson condo, and cocked my head, trying to place the sound. That was when the first gust of wind hit, and lightning flashed crimson-close outside my window.

The instantaneous thunderclap might have knocked me out of my chair if I hadn't already been moving. Hearing the wind now, I hurried into the kitchen, and out through the back door, into my tiny backyard. The yard was walled on one side by the house, on another by the attached garage, and on the other two by eight-foot stockade fence. Ordinarily it was nicely protected from the wind, but a gust knocked over my trash cans as I went down the steps.

There was all kind of stuff blowing in the air. I could smell dirt and rain and ozone, and my skin prickled. Overhead, continuous veined lightning pulsed and flickered an evil greenish white. The siren was louder out here, and I finally figured out it was the tornado warning siren for the complex.

I took about two steps toward my garage door. The wind suddenly increased by a factor of a thousand, and the garage roof started flapping at one corner like it was made out of rubber, and then part of it blew into the blackness and my stockade fence started to come apart and the howl overhead became a throaty, railroad roar, and my dimwit brain finally realized, *This could get serious.*

I turned back toward the house. The wind became unbelievable, with a ferocity I could not have imagined. It knocked me against the wall of the disintegrating garage and hit me with a piece of a tree and started burying me under uprooted sections of the fence.

The fence, as it turned out, probably saved my life. But when I regained consciousness a little later, with torrential rain half-drowning me, I didn't feel thankful. What I felt was shell-shocked. Spitting dirt and plaster-dust, I threw broken fence and roofing off of me.

The world I crawled out to was pretty radically altered, and not for the better. My garage had been half-flattened. Two-by-six wall studs stuck up like broken trees after a forest fire. I turned toward the main part of my house, squinting through the driving rain, but instead of seeing the back wall I saw the front streetlight.

The mind boggles at such times. *What did they do with my house?*

A series of lightning flashes showed me rubble, half a standing wall, and part of the collapsed roof where the floor was supposed to be.

That was when I heard a woman screaming somewhere nearby. I was bleeding from the head, but the rain kept it washed out of my eyes, and I felt okay if you ignore almost total confusion. I staggered across rubble into an adjacent yard, looking to help.

Most of that condo unit was gone, too. I didn't see anyone. I looked across the alley toward the apartments on the other side. Orange flames thirty feet high roared behind a swirling maelstrom of smoke, steam, and wind-driven rain. *The lightning that had jarred me: it had hit here.*

OVERHEAD

A little dazed, I crossed the alley, splashing through ankle-deep water. The rain was still coming down in sheets, and it felt like somebody had dumped an icemaker. There was smoke mixed in. Through the mix I made out hazy figures back-lit by the orange and crimson glow of the fire. I struggled closer and made them out: a rotund older man and a couple of women and a child, a little girl of maybe four, in her nightgown. One of the women was screaming, and the man was holding her back.

She spied me, ran to me, clawed at my chest. "My husband, my husband! He's in there!"

I looked from her to the burning apartment. Long red tongues of flame gushed from the upstairs windows. The smoke and rain were too dense to allow a good view of the lower floor. The heat reached out through the rain, sharp against my face. I wondered despairingly where the firemen were.

"Do something!" the woman cried. "*Please!* In the living room!"

The fat man tried to pull her away from me. In her hysteria, her face resembled one of those demons engraved forever on gothic cathedrals. The flames changed, going redder, making everything crazier.

"Please! Please! He's dying!"

Damn, I thought.

"You can't go in there!" the fat man yelled after me.

I ran to the back door. It was closed. I hauled it open. A lick of flames came out like there was a maniac with a flame thrower on the other side. It staggered me back, scared badly. But then the flame puffed out and only dense smoke rolled. Putting my arm over my face, as if that would do me any good, I went in.

Couldn't see a thing. Smoke like needles in the eyes, rasping in my lungs. *I can't do much of this.* Massive roaring all around, the fire going wild. The hair on my head and arms began to singe. The hot, smoky air hurt going down. I staggered forward and bumped into something. The refrigerator. So I was in the kitchen. I felt along and found another doorway. I went through.

The living room: some bookshelves, a couch, a couple of overstuffed chairs, carpet on the floor burning here and there like a summer grass fire. On the far side, a sheet of flames, and from overhead, chunks of burning stuff coming down out of the ceiling. My clothes were going to catch fire and/or I was going to start blistering any second. I didn't have all night. *Where was he?*

I found him by falling over him. I sprawled headlong into a puddle of fire eating at the carpet. Ah, the graceful world-class athlete at work. I jumped up, beating the fire off my clothes.

The man unconscious on the floor was as big as the fat man outside. He lay face-up. He looked a little like Lou Costello. I did not have to remind myself that this was not funny.

I grabbed him by the shoulders and hefted, and it was just like trying to lift a floor you're standing on. All I managed to do was rip his T-shirt.

What I might have done next if I hadn't gotten more scared is anybody's guess. Luckily for me, the living room ceiling started coming down—not just little piddling chunks, but great gobs of flaming sheetrock and insulation and some of the furniture from the upstairs bedroom and everything else. I saw it start as if in slow motion, and somehow—call it the panicked strength of a coward—I picked old Lou off the floor and got him into a staggery fireman's carry and was just bolting out through the back door of the kitchen, with hell on my heels, when the first firemen came charging up onto the little porch and caught the both of us just about the time I was starting another graceful face-first plow-in.

Two of the guys in glistening rain slickers grabbed Lou and hustled him into the backyard. The other one supported me under my left arm.

"You okay, bub?" he demanded. "You shouldn't of gone in there!"

"Tell me about it," I rasped.

"*Louis!*" the woman screamed through the rain. "*Oh, thank God!*"

Or Lou for short, I thought. "I'll be damned," I said, and lost control of my legs and sat down in the mud.

The tornado that went through the north Dallas area that night killed five. Why it didn't kill five hundred, I'll never know. My own injuries were negligible: some scratches and bruises, a small knot on the head. I was missing most of my eyebrows and the hairs on the back of my hands, and my lungs felt like somebody had scrubbed them out with a wire brush. But I was lucky. Not everyone is stupid enough to run out into the open under a funnel, and then into a burning house, and live to tell about it.

OVERHEAD

It was about four in the morning when I got out of the emergency room and remembered to call my special lady in California and tell her I was alive.

"My God, where have you *been*?" Beth demanded, her voice shrill with uncharacteristic panic. "The news here said your area of Dallas was *wrecked*, and hundreds of people hurt, some dead, and when I tried to call your apartment I kept getting an out-of-service recording—"

"No problem," I told her. "My place is wrecked but I'm okay."

"Why didn't you *call* me?"

I explained.

"I've been worried sick!"

"Hey, listen, I've got a solution. Come live with me, and you'll know where I am all the time, almost."

"Oh, you bastard," she said, but it was relief talking, not anger, and then, level-headed lady that she is, she wept.

As far as possessions go, I was left with most of my clothes, soaked; most of my old tennis trophies, many of them bent and scratched; a few cartons of soggy pictures and mementos, and the stuff that had been in the back of my now-squashed Bronco inside the garage.

The Bronco went into the body shop and most of the other salvageable stuff into a new, smaller apartment a mile or so away and a little closer to the tennis club where I worked as assistant pro. I told myself I had been meaning to simplify my life anyway.

It didn't entirely work. I was feeling a little sorry for myself a couple of weeks later when I got the telephone call, person-to-person for Mr. Brad Smith.

"Brad?" the familiar male voice said. "How did you enjoy your tornado? This is Collie."

The moment I heard his voice, the unwelcome chill started at the back of my neck and spread down my body. The unreasoning fear that plagued—and shamed—me despite my best efforts to shuck it.

"What is it?" I asked sharply.

Collie paused a beat. Then: "It isn't about Sylvester." His voice sounded a little flat with disappointment. Or disapproval.

"I didn't think it was," I lied.

"Right. Something else entirely."

"The last couple of times I heard from you, Collie, I ended up in jobs that turned out a lot more exciting than that tornado was."

"Would I call only to ask you to do a job?" Collie asked piously. "Would I contact you only when I needed you?"

"Yes."

"Well, listen, man, how are you? I just heard you almost got blown away down there!"

"It was a thrill a minute, Collie. Everything is fine now."

"Good. Great. In a new place, are you?"

"Yes."

"And all settled in?"

"Fairly so."

"A man needs some rest and relaxation after undergoing such a harrowing experience."

Collie was the only person I knew who said things like that: "undergoing" a "harrowing experience" indeed. Trouble was, the more formal Collie's diction became, the more likely it was that he had something devious on his mind.

I said, "What's on your mind, Collie?"

"Have you heard lately from Ted Treacher?"

Ted was a tennis pro like me, roughly the same age, starting what sometimes seemed like a downhill slide from having the world on a string to having a wheelchair in your living room. In Belgrade not so long ago he risked his life to help me get someone out of Yugoslavia when the secret police—the UDBA—would have killed to prevent it. I owed Ted one. More than one. But I hadn't seen him in over a year.

I told Collie, "I had a long letter and a phone call from him when Danisa was killed. I haven't heard from him since that time."

"Okay, Brad, fine. I've got an idea you'll be hearing from him soon. When you do, I hope you'll be able to help him with a little problem."

"What kind of a problem?"

"He can tell you about that."

"Something you're also interested in?"

"Put it this way, Brad. He was a big help to us in Yugoslavia; now he has this problem and we would just like to see that he gets good help—sort of a payback."

"Collie, why don't you help him yourself?"

"Hell, *I* can't do that. You know the kinds of restrictions we work under inside the United States. Besides. It isn't even our kind of problem."

"What kind of problem *is* it, Collie? If you don't mind my being repetitious."

"Ted will tell you all about it. He just needs a little help with a business deal, and when I heard about it, I told myself, 'Hey. Brad Smith owes him, too. I'll just give old Brad a call and make sure he's receptive, if I can.'"

"Collie, you are the soul of human kindness."

"Hey, I'm just touching base, making sure you're okay, letting you know old Ted may need a hand."

"That's all?"

"Absolutely. No problem. I guarantee it."

I didn't believe that for a minute. The last time Collie Davis had guaranteed something to me, I had almost been killed. I certainly don't want to imply I'm a hero, because the only real heroes I've ever known are still in Vietnam, or crippled. But I scare easy, and Collie had gotten me scared more than once, and when he said something was no problem, "guaranteed," you could be reasonably sure you were being set up again.

Quite a while ago, when I was in the computer as one of the top ten professional tennis players in the world, a man much like Collie Davis contacted me and asked me if I would do a small favor for my country. He knew a lot about me, from high school through college and Vietnam right up to the present. I never did learn much about him. Somebody had done a lot of checking on me, however, and had evidently decided I was trustworthy.

I accepted the assignment, and was sort of let down when all it involved was carrying an envelope across town and handing it to somebody in the Wimbledon locker room when no one else was looking. After that, from time to time, my first case officer or one of his replacements contacted me somewhere along the professional tennis tour and gave me some other seemingly innocent task to do. I did them. It was no big deal.

It was a long time later, when my knee took me out of competitive tennis for many months, that they got around to formalizing the deal and even sending me to that place in Virginia for some elementary training.

Later, after my knee blew out again and my reflexes frazzled, I left competitive tennis. With my cover gone, I assumed I would hear no more from the Company. I was mistaken. Some years passed, and then Collie Davis—with whom I had worked on some earlier deals—made contact. He outlined this plan whereby I would go to Yugoslavia and help a star female tennis player named Danisa Lechova defect. I did that. Then on another occasion there was a job somewhere else where my rapidly tarnishing tennis reputation and part-time work as a freelance tennis magazine journalist gave me entrée into something spooky. I had thought *that* was the last time, too.

I thought every time was the last. But when Collie called, you knew better.

I thought about his latest call the rest of the night and much of the next day. Slowly it dawned on me that I was not as irritated this time as I had been the last. I was getting thoroughly burned out with the little job at the club. Losing most of my stuff in the tornado and having to move had stirred me up, left me feeling uneasy, restless, dissatisfied. As much as I loved Beth, and as determined as I was to let our relationship work out as best it could without pressure from me, I felt uneasy about that, too. And maybe a little sad. We seemed to be getting nowhere. A new challenge might be just what the doctor ordered.

Also, I was fascinated as always when Collie contacted me. I am cursed with this archaic sense that my country has given me a lot, and I owe it. When they call me and say I can help with something, I feel like it's my duty, even when I don't much feel like making the effort. They have many better people. But if my particular background and reputation occasionally might come in handy, should I say no? Shouldn't I be flattered, and glad I can make a little payback somehow?

Of course there was no guarantee in this case that Ted Treacher would even contact me, right? Collie might be mistaken, right?

Wrong. Four days later, Ted strolled into the club pro shop.

I was struck at once by how he had changed in the two years since he had helped me get Danisa Lechova out of Belgrade. He had always been tall and thin. Now he looked taller because he was so gaunt. Wearing the kind of African safari canvas jacket and hat he had always favored, with high-cut turned leather shoes and faded, many-pocketed khaki pants, he looked like an aging white hunter. But even the cigarette holder sticking out of his wide mouth at a jaunty angle did not make him look happy, or even devil-may-care. His cheeks were sunken, his skin sallow under the usual leathery tan. His eyes had seen ghosts.

"Ted," I said, offering my hand.

"Brad, my friend," he replied, the old slow smile creasing his long, sun-battered face. "How in the world are you?"

"Better question: how are you?"

His eyebrows went up frantically. "Fine, of course. Why do you ask?"

"Mainly because you look like hell."

"Thank you, sir. I heard you almost died in a tornado recently?"

"Yes," I said. "It was very dramatic."

His eyes twinkled. "And I hear also you performed some heroics?"

"Oh, yes. They may erect a monument to me at the site."

"Nothing embarrassing, I trust?"

"I've told them a modest statue and a small amphitheater should do it."

He looked a little better, smiling like this. He removed his cigarette holder, ejected the tiny butt into a sand container beside the counter, and pocketed the holder. I noticed that this man, who until recently had been a world-class athlete, had a bad case of the shakes.

"How," he asked, "would you like a paid vacation in the mountains?"

Ah, so. But before I could reply, the pro shop door opened and two of our more affluent members came in with that look in the eye that said *Buy a new racket!*

"Dinner tonight?" I asked Ted.

"Excellent," he said. "I know just the place. Modest French cuisine, very expensive. You can buy."

Because it was a weeknight, and the restaurant off the beaten path, we had the place almost to ourselves. Ted Treacher had changed clothes—bulky linen suit and broad-necked white shirt open at the collar—and his gray hair shone, still wet from the shower. His shakes were, if anything, worse.

We ordered drinks.

The way Ted plunged into the conversation showed how intensely he was preoccupied with the subject. "I've made the investment of my life," he told me. "Eighty acres, with exclusive use and control of an adjacent golf course and an option to buy another sixty acres beyond that. I'm calling it Bitterroot Valley. I know there's really a Bitterroot Valley upstate a ways and it's not quite in the Bitterroots but it's close enough, you can see them, and there are other mountains on all sides. And it's a good name, right?"

"Where are we talking about?" I asked. Geography has never been my strong suit. "Wyoming?"

He shook his head. "Montana. Close to the Idaho line. Beautiful country. Just beautiful. It's close enough to draw some motor traffic from Yellowstone and Jackson Hole. People will fly into Missoula, too, and come down on buses we'll operate. Elk City—that's the name of the little town nearby—has an airstrip that I hope one day to pave and lengthen to six thousand feet for the small corporate jets. Once we get big enough, somebody will put two-a-day commuter-type flights in there, I know they will. Brad, this is one hell of a gamble for me, and I'm not saying it isn't touch and go. Especially with the local opposition, it's decidedly touch and go. But it's going to go. I'm going to *make* it go. Hell. I've got to. I've got everything sunk in it now. The timetable—"

"Ted," I cut in, "I am not clear what the hell it is you're talking about."

"Oh." He flushed and fumbled with the cigarette holder. "Sorry. I'm getting ahead of myself."

So then he told me, and I interrupted often enough with questions to keep him on a track I could more or less follow.

Like most of us who had had our best years in tennis before corporate sponsors and television made instant millionaires of practically everybody, Ted Treacher had had to invest his winnings carefully, and make them grow. Unlike me, he had made wise investments. Now he was finally ready to call it quits on the tour—even the celebrity and corporate playing circuit—and settle down. What he had done was pull all his money out of everything, stand on his considerable tiptoes to stretch, and buy a failing, partly developed resort.

An earlier owner had built a lodge, a handful of cabins, some condominium-style living units to be sold, a swimming pool, a dozen tennis courts, a parking lot and a new pro shop for the existing golf course. Then he had run out of money and been forced to sell out. Ted had gotten in with the high bid. Now he was the proud owner of all of it—plus a multitude of problems and a debt burden that would bury him, too, unless he could get things going as a paying proposition within a year or two.

"This thing is enormous, Brad. The golf course alone can make me a millionaire. Once we make a few minor improvements and start drawing in the traffic, it can support thirty thousand rounds a year, easily. That's over half a million dollars right there, and that doesn't include driving carts, equipment, food, drink, any of the extras. The margin on the living units and the new houses we're going to be building is even bigger. Once the place is established as a tennis *and* golf resort, we can put in another thirty courts, sprinkle a few more back among the condos and private homes, start both tennis and golf schools, and *really* watch the profit roll in. The local opposition will vanish like smoke once they see what a boon this will be to Elk City. That's—"

I cut in again, "What form does the local opposition take?"

"Oh," he said vaguely, "just grumbling, mostly."

Which obviously was a lie, but I let it go. A long time later I would look back at this oversight on my part as Big Mistake No. 1. First in a long series.

We had two drinks and dinner. Ted talked almost non-stop throughout. He was devoured by Bitterroot Valley, obsessed by it, driven. Maybe I should have been happy for him. But when I see someone this consumed by anything, it worries me a little. I loved this guy. The pressure on him was terrific. It showed.

None of which gave me a clue as to why he wanted to see me—or why Collie Davis had shown an interest in the situation.

But that point, too, finally came.

"I need a household name," Ted said at last, watching me warily. "You."

"I'm not exactly in the Boris Becker class anymore, Ted."

"People still know your name. They remember you. And I don't have to have you for long. But I want your name as resident professional for some stationery I'm having printed for promotion letters, and so on."

"Hell, Ted, you want to use my name? Is that all? Go ahead."

His mouth twisted. "Well . . . there's a little something more."

"I thought so. What?"

"I want you up there. Just for a few weeks."

"When?"

"As soon as you can get free here."

"*Why*, for God's sake?"

"It will show the townspeople I'm serious. Solid. Your prestige—I mean, here you would be, right on-site—would help my PR immeasurably."

"That's all?"

"Well . . . no."

"What else, Ted?"

"Number one, I've got a potential major investor coming in. Someone who might buy big into the limited stock offering I'm making. Your presence would help a lot. Impress the investor."

Wary now, I watched him. "And *that's* all."

"Well—no."

"What else, Ted?"

"I'm in the process of setting up a small tournament. Eight or twelve professionals, and some local doubles, something like that. I want you to help me contact some of our old pals and get them to come play in it."

I hardly knew what to protest first. "It's too short notice for touring pros, Ted!"

"Yes, but there's a natural hole in the schedule. Some of them could make it. They would have fun, a vacation. I'm putting up sixty thousand prize money. They would come, some of them, for you. You're universally respected. Revered, even. I—"

"Cut the crap, Ted. When are you thinking about on the tournament?"

"I've set a tentative date the first weekend of next month."

"That's four weeks! You're out of your mind!"

"You could bring it together, Brad."

I changed tack. "Who's the potential major investor I would impress?"

His eyes slid away. "I'm not at liberty to say just yet. I need a few more days."

Why, I wondered, the sudden deviousness? Was the investor someone he had to protect, and if so, why?

Or was there a major investor at all? Was this worried old friend across the table whistling in the dark?

Sanity said to blow him off. But he had saved my life once.

"There are a lot of questions," I said lamely after a long pause.

"Think about it," he urged. "We'll get together again tomorrow and iron it all out. It's beautiful up there, Brad. You'll love it. You'll fall in love with it, just like I did."

"Just one more question right now," I said.

He stopped fiddling with his cigarette holder. "Shoot."

"Where does Collie Davis fit into all this?"

"Who?"

Either Ted was a good actor, or he really had no idea who Collie Davis was. But then I knew he was a good actor. His acting ability had been crucial in getting me out of Belgrade two years ago.

I didn't press it. We left it at that, and shortly afterward split up for the evening, with him promising to be in touch before noon tomorrow. I went home to my new apartment that felt about as cozy as an elevator in an insurance building, double-locked the doors, set the motion detector, put the pistol under my pillow, tried to sleep.

Sleep would not come. I wanted to help Ted Treacher. I owed him one. A big one. He was a worried, driven man and obviously needed all the help he could get. But things kept humming past my consciousness like Texas June bugs, nasty, baleful, persistent.

There were things Ted hadn't been straight with me about. Who was the big investor that a question about made his eyes slide away? He had let slip a comment about "local opposition." What did *that* mean, and how serious was it? And then there was Collie Davis. Why was a dedicated career man in the CIA involved in something like this?

Was I being had again?

I found out the next day.

"Brad, old pal, old chum," Collie Davis said, walking into the club pro shop.

"Oh, hell," I said.

"Ted contacted you, right?"

"Did you put him up to it, Collie?"

"No." He looked like he might be telling the truth for once.

"What do you *want*, then?" I asked.

"There's a man I want you to meet."

We met that night at a restaurant in nearby Plano. Collie's friend was a bulky gent, red-haired, sad-eyed, dogged, with enough freckles to resurrect the old Andy Hardy series. His name was Skurlock and he showed me a card which convinced me he was FBI.

"There's a research facility—air force—not far from where your friend Treacher bought the resort," Skurlock told me over coffee. It was good coffee but he didn't seem to be enjoying it. He was a dour man who probably didn't enjoy much. "No connection between the lab and his buying the resort. Coincidence. But maybe we can use it, if you'll go up there."

"Why should I?" I asked.

"Top stuff going on at the lab. We have reason to believe the Soviets are trying to infiltrate."

"In this day and age? Isn't that all behind us?"

Skurlock's beefy face colored. "It's Star Wars stuff. They still want that. And they *did* get inside. We caught the agent, a woman. Had her up there interrogating her. Thought we might break her. Then one night a man came by the building where we had her. Killed three guards and one of our people. Killed her. Used an automatic weapon of some kind. Got away clean. We found a phony AT&T repair kit—empty—downstairs at the front desk."

Collie said much too casually, "Same MO used by Sylvester a couple of times. Notably four years ago when he took out a Ugandan diplomat to the UN who was about to tell us everything about Russian missile-testing in his country."

I felt a chill. "You think *this* was Sylvester?"

Skurlock let Collie answer. Collie did not flinch. "Yes," he told me simply. "And we theorize he's probably still up there."

"Well, God damn it," I spluttered, "go get him, then!"

"That," Skurlock said, "is where you come in. We hope."

I looked at the two of them. Tweedledee and Tweedledum in

gray suits off a pipe rack. The thought of Sylvester up there someplace started eating a cold hole in my stomach.

I had wanted the bastard for so long. Since he killed Danisa Lechova. Since he almost killed Beth and me on St. Maarten. But my hate was mixed with knowledge that he was a pro and I was an amateur and it was a miracle he had not killed me the last time.

Into the long silence Collie said, "This is the deal, Brad. You go up there and work with Ted Treacher. Help him with his resort. But at the same time you sort of nose around, help us try to locate Sylvester."

"That's bullshit," I said instantly.

"Why?"

"He has to have had plastic surgery after the mess I made of his face on St. Maarten. I couldn't recognize him if he walked in here right now."

"They wouldn't have changed his voice. You've always made a big thing of his distinctive, high-pitched voice."

"You expect me to walk around asking people to *speak to me* so I can sniff him out?"

"Look at it this way," Skurlock said calmly. "From everything we've heard, he wants you. Your arrival up there will be publicized. He'll see that. With any luck, he'll come to you."

"With any *luck*!" I said. "Jesus! What you're asking me to do is go up there and present a moving target!"

"A fast-moving one, we trust," Collie said with his thin, asshole smile.

I told them I would think about it.

I did not want to go.

Maybe he wasn't there anymore. I could always hope that.

Or maybe he was.

Either way, was I going to stay in my scaredy-hole?

I did not like the idea of going up there at all. But Sylvester *knew where I lived*. In a pocket at the back of my mind, for all these months, had been the fear that I would turn a corner and there he would be, when I least expected it. Maybe, I thought, the only way I might ever get rid of the fear was to go face it.

Which line of thinking felt real stupid. But I also knew I would feel ashamed of my cowardice if I declined the assignment.

I tend to think like that, being a simplistic jock with a closetful of weird anachronistic habits like flying the flag on my porch on the Fourth of July and standing up when they play "The Star Spangled Banner."

But—go to Montana to smoke out Sylvester? Why not something easy, like trying to stop a semi-trailer truck by standing in front of it at speed on the LBJ?

I stewed and fretted all night. Told myself I needed a break, new scenery. I had been increasingly antsy at the Richardson club ever since my friend Jack Stephensen left, to be replaced by a guy with a Hitler complex. I was almost as sick of him as I was of myself, sitting around waiting for Sylvester to decide it was time to come around that corner.

So by morning I had made up my mind. I didn't like it, but I had.

Ted Treacher called me again at the club around noon.

"You know, Brad," he began earnestly, "the one thing I failed to mention clearly—and it's significant—is this: you can invest in this thing at any point you wish. You might make a lot of money here."

"Sold," I said.

"What?"

"I'll do it," I told him. "Assuming my boss at the club doesn't object, I can be there in a couple of weeks."

His outrush breath of relief was audible over the line. "Oh, that's great, Brad. I appreciate it. You'll never regret it, I promise you."

"When are you heading back?"

"In a day or two. There are some people I still need to see in this area . . . drumming up enthusiasm for our condominiums up there, you know."

"I'll talk to my pro and call you later today to confirm."

And I hope you'll be pleased, Collie, I thought. *You're going to owe me one. If I live long enough to collect.*

two

Doug Twyle, our new head pro at the club in Richardson, was not pleased.

"Spring," he said dourly, "is the time when we get the busiest."

"It's still early," I countered. "And I'll only be gone a couple of weeks. I'll be back in time for the real heavy inflow."

Doug, never a man anyone would accuse of being the life of the party, rubbed a bushy black eyebrow. The nervous affectation usually showed when he was the most irritated. "You insist?" he asked finally.

I insisted, mildly but firmly. In my mind I was already on the way to Montana—and Sylvester. I didn't need Doug Twyle's nonsense. But I held my temper.

Doug thought about it, transferring his attentions from his eyebrow to his Wild West handlebar mustache. Finally he said, "I'll look for a replacement. I'll want you to interview him and approve him."

"Fine."

So I called Ted Treacher and told him I would be in Montana soon.

As it turned out, I got on my way sooner.

Perhaps Doug didn't do it on purpose, to hack me off. Perhaps.

But it was only three days later when a young area pro named

Ferguson sauntered in early, finding me alone in the pro shop, to announce he was my replacement.

"You mean you're here for an interview?" I asked.

He gave me a slow, insolent grin. "Hey, man, I'm on board. Show me where the coffee is."

We had never met before and I knew him only from newspaper pictures. Already I didn't like him. But I started showing him around and doing a slow burn at the same time.

"So you're Brad Smith," he said. "You used to be pretty good."

"I guess so," I said.

The back door alarm blipped and then went off, a sure sign that Doug had come in through the back way. I started in that direction.

Behind me, Fergie said, "I'm looking forward to that match tomorrow, Pops."

I turned back. "Match?"

"Yeah, didn't old Doug tell you about it? You and me, a friendly little exhibition to introduce me to the customers and get some pub in the local press."

Doug Twyle had a handful of mail when I banged into his office. He looked up, irritated. "Knock."

"You said I was going to have approval of my replacement," I said.

"Well, this came up quick. Too good an opportunity to miss."

"And what the hell is this I hear about some kind of a match you've set up between him and me?"

"Calm down. It's no big deal."

"You *said* I was going to interview and approve the replacement."

Twyle tossed the mail onto his littered desk, the envelopes scattering, and then looked up at me with sagging, hostile eyes. "And *you* said, Brad, that the last unscheduled vacation was going to be the last."

"Oh," I said. It began to come clear to me. I was being punished.

I added, "It's only for a few weeks, Doug. And I haven't bugged out on you that often."

"This is your second unscheduled jaunt in the last year. And that doesn't count all the goddam long weekends—extra days here and there—to allow you to do some of your bigshot tennis magazine stories. Maybe it's time you realized I'm a little tired of it."

"So you're within your rights to hire a replacement without checking with me, after you said you would."

"This isn't your club, Smith. It's mine."

"I see, sir," I said. "Thank you, sir."

"So just get out there and get along with him."

"Yes, sir." I started for the door. Steaming.

"And try to hold up your end in the match tomorrow," he called after me. "I'm using it as a gimmick to get some publicity. Some of the big boys from the *Morning News* said they'd be here. We might get a nice story in about it if you can stay on the court with this kid."

I looked back at him. "I'll stay."

"Will you?" His grin looked like a death mask. "You've been away from the big time for a long while now, my friend. You look a little flabby. I'll be interested to see if you've got anything more than your old rep going for you any more—not that it's so big anymore either, now that I think about it."

Twyle's intensified hostility bugged me. I didn't need anything else to think about right now.

He was right about my status in the tennis world. It had been a long time since Wimbledon or the U.S. Open. I knew I was washed up as a major tournament player. But the local members got a kick out of having a former world-class star on the staff of their crummy little club, and the job was just right for a man who wanted to stay active but not competitive, and out of the limelight.

I had assumed that since it was okay with me, it was okay with everyone.

But that, I saw now, was wrong. My reputation ate at Doug Twyle, jealousy refusing to go away. Looking back now, I could recall several occasions when he had made some crack about my freelance journalism for *World Tennis* or some other magazine. At those times, I had taken the jibes as the kind of good-natured kidding we all indulge in with our friends. But now I saw that the bylines—the sad little prestige that might flow from bylines—had been eating at him too.

Twyle had never been a star player. He had been a fine college competitor who never quite made it on the tour of those days. I had heard him complain (good-naturedly again, I had imagined) about how he had been born too soon to become a millionaire with his racket. Seeing the kind of game he played in later years, I knew that he would never have been world class. But he didn't know that, and my successes later on must have always gnawed at him, too.

Add my short-notice trips away, and you could see how he had been itching, stewing in his own jealous juices, for quite some time. I had thought I was being low key, low profile, relaxed. I saw now that he could have interpreted a lot of my behavior as insolently lazy.

Overnight, I decided to swallow my own twitchy pride and be a good fellow, play the silly little match with hotshot Ferguson, and not worry any more about it. After I got back from the mountains, maybe I could sit down with Twyle and try to make amends.

No problem, I thought.

Wrong as usual.

The next day was cloudless, with the sun feeling the fiercest it had felt since the previous October. There wasn't a breath of wind. The courtside thermometer slid well above 90, far enough above that I didn't check it after 11 A.M.

Worse, Twyle hadn't just invited somebody from the Dallas *Morning News*. He had gotten to several of the local TV stations, and the afternoon daily as well. He had also managed to let some of our best members know. So that when I walked back to the club after a light lunch, there were about forty people in the rickety green bleachers beside the No. 1 court, and good old Fergie Ferguson was already out on court, hitting with none other than slightly rotund, immensely sweating Twyle himself.

Telling myself to stay calm, et cetera, I resignedly went into the locker room and changed into playing gear, then strapped on my knee brace. A couple of members stood nearby, naked after emerging from the showers.

"Don't start until we can get out there, Brad," one of them, a banker named Murphy, called across the dank little room.

"Wouldn't think of it," I said, smiling.

"The youngster plans to give you a real test. I suppose you knew that?"

"I didn't figure he would take it easy on me."

"Anything but! He was telling some of us a while ago how he plans to wipe the court up with you."

I got out my rackets and started for the court door. "Wouldn't be the first time somebody did that."

Their relaxed laughter followed me out. *Stay calm,* I told myself. *You're a big boy now, and it just doesn't matter.*

It did matter, though. At least a little bit. I had done my best for the club and had felt loyalty to it. I thought maybe I deserved better than the treatment Twyle was giving me. And the idea of going out to get slaughtered by a kid irritated me no end.

I knew how Ferguson was thinking. Years from now he would be saying, *"Hey, I remember the time I took old Brad Smith apart down in Dallas . . ."*

Courtside, Doug Twyle introduced Ferguson and me to the local press. Some of the TV boys turned on their cameras. A pretty little news anchor from one of the stations stuck a microphone in my face and asked me how it felt, not having any corporate sponsors anymore. I told her it was such a profoundly important question, I would have to think about it for a day or two. Then Twyle got on the PA and told the assembled curious that Ferguson and I would play best of three sets, to introduce Ferguson to the Richardson club, where, he was proud to announce, Ferguson was taking my place "for a while."

We went oncourt. Ferguson was already well warmed up, his shirt soaked with sweat. He had that look in his eye. Probably in the olden days the best gladiator saw that look in the eyes of every new, hopeful challenger. If we are to believe mythology, gunfighters in the Old West seldom got to retire because youngsters had that look, were always searching them out, intent on giving them the ultimate life–death test. Boxing champions always get goaded by ambitious drunks in bars, and senior business executives probably see a look like Ferguson's in the eyes of new, on-the-make junior partners.

It's the trophy hunter look. It says, *Man, I am going to have your balls.* I don't know if it comes from the universal male macho drive or what. It certainly isn't a solely masculine attribute. Since women gained their "equality" in the workplace, you can see it in their hungry, spiteful eyes as often as in men. I don't get it. As far as I know, taxidermists have little or no success trying to preserve, stuff, and mount testicles. I've never seen any on a wall yet. Further, most ball-cutting competitions are stupid, like the one I had been roped into here. I had played *serious* matches. For *serious* stakes. Who cared about this stupid exhibition Doug Twyle had set up?

Ferguson, that's who.

Twyle introduced us over the portable PA like it was a big deal. We would call our own lines, no referee, just a friendly little match to let everybody get to know more about my replacement. We warmed up. Ferguson was so keyed up he even hit a few winners during the warmups. I stayed nice and calm.

Right through the fourth game of the first set.

At which point, down 0–4, love–30 on my serve, and getting more discouraged by the minute, I hit a weak backhand and he made it up to the net and slammed a volley crosscourt. I chased it and saw to my great relief that it clearly hit an inch beyond the backline.

"Out!" I called.

"*What?*" Ferguson yelped.

I looked up to see him standing at the net, hands on hips, the old incredulous McEnroe look. Not wanting a scene, I strolled up to face him and said quietly, "I called it out. It was out at least an inch."

"That ball," he said loudly, "was clearly in!"

He had already made two awfully close calls in his own favor at his end. Now he was questioning *my* honesty. I told myself to cool it.

"Of course," my worthy opponent went on, sweat dripping off the end of his nose, "if you *really* believe the ball was out, we'll let the wrong call stand, or play a let."

There are so many fourflushers in sports, so many college and even high school kids throwing tantrums—and rackets—cheating on line calls, berating and browbeating referees, shooting off their mouths and then screaming about press prejudice when the press has the temerity to print *exactly* what they said and what they did. There was a time when tennis was a cleaner, better game, and we should get back to it. I feel strongly about this. So my reaction was undoubtedly out of proportion to Ferguson's provocation. Suddenly I was quite angry.

"No," I said through my teeth. "I'm sure you must be right. It's your point."

His eyes widened in sincere shock. "We'll play a let."

"No," I said. If he was to steal my point, he would not be allowed to trick his conscience by only taking it from me and playing another ball. He would take his stolen merchandise and put it in his column. "The score is now love–forty," I told him, and walked back to the baseline.

One of the members, serving as ballboy at my end, tossed me two yellow Penns. I put one in my pocket and bounced the other. Looking up at Ferguson at the far end, I saw him swaying back and forth, eager to put my next serve away. And it simply made my good intentions about an easy exhibition vanish like water colors on a rain-washed pane of glass. Quite suddenly I was so hot and dizzy from the adrenaline rush that I had to step back from the service line for a few seconds.

I tossed the ball and when it was in the air I knew it was an ace. It went like a bullet past his outflung racket.

He managed to touch my next serve, but only to dump it helplessly into the net. My next serve was another winner. Quite suddenly I was into the stupid match, and who it was or where it was—or for what—didn't matter a whole lot anymore because when you get into the zone, nothing matters but the ball.

I hit him another ace on the deuce side. At add-in, I hit a clean service winner. Belatedly, he yelled "Out!" Seething, I hit the second serve just as hard as I could and blew it right by him.

We changed ends. When we met going around the net, his smile looked a little sickly. It gave me childish satisfaction. Instead of being up 5–0 on his serve, he was up only 4–1, and the latter part of the last game had been quite unlike anything he had seen from me earlier.

In the sixth game I broke him at love, and then accepted two bad calls on my serve to win at 40–30. Suddenly I was only back 3–4, and playing out of my mind. I broke him again to tie, served a love game, and hit three straight winning returns off his now-wobbly service before catching his weak lob near the end and hitting a very satisfying volley to end the first set, 6–4 for the good guys.

We took a short Gatorade break and toweled down. It was hot. I was shallow of breath, but my bad knee felt strong. Ferguson looked long at me, his eyes beginning to be haunted by self-doubt. *I can't handle this guy. He's beating shit out of me.*

A real pro would have rallied on courage and pride, if nothing else. But he couldn't bring it off. He went entirely to pieces in the second set. His name should have been Custer; it was a massacre, 6–0 in 31 minutes.

All right, I admit it. I don't like braggarts and bullies, and I thoroughly enjoyed beating his brains out. For a few minutes there, I played as well or better than I had in years, and that felt good, too.

Beating him 6–0, however, was not cruelty, once I was in the zone and his game collapsed. I would have played the set the same way, with no more "mercy," against my best friend. There is no dishonor, really, in going down 6–0. You simply had no chance. What's insulting is to get ahead 4–0 and then coast, maybe dump a couple of balls into the net, and in effect try to make your opponent look good. It never makes the opponent look any better. It's the ultimate insult and—if he has a stitch of pride left in him—the ultimate cruelty. At least he deserves the best effort you can put out.

Walking off the court, however, my friend Ferguson obviously didn't share that view. His handshake was briefer than a whore's wink, and less sincere.

And Doug Twyle, in the locker room a few minutes later, was seething, his face mottled red, his pupils at pinpoints of badly controlled rage. "You didn't have to make him look like a fool!"

"I didn't," I said. "He did that."

"Smith. I'm fed up with your ego."

Looking into his sickly angry face, I realized I was fed up, too. "Doug," I said, "shove it. I quit. Have a nice day."

I tracked down Collie Davis by telephone and told him of my slight change in plans. He sounded pleased and said he would notify Skurlock. I then called the resort in Montana. Ted had not gotten in yet on his return trip. I left word that I would be arriving sooner than expected, as soon as my storm-damaged Bronco got out of the body shop. He called back the next day to say he was delighted; he had a potential big investor coming in soon, and my early arrival would help with that. Maybe with my help we could get the tennis tournament set up, too.

It felt weird a few days later, driving out of Dallas in my newly uncrunched Bronco II. Most of my stuff was still stacked in the tiny new apartment. But that wasn't home and now nowhere was. Feeling at loose ends, rootless, and unsure of a lot of things, I shoved a Statler

Brothers CD into the dashboard player and pointed the hood north and west. Bitterroot Valley, here I come. And if I am starting this assignment partly out of job frustration, or my sudden new rootlessness, or fear of old age, or because of frustration about Beth Miles, so be it.

Sylvester filled my mind. It was not pleasant. Part of me wanted to run in the opposite direction. I kept driving. Maybe this way I could finally find a way to confront the acid hate and fear standing around in the dark corners of my mind. In Montana I might find a conclusion to many things that had been eating at me.

three

Elsewhere

Kansas City, Missouri

Fred Skurlock left the Federal Building in downtown Kansas City, walked to his dark red Buick Regal, and drove to his apartment. Muttering to himself about the ways of bureaucracy, he packed: slacks, summer shirts, one sportcoat and tie, Levi's, flannel shirts, heavy socks, hiking boots. It was late afternoon by the time he was ready to proceed on his orders, and he waited two hours to let the rush-hour traffic abate. Then he carried the last of his gear out to the Buick, including the hard leather guncase with the Browning pistol and the .357 Colt revolver in it. He put the guncase on the floor of the car in the back seat, and covered it with an old blanket and his AAA map book. Then he went back to the apartment, checked it over, and made sure the deadbolts were fixed on his way out.

Skurlock drove west, and soon he was in Kansas. He had that uneasy feeling one gets when there has been a hurried departure and the worry keeps arising that something important has been forgotten and left behind.

Skurlock had not planned to leave for Montana until the first of the next week. His FBI colleagues already in the area were handling things adequately. His special assignment—searching for Sylvester—was to have waited until Brad Smith arrived on the scene. Smith's earlier departure had thus hurried up Skurlock's own.

Driving on, Skurlock reviewed plans and equipment, and decided his feeling of having forgotten something was inaccurate. Things left undone at the Kansas City office could wait. He intended to drive until midnight. Tomorrow he would see the mountains. He realized he was anxious to get the show on the road. He wanted Sylvester pretty badly. Of course, he thought, he was not the only one. People had been wanting Sylvester for years. Some of the ones who had wanted him worst were dead.

Elk City, Montana

Sylvester stood out by his pickup in front of his mountainside cabin and took his time assembling his flyrod and reel. He had seen his landlord's truck pull away from the old farmhouse far below at the foot of the elevation, then turn onto the gravel road leading up here. Good thing, Sylvester thought, to let the moron find him engrossed in fishing tackle.

That was Sylvester's story. He was a businessman recuperating from a heart attack while on a solitary fishing sojourn of indeterminate length. The heart-attack story covered his gaunt weakness. The fishing yarn provided adequate explanation for driving around wherever he saw fit, and for keeping no regular hours anywhere.

In the days since his successful work at the old fort, Sylvester had made some progress on the operation. His KGB colleague remaining inside the air force lab appeared secure, and was proceeding cautiously toward learning the best time and procedure for copying the key schematic diagrams on the new EMP transmitter circuits. Killing the woman had been unfortunate, but it had guaranteed continuation of the effort. In addition, Sylvester had gotten a solid lead on another female employee inside the lab who might be tricked into providing additional information. He was scheduled to meet with her later in the day.

Fortunately, too, it had not all been work, and there had been no undue pressure. Sylvester had actually had time to establish his fishing trip cover, walking to the nearby mountain stream. With exercise here in the fine mountain air, he could feel himself gaining strength daily.

Waiting for the man who had rented him the cabin to finish the drive up the twisting mountain road, Sylvester allowed himself to breathe deeply, testing the residual pain in his chest, and enjoy the scenery. It was a fine, almost cloudless day. Great conifer and aspen woods cloaked the nearby hills in dark green. In the valleys higher up, and on distant peaks, winter snow still shone brilliant white. Bluejays and mockingbirds yelped from some of the trees near the rocky abutment site for the cabin. Little more could be asked for.

The landlord's faded red Ford pickup truck appeared in the rent of the woods where the narrow driving path emerged. It trundled across the grassy field, headed directly toward the cabin. Sylvester busied himself with tying leader and pretended not to see until the sound of the engine was loud. Then he put his rod down in the back of his opened Dodge truck and made a show of surprise to have a visitor.

His visitor got out of his vehicle. A big man, broad across the chest and shoulders, with neanderthal features, he moved with the ponderous grace of a former athlete. He was in his brown uniform, so Sylvester surmised that it must be time for him to start his drive into Elk City, where he was the number-two man on the town's two-man police force.

"Morning!" Sylvester called, smiling.

His landlord lumbered over. He had a small American flag sewn over his left shirt pocket, under the nametag that read LASSITER. He also wore small enameled flag pins on both lapels. Sylvester had already heard more than he wanted about Lassiter's service in Vietnam, his wounds, and his super-patriot attitudes. Sylvester consoled himself with the amusement derived from duping such an American.

Lassiter's small, suspicious eyes scanned Sylvester's fishing gear. "Getting ready to try it again?"

"Thought I would," Sylvester told him in perfect idiomatic English.

"Done any good yet?"

"Yes. I located some nice browns in that pool you told me about. Had one for dinner last night. I also caught a couple of fish that look a little like trout in the deep water, but they're ugly bastards and very bony."

"Aw, hell, that would be squawfish. You don't want to eat them."

Sylvester grinned. "Now you tell me."

"Listen, Mr. Mason, you stay away from them squawfish. You might as well eat suckers as them."

"I appreciate the tip."

Lassiter hesitated, slapping a thin rolled newspaper in his palm. "Well, you're doing fine, then?"

"Fine, yes."

"No problems?"

"Nary a one, my friend."

"Want to make sure. Like having you up here, using the cabin. Like to see a man have a good time in the great out-of-doors."

And pay me far too much rent, Sylvester thought. "I'm having a blast, Officer Lassiter."

"Good." Lassiter handed over the rolled paper. "Oh. Thought you might like to look at the latest paper."

Sylvester accepted it with thanks. He unrolled it and glanced at the front page. The Elk City *Pioneer* was not long on news, giving most of its twice-weekly space to historical items or puffery for local businesses, and he saw that the latest edition was no exception. There was an item on a raft race and another on summer rebuilding plans at a ski lift and a smaller item at the bottom of the front page that caught Sylvester's attention and jolted him to the core.

"What's the matter?" Lassiter grunted.

"Me? Nothing."

"You sort of jerked, there." The policeman's eyes bored in. "You've lost what little color you had."

Sylvester's mind raced as he assimilated the bad news and considered how to deal with Lassiter about showing his reaction. He decided. "It's this item here."

Lassiter squinted at it in the bright sun. "That? Yeah. Goddam Bitterroot Valley Resort. If they make a go of it, no telling how bad it will spoil our town. Let the tourists go someplace else. We like Elk City the way it is. But them resort people are already starting, bringing in these so-called big-name stars."

Sylvester had earlier heard Lassiter rant against the resort, but had no idea what was really behind the animosity toward it. That was not at issue right now. Sylvester pointed at the story. "This man they mention here, this man Brad Smith."

"Never heard of him," Lassiter muttered disgustedly.

"Maybe you're lucky," Sylvester said.

"Yeah?" Lassiter looked suspicious. "How come?"

"You're a Vietnam veteran," Sylvester told him, ad-libbing the approach as he went. "I appreciate you and all the men like you who did their duty—went to Nam and put their lives on the line for the American way of life."

Lassiter straightened perceptibly. "I did my duty. Yeah. So? what does that have to do with—"

"This man Smith." Sylvester tapped the newspaper again. "You don't know what *he* did?"

"No. Tell me."

"He went to Vietnam too. But he used his influence to get taken right back out again. Then he bought his way out of the army. While brave men like you and my dead brother were giving their all against the gooks, this man Smith was back in this country, a civilian again, *playing tennis.*"

Lassiter glowered at the newspaper in Sylvester's hands. "Playing tennis," he repeated.

Sylvester nodded. "Making millions of dollars. While you were over there, fighting his battles for him."

Lassiter's teeth grated audibly. "And now he comes here."

"And now he comes here," Sylvester echoed.

Lassiter shook his head. "I'd like to catch him trying to pull any of his phony rich-man stuff around *my* town."

"Let's hope he doesn't stay long, my friend."

Lassiter glared from under the shelf of his eyebrows. "Maybe he won't."

After the policeman finally trudged back to his truck and drove away in a sullen rage, Sylvester congratulated himself. It had been a shock, seeing Brad Smith's name. If Smith was coming here, it had to be part of some kind of counter-espionage operation. Which put Sylvester and his colleague inside the lab squarely in the cross-hairs.

It changed everything. They had to be supremely cautious now. Brad Smith's impending arrival "to help at the new Bitterroot Valley Resort" meant Sylvester was the object of a search. New contingency plans had to be drawn for this.

Immediately, however, Sylvester decided he had done a clever thing, pulling Lassiter's patriotism chain and making him hostile to Smith even before his arrival.

They could talk again about Smith. Perhaps the policeman could be led into keeping Sylvester informed of Smith's movements. And if Lassiter, out of his misled patriotism, could be induced to make life slightly miserable for Smith, impeding his investigations, so much the better.

Sylvester went fishing for an hour. He then returned to his cabin, changed clothes, and drove to a café on the highway outside Elk City, south of town and well away from the air force site to the north.

His lady was waiting for him: sad-eyed, fortyish, with crow's-feet and a beehive hairdo and a dowdy cotton dress. She had just gotten off her office shift at the lab.

"It's very kind of you to meet me, Mrs. Hill."

She sighed. "It's not as if I was important. To anyone. I'm really not well. I have so many debts. I have two children, you see. I have to work. If there was anyplace else to work except that lab, I wouldn't work there at all. They're making some kind of terrible weapon. I don't think that's right. There shouldn't be any wars."

"I couldn't agree more," Sylvester said smoothly. "In addition, our organization, the League to Preserve Our Environment, is quite sure they are polluting the groundwater out there, and possibly destroying the ozone layer with their lasers or whatever they are."

She sighed again. "I wouldn't be surprised. —But your friend said you might have an idea of how I could be of help . . . for money?"

Sylvester explained how his "LPOE" needed information about the nature of the work being done at the lab—"any general information, you see, to let us have enough to go public and blow the lid off the whole awful mess up there"—and how Mrs. Hill might help by keeping her eyes open for proofs of secret tests. The lady seemed unsure, reluctant. Sylvester handed her an envelope containing ten fifty-dollar bills "as a sign of our sincerity, and in compensation for your time."

Hesitancy vanished. Spots of color appeared on the woman's face. Her eyes came to life. "I will do everything I can for you and your wonderful organization, Mr. Jones! It's time to stop wasting our tax dollars on war."

"I agree, Mrs. Hill. And I will be in touch."

With that meeting concluded, there was one more item of business. A telephone call put him in touch with someone who could report when Brad Smith arrived, and what he was doing.

Then, satisfied with a good day's work, Sylvester drove back to his mountain. A fine trout hit his fly on the third cast.

Chicago, Illinois

"The plan," Paul Dominick said angrily, "is not just unethical. It's getting more and more dangerous. We've got to stop this approach and do something responsible for a change!"

"I'm being responsible to the firm," Ardis Allen told him. "Nothing else counts."

Dominick glared at her across her big desk. "Are you sure you're not afraid of losing the chairmanship if this ever becomes general knowledge?"

"Paul, that's uncalled for."

"This entire goddamn obscenity of a coverup is what's uncalled for!"

"It's too late to turn back."

Dominick winced. "You won't listen to reason?"

Ardis allowed herself a long moment to study his face. He had been her vice president for operations for four years, her lover for three. She knew him very, very well. She noted his slight pallor, angry eyes, tightened hands—signs that went beyond normal frustrated dissent. She felt a little sad.

"Paul," she said in a gentle, cajoling tone that was wholly uncharacteristic, "I've made my decision."

He looked down at the planning paper she had personally prepared. The silence extended. Ardis left her desk and walked to the draperies behind it. A touch of a button retracted the ceiling-height draperies on two walls of the office, revealing the city. It was dusk, and a deep blue crept over other skyscrapers nearby. On the streets far below, car headlights made diamonds among the rubies and emeralds of signals and signs. Because the Allen Industries Tower was among

Chicago's tallest, Ardis could see through a canyon formed by other buildings and get a glimpse of Lake Michigan, already midnight blue.

Ardis Allen was intent on giving Dominick all the time she possibly could. She needed him. She did not want to force him to go along with the extension of her plan, although of course she would if she must.

She was a slender woman in her thirties, very young to hold such power. But other corporate executives who had once complained that she inherited the power from her dead husband—and who challenged her—were no longer with the far-flung petrochemical empire. She was wearing a severe dark blue suit that contrasted sharply with her beautiful flaxen hair and the glitter of discreetly fabulous jewelry at her earlobes, her throat, and her long, slender fingers. In no way did she look like a woman who would do anything to consolidate and hold her power.

Dominick was near fifty, broadly muscular in his pale spring-wool suit, his leonine head beginning to go gray, his handsome features set in a frown of worry. Only an insider could have guessed from appearances that the slender younger woman was at the center of power here, and the slightly bulky older man on very thin ice indeed.

Dominick finally spoke: "We can't continue this. We have to take more vigorous action. We can't hide everything any longer. It's dangerous—we could be found out any moment—and damn it, Ardis, it's—it's immoral."

Ardis allowed herself the thinnest smile. "What a deep pronouncement, Paul darling."

"Damn it, Ardis. People are *dying*!"

"There's no proof of that. You're being melodramatic."

Dominick tossed the planning folder onto her desk. "I'll have to fight you on this, Ardis."

"Paul." Ardis's voice lowered. "Don't do this. Please."

"I have no choice."

"It's *my* company, Paul."

"People like me were giving their lives to this company long before Anton died and left it to you!"

"But he did die. And he did leave control to me. I don't intend to relinquish it. You would be well advised to remember that."

Dominick straightened. "Is that a threat? Have we come at last to threats?"

"*No*, darling! Listen to reason! After all we've meant to each other . . . all the wonderful times we've had together—"

"None of that enters into this, Ardis. I'll fight you."

"Paul—!"

But Dominick had turned and walked angrily out of her office, the heavy oak door closing behind him with a resounding thud.

Ardis Allen sat behind her desk and remained quite still for several minutes. It was now well after normal working hours, and none of the lights on her telephone blinked, no sounds penetrated the vast office from the other offices and cubicles all over this floor of the tower.

After a while Ardis got to her feet. She walked to the windows and looked again into the gathering night, the constellations of moving lights on the streets far below. She was not a tall woman, and looked both beautiful and slender in her gleaming high heels. She also, to an outsider, would have looked fragile, vulnerable, and very much alone.

She seemed to come to some decision. Returning to her desk, she touched keys on an IBM OS–2 computer, bringing up a program. She reached for her telephone, which was connected through the computer for messaging, and punched another set of codes into the computer with the telephone touchtone pad.

A cursor began to blink on the color screen.

"Betty," she said, recording the message for her executive secretary, "please type this letter immediately and bring it to my home tonight for my signature. To: Paul Dominick, et cetera, et cetera. Dear Paul. After serious consideration of our conversation of this date comma I have come to the conclusion that I must request your resignation effective immediately period. Paragraph. Under the terms of your contract dated—fill in the date from the file, Betty—comma, your retirement option package including separation bonus comma continued participation in the insurance programs comma and stock benefit options comma will of course remain in force. Period. Paragraph. In addition comma Paul comma let me thank you personally for your years of dedicated and devoted service to the firm period. Your unquestioned loyalty and effort on our behalf have been an inspiration period. Good luck in your future endeavors period. Sincerely et cetera. End of letter.

"Betty, after preparation and signature, this confidential letter is to be duplicated in sufficient number for Mr. Dominick and each member of the board. Mr. Dominick is to receive his copy by messenger *tonight*. Members of the board must receive theirs by overnight personal delivery.

"Also, Betty, please see to it that the contents of Mr. Dominick's personal office are packed and crated and placed in departmental storage overnight, so he or his representative can pick them up at his leisure. Also tonight, have the locks changed throughout the executive suite.

"I'm going to dinner and then I'll be at home. Fax a copy of the letter to me there."

Ardis thought a moment, then punched in another telephone code and hung up. A flick of crimson-tipped fingers over the computer keyboard sent the recorded instructions to her secretary.

With a sigh, Ardis got up from the computer. She looked around the office. For an instant her shoulders drooped, her eyes became bleak. Then, however, with obvious mental effort, she squared her shoulders. In the instant of self-control she looked strong and confident again. With a last glance around her office, she walked out. Her perfume lingered in the air.

Elk City, Montana

Something had moved inside the fence, where no creature was supposed to be.

Clarke Higgins was sure of it, and it troubled him.

The setting sun had just slipped behind the distant Sapphires, leaving a sullen, red-amber light. There was no wind, and the Ponderosa pines and Douglas firs stood silent, darkly unmoving against a darkening, cut-glass sky. An eagle turned high above, restlessly searching, and along the rocky creek bottom magpies swooped through branches. With the sun's disappearance the late-afternoon chill deepened with magic speed, and it was cold.

Leaning against the muddy front fender of his Jeep, construction supervisor Higgins rolled the architect's plans showing how earth was to be moved to lengthen and beautify two of the holes on the adjacent golf course. He had driven away from the old course to this grassy knoll thirty minutes earlier to give himself a vantage point from which to view progress of the work. He was satisfied; in the distance to the east he had been able to see clearly how the new fairway had been cut out of the lodgepole pines and recontoured, and how the new greens would blend in. After reassuring himself, he had watched the distant bulldozers and bladed trucks trundle away like Tonka toys, signaling the end of the day's work. Then he had allowed himself a smoke.

Then, moments ago, he had seen the movement out of the corner of his eye.

Feeling the chill dig in, Higgins tapped his pipe out against the heel of his hand, making sure the remaining sparks fell on bare dirt only recently churned and cleared by the bulldozer. The fire season was not on yet and it had been a good winter with plenty of snow. But fires had gotten started this early in other years, thanks to careless smokers or bad-luck lightning, and Higgins took no chances.

In his thirty-four years, the tall, powerfully built Higgins had learned to be a good outdoorsman. He prided himself on being able to take care of himself in any situation. His nerves were excellent. He did not have a very active imagination, but that wasn't all bad; it kept him from worrying about things he could not control—seeing boogeymen in the dark.

But from the slight grassy knoll that poked up on the edge of the woods west of the creek—with the new golf course construction well off to his right and the rocky hillside five hundred yards to the west—Higgins had definitely seen something.

The golf course property ended near the bottom of the wooded slope to Higgins's left. There was a fence there. The high cyclone fence had barbed wire along its top. It enclosed most of the next rocky hill, and the old mine property.

Inside the fence, except for the derelict shacks and rusting equipment standing around the mouth of the old mineshaft, there was nothing but weeds and strewn rocks and a handful of scrubby lodgepole pines trying futilely to get a foothold.

People didn't get in there. Animals didn't get in there. But Higgins, to his surprise, had seen some kind of movement in there. He had seen it near the mine entrance shack—tumbled black boards and scattered barrels and boxes—and the movement had not been a bird or small animal that might have burrowed beneath the fence.

Higgins, a man who usually minded his own business, stood by his Jeep a few minutes and worried about it. Part of himself said to forget it, it was probably an optical illusion, and even if it wasn't, it was not his affair. But he was mightily interested. The one thing that had been made clear to him was that the abandoned mine—"the ghost mine," locals often called it—was dangerous in the extreme. Not even Ted Treacher, the owner of the resort, who had hired him to improve the old golf course, had ever been behind the fence. The big signs made it clear snoopers were not welcome.

So who or what was inside?

Higgins could not see anything unusual now. But he was pretty far away. He decided to take a closer look. He got back into his Jeep and drove down the wooded hillside toward the fence. He drove carefully between the tall pines, staying in low gear and bumping gently over the rough ground. His path took him gently downhill and across a rivulet of stream (wheels spinning briefly in the rocks and clay), and then out of the trees and through sagebrush and weeds on down the slope to where he knew the locked main gate to the mine property was located.

Darkness was spreading fast and he was cold. He turned on his headlights and moved on. In moments the headlights sprayed across the board sign, red on white, with a blue insignia in the top right:

DANGER—RESTRICTED AREA—DANGER
Barnwell Mining Co. Property
Entry Positively Forbidden
DANGER—STAY OUT—DANGER

Higgins pulled around the sign and poked the jeep nearer the fence, following it to the north. Darkness came on fast in the mountains, and the trees were obscure now in the gathering blackness. He realized he would not be able to see an elephant beyond the fence now.

He was about to turn back when the headlights lit the sign on the fence beside the gate:

DANGER! STAY OUT! DANGER!
Cave-In Area—Hidden Deep Holes
Possible Explosive Gas in Unstable Shaft
STAY OUT!
Private Property, Barnwell Mining Co.

They did not, Higgins thought with a wry smile, believe in being subtle. He put the jeep in reverse to back around. Which was when he saw in the distant illumination of his headlights that the heavy mesh gate was standing slightly ajar—unlocked and open.

"Funny!" he said aloud, and stopped the Jeep.

The big gate definitely stood ajar—the heavy chain and padlocks hanging on the post, and the gate swung open just about far enough for a person to slip through.

Higgins had never entirely believed all the warnings. He had heard both the silly superstitions about a "ghost mine" and the more recent and—to him—more credible stories of strange doings out here in the night back a few years ago: moving lights and the distant sounds of heavy machinery.

He had always sort of wanted to see for himself. Would he ever have a better chance than this? Whoever was in there had no right to be there; Higgins could always claim an innocent motivation to "save" the intruder from all the dangerous things mentioned on the signs.

Higgins thought some more about it, then rummaged under the seat and brought out his soft guncase. Unzipping it, he took out the .45 Colt pistol. Its full magazine was in place and he knew there was one in the chamber. He cocked the pistol and put the safety on, then got out of the Jeep and walked to the gate. In the gathering darkness he could make out the bootprints in the soft dirt there.

It was probably a kid inside, he thought. Or a curious rockhound who jimmied the locks. Higgins figured he could go in, take the intruder by surprise, terrorize the shit out of him with the .45—and seize the perfectly defensible opportunity to have a look-see for himself.

So Higgins slipped between the gate and the fencepost and hurried up the slight, scrabbly incline toward the mineshaft and the black clutter of rubbish and shadows around it. His boots made a little noise in the gravel, but he didn't worry about that.

There was certainly no one in sight now.

Slightly out of breath from the climb, Higgins reached the immediate area of the shaft. There was some track and even two aged, rusting steel cars, one of them still piled high with perhaps the last batch of dirt ever pulled out of this hill. There were rotting crates and some boulders and broken barrels and the falling-down shacks, and the overhead conveyor arm. Higgins could scarcely see the conveyor arm. It was getting really dark.

Quite suddenly, Higgins began to realize that maybe—just maybe—he was not being very smart. The short hairs stood up on his neck. His mouth went dry. Out of his memory tumbled some of the spook stories he had heard as a child: the ghost of the old miner who still prowled these grounds; the spirits of the Nez Percé killed here long ago in a vicious ambush by drunken settlers; the story that it was the government that closed this area not because of the danger of drop-holes or avalanche, but because things walked here by night which no scientist could understand . . . abominations.

Higgins stared for a moment at the black maw of the mineshaft itself, and his uneasiness became worry became fear became something close to galloping panic. *I don't think I'm all that curious anymore, this is horseshit.* He turned to head back downslope toward the gate, and the safety of his Jeep beyond the fence.

Something made a scrabbling sound in the rocks and dirt behind a hulking old water tower to his right. Higgins turned. His fear peaked. A cloudy grayness seemed to envelope him. Then the pain.

"*No!*" He dropped his pistol.

He fell.

four

It was cooler in the mountains and I enjoyed the drive as much as you can when you're that apprehensive. Your unconscious can conjure up boogeymen when you're driving long distances alone, and you can think about a lot of ghosts.

Some of my thoughts went to Danisa. She had kept her maiden name—Lechova—on the professional tennis tour after confounding a lot of people by marrying a much older gent, namely me. My thoughts of her were as vivid as ever . . . as they would always be. Sometimes it seemed ages since her chartered jet had gone down in the Rockies. But it hadn't really been that long. Sometimes my mind does a trick and I turn and think I almost see her, golden hair laughing in the sunlight—astonishingly, my *wife*—but then I snap back to reality and the pain is shockingly sharp and fresh.

Once upon a time I imagined that people mercifully sort of forget the pain surrounding loved ones they had lost. But now I know better. Memory is too good.

Many months after Danisa's death, I had gone on another mission that Collie Davis was mixed up in. That was when I met my California lady, Beth Miles, and that was when my KGB man named Sylvester showed up again and almost killed both of us.

OVERHEAD

And now he was back again and I was driving toward a possible new meeting with him. I didn't want that. But you do what you have to do. I was awfully sick of the memories that made me fear and hate him about equally. Maybe I was driving toward some kind of catharsis.

Not that all the driving time was bad by any means. I had good company of a more real variety. In addition to the Statler Brothers, there were friends like Alabama and Sonny Terry and Brownie McGhee on the cassette deck, and National Public Radio sometimes when the Bronco cruised within range of a member station. Did you know that six years after a world ban on commercial whaling, Iceland's "scientific research program" shipped 197 tons of frozen whale meat to Japan? Or that Francis X. Beidler, vigilante, was born in a place called Mount Joy, Pennsylvania? N.P.R. is great for such trivia.

Having camped out west of Yellowstone on Sunday, I followed the gray, squiggly line on the road map and approached my destination shortly after noon Monday. Ted Treacher had said the turnoff for the resort south of town was well marked. I managed to miss it, and the next thing I knew I was driving past the sign that said I was welcome to historic Elk City.

Low, mostly wooded mountains to the north and east formed a crescent that tightly enclosed the river valley. Dense, dry-looking woods, mostly lodgepole pine, covered the rolling terrain to the south, and to the west were more lumpy hills and sagebrush country extending out toward a mountain range whose majesty was diminished by distance. The valley was itself in high country.

After the welcome sign, the next thing that greeted me inbound on the south road was a gully half-filled with rusted car bodies, piles of old tires, and some ancient farm machinery. On the left, a beer joint with two more junkers in the side yard, and beyond that a half-mile, a deserted farm with the barn flat and the house a leaning black skeleton with wind and sunlight showing through: a real fixer-upper.

The valley floor narrowed somewhat after that. I drove past scattered houses on the outskirts of town: small frame structures, mainly, with faded shingle sides and tarpaper roofing, and lots more trash in the yards. Then I passed a dusty brick elementary school with kids playing softball and tag in the yard; then a McDonald's, a convenience store, a funeral parlor, four gas stations, some old brick buildings with falling-in roofs, then more gas stations and a lumber yard and a humpy railroad crossing, and past a grain elevator company and feed mill into the main part of Elk City.

It was composed of six or seven streets in either direction, no building taller than the second story, most of them the aging pink brick, with a commercial radio tower sticking up from the top of one business bulding in a block ahead, and a traffic light, and a local police car in my side of the intersection, blocking the way. I pulled up short of the cruiser.

A funeral procession was passing. It had just started and I got a look at the hearse, a gray Cadillac several years old but in perfect trim, and behind it a couple of Cadillac limousines. The hearse and limousines had pink paper streamers on the radio antennas, which struck me as weird. The local cop just ahead of me stood beside his car, his cap over his chest. He was tall and heavy, his once-athletic body ruined by hamburgers and beer. Red-faced from too much sun, his uniform stained under the armpits by dark sweat, he was obviously trying to hold his stomach in. He looked dull, brutish. His big revolver and handcuffs seemed out of place at a funeral.

A lot of cars trundled past. I saw the faces of young kids peering out of many backseat windows. Which tipped me off about the pink streamers: it was a child's funeral.

Some pedestrians, looking like locals, had paused along the sidewalks. I watched them. They looked sad and forlorn. A dull wind riffled their clothing and fluttered the American flags atop the bank, a hardware store, the telephone company offices. It was a very long procession across my street.

When the last car had finally passed, the cop got back into his old Ford cruiser and pulled it forward, against the curb to my right. He got back out and walked over to the traffic light control box, which he had set on blinking red. He fiddled in the box and changed it to blinking yellow. I nosed up into the intersection, looked both ways up and down the short, lumpy street, and drove across. Intent on getting directions, I headed for the gas station sign on the next corner. Didn't get there. Flashing gumball machine lights on top of the cruiser rocketed up behind me, filling the rearview mirror. Puzzled, I pulled over.

Same cop, but he looked redder and larger peering in through my side window. A tic jumped near his left eye. He seemed to be fighting a great rage, trying to be courteous. "May I see your driver's license, please?"

I dug it out and handed it over. "What did I do wrong, Officer?"

He studied my Texas license. His mouth worked and sweat coursed out of his shaggy hair under the police cap and rolled stickily down his glistening cheeks. He was steamed. "You just broke through a funeral procession."

"The procession was past."

You could almost hear his teeth grate. "Did *I* wave you through the intersection?"

There are wonderful cops, and I wouldn't have their job. There are others like this guy, whose nametag said LASSITER. They thrive on humiliation and intimidation: yours, not theirs. I think they get an erection every morning when they strap on their shooting iron. The best policy with such Wyatt Earps is to act just as stupid as they are, and be very, very meek. "I thought the intersection had been opened, Officer. I'm sure sorry!"

"Where are you staying locally, sir?"

"Bitterroot Valley Resort. I'm working there." Lassiter's face changed. He moved back two steps and put his hand on the butt of the .357. "Please step out of the vehicle, sir."

Shit. "Yes, Officer."

We then went through the routine: back to the cop car; sit inside and gawk at all the radios and radar and things; produce registration papers and insurance card. Answer stupid questions like is this your correct age and address, which in the case of the address it wasn't, but I didn't admit it. Wait while he calls in your ID, tag, etc., and asks the local dispatcher to check locally, at the state level, and possibly with the FBI and Interpol about possible outstanding warrants.

It took a long time. Local folks strolled by and peered at me, evidently wondering if I was an ax murderer.

Finally, assured by the radio that I had no warrants outstanding, he wrote a citation and handed it to me.

I looked at it. "Reckless driving?"

His eyes dulled with the animosity I couldn't figure. "If you want to argue, Mr. Smith, we can go to jail."

"No, Officer. Thank you very much."

I got my directions at the gas station and headed south again, wondering what Ted Treacher had done to make people so mad at him.

The southwest road wound mildly uphill beside a small, heavily wooded mountain stream, into a higher section of the valley featuring rolling terrain covered by tall pines, with a sprinkling of fir and tamarack. Beautiful country, with the mountains still snow-touched, sunlight brilliant, on either side. I passed a few isolated log homes set far back from the road, then drove through empty country a mile or two where the river crossed under the road and boiled downstream, the way I had come, over white boulders and rocks.

The country made something ache inside me. Once I had imagined I would end up in a place like this: mountains, clean streams, clean air, deep woods. All of us get off-track.

Tennis players, even the best in the Seventies, made nothing like the money they make today. I had done awfully well, and thought I was investing most of it wisely. When the bottom fell out of the oil industry in the early 1980s, all my "growth investments"—about 75 percent of everything I had—went the way of new oil drilling, stripper wells, deep exploration, and offshore activity: right down the tubes. Some of my presumably conservative investments in Houston real estate went down right after it. So one day I woke up and looked around and joined a lot of other fine people in Texas, Louisiana, and Oklahoma: not ruined in my case, but wondering what the hell had happened and why I hadn't put more in coffee cans buried in the back yard.

I had already long since retired from the circuit in those days except for occasional appearances as a sort of symbolic player, the kind of role Jack Nicklaus later adopted in the golfing world. I was learning how to write tennis journalism and enjoying that, and working with an old friend at the Richardson club, and enjoying the low pressure of that, too. Amazing, how part-time retirement jobs begin to look different when the bulk of your retirement money has vanished and you *need* to work in order to save your remaining meager capital.

I was by no means poor. Compared with most people, I was very well off. But seeing a couple of million vanish overnight does tend to make one cautious. Evidently Ted Treacher's earlier investment program had been much smarter than mine, and now he had found a place worth risking it. Part of me already envied him.

When I reached the sign indicating the Bitterroot Valley turnoff and then found the resort, I started envying him more.

It was a long, rambling Alpine-style central building, white with dark brown cross-members and vertical trim, two stories, with deep gables, shambling rooflines, and bric-a-brac around doors and windows that would have flattered any Austrian guesthouse. Ted even had the geraniums in flowerboxes under all the windows. Off to my left as I pulled into the nearly deserted main parking lot, I saw a swimming pool and the fencing of many courts. A sign pointing right showed the way to the golf course. I could see the open expanse of one fairway over there, and a side roadway leading down into a treed area where there were A-frame cabins and, farther down, some nice-looking contemporary condominium units. Some construction still going on down there. Nearer the parking lot, workers hard at it with hand tools in some of the immaculate flowerbeds. Through my open car window came the sound of mowers or tractors not far away. Everything looked fresh and clean and ready for occupancy, but except for some people on a couple of the near courts, and a family piddling around their big camper in a corner of the lot, we might as well have been on the moon: there are few things as naked-looking as two acres of asphalt with fresh diagonal striping all over it to direct the cars that haven't come.

I parked near the sign designating the office and went inside. Nobody in the lobby. I bonged the counter bell. A flurry in the rear office brought Ted Treacher out. He grabbed my hand like it was a lifeline. "Brad! Damn, I'm glad you got here early! Come on back here! How about coffee?"

His barren back office reeked of stale cigarette smoke. I looked around: tile floor, ugly paneled walls, naked windows looking out through a utility area stacked with trash cans toward the courts to the left behind high metal fencing, a garden and patio area straight back, a wing of the building on the right. Ted had some filing cabinets, but it looked like most of the paperwork that mattered was stuffed in cartons on the bare floor. His desk looked like a bear had gone through it, looking for a handout. Another open doorway looked into a smaller adjacent office, and I saw the end of a Xerox machine and some computer stuff, as well as a steel worktable as littered as his desk. Ted hustled in there and went around the corner and came back with a white plastic cup of steaming coffee.

He looked haggard, with circles under his eyes and unkempt hair, tireder than he had been in Dallas so recently. His tired grin, though, was sincere and wall-to-wall. "Sit down, man, sit down! Am I ever glad to see you! Can I use your help!"

I perched on one of the steel folding chairs facing his desk. He shoved piles of brochures and bills aside to make room for his cup. "I was hoping you would arrive today. How was the drive?"

"Fine until I got on the wrong road here."

"I know. We've got to get more signs up. But you've got to rent a piece of land adjacent to the right-of-way, you know? And it's not the easiest thing in the world to find a landowner around here who wants to rent space cheap."

It occurred to me that he was in deep trouble if the cost of renting space for a roadside sign was a factor for him. I filed the information, but didn't comment.

Ted, however, seemed to sense my thoughts. "No problem! We're rolling! Our courts are in top shape, we have a hundred and twenty rooms in the lodge, we have thirty A-frames ready for occupancy, plus eight condominiums ready now and six more nearing completion. All we need is to bring the people in. This place will sell itself. Here. Look at this brochure we're mailing out." He grabbed up a colorful folder from the desk litter and handed it over.

I examined it. The print job was first-rate, expensive. It made Bitterroot Valley look better than Vail. "Looks like you've got everything but business."

"That will come, that will come. We've advertised the golf course all over the place. We ought to have a lot of players this weekend. The course modifications are almost complete despite the setback."

"What setback?"

He frowned at his coffee cup. "Strange thing. Supervisor for my golf course architect. Fellow named Higgins. Disappeared last Friday night."

"Absconded?"

"Nothing like that. They found his Jeep over on the far side of the construction area, nose-down in the creek. Looks like he tried to drive across it and got stuck, four-wheel drive and all; it was buried to the transfer case. But Higgins wasn't around anywhere. Nobody has seen hide nor hair of him since. There were some bear tracks not far away, but a bear would have left the body, even if it was badly mauled. Nobody knows what to make of it."

"What does the law say?"

Ted sighed. "They came out, poked around, asked questions, made notes, filed reports, went back to town. We've got a deputy sheriff who's about as worthless as a tit on a boar hog. The local constabulary consists of a police chief who's semi-retired and two officers, brothers, one of them part-time, whose main claim to fame is that they played football once upon a time over at Bozeman."

I nodded. "I met one of them when I got lost and ended up in town. He was directing traffic for a funeral."

"Sad situation," Ted replied. "A youngster, I heard. She was the second young person to die here this year."

"Bad luck."

He shook his head. "There's been a lot of it around here, from what I've heard. Some people are upset. Some of them say there's something wrong. Several cases of childhood leukemia. Some say there's too much cancer of other types and things like lupus, too, but maybe that's just the kind of rumor that can get started in a small town. I asked around, and there are certainly no statistics on it. They had three or four childhood deaths last year too, and evidently the year before that. There used to be a pulp mill up north. It's closed now. Some people believe it poisoned the atmosphere when it was in operation."

Again I had a random reaction. I had been told the air force research work was harmless. *Was it?* I decided I was getting paranoid. Collie wouldn't lie to me about something that crucial.

Ted went on, "No problem of that kind anymore. Look at that sky! And the creek that runs through this place is so clear you can dip a cup into it and drink it straight off. Whatever might have been wrong is in the past, thank the Lord. This is God's country now!"

"Want to show me around?"

He did, and he did. He fed me history and business along with his worries and enthusiasm as we went along.

"Gosh, I wish Sally was back from town."

"Sally?"

"Sally Wallis. She's my business manager. Wonderful woman. An absolute marvel. Intelligent, loyal, hard-working, and simply beautiful to boot. She's in town, delivering another load of our brochures to the post office. Wait till you meet her. You'll love her."

Going outside, we walked through the service area, which turned out to be the only part of the entire resort that I didn't instantly fall in love with. Once beyond the tarmac, we walked through broad gardens with bricked sidewalks, a meandering artificial creek, and stands of lodgepole pine. The tennis courts, sixteen of them, were mostly unoccupied. Ted said he had refenced and resurfaced, using dense, dark green rubberized paint on ten courts and Tartan Turf with sand swept into the surface on the other six. New nets, new vending machines, and a neat new pro shop with a cheery young man behind the counter.

"Ted, all these improvements must have cost a bundle."

"They did cost quite a bit, yes. But I got wonderful terms on almost all the loans. With good business we can handle all the overhead."

We went by the swimming pool area. The pool had been another of the unanticipated problems, Ted said. New plaster, paint, decking, and filtration equipment was unbelievably costly, he told me.

"But it's fine now."

The new cabins and condominiums nearest the lodge had been completed, I saw when we walked down that way, and sparse grass had begun to cover the sandy berms and lawns. The winding asphalt paths were attractive, the structures well separated.

"How many of these are sold, Ted?"

"Well, actually . . . none, yet. But we have prospects!"

Farther west we encountered bare earth, mud rivulets across the paving, and construction crews driving bulldozers and hammering on walls. Plumbing and electrical contractors' trucks dotted the landscape.

"We need to get this work done," Ted told me. "*Then* things will pick up, saleswise. The brochure and the publicity we get out of the tennis tournament will turn things around."

Beyond and behind many of the condos and cottages I could see the green fairways of the golf course. There was a separate pro shop for that, also spanking new. It had a good supply of equipment. Outside its doors, two dozen new electric carts gleamed on the apron separating it from the beautiful large practice putting green.

Ted took me to the first tee, an elevated vantage point that provided a view of several holes. No. 1 was a 445-yard par 4, down a hundred yards to a meandering stream that wound its way up the righthand side of the rising fairway, bounded by spruce and firs on the left, to a plateau green with traps left and right. From here I could see a part of the No. 2 fairway, tightly tree-bound; the No. 6 green with water in front; and all of No. 10, a pretty par 3, elevated tee to elevated green, a 124-yard carry over a ravine filled with dense brush and fallen rock. Ted explained about construction work he had going to improve some of the outlying holes. He said the loans for that work were at a good rate of interest, too.

He seemed to have a great many loans.

We finished our outside tour and walked back up the curving cart road to the lodge. The high mountain air left me slightly out of breath, which disturbed me; retired or not, I'm supposed to be an athlete. I was about to mention it and ask the elevation here when Ted pointed toward a red Mazda sportscar zooming into the small back parking lot behind the office area of the lodge.

"That's Sally," he said with transparent boyish delight. "Come on!"

I had to hurry to keep up with his long-legged strides. The door of the Mazda popped open as we approched, and the renowned Sally Wallis climbed sinuously out.

I saw why Ted was smitten. The lady was indeed gorgeous.

Tall, perhaps in her middle thirties, she had lustrous, medium-length dark hair. She was wearing wine-colored shorts that revealed wonderful tan legs over fluffy sports socks and Nikes, and a sleeveless white cotton shell. Her breasts might have been too large for her slender, athletic body if she hadn't had such an erect, graceful carriage. She had been wearing big, blue-framed sunglasses, but she removed them and smiled brilliantly as she spied us coming. She had bold, dramatic features—very large, dark eyes, and a handsome mouth accentuated by her dark red lipstick. She would have changed the heartbeat of almost any man, anywhere.

"Ted. Hi." With a glad shiver, she moved close to him just long enough to brush her lips against his cheek . . . press briefly against him. "Damn! I got the brochures all delivered, but some of them won't get trucked out until Thursday or Friday. That's the penalty we pay for using the cheaper bulk rate."

Ted stared at her like a man dazzled by the sun. "I still think you had a great idea, mailing them that way, Sally."

She turned toward me. "Hi. You must be Brad Smith." She strode toward me, holding out a hand. "Welcome!"

Ted introduced us. "Anything you want to know, you can always ask Sally. She knows this place like no one else. She managed for Avery Whitney, the previous owner—the man who started this whole thing out here."

She laughed and shook her head. It was a pretty gesture, beguiling and seemingly spontaneous: the kind of unstudied perfection that comes from endless practice in front of a mirror. "Poor Avery. We fought 'em hard and we fought 'em fair. But when some of his backers got cold feet, he decided to sell out just when we might have been ready to turn the corner."

"How long were you with the previous owner?"

"The whole time. Over five years. My husband was a geologist. When he died in 1983, I took some night business courses and then started to work. And gosh, I love this place. I guess I'll work here as long as anybody will have me." She looked at Ted. "As long as . . . I'm welcome."

Ted flushed. "You'll *always* be welcome here. You know that."

She turned back to me. Her lips curled winsomely. "Isn't he *sweet*?"

It was a bit much, this part of the performance. But Ted obviously ate it up. He told her, "I'm going to put Brad in Cabin Four. I'll go down there now and make sure everything is in order. Why don't you show him around the lodge building, here, and then bring him and his luggage on down in the golf cart?"

She nodded. "Great. Come on," she said to me, and bounded up the steps at the back of the building.

I followed her inside.

It took about twenty minutes for us to walk around and look things over. Ted had not spared expense in making everything first class, from the dark-stained heavy beams of the hunting-lodge-style lobby to the thick carpet on the floors of the upstairs hallways. The dining room, empty at the moment, appeared top notch. The help we encountered seemed friendly and cheerful. Sally pointed out everything with buoyant optimism. All Bitterroot Valley lacked, that I could see, was customers.

"We'll get it going," she assured me as we returned to her office. "Things have been slow, and I know how much Ted worries. But your being here will help a lot. We've put an item in the local paper about you, and they want to do an interview. It's just a little paper that comes out twice a week. But any publicity for the tournament will be wonderful."

"How much has been done so far on the tournament?" I asked.

"Well . . . some."

"Like?"

She reached behind a work table and pulled out a large, lobby-sized poster, big black letters on cream-colored cardboard.I read:

First Annual
BITTERROOT VALLEY TENNIS TOURNAMENT
Professional Men
Amateur Mixed Doubles
Exhibition Matches
PROFESSIONAL DIVISION FIRST PRIZE: $60,000
Bitterroot Valley Resort
Elk City, Montana

"Impressive," I said. "But there's no date."

"Oh, that's set. This was just an early poster when we weren't sure."

"When is it going to be, then?"

"The thirteenth, fourteenth, and fifteenth of next month."

I stared at her.

"What is it?" she asked.

"I had hoped he would postpone it."

"He did. One week."

"That's like no postponement at all!"

She shook her head. "I know. That's another reason I'm so relieved you're here. Ted said you were a wizard at getting things set up."

I began to get a bad sensation in the pit of my stomach. "Is there a lot that still needs to be set up?"

"I'm afraid," she said ruefully, "almost everything."

I pursued it although I was not sure I wanted to. "Ted told me in Dallas he might need a little help from me in making a few calls to round out the brackets with name professionals. How many have accepted so far?"

"Well, there's Terry Carpoman."

I waited. Finally I prodded, "Who else?"

"Well, no one else, actually."

five

I took a minute to think about it. "*No one else?*"

Sally made a little hand gesture that could only mean futility. "Well, *I* don't know who to call, and Ted is the only other person who could do it, and he's been running all over the place, making other kinds of arrangements—rearranging loans—"

"How in the *hell* does he think we can get top tennis pros in here on less than a month's notice, and for no more prize money than that?"

"Well, the posters aren't dated. We haven't—you know—made *real* definite commitments yet!"

"Christ!"

"He said *you* could convince them."

I smacked my hand to my forehead. This I could not believe. I looked around. "Where did he say he was going? I need to find him and kill him."

With a little murmur of worry, Sally moved close to me. Her Shalimar wrapped itself intimately around me. She put her hand on my forearm, another of those "unstudied" gestures of hers that took endless practice to get just right. I looked down at her long, graceful fingers on my arm, then into her eyes. Ah, the power of feeling over intellect. I *knew* what she was doing to me, but it worked anyway. Her hand had sent pulses of electricity all through me.

"Please, Brad," she said. "Don't tell him I blurted out how far behind we are on this. I know he wanted to break it to you in his own way. He would *hate* me for being so dumb. He's had so many setbacks. He would practically take it as a betrayal." She squeezed her beautiful fingers. "Please."

"You care a lot about him," I said, testing.

"Of course I do! Isn't that obvious?" She paused a beat and her eyes swept up, the down-from-under look. "I would never do anything to hurt him. Of course . . . I'm my own person, I'm free. I do what I want. I'm not . . . taken, if you see what I mean."

I saw what she meant, all right. But before I could reply, the telephone rang, quick bursts from the lodge switchboard. Sally turned away from me and picked it up. "Sally Wallis speaking?"

She listened. I saw how she tensed slightly—her quick, reflexive intake of breath. "Yes." Her eyes darted toward me, then away again. "I, um, believe that might be all right, but this is not a good time for me . . . That's correct . . . Something like that, yes . . . All right. Goodbye." She hung up and turned back to me. "Vendors! They drive us crazy!"

I knew it hadn't been a vendor.

The back door slammed and Ted Treacher breezed back in. "All set, friend. I decided to come back and collect you personally. Golf cart is right outside. Let's get your things from your car and take a ride back to your cottage."

We walked out together, went down the steps to a golf cart, climbed in. With Ted at the wheel, we hummed around the east end of the lodge, following a path that led toward the parking lot where I had left the Bronco.

"Beautiful afternoon, isn't it?" Ted said.

"Tell me about the tournament."

He frowned. "We're a little behind on the arrangements for that, actually. I certainly hope you can help me get caught up."

"How many players are committed?"

"Well, there's Terry Carpoman. And there's you. And I can play in a pinch, of course. So we're almost in pretty good shape there."

"You've got to have a dozen players to make it a genuine tournament, Ted, and sixteen would be better. How the hell can you be advertising the thing when you don't have more commitments?"

"Time got away from me," he admitted glumly. "By the time I put a description of the tournament and the dates and everything in the stock prospectus—"

"You promised a tournament *in your stock offering*? Isn't that false advertising?"

His face stiffened in offense. "Certainly not. I plan to have the tournament."

"You don't have any players. You don't have a big enough purse. You don't have brackets or supplies or a corporate sponsor. You don't even have any *bleachers*, Ted!"

"Well," he said grudgingly, "that's what I've got you for. The details."

"Those aren't 'details.' Those are *necessities*."

"Well, we just have to work it all out."

He had pulled the cart up behind my Bronco. We collected my stuff and put it in the luggage compartment of the modified golf cart. Ted kept up a running monologue, baloney to prevent me from pressing him about his lack of planning—lying to me down in Richardson. We drove down an asphalt path through woods, passing a couple of widely spaced A-frame cabins. He pulled up in front of the third one about a hundred yards downslope from the lodge and out of its view.

"Here we are. Number Four. Spiffy, what?"

It seemed to be the most isolated cabin, on a slight knoll that gave it a partial view on downhill through the trees toward the distant golf course. I couldn't see another sign of human habitation, just the Ponderosas and a light sprinkling of tamaracks, with not much underbrush.

From long and hated practice I scanned and approved the lack of underbrush. It would be hard for a man to crawl unobserved up to the cottage. A couple of the huge pines overhung the shingle roof of the place, but the roofline was far too steep for someone to drop onto it and hold. There were no windows on the north side, only a door that had no glass in it to weaken it. I could hope there were only one or two windows on the other sides I couldn't see from the cart. The front door looked sturdy and so did the one on the side. Walls: heavy logs. Good. *Of course he could walk right up from the north side and be on that little porch, kicking the door down, before you knew he was there—*

I caught myself, tasting the acid in my mouth. I told myself I had to stop thinking like that.

Angry, I got Ted to leave me alone for a while. He didn't seem to realize he had screwed me by getting me here under false pretenses. I realized that was another measure of his desperation because he was a good man, a decent man. But I was still hacked.

There was a telephone in the cabin. I called my assigned number and got a neutral recording, one of those AT&T machines that sounds like the voice of a robot built in the Bronx. I left my verbal bona fides for Fred Skurlock and an obscure-sounding message to let him know I was here and ostensibly on the job.

I wondered how I was supposed to work on the job when my cover assignment already had me knee-deep in complications. I was supposed to be watching for Sylvester and checking out the lab as best I could without actually going in and making a spectacle of myself. But I had to attend to my cover, and Ted's ineptitude threatened to leave me no time for anything but trying to bail him out.

A little later, after putting a few things away in the cabin and allowing myself one more cigarette—which put me into my quota for next Wednesday—I walked up to the courts. The late afternoon had turned even more beautiful and I soaked up the slight cool breeze through the pines, the scents of grass and water and trees, the thin sunlight filtering down out of a crystal blue sky. It made me remember briefly how hot the days were already getting in Richardson, and how the tornado had made me feel homeless down there. This place, on the other hand, felt *right*.

I wished Beth were along to share it with me. I felt a thump of frustration about that. I believed in sexual equality one hundred percent, right? And equality in a relationship, right? So it was right and proper for the lady to stay in California and continue her convalescence and prepare to get back to her law practice, right? And fulfill her own destiny and all that. And I had no right at all to feel frustrated, right?

Wrong. Wrong. I wanted her here with me. Down deep, underneath all the should-be's, I didn't care about her rights and individuality and all such good stuff. The hidden man inside me—the one I try so hard to ignore—wanted to go find her and grab her and drag her here by the hair of her head. *Listen, Beth. Like the man said, read my lips. You just shut up, this is the way it's going to be. Now take off your clothes.*

Sometimes I despair of ever becoming noble enough to live with a modern woman. Betty Friedan, forgive me.

At the courts, Ted Treacher had assembled a small crowd of about twenty patrons. All but a couple were lodge guests. We visited a while and then I borrowed a racket, mine having been left in the Bronco, and rallied with a few of them. I worked up a nice sweat and got thoroughly loosened up, and then the patrons urged Ted and me to play a few games for their edification.

"I'm not warmed up," Ted, who had only been watching, protested.

"Oh, come on!" a pretty blonde urged. "It will be fun!"

"Sure, Ted," I said mildly. "It will be fun."

He looked at me and I think he saw my expression. But he couldn't get out of it. "Well, six games, then," he said reluctantly.

He had been off the tournament trail a shorter time than I had, and he was a fine athlete. But he obviously hadn't been playing. Even favoring my gimpy knee because I wasn't wearing the bulky brace, I saw at once that I could take him without much trouble. Of course a nice guy—me—would never even think of beating up on a friend just because I was hacked off at him.

So we played our six games and once he led a game 30–15 before losing that one like all the others.

"Bastard," he muttered with a sheepish grin as we walked off the court.

"Who? Me?"

We found Sally Wallis waiting for us outside the courts. She had two people with her: a slender, youthful brunette wearing jeans and a pale yellow cotton blouse, and a lank, musty-looking youth with more facial hair than I had seen since about 1971. The girl had a notebook and the boy had a 35 mm camera. She had smashing green eyes. He needed a bath.

Sally Wallis introduced us: "Brad Smith, may I present Lynette Jordan and Bobby Winkleman. They work for the local paper, Brad."

We shook hands. I liked Lynette's wide, enthusiastic grin and firm handshake.

"I'm thrilled to meet you, Mr. Smith." She beamed. "Is there someplace where we can talk—do an interview?"

"Sure." I glanced at Ted for an idea.

Lynette beat me to it. "How about over there?" she suggested, pointing to a small gazebo under the pines of the open parkway next to the courts. "Wouldn't that be good for your pictures, Bobby?"

"Far out," Winkleman murmured, and started fiddling with his camera.

Our patrons waved goodbye and discreetly withdrew to the courts. Ted said he would be in the office. He and Sally Wallis walked off, and I went with Lynette and Winkleman to the gazebo. The benches inside the pretty, white wood structure were fairly comfortable. Lynette started shooting me questions while Winkleman squatted and perched here and there, abusing the motor drive on his Nikon.

Lynette struck me as a little jewel. I liked her immediately. She had more energy and vivacity than an Olympic gymnast. She asked a lot of the right questions and I gave her the quotable answers. No, I had never been in the Elk City area before, but I thought it was beautiful. Bitterroot Valley was a great resort and I knew Ted Treacher was going to make a lot of money for the whole area with it. When I missed that dropshot in the championship match against Borg at Wimbledon? Well, it was a bitter disappointment, of course, Lynette, but Borg was a great player and maybe he would have won the match anyway. Yes, I expected to stay a month or so and help manage the tournament. No, we weren't ready to announce the brackets. The golf course? I was anxious to play it. I had brought my clubs, yes. Not too bad. I used to play to an eight, but I hadn't played much in a long time and I would probably be lucky to break 100. And so forth, and so on.

After a long time, Winkleman said he had enough, and wandered across the green to a nearby pond, where he changed to a long lens and started shooting pictures of the ducks. Lynette filled up more pages of her notebook, and I began to slip in a few exchanges which answered some of my curiosity, too. She was 21, a senior in the journalism school at Missoula, working at the Elk City paper this semester as part of an internship program that gave her experience, a small income, and academic credit. She expected to graduate in August. She was ambitious. She loved journalism. She wanted to work for the Denver *Post*.

"Don't you like Montana, Lynette?"

"Well, sure, a lot. But nothing ever happens around a place like little Elk City. My gosh, the biggest thing that's happened around here in the last ten years was a few years back, when some of the satellite dishes failed during the Super Bowl! I want to cover some *news*!"

I said I was sorry I didn't have any.

She asked me some things about my magazine freelancing, betraying ambitions in that direction, too. I asked her about the previous owner of the resort. She said he was a grand eccentric named Avery Whitney. He still lived outside of Elk City in a big log home. Some people didn't think much of him, but she thought he was kind of cute. He drank whiskey and smoked big cigars and had made a pass at her once.

After she got some biographical facts about me straightened out, it was my turn again.

The other resort north of Elk City was doing okay, but it catered to skiers and hunters and fishermen, mainly, and Lynette did not understand why the owner, John Lis, and some of the other local businessmen seemed so dead set against Mr. Treacher and Bitterroot Valley. She had heard that Mr. Lis had bid on this layout when Avery Whitney let it be known he would sell. She had also heard rumors that somebody else local had also made a try to buy it. Maybe people were mad because Ted had outbid them.

"Hey, wow!" She grinned finally, tilting her head to examine my expression. "Who's getting interviewed here, anyway?"

"Natural curiosity, Lynette, sorry."

She sighed and closed her notebook. "I've stayed longer than I was supposed to. Thanks a bunch. I'll write this up right away. It's too late for the Tuesday edition; that's already being printed this afternoon. But it'll be in Friday, if we have any room." She shook hands vigorously. "Where's that darned Bobby? The last time I saw him he was trying to interview a mallard . . ."

* * *

Later Ted drove me around most of the golf course in his lodge cart. It was virtually deserted, a middle-aged vacationing couple on the third green, a male foursome putting on six, a lone player—short, whip-slender, with bushy gray whiskers and hair partly obscuring his sun-darkened face—on eleven. It was a shame. The course cried out for play. It was beautiful and it looked challenging enough for anyone. The new holes that had just been seeded in were an improvement in an already excellent layout.

Dinner in the lodge dining room that night was excellent: trout and new potatoes, a California Chardonnay, peaches and Courvoisier. Our voices tended to echo. I counted all the other customers in the vast room; there were twelve of them.

After that it had been dark a long time already, and I had a bad case of the yawns. I left the lodge building and started back through the woods on foot, lugging my small blue duffel. Before going far I stopped long enough to dig the .38 revolver out from under my tennis shoes and sweats.

The vast darkness around the cottage was punctuated only by a distant light in a condo and the tree-filtered stars overhead. I double-bolted myself inside, opened one of Ted's courtesy New York Seltzers, and stretched out on the couch to call Beth. The call went through and she sounded glad to hear from me.

I told her most of it.

"Brad, you sound really tired," she told me.

"Long day."

"You sound worried, too."

"A little."

"But you're okay?"

"I would be better," I told her, "if you were here."

She didn't say anything to that.

I went on, "It's beautiful here, Beth. Really. And they've got fine courts and a pretty golf course, not to mention a swimming pool and all the other amenities. Why don't you change your mind and come join me for a few days, or for the whole time I'm here? You'd love it. Okay?"

There was a pause, and then she said, "Brad, I have another doctor appointment in a few days. I expect him to turn me loose to go back to work. You know I've already been going in a few hours every day, getting reacquainted, getting up to date."

"This wouldn't be long," I said, "and the vacation might do you good."

When she replied this time, I could hear the slightest ping of impatience in her tone. "I've been doing nothing but have a damned vacation ever since that madman shot me down there in St. Maarten. I want to get back to *work*, Brad! Is that so bad?"

"No," I said. "Of course not."

"Now you're pissed at me."

"No. I'm not pissed. I understand."

We talked a while longer. I put in one more plea for Bitterroot Valley. She responded with one more commercial for the Work Ethic. End of conversation, she hanging up first and me listening for a few seconds to the whine of the dial tone . . . the sound of a couple of thousand miles I detested.

Ten minutes later I heard the person on the porch.

I moved fast. Then the person outside knocked. Holding my right hand behind my back, I cracked the heavy door on its security chain.

Sally Wallis blinked at me in the glare of the little porchlight. She had changed into body-hugging lavender sweats and Nike running shoes. She still looked beautiful and exotic. A lodge golfcart sat on the lawn behind her like a misshapen ornament. "Hi! You got a minute?"

"Sure," I said, puzzled.

I unchained the door and got the .38 hidden in my back pants pocket as she came in, moved silkenly to the couch, and perched on one end of it.

"What's on your mind?" I asked.

"I was worried about your concern about the tournament and everything. I just wanted to make sure you're okay."

"I'm a little hacked, but I'll get over it."

Her eyes enlarged. "I don't want you mad at me."

"No."

She sighed with exaggerated relief. "Whew!"

I stood across the table from her and refused to say anything.

She crossed her legs and looked around the cabin interior as if she had never seen one before. "These are really nice, aren't they? I've always sort of wanted to spend the night in one to get the feel of the place."

I yawned.

She was watching me most carefully. "You *are* comfortable?"

"Yes. Thank you."

She got to her feet, innocently stretching in a most fetching way. "That's nice. I just wanted to make sure you weren't too upset . . . or didn't need anything. I know how lonesome it can be in a new place, all alone."

Our eyes met and she waited. I knew how it was supposed to go now.

I was supposed to say, "It wouldn't be lonely if you stayed, Sally."

And she was supposed to say, "But I don't know if I should . . ."

And I was supposed to say, "Please, Sally. I want you. A lot."

And then she would say, "I have to be back in my own room by daylight, darling."

Anticipation hung thick in the air like a rank jungle spoor. Sally would be a handful. Her snug costume couldn't have better shown off her sleekly exercised body, those long arms and legs. After the frustrating conversation with Beth, and looking Sally over from head to toe, I was tempted. But I was also a little tired and a little disgusted. Poor Ted.

So I told her, "Drive carefully on the way back to the lodge, Sally. That cart doesn't have any lights on it."

She stiffened with surprise. For an instant I thought I saw the anger of a rejected lady in her big eyes. But then she got control. "I will, Brad. I'm glad you're not mad." By this time she had recovered enough to make another try. "Maybe some other night . . . soon . . . we can have a nice long time together."

I yawned again and walked her to the door and closed it behind her, and then decided maybe I needed something stronger than New York Seltzer. I didn't like what I had gotten into here. And Sally had been right about one thing: it *was* lonely.

But that was not entirely the reason why I nursed my new drink and felt the gnawing, reluctant regret that I hadn't played her little game and asked her to stay. Having someone here might have made it easier to sleep; more ears to listen for the footsteps that meant he had come after me at last.

Yes. Brave Brad Smith. Thinking that even a cheap roll in the hay might make him feel more secure for just a little while.

Taking my Smith & Wesson out of my pants pocket, I examined it. I was sick of the lurking fear. When was it going to *get better*? When was I going to find enough manhood inside me to *make* it get better?

I nursed the highball and smoked more cigarettes and tried to concentrate on Ted Treacher, and what was obviously a very tight fit he was in. But Sylvester kept creeping into my mind.

Finally, gun in hand, I spooked outside and looked around. It was very dark under the trees, only the faintest light scattered through the woods from the unseen security lights surrounding the lodge. I went all the way around the cabin, pulse speeding, imagining ghouls and ogres.

At the back end of the cabin near my woodpile I happened to see something off to my left, downslope, toward the golf course. I stopped, squinting to see better.

It had been two brief flashes of white light. Far off through the woods. Perhaps even beyond the golf course. I wondered what they were. They did not repeat. I watched in that direction for a minute or two, then began to get the galloping cowardlies. I went back inside.

Skurlock had not returned my call. I guessed that meant he must think I was doing my job.

After locking up with all the care of a ghetto widow woman, I brushed my teeth, rechecked the locks, and piled into the big, oversoft corner bed, the pistol making a friendly hard lump under my pillow. Pictures of Sally in here with me flashed across my imagination. I worked on thinking of other things.

Finally I slept. Then I dreamed. Same dream. I was walking down a street in a city I had never been in, and I was about to turn the corner around a building, and suddenly *he* came around the corner from the other direction: Sylvester. I recognized his body bulk and the animal-smooth way he moved, but he had no face at all, only a lumpy, featureless mask of flesh. In his hand he held the weapon he had had on St. Maarten. My nervous system went crazy with terror.

Then I realized Beth was beside me and he started firing the pistol and the first bullets hit her and then they started hitting me and I yelled something. The sound of my own voice jolted me awake.

I found myself sitting up in the big bed in the dim cabin—the bathroom light throwing faint illumination over unfamiliar, grotesque outlines and shadowy features. I was sweat-soaked.

I got up and padded into the bathroom and got a drink of water, went back into the main room and smoked again. The sweat cooled and dried on my naked body and my heart rate slowed down. But it was a long time before I tried to go to sleep again. I filled some of the scare-time by worrying some more about the tournament, and some other minutes by wishing I had more courage.

The travel alarm said 3:15 when I turned in again.

six

Elsewhere

Chicago

The telephone on Ardis Allen's sprawling desk blinked. Ardis looked up from her financial statements and picked it up. "Yes, Betty?"

"Mr. Matthew Cliffton on line one, Mrs. Allen."

"Thank you, Betty." Ardis stabbed the button. "Yes, Matthew."

"Mrs. Allen, this is Matt Cliffton out in Elk City."

Ardis imagined the rotund attorney sitting in his crummy office. She imagined he had a moose head on one wall and a stuffed fish on another. He was not the brightest man in the world, she thought—evidence being that he had to announce himself after the secretary had obviously screened the call—but he had done Ardis's bidding satisfactorily, if not brilliantly, so far.

"Yes, Matthew. What is it?"

The nasal voice sounded unctuous. "I thought you would be interested to know that three of our local suppliers have ceased all deliveries to our acquaintance, demanding full payment of bills before they'll resume."

"Excellent, Matthew. About that request for extension of loans from the S&Ls in Butte and Missoula?"

"I am assured both requests for extensions are being denied."

"That's good news. Anything else?"

"I'm working on mechanics' liens and possible court action *in re* the roof repairs and swimming pool work. When I have something definite—"

"Fine," Ardis cut in crisply. "Now, is there anything further on the missing man at the site?"

For the first time Cliffton's voice sounded tight, worried. "No, ma'am. It's a total mystery. He's simply . . . missing, still. We're all puzzled."

Ardis was puzzled too. A missing person near the mine was hardly the kind of attention-getter she wanted right now. The clean-up work had to continue quietly, out of the public eye.

She said, "Anything else, Matthew?"

The Elk City lawyer had nothing more. Ardis assured him that their contingency agreement would remain in force. "A new retainer check will be mailed at once, Matthew. And thank you again for your good work."

Hanging up, Ardis thought about it. Except for the missing man—which worried her a good deal—things were progressing faster than she had hoped. The new financial developments engineered by her Elk City lawyers were surely tightening the screws on Ted Treacher.

Now Ardis would tighten them more.

She summoned Betty, her secretary. "Betty, please call Mr. Treacher in Montana at once. Inform him that other developments require that we move my inspection visit to this coming weekend."

"Yes, Mrs. Allen."

"If he wants to talk to me or anyone else, tell him we're in conference. No, better yet: tell him we're out of the city. Then please notify my pilots and make the other necessary arrangements. And send in Mr. Lyle immediately. Thank you, Betty."

As her secretary hurried out to do her bidding, Ardis opened a desk drawer and allowed herself a rare cigarette. Touching its tip with the flame of her gold Colibri lighter, she smiled. She enjoyed times when she could increase pressure to her advantage. The weekend, she thought, would increase the pressure on Ted Treacher to the point where there would be no way he could turn down her offer to buy the resort—and secure the security buffer zone her cleanup operation desperately needed.

Elk City

Sylvester, too, got a telephone call at his mountain cabin.

"Yes?"

"I have information," the familiar voice said.

Recognizing the voice, Sylvester snapped to attention. "Go ahead."

"He had a visitor this morning. A man named Skurlock. I have the license number from the man's car if you need it."

Sylvester had already tightened. "I know who the man is. Were you able to hear anything they said?"

"No, I'm sorry, that was impossible. Except for one thing. I did hear them say they were going to drive past 'the place.' I don't know what that means."

Sylvester thought he did. "Anything else?"

"No, not really. They left in Mr. Skurlock's car and were gone almost three hours."

"Anything else?" Sylvester repeated.

"No."

"Thank you. Keep up the good work." Sylvester hung up.

It was a day, he thought, for good news and bad news.

First had come the report from his colleague inside the air force lab: he had finally managed to slip an inside key off a janitor's key-ring. The janitor had been sleeping on the job, and Sylvester's colleague felt sure the man would be too guilty and scared to report the loss, even if he was intelligent enough to notice it.

Having the key was a critical breakthrough. Even security areas tended to make a fundamental mistake with their keying. Keys to related areas—and to outside masters—tended to follow a general pattern. In the hands of an expert, a room key or sub-master gave crucial hints about the tooth and indention patterns of all other keys in the related set. And Sylvester knew such an expert, one who had done work for him before.

The key would be delivered to Sylvester tonight. He had already made a long-distance call and would have it express-mailed to Seattle overnight. By tomorrow night this time, he would have back a set of new keys, one of which almost surely duplicated the lab's master key.

If that was exceptionally good news, however, word of a meeting between Brad Smith and the FBI man named Skurlock was equally bad. Sylvester thought there was at least one other FBI man in the area, but had so far been unable to identify him; Skurlock, however, had arrived with the thinnest cover, and had made himself conspicuous almost at once by asking too many questions around town.

If Skurlock and Smith were meeting, it could mean they were onto something—some lead Sylvester was not aware of.

What to do? Sylvester paced the floor of the cabin and finally decided that it was too risky to take any overt action yet. But a bit of hassle, designed to distract Smith from his work, might be in order.

Sylvester drove into Elk City. He had little difficulty locating Jack Lassiter. As expected, Lassiter was parked in his car under a shade tree near the high school, grimly watching his radar screen with one eye while gloating over the long-legged girls with the other.

Sylvester pretended surprise at seeing Lassiter here, and pulled over, then walked back to the policeman's open side window.

"Afternoon, Mr. Lassiter! I'm on my way to fish upriver, and just wanted to say hello!"

Lassiter watched his radar unit register *19* for a passing car loaded with teen-age boys. He seemed disappointed. "Hope you have good luck, sir."

"Oh, I will, I will." Sylvester paused. "Say, you must have really made that Vietnam shirker angry since we talked about him!"

Lassiter's eyes narrowed. "Who?"

"You know! The shirker! Brad Smith! Say, I was in the café awhile ago, and he was in there really shooting off his mouth, saying what a hick town this is, what a . . . well, I hate to use his exact words, but . . . what a bad person you are, and so on."

Lassiter was all attention now, and there was that crazy light in his eyes. "He said that, did he?"

"If you ask me," Sylvester said blithely, "a man like that needs to be taught a lesson. A *serious* lesson. I tell you, sir, if I wasn't a peaceful man recuperating from a heart attack, I would be tempted to go out to that rich man's club myself and invite him out into the nearest alley!"

It was a transparent trick, one that no totally normal person would have bought. But Lassiter's jaw worked and his eyes got crazier. "Talking about me and the town, huh?"

Sylvester sighed. "I hate people like that. Well, I should be going. Those trout are calling my name. If I get two big ones, I'll bring one by your house tonight for you and your brother! Have a nice day, Mr. Lassiter!"

Who knew about such things? Sylvester wondered, driving north. Lassiter was crazy enough to do anything if sufficiently goaded. At worst he was almost sure to give Brad Smith a troublesome diversion from his major task in Elk City. At best, a man like Lassiter might even really go off the deep end and kill him.

That thought made Sylvester chuckle.

Watching his renter's pickup vanish around the next corner, Lassiter rubbed his callused hands over his face, trying to make the ringing in his ears go away. He had had the ringing all the time since Nam, and the plate they put in his head after the mortar attack. It was always worse when Lassiter was angry or scared.

Now he was both.

If Chief Hamm or anyone else ever found out the bad things that had already happened in the last few days, Lassiter knew he was not only finished as a cop, but doomed to prison. And he could not abide the prospect of prison. To be locked up, held in one of those concrete tombs so small you couldn't even stretch your arms out without hitting the walls or ceiling—! Even imagining it made his insides shrivel and fill with screams.

Lassiter did not think he had really done anything wrong. Accidents happened. People got in your way and sometimes they got hurt. And it was not like anybody influential in Elk City, from the mayor on down, seemed too eager for Treacher and his new resort to succeed. *Something* was going on, Lassiter knew; he just didn't know what. But first there had been happy, optimistic talk about how reopening of the resort would help the town, and then overnight all that talk stopped and everyone started muttering about bringing in too much traffic, an undesirable element. Or they said nothing more at all. Hassling Treacher's guests was tacitly approved, as long as you weren't too obvious about it. Eager to make people in power like him, Lassiter had been hassling pretty consistently.

Having the man named Brad Smith here, however, had upped the ante. Especially since Lassiter had been told how the son of a bitch had dodged honorable duty in Nam—letting people like Lassiter fight and get hurt or die for him. And now came this latest word that the bastard was going around, talking behind Lassiter's back.

The anger and confusion dinned in Lassiter's ears, making it hard for him to think. Sometimes when he felt like this he went out and found a stray cat or dog, and took it into the woods where no one could see, and did things to it. That helped, a little. But the relief was always temporary. The ringing always started again, along with the confusion and the pains inside his head.

Lassiter brooded about it.

Later he consulted his watch. Time for his shift to end for the day. Time to hurry over and start his other job watching the fence around the old mine.

Maybe, he thought, he would find time to go to the lodge. There had to be some way to get back at Smith. He had to find the way.

seven

By Thursday, just three days after my arrival at Bitterroot Valley, I had worn calluses on my ears with the telephone, and some things were looking up.

Some weren't.

Good news: I got lucky with a couple of top players. Knowing Ivan Lendl's fondness for golf, I got my telephone call past his manager and talked to him directly, extolling the beauty of the area—and our golf course. Ivan said yes, and suggested a couple of other players who might be interested. I started trying to track them down.

Bad news: I asked Sally Wallis about other arrangements—court arrangements, ticket printing, programs, outdoor concessions, food service, ushers, and so on. She looked blank. I then asked Ted. He looked blanker.

Good news: Ted came back from seeing some creditors in Missoula, confident they were going to extend his time to repay some notes, about which he was vague with me.

Bad: He got a telephone call from Allen Industries, the Chicago firm scheduled to visit later in the month, saying they would be on our doorstep in forty-eight hours. That sent him into a new nervous tizzy, and any thought I had had of his helping me on the tournament went right out the window as he started running in all directions to make preparations for the investor visit.

The worst news came when Fred Skurlock showed up Thursday morning. He said security people at the air force lab had missed a key.

"An important one?" I blurted.

Skurlock stabbed his spoon into his coffee cup. "Inside office door, so you wouldn't think so. But the idiots out there had never installed a decent random-coding key system."

"Meaning?"

"Meaning any key might provide the pattern for a master key."

"Great."

"It's being fixed right now," Skurlock told me. "New locks all around, and a random key-form pattern. So *that* can't happen again, anyhow. And the old key couldn't have been missing more than a day."

"Long enough for somebody to make off with something," I pointed out.

"I know that, I know that," he replied testily. Then he glared at me. "You're not pulling your weight, Smith."

I just stared at him.

"You haven't come up with lead one. Not one. From what I can see, you're sitting around out here all the time on your dead ass, talking to your country club buddies or squiring that piece of fluff from the newspaper around."

"I can't get out of helping Ted. That's my cover."

"You could do *something* on the security problems we've got here."

"That's the reason I've been nice to the girl from the paper. She's smart. I've been asking her a lot of questions, getting her to drive me around on back highways and byways. With her at the wheel, I was even able to get up to the air force station front door, and get a small first-hand idea of what we're dealing with here."

Skurlock studied me suspiciously. "With what results?"

"With no results yet. But I'm working on it. I've set up a golf game in a little while—"

"Oh, *that's* going to help our case!"

I was losing my temper. "It could. It could. This guy Avery Whitney, who used to own this place, is said to know everybody and everything around here. I rustled up a game with him, hoping to question him while we play. He might be able to tell me something that will give us a lead."

Skurlock seemed somewhat mollified. "Well. You hadn't told me you were doing any of that."

"Am I supposed to report bowel movements too?"

That hacked him. He stood, sloshing out remaining coffee into the saucers. "Keep me informed."

"Yes sir, boss."

A couple of hours later I collected my equipment at the cabin and hiked down into the gentle ravine where the golf pro shop was located. The only person around, other than young Max the pro, was a tall, slightly corpulent gent of about sixty putting some balls on the practice green. He was wearing a tam-o'-shanter, vivid green sweatshirt, and plaid knickers with high white hose and white spikes. His putter was an old-fashioned blade with what looked like a hickory shaft, but the irons sticking out of his kangaroo-leather bag on the edge of the green were state-of-the-art beryllium-copper Pings. He was either an avid throwback or the senior president of the Payne Stewart fan club.

He rolled in a forty-footer, looked up at me to make sure I had observed, and nodded. I nodded back and walked over. "Mister Whitney?"

He peeled off the tam and ran a ham-sized hand through long, bushy gray hair. His face looked like something peeled off Mt. Rushmore. One of his protruding dark eyes did not quite track, so one side of his face always looked like he was peering in some other direction. He took a long look at my old Haig clubs in the battered canvas bag on the back of the cart. "That's me."

I held out my hand. "I'm Brad Smith."

He shook, mangling my knuckles a little. "You play golf as good as you play tennis?"

"Never have."

"What's your handicap?"

"Used to be eight," I told him. "Might be thirty now."

"How are you hitting the ball?"

"Don't know. I haven't been playing."

He leaned on his driver. "Well, sir, let's put it this way. Number one is a four-par. If you hit a good drive, what iron do you think you would be hitting on your approach?"

His cross-examination was getting so outrageous I stifled a smile and played along with it. "Well, sir, let's put it *this* way. Every time I club myself for an iron shot today, I'll have to pick on the basis of the shot I know I can hit if I hit it right, or the shot I think I'll probably hit, or the shot I'm afraid I *might* hit."

The laugh issued from deep in his chest like a subterranean echo. "Let's play some golf."

We rode in his cart down the path to the first tee, which looked up a long slope between woods toward the distant green. Both of us took a few practice swings.

Whitney teed a ball up. "I might as well hit first. I'll have the honor the rest of the time anyhow."

He took a couple more practice swings. I hauled out my No. 1 wood and loosened up. There was a weedy creek out there, angling across the fairway about 130 yards out. The creek then ran alongside the fairway toward the distant green. Bunkers left and right of the slightly elevated green, and perdition—a sharp dropoff—beyond.

Whitney moved up to his ball, took a bent-knee stance, and swung back with the slow caution of many, many lessons. He came around with a vicious, accelerating turn that made the shaft whistle. *Crack!* The ball screamed across the creek and down the right side of the fairway, bounding and rolling about 255 yards out.

"Gave you an opening right away," he said with a grimace, shoving his driver back in the bag.

Even the great pros have told me that the first tee shot is something special every day. The old man had stirred up some of my competitive instincts, and nobody wants to look like an idiot on the first tee. I sensed that the better I played, the more likely he might be to relax and answer the questions I intended to work into our talk between shots. So, concentrating on about sixteen fundamentals at once, I took three more careful practice swings. Then I moved up to the ball, looked up the fairway, and made my mind a blank, working on feeling. It was far from a great shot, but I would take it: a slight draw, hitting in the middle about 190 yards out and rolling left another twenty through the lush green grass to the edge of the fairway.

"Not bad," Whitney said as I got in the cart beside him. "You want to play for money?"

"No thanks."

"Why not? You played for millions when you were a tennis star."

"That was tennis, and it was also then."

We started out. He floorboarded the cart accelerator and we whizzed down the path, the wind cool on my face. I said, "You like it around here?"

"Oh, sure. It's a good place to almost go bankrupt."

"You've been here a long time."

"Yep." He didn't elaborate.

"Lots of visitors around here?"

"Lots." He glowered, obviously wanting to think golf.

"I think a friend of mine is up here somewhere," I pressed. "Sure would like to find him. He's a little bigger than normal height, real thin. Last time I saw him, he had fairly dark hair, some gray. He's been sick. You'd notice that."

Whitney kept driving.

"He has a very distinctive, high-pitched voice," I added.

Whitney stopped the cart. We had reached my ball. "Hit."

I pulled out my 5-wood. "Seen anybody around who matches that description?"

He glared at me with his good eye. "What description?"

Damn. I addressed my ball, sitting down in the lush spring grass, took my time, remembered to swing rather than hit, and watched the resulting shot leap out of there and fly toward the green on a perfect trajectory—but stop a little short.

"We ought to play for something," Whitney told me as we drove on up to his ball. "Just to give it flavor, you know."

"How much?"

"Let me think about it." Then he hit a 5-iron halfway to the sky and down onto the middle of the green perhaps twelve feet from the pin.

I chipped badly and two-putted for a bogey five. The old man walked all around his putt like a restless caged lion, then stroked it in for a three.

"A dollar," he told me, replacing the flagstick.

"Fine."

"A dollar for longest drive, a dollar for first on, a dollar for every stroke you win the hole by. Let's see . . ." He licked the stubby pencil and marked on the scorecard. "That means so far you owe me four bucks."

By the time we were halfway through the back nine, I was thinking I might have to get a GMAC loan to pay him off. He was an outrageous old bastard and a fine, reckless golfer. At that point he was one over and I was only seven over, good for me. But his scorecard had marks all over it, totaling all I owed him.

It was not worth it. Sifting through his hyperbole, I had collected a lot of information, none of which seemed useful.

"Going broke," he pronounced at one point, "is truly horseshit. It attacks a man's masculinity, if you ask me. It also makes it impossible for you to do practically anything else that requires any kind of financing for a few years. Being convicted of a felony may be worse, but you can petition the governor for a pardon for *that*. You go bankrupt, it's always on your record, a big green 'B' as bad as Hester Prynne's scarlet letter."

"Avery, how did it happen?"

"You can call me Spud if you want. Anybody that owes me as much money as you do, it's the least I can do for you. Well, I would say my loss of this resort and my close encounter with bankruptcy came from three causes: my failure to see how much operating capital I was going to need in the first two years, my failure to realize how bad the town was going to get depressed financially, what with businesses going under and young people dying all over the place, and my failure to be smart enough to realize it when I first started getting in over my head in debt."

A worry that had been ticking in the back of my mind came to the front. "Was that old pulp mill the source of pollution? Do you think that's what makes kids sick around here?"

"Don't know. Is it my honor as usual? I'll hit."

He kept talking. He struck me as an unusual man, not merely colorful, but with surprising depth. The failure of the resort under his ownership had hurt deeply. He said he thought some local suppliers screwed him on purpose, but he couldn't prove it.

"Why would they do that?"

"Dunno. Good shot. For you."

"And yet you stayed around here."

"I came here many years ago. When I say 'they,' I only mean a half-dozen of the bastards. Everybody else around here—good people. *Good* people. They ain't going to run me off."

We finished the fourteenth hole and drove up to the elevated fifteenth tee. From this point I could see how far the fairways had been recontoured and new greens installed with berms and embankments along the ever-present creek. Because it was high ground, I could also look over woods on my left and get a distant first look at the old mine I had heard about, bare dirt and rubble strewn on the hillside surrounded by a high security fence.

Whitney lit a prodigious tee shot about 300 yards offline to the right, and well into the pines. Given a fine opening, I pulled mine straight left into those woods.

Whitney looked disgusted. "Shit! Well, you take the cart. I'll walk down there and see if I can find my ball."

I drove alone partway down the hill, then turned the cart off the path and barrelled into the trees. By luck I found my ball at once, nestled in pine needles. I guessed the line to the green and got a four-iron over the trees and headed in the right direction. Then on impulse I drove on through the trees to get a closer look at the mine property.

The gleaming new fence interested me. I wondered why the firm kept things up so well when obviously the mine had played out. It struck me that some well-placed dynamite would have closed the shaft once and for all and saved money for fence upkeep, etc., in the long run. Repainting the warning signs alone must be a yearly job for somebody.

That was when I remembered the lights I had seen from behind my cabin. Had they been over here—behind the fence?

But that didn't make sense. This place was closed up, deserted. Maybe . . .

I pulled the cart up by the gate and read the sign there, wondering what had happened to the construction foreman still missing. Was this, I thought, one of those mysterious accidents of the type that had haunted—and finally doomed—Avery Whitney?

Which was as far as I got in my thinking before the voice startled me: "*What the hell do you think you're doing there?*"

I turned sharply and saw what I hadn't seen from the crest in the woods or from my position driving the cart along the fence: a battered red Jeep, no top, parked in the shade of a little grove of aspen, and a familiar bulky figure coming toward me at a lumbering high rate of speed. Hatless, sweaty, he was otherwise in full brown uniform. And he had one of those old-time billy clubs in his right fist, the kind cops on the beat used to carry. My dear friend officer Lassiter again. Wonderful.

"Hello, Officer!" I sang out cheerfully.

He crunched up to confront me at a distance of about a foot. It's a trick cops and other bullies sometimes use: violate your space and make you immediately back away by reflex, with the conjoint sense of inferiority.

"What," he demanded, "do you think you're doing here?"

"Looking at the fence," I said in total honesty.

Lassiter's close-set eyes narrowed as synapses sluggishly fired somewhere behind all the ridges of thick bone and muscle. "You're the same guy that broke through the funeral procession."

"Mistakenly misunderstood your signals, you mean."

"Don't get smart, buddy!"

"I'm not, Officer. I'm being factual."

He raised the billy club and shoved me none too gently in the stomach with the blunt end of it. "You might be lucky this is my day off, buddy."

I should have shut up right then, but I was getting steamed. "Is this what you do on your day off? Drive around in search of people to try to intimidate?"

"Listen! I *work* for a living! Just like I by God fought for my country! I love this country. But I guess you wouldn't understand that."

"What are you talking about now?"

He crammed the business end of the club into my sternum, painfully staggering me backward a step. "I work part-time as a security guard here because officers don't get paid enough. But I can change hats fast and take you in and arrest you on my own complaint of trespassing."

"Wouldn't that be a little hard to make stick, since I haven't even so much as touched a finger to your precious fence?"

The eyes got narrower and crazier. "Don't smart off. I'm warning you again."

The temptation was very, very strong. Oh, how strong. To wrench the club out of his hands and turn around and apply it to *his* midsection. I knew his type and just how fast he might react, and the old training I had been given once in Virginia by the best in the business made me reasonably sure I could carry it out.

The wiser part of me prevailed. So you do that, I thought. Then what? He's your enemy from then on. You win this round, possibly, but he puts on his badge, sooner or later, and takes you to jail, where you fall on his flashlight or the end of his club in some regrettable midnight "accident," and if you're very lucky you start tracking mentally again in about a month, or maybe you stand up later in the misdemeanor court with a lawyer beside you to plead guilty because your eyes won't focus any more, and neither will your mind, and when you try to speak, you make embarrassing slobbering noises.

"Sorry, Officer," I said through my teeth.

Naturally he took that as weakness, so he shoved me again, making me stagger back against the unyielding chain link fence. "This is private property, very dangerous, and you're trespassing."

"You said that before," I pointed out. "But I hadn't so much as touched your precious fence until you just pushed me into it."

"The property line," he flared back, angrier than ever, "is clear over there." He pointed to an invisible line ten yards from the fence.

Before I could answer that, there came the sound of some brush rustling and rocks tumbling upslope to our right, in the direction of the golf course. We both looked up to see Avery Whitney, 7-iron in hand, coming down the steepest, shale-strewn part of the embankment like a gored water buffalo.

"Thought you might be having an adventure," he muttered, and then turned to Lassiter. "Hey there, Lassie. What's going on here?" He stared at me. "Did you find your ball? You didn't hit it this far out of the fairway!"

"Spud," Lassiter growled, "don't call me '*Lassie*'! I've told you that before!"

Whitney stood first on one foot, then on the other, screwing up his face in pained confusion. "I'm sorry, Las—I mean Jack. It seems like such a natural nickname for 'Lassiter,' but I guess you don't like it because it makes it sound like you're a collie. Like, 'Here, Lassie! Here, Lassie!' Or *Lassie Come Home.* I guess if my name was Lassiter I wouldn't want to be called Lassie either. It's stupid, how I keep forgetting."

"What the hell are you doing here, anyway?" Lassiter, beet-faced, demanded.

Whitney pointed at me with the 7-iron. "Trying to play golf with this jackass. But he hits the ball everyplace but the golf course." He glared at me like Jack Elam. "Did you find the ball? Have you been smart-mouthing Officer Lassiter, here?"

"Mildly," I said.

"Well, stop it. Jack, please forgive the dunce. If you'll just overlook this incident, we'll get back over the hill to the golf course, and I'll *try* to keep him in line for the rest of the round."

Lassiter glowered at Whitney, and then at me. "Don't come around here again," he said.

"I won't, sir."

"I'm warning you!"

"Yes, sir."

He hawked something up and spat it into the dust between us, sort of like one of the bad guys did to Shane early on, before Shane lost his temper and fought back. "Go on. I'm letting you off this time."

I climbed into the cart. Whitney climbed in beside me, rocking the contraption dangerously on the sidehill. "Thanks, Lassie—I mean—sorry!—*Jack*. No more balls hit clean over here, I promise you! Have a good day! Give my regards to Chief Hamm for me, all right? Bye bye! You take care now!" Under his breath as we started up the hill he hissed at me, "Get us *out* of here!"

With one glance back at Lassiter, I did. Under some circumstances I would have been amused by the comic-book melodrama of the thing. But there was something about Lassiter that made it not funny at all, not down deep. I had known a few men like him. Real violence—dangerous stuff that might be truly crazy—lay just under his surface.

We hummed over the rise and into the woods, hidden from view.

Whitney said seriously, "You watch that man. Don't smart off to him. He's a bad-ass."

"I wasn't doing anything."

"That doesn't *matter*. Believe me. Oh, I know he's got the IQ of a turnip. But don't underestimate him. He can be mean and nasty. Real mean and real nasty. There have been local tough guys who crossed him regularly in the past. Two or three of them just . . . went away one night or another. No sign of 'em anymore. Everybody looked at each other and said, 'Well, I guess old Sammy decided to try it in Missoula.' Or: 'Wonder where old Archie went; must have went off to look for a better job somewhere else.'"

"You teased him, Avery."

"I live here. I'm too old to threaten him. Also, I know just how far to go—what I can get away with. You don't. And he *knows* me. He figures I'm crazy. You're a different proposition, entirely."

We reached my ball in the fairway. I got out and pulled out my wedge and walked around the cart, and my eyes met Whitney's stare for a moment. There was not a trace of humor in his look. I had never seen a man more serious.

"A word to the wise," he said. "Some of these people can work against Ted Treacher all they want. Just like they worked against me, for reasons I don't fathom. That's his problem. Or yours, too. But no matter what happens, there is *no* reason for you or anybody else around here to take a man like Lassiter lightly. Because if you do, you might regret it all the rest of your life. All ten minutes of it. Do I make myself clear?"

I studied his expression, and especially his eyes. This was not a stupid man, nor a weak one. He had taken a battering and kept on. He was brave, too, but there was a black fear underlying his stony eyes. His warning was as serious as he could be. He meant it.

"You're clear," I told him.

"Also," he added heavily, cocking his head to keep me in focus with his good eye as I moved around, "you need to understand something about Montanans. They treasure their privacy. They don't like people who walk around giving descriptions of somebody, asking if they've been seen. This used to be frontier country, son. Vigilante country. Francis X. Beidler. All that. Why, hell. If I *had* seen your skinny, sickly-looking feller with a high voice, I probably wouldn't tell you, just to be shitty about it. A lot of people, you ask them something like that, they'd kick hell out of you, or at least let the air out of your tires when you were in the toilet. Then, if they did know your man, they'd go warn him you were asking about him. People here like to be *let alone*, son. Remember that."

"Even if the man I'm looking for is my friend," I argued.

The old man made a harumphing sound. "Shit. Don't insult my intelligence." He reached for a cigar and lit it with a wood match cracked across the back thigh of his knickers. "Hit the ball. Let's get going. Oh, by the way, I couldn't find my ball over there so I played another one, which puts me over the green in three. It's a sonofabitch back there; trying to pitch back will be like trying to stop it on the parking lot. So if you can by some miracle get this one on, you might stand a chance to win back three or four dollars."

He consulted his scorecard hieroglyphics. "Mmm, boy. That would be really good for your side. It would get you down to where you owed me under forty for the round so far. Go ahead! Hit! Take care you don't push it, though, that bunker on the right is a bastard. I knew a man took seven in there one time. We ought to put up a marble stone in his memory. So my God, do be careful and don't hit it in there, son. Remember what I just told you. Let's keep moving, here, keep moving. Don't let me hurry you, though. I know how important this shot is to both of us."

The wind suddenly freshened as I addressed my ball. I glanced overhead and saw that the sky had quickly begun to cloud over. The breeze suddenly felt sharply cooler. Thinking equally about the bunker and how I had wasted part of a day, I swung. The ball went right. Into the bunker.

Avery Whitney smiled beatifically through the cigar smoke. In the mountains to the west, the first rumble of thunder rolled.

eight

Elsewhere

Elk City

The first sound of thunder reached Sylvester's ears as he got out of his truck beside the café in Elk City's downtown. Glancing at the clouds over the flat roof of the cinderblock building, Sylvester calculated that the heaviest of them would pass to the west. It was an automatic deduction, given no thought; he had far weightier matters to worry about.

Entering the café, he swept it with his eyes: high tin ceiling, worn yellow linoleum floor, scattered plastic tables, and a lunch counter to the back with stools on one side, the usual clutter of cups and drink dispensers on the other. A couple of young tourists studying travel brochures at one table, three older men—townspeople—at the far end of the counter with their coffee cups.

Sylvester walked to the other end of the counter, taking the end stool next to the door that led to the toilet. The owner, a rotund man wearing Levi's and a red flannel shirt, ambled over.

"Just coffee, please," Sylvester said.

"How they biting today?"

"Not bad, not bad. Caught a couple."

The owner squinted toward the front windows. "They always hit better on a falling barometer."

Sylvester grinned at him. "I've heard that. I've been skunked on days like that, though."

"Haven't we all, brother!"

Sylvester nursed his coffee for a few minutes, reading some of the placards and signs thumbtacked to the back-counter wall among the shelves of cups and paraphernalia. It seemed fishermen had stiffer rods. My wife said to choose between her and fishing, and I'll sure miss her. Et cetera.

At precisely the appointed time, Sylvester's KGB colleague from the air force research station walked in. He perfectly looked his part: tall, sandy-haired, with a sun-reddened face most people would have branded as Irish; he had mild eyes that made him appear lazy, easygoing, perhaps stupid. His tan slacks were cheap and rumpled, his open-collar wool shirt faded. In the left breast pocket of the shirt he carried one of those white plastic sleeves; it had eight or nine ballpoint pens and a pencil or two crammed in it. His cap had come from an electrical workers' union local in Oklahoma City. That was a nice touch, Sylvester thought, for an hourly-wage electronics scut.

O'Connor—his cover name—paused inside the door, looking around aimlessly, then strolled toward Sylvester's end of the counter. He sat down, putting one stool between himself and Sylvester. "Java!" he said stupidly when the owner approached. When the mug of coffee came, he stirred in far too much sugar, removed a battered paperback novel from his hip pocket, and began to read.

Their conversation was in the lowest tones, and without looking at one another.

Sylvester raised his mug to his lips. "Your code said trouble."

O'Connor replied without moving his lips. "The key was noticed. All locks have been replaced."

It was all Sylvester could do to prevent a change in his expression. "Is theft suspected?"

"Don't know. No sign of that. But I got nothing out before the locks were changed."

So they were back to square one. It was as bitter as the coffee. "You will have to risk a direct approach."

"Understood. New testing commences this weekend. I will watch for an opportunity."

"We *must* have those diagrams."

"Understood."

Sylvester reached into his pocket to pay for his coffee.

His colleague added, "They may be closer to us than we thought."

"Why do you think so?"

"I was questioned."

"About?"

"If I knew anything about the key."

"Were you the only one questioned?"

"All civilian employees."

"Then it is of no consequence. Press on."

"Understood."

Sylvester slipped off his stool and paid for his coffee. After some fishing repartee with the owner, he went back to his truck and drove directly to his mountainside cabin.

The heavy weather was definitely passing far to the west. Breaks had appeared in the clouds overhead, with sunshafts bright against the nearby hills. It was colder. All he needed, Sylvester thought, was a late spring storm that would force him to hole up in the miserable cabin.

He walked into the cabin. The telephone was ringing. He picked it up.

The familiar voice said, "You are there! I was about to give up again!"

"What is it?" Sylvester demanded testily.

"The man you know. He visited here this morning. He had coffee with, uh, our Mr. Big."

God, dealing with such ignorant people! Only an untrained idiot mercenary would call Brad Smith—or anyone else, for that matter—"Mr. Big." But Sylvester hid his irritation. "Their conversation?"

"I couldn't hear a word. But I also knew that, uh, *he* has been asking people if they've seen you."

Sylvester chilled. "How do you know that?"

"It sounds like you. He tells people he has a friend he would like to locate: thin, having been sick recently, with a high-pitched voice."

"Anything else?"

"No."

"Thank you. As before, you will receive an envelope."

Hanging up, Sylvester paced the cabin floor. The use of a key at the lab was now impossible. More time was needed. But Smith was working hand-in-glove with the FBI man—and now was openly searching for Sylvester.

To establish his cover, Sylvester had had to make some appearances in town, as any regular tourist would do. He had to continue that. Given time, Smith would give his description to the wrong person and they would say, *"Oh, sure, I know him, he's renting a cabin up on the side of Lumberjack Mountain from old Jack Lassiter!"*

And then, as the old saying went, the fat would really be in the fire.

Sylvester examined his logic and his options.

With the delay at the lab, Smith simply posed too serious a threat. He had to be taken out at the first opportunity.

The decision was a relief. Sylvester had already grown weary of waiting, wanting Smith as badly as he did.

Getting his Makarov out of the false-bottom compartment of his creel, Sylvester fitted the silencer and double-checked the magazine. Wrapping the gun inside his lightweight black jacket, he went out to his truck and drove away. Fifteen minutes later he turned onto the paved road below, heading toward the resort.

nine

The storm had passed to the west and the sky was clearing again by the time we reached the No. 18 tee. Avery Whitney hit his usual gorilla drive, winning another dollar from me by forty yards or so, but then he duffed his 6-iron and I hit my 5-wood onto the green twelve feet from the pin. When I lucked the putt in for a birdie, I had shot 89, he had shot 77, and I owed him thirty-six dollars.

We drove the cart back to the pro shop, where I gave him his money in cash. He counted it out loud twice, with maddening care. "Thanks, son. Any time you want to play, lemme know. My cabin's only ten minutes from here and I'm in the phone book."

"I'll keep it in mind," I told him.

"Oh, and one other thing," he said, shouldering his clubs. "I really haven't seen that fucker you described for me. But if I do, maybe I'll let you know."

I studied his face. This was not a tease or a gambit of some kind, and he had not spoken casually. Those wise, beat-up, sardonic eyes carried more meaning than the words alone conveyed.

I said, "I might have other questions."

"Me too. Like what you're really doing around these parts."

"Just helping out a friend."

"Right, right." He dug out a fresh cigar and lit it with a kitchen match. "Just poking around, driving around with that little reporter-girl, asking your questions of folks, getting them gossiping about what you might *really* be doing here, et cetera."

"Avery, I'm just trying to help Ted. I don't like seeing him get screwed like you were."

"Smith, when you get as old as me, you'll have learned that living life and getting screwed are two terms for the same thing. My only mistake was learning too late how many screwers there were around here, and letting myself get set up to be the screwee. I'll help you and ol' Ted, too, if I can. I just ain't going to put my head up too high. Turkeys do that; get shot. So do giraffes in Africa. You ever think about giraffes? They're the tallest thing out there. They stick their heads up and walk around in thunderstorms, getting struck by lightning. Did you ever think how it would be to be a giraffe? If they had an ounce of brains they'd lay down at the first distant sound of thunder. But do they? No. They stick their heads up higher, sort of, 'Hey, what's that interesting sound out there, I want to see!' Then, whap. I want to help, but I ain't going to impersonate no giraffe."

"I'll be in touch," I said.

"Good. We can have a nice visit. I'll get my little girl to pour us some whiskey. You'll like her. Cute. Your little reporter-girl is saucy, but mine is outta sight. Of course it does get tiresome, having to explain to her who people like Adlai Stevenson were, and which came first, Teddy or Franklin D., and was Jack Kennedy ever President. But she has good taste in men, namely me, and the young ones never get enough, if you know what I mean, and oh, has she got a set of legs on her. Call me."

"I will," I promised.

We walked to the shop parking lot, where he put his clubs carefully into the back of an early-Eighties white Cadillac with the trunk door removed and a metal box welded in to make a kind of pickup compartment. He waved as he drove off, the tailpipe leaving a blue curl of oil smoke.

There was a note on my cabin door from Ted Treacher, saying we were to have dinner at the lodge with some of the guests at seven. I showered and changed into clean slacks and shirt. I was half-expected to call Skurlock and report, but I decided I was not quite ready to report another failure, and listen to more of his FBI-style sarcasm. So I locked up, concealing my revolver in my belt in the back, and walked up to the lodge in the gathering darkness, thinking about Avery Whitney, small-town cops who liked to bully people, and giraffes. The pines cast long, spooky shadows, and I had Sylvester in the back of my mind, too. I tried to ignore that. With the sun going down, the evening was brittle-cold.

It crossed my mind, walking, that Beth Miles, with her logical lawyer mind, might have been a lot better than I at prying information out of people. But this rather logical thought instantly short-circuited into loneliness for her, and the old frustration that I couldn't get her to do what I wanted.

At which point my imagination did another of those irritating jumps, and for a few seconds, walking the dark pavement toward the glow of lodge windows ahead, I imagined what it would have been like if Danisa had lived, if *she* could have been here with me. *She*—the childlike part of me huffed—would not have stayed half a continent away when I needed her. She would have been right beside me, quick smile responding to every halfass joke I made, touching my arm with her keen, gentle fingers, getting out on the court with the customers and gliding right and left as she rallied with them, stroking those elegant backhands to the corners and occasionally forgetting she was supposed to ease up, and instead hitting one of those howitzer forehand winners down the line.

I could see her, in this moment, sweat gleaming on long, beautiful legs, trademark ponytail bobbing, every muscle and cell of her achingly alive, moving to the ball. And then, later, coming out of the shower in the dark, murmuring and coming into my arms all quicksilver chills and murmurs of desire and pleasure . . .

At which point I stopped myself.

Facts, I lectured myself, were facts.

I had managed to help Danisa defect from Yugoslavia. By some miracle she had fallen in love with me. We had had those months that were like none other I had ever imagined. And then her plane had gone down and I had seen those CBS television pictures of the fire-scarred mountains, and the orange body bags. And then I had buried her.

She was *gone*, and that was the end of it. I knew now that the man called Sylvester had engineered her murder. He had almost killed me, too—and Beth. I had had my chance to kill him and I had blown it. Missing Danisa, remembering how Beth had almost died, living with my own rusting load of anger at my failure and fear of his revenge—wanting to face him and have done with it, and at the same time dreading what might move out of every shadow because of the lurking fear that I was not man enough to handle him—they were all *normalcy* now.

Admit it, Smith. You half hope you *don't* get a lead on him. Maybe Skurlock is right and you really are dragging your ass. Because you're scared.

I cast around in my head for a way to cope. From somewhere in there came the voice of my father. *Shape up!* he said sternly. *Quit whining. Be a man. For once.*

Wonderful. All I needed right now was to let my father out of the shoebox of memories. That would be the ultimate in self-indulgence, in weakness. And if he had taught me anything, hadn't it been that you kept a stiff upper lip and didn't allow yourself any weakness? You did something—anything; you kept on keeping on.

Long after my father's death, we went down to the little storage building he had kept at the back of the property, and there on the dusty concrete floor was the big antifreeze can of old nuts and bolts he had bought at a junkyard somewhere, and all around it the little piles of pieces he had been laboriously sorting according to size. It was so like him: a totally unnecessary job being done *perfectly*. I could imagine him sitting there in the shed alone, in the hot, hermetic quiet, sorting nuts and bolts and thinking his thoughts. I wondered what thoughts he had thought. Were they plans for building things, Pop, or pictures out of the past like the ones that haunt me, or ideas for your golf swing, or plans for manipulating your stocks? Did you ever think of me, and if you did, did you ever think maybe I was okay, or was I always still a disappointment?

Many of the guests had elected to use the dining room this evening, and it looked more festive and happy with all the lights on and a fourth of the tables occupied. Waiters scurried around and there was a pleasant hum of voices. I spied Ted Treacher, waving at me from a table near the windows, and walked over to join him and his dozen guests at a big oval table.

"Brad!" he said with bright, hectic gaiety. "Join us!"

He was dressed in dark slacks and a white dress shirt open at the throat, with a crimson ascot, the old Ted Treacher Britisher role. I was glad to see this hint of normalcy in him, but it might have worked just a little better if he had not had that gray, driven look as well. "I was just telling everybody," he went on, "about some of the big-name stars you're lining up for our tournament."

"We're *excited*!" a pretty blonde on Ted's side of the table cried. She was fluffy and pink in her soft jersey dress, with lots of silver bangles and dangles. If she was just a little overweight, and the color of her hair might have been taken from a bottle to blend with encroaching gray, it didn't matter a lot. She was bouncy and cute. She patted the empty chair between herself and Ted. "Do sit here and tell us all about it!"

I took the proffered chair, descending into a gentle ocean of White Linen.

"Brad," Ted went on, "have you met everyone?"

"*I* haven't been introduced," my bouncy blonde cooed. She held out a round, firm little hand carrying three slender silver bracelets and a sapphire ring. "Hi! My name is Maryann!" In such proximity she was almost overwhelming, all perfume and creamy-firm brown skin and soft, lush curves in abundance. "I'm thrilled to meet you, Brad. Really."

I shook her hand and met some of the others I hadn't encountered earlier on the courts. There were four married couples and a couple of other evidently unattached ladies like Maryann—indeterminate thirties, determinedly pretty and fetching—and one sad-looking little guy, obviously without a partner, whose self-pitying smile said he fully expected to stay that way. One of the married gentlemen asked about my personal plans for the tournament, and one of the married ladies said she certainly hoped it was a success, and Maryann jumped in and touched my arm with seeming artlessness to ask if I could please, *please* find some time tomorrow or Sunday to show her *what* in the world she was doing wrong with her backhand.

"With the possible exception of the golf swing," I told her, "the tennis backhand is the most unnatural movement in sports."

She stared at me with eyes as round and worshipful as if I had been reciting *Paradise Lost*. "Oh, I couldn't agree more!" she breathed.

"But maybe I can be of help."

"Do you *think* so? Would you really be willing to *try*? Oh, that's *wonderful*! Thank you!"

Waiters appeared, bringing drinks the rest of them had ordered earlier. My waiter took my drink order and offered menus all around.

"The trout," he announced, "is not available this evening. And neither, I am sorry to say, is the venison. However, our special is a ten-ounce strip steak for twelve ninety-five."

One of the guests, a slender banker-type named Dan something, grimaced up from his menu. "Ted, dammit! Why have a menu when you're always out of most of the things on it?"

Ted colored. "We're having trouble with some of our suppliers in the area. They promised delivery but they've disappointed us again. I hope the complimentary drinks will make up in a small way for the shortcomings of the menu."

"I," Maryann announced, with a purportedly accidental but decidedly firm bump of her thigh against mine, "think free drinks can make up for just about *anything*!"

Ted's grin came back, lighting his pallor. "That's the kind of talk I like to hear. Now. How many of you plan to go on that bus trip to the stables in the morning?"

They talked briefly about that. I wondered if the shortages on kitchen supplies were an accident of small-town inefficiency or part of the local resistance designed to make Bitterroot Valley go down. Then I wondered if I was paranoid. My drink came. After everyone had ordered, Ted talked about Sunday's guest round-robin on the courts. Maryann managed to bump me again. Her complexion was suffused with pink excitement. It was all pleasant enough, and other conversations quietly hummed at tables all around us. A few guests left and more came in. The dinner seemed to be a long time in arriving, but then it came out and looked good.

We had just started eating when the trouble started.

Ted Treacher saw him first. I reacted when I noticed the way Ted stared toward the dining room entrance across the room behind my back. Then a couple of the guests on the far side of the table looked up, and the conversation stilled. I half turned to see your good friend and mine, Officer Jack Lassiter, striding toward us.

He was in full uniform this time. Tan pants with a brown stripe down the side, brown shirt with nametag and American flag over the left breast, black lizard cowboy boots that hiked the pantlegs up. Enormous .357 protruding from his holster, suspended on a blast belt studded with brass bullets. He had his hat clutched in his left hand.

He strode up to Ted. "Mr. Treacher, I need to talk to you, sir."

Ted looked dubious. "Right now?"

"Right now." Lassiter didn't blink.

Ted sighed, pushed his chair back. "If you'll excuse me, folks? Please go right ahead. Brad, keep everyone entertained, all right? I'll be back soon."

He followed the hulk out of the dining room. Every eye followed them.

"What in the world?" a woman named Martha something murmured.

"I hope there isn't any trouble!" another woman said.

I stepped in with my best host demeanor. "I doubt that it could be any trouble. Just routine, I'm sure."

"It might be about those car break-ins the other night," the man named Dan observed.

"I *heard* about those!" Maryann said. "How *awful*!"

One of the other men must have noticed my vacant expression. "Kids, probably. They broke into four cars—broke the side windows—and stole some cigarettes and clothes. They also vandalized three of the cabins, from what we heard: broke in through windows, spray-painted walls and broke furniture, really made a mess. Luckily no one was staying in any of them at the time."

Maryann bumped me again, and this time allowed her leg to remain pressed against me. "I suppose you knew all about that, though."

I moved to get away. "Of course," I lied. "Nothing to be worried about."

We resumed eating. One of the men wanted to talk about America's younger tennis hopefuls, and we got off onto that for a few minutes. I kept expecting Ted to come back. Finally he did, but he didn't sit down. Instead he leaned over the back of my chair. "Everybody, I'm really sorry, but I have to take Brad away from you just for a minute or two."

I looked up at him. A film of sickly sweat covered his pallor, and his tight mouth betrayed the tension he was trying to hide. "What's up, Ted?"

"Come with me just for a minute."

I excused myself and went with him, leaving a table of guests who were getting more puzzled and concerned by the moment. In the foyer outside the dining room I asked, "What's it all about, Ted?"

He was already starting in through a doorway that led to a small concierge-type room. "In here."

Inside, standing beside the postage-stamp desk, was Lassiter. He had his storm-trooper face on. Ted closed the door to the foyer, shutting the three of us off. He stood between Lassiter and me, staring at the floor. Sweat dripped off his nose. I realized he was making a supreme effort to hold back some almost-overpowering emotion.

He said, "Officer Lassiter is concerned about your alleged trespass at the old mining company property today."

"What?"

"He says," Ted said unsteadily—and now I could see the emotion was a towering, frustrated rage—"that you trespassed on the mine property, and unless we can guarantee that no other golfers will do the same, he intends to demand that we put up a fence along the golf course out-of-bounds line."

I stared at Lassiter. "You come in here and interrupt our dinner with *this*?"

"Don't get smart," Lassiter warned me.

"Calm down, Brad," Ted added uneasily. "No need for anyone to get angry here—"

"My ass!"

"I am here," Lassiter intoned, "in an official capacity, acting on knowledge from our earlier meeting today when I was working as an off-duty security guard. What I have to have is some kind of definite assurance about the integrity of that property. Otherwise—"

"What do you want?" I asked. Few things get me going faster than bullying. "A signed statement? A public apology?"

"Maybe," he said, "you would like to come downtown and talk about this."

"Maybe so," I told him. "I've got two lawyer friends in the next room. We'll bring them along as witnesses."

He stared at me. A pulse thumped in the side of his face. Clearly he wasn't accustomed to resistance, and the mention of witnesses was not the kind of thing that encouraged him.

Ted seemed to get a little braver. "It may be that Brad is right, officer. If this was all a misunderstanding, we can let it rest right where it is."

"I don't want any more problems," Lassiter said.

"There won't be any," I told him, "if you'll stop being an asshole."

"You—!" He caught his move toward me. "I'll—"

"What?" I asked. This was really stupid, really dangerous. But my temper had the better of me.

Surprisingly, he controlled himself. Maybe he realized this was not the place to push it any further, with guests staring. He swallowed. The rage was there, but we had witnesses and he had been cooled by the mention of lawyers.

After another minute he jammed his hat onto his head. "We'll consider the matter closed for now." He walked out.

I took a deep breath.

"My God," Ted said quietly. "Was that *wise*?"

I breathed deeply again, and felt the hot weakness that came with the adrenaline rush. "Probably not," I admitted. "I guess I lost my temper."

We got ourselves back together and returned to the dining room. My food had gotten cold, but I ate it mechanically. There was a spirited discussion of racket designs, everyone agreeing that the larger heads were harder-hitting and generally more forgiving, and then they asked me and Ted questions about the relative merits of metal, graphite, boron, etc., which we probably did a bad job of answering, given the fact that the best racket for you is usually the one you have confidence in, even if it's an old Maxply Fort.

I didn't have any heart for the conversation. It was not bad enough that I had gotten absolutely nowhere toward uncovering useful information about Sylvester. Now I had lost my cool and further antagonized Lassiter. When was I going to get on track, here?

The blonde named Maryann did not take part in much of the conversation. That wasn't what she was concentrating on. I was aware of her keen, silent appraisal, close beside me. She seemed like a sweet enough lady, and I felt sort of sorry that she had evidently focused on me this way. There would not be anything in it for her and I didn't want to hurt her feelings.

We had two after-dinner drinks. Ted seemed to cheer up a bit, and told some old tennis yarns. It got late. The party began to break up. I said good night and ignored the sudden look of disappointed surprise in Maryann's eyes, and headed out of there.

After stopping in the men's room off the lobby, I found the cigarette machine and bought a fresh pack. It was about midnight and the lobby Muzak had been turned off, and the building echoed with my footsteps as I crossed to the back door and went out into the vast black. The sky overhead was brilliant and clear, lighted by more stars than I had ever seen, and I was looking up at them as I walked when he hit me.

ten

He had a weapon: a blackjack, a sap, or some similar resilient sack-type weapon filled with lead shot. I heard the rustle of the loose pellets along with its whistle through the air for a fraction of a second before it hit me with stunning force.

The fact that I had my head back, gawking at the stars, may have saved me from a fractured skull. Perhaps he made the slightest sound, stepping out of the shrubbery beside the road behind me, or it might have been a sixth sense that warned me just in time enough to jerk my head forward and start to turn. It was in that nanosecond that I heard the macabre sound of the weapon: not enough time for me to duck or register anything rationally, but my head-forward movement of alarm caused him to hit me a glancing blow rather than the bone-crusher he might have intended.

There was also the possibility that he never intended to do more than stun me. Whatever. It was plenty as it was. Pain exploded through my brain. For a second I lost consciousness. The next thing I knew, I hit the pavement on hands and knees, my vision full of red-and-yellow stars.

He followed up instantly. Hit me a second time, missing my head in the dark and smashing onto the tip of my right shoulder. I rolled, trying to get out of the way. I still had little idea of what was going on, but instincts had taken over. Even with my eyes adjusted to the dark, all I could see was a big figure, and then a rough, jeans-type pant leg as his foot exploded into my chest, knocking me over backwards. Hightop boot, the lace-up kind, maybe black. I tried to roll again. Getting boring, my numbed brain thought. He kicked me in the midsection. The pain said a rib might have cracked. I managed to grab his leg and try to twist, but he pulled free and kicked me again, this time in the groin. I think I yelled as I doubled up. That made the next boot-shot carom off my back.

I tried rolling again. My wind had been knocked out of me. I couldn't get collapsed lungs to open for air. My stomach rebelled. I upchucked. He hit me again, somewhere, and things started to change from normal blackness to a furry, distant dark that I knew was unconsciousness . . . maybe death.

I braced for the next blow, the one that would be the last I could feel. It didn't come. I realized he wasn't hitting me. I heard his muffled exclamation. Shoe leather scraped on the asphalt. I got my eyes open. Nobody. Nothing. Pale streetlight shadows on bushes still rustling from the way he had rushed off.

What—?

That was when I heard the screaming. A woman's voice.

Footsteps, little quick sounds like high heels. A small, gyrating light. I fought my way up through ten atmospheres of confusion and darkness. I lay sprawled on the asphalt, in my own vomit and blood, and the light danced around on me, lancing my eyes. She was right beside me—pretty legs and heels—and she was still screaming.

I managed to suck in a little blessed air. "Turn it off! Turn the light off! Be quiet!"

The screaming stopped. The light veered sickly off me and onto the pavement nearby, and then onto the bushes. The figure behind the light—it was a small flashlight—knelt beside me. Heels, legs, dress, White Linen.

Her bracelets jangled as she plucked meaninglessly at my shirtfront. "I thought he was killing you!"

I pushed her hands away, choked breath into my tortured lungs. "Who was it?"

"I don't know—all I saw was his back. He was big. That's all I know."

I scrambled to a sitting position. "Okay, Maryann. I'm okay."

"You're *not*! You're sick! You've got blood on you and I saw him kicking you—hitting you—and you were all crumpled over and I thought you were dead—"

"Hold it," I pleaded. I shut her up by grabbing her wrist, hard.

"But who was it? What—?"

"Maryann! Shut *up* a second!"

She froze, bent over me. Everything clicked into clarity, like a camera lens suddenly brought into focus, and I saw her terrified, tear-streaked face, her little flashlight, everything. Nobody else around. Back behind her somewhere, lights had begun to flash on in the lodge compound.

I released her wrist and turned over, lurching to a kneeling position. "Help me up."

"I'll get a doctor!"

"Help me *up*!"

Issuing little sobs, she obeyed. I got to my feet and leaned heavily against her, feeling her nice softness, while the world swam around. She was stronger than she looked and she did not let me fall down and go boom again.

My mind was going a mile a minute. *Where are we going? I don't know, sir. We're lost, but we're making good time.* I knew my cabin was just ahead, not ten yards away. "Help me inside," I told her.

"But—!"

"Will you just for Christ sake do as I say?"

She did. Once inside, I sank onto the edge of the couch. She looked down at me with tear-streaked apprehension and shock.

"Are you going to faint?" I demanded.

"No—I don't think so—"

"Will you help me?"

"Yes—"

"Good. People are going to be coming to see what your screaming was all about. Go meet them. Apologize. Say you thought you saw a bear, but it was only a shadow. Get rid of them. Then come back here."

"But you—" she started to protest.

"Maryann, do you want to help or not!"

She stared, sniffled, turned, fled out of the cabin, leaving the door ajar.

I closed and bolted it, then walked dizzily into the bathroom. The flare of the overhead light hit my eyes like daggers. Through a pink haze I looked at myself in the lavatory mirror. I had an egg on the side of my head, low down and toward the back, where he had gotten me with the sap. The skin was split and I had bled an amazing amount, down my neck and all over my shirtfront. Otherwise, except for a couple of minor gravel scratches and a whole lot of dirt, my face was unmarked. I had red dirt, traces of motor oil, and vomit all over. Shirt torn at the shoulder, and the start of an angry bruise showing through. Both pant legs ripped at the knees, and the knees scratched and bloody. Considering how bad I was starting to feel, the obvious damage was minimal.

Good work out there, Mr. X, I thought. Beat a man and leave no marks on his face. Professional.

Leaning over the lavatory I shakily poked at the sticky mass of blood and hair where the sap had hit me. It hurt and looked horrendous, but the swelling had already pinched off most of the bleeding and I couldn't see any clear fluid leaking out. The bone felt intact: no give, no crunching sounds.

I stripped out of my filthy clothes and stepped into the shower and let 'er rip, allowing the cool fingers of spray to needle into the head wound and get it clean. When I stepped off and toweled off, patting the head injury, not much fresh blood got on the towel.

A spasm of pain and nausea bent me over. I leaned over the toilet and brought up a thin, acid stream of mucus, all I had left in there. It had been such a good dinner, too. I shuddered, wiped my face with the cool, wet towel, and sent down a glass of water and four Tylenol.

I was vaguely disoriented and slightly dizzy going back into the main room and poking around the closet to come up with cotton slacks and T-shirt. Barefooted, I poured a water glass half full of Canadian, dunked in three ice cubes, sat on the couch, and really began to shake.

For perhaps a few seconds during the attack I had thought it could be Sylvester. But now I did not think so. The attack had been too crude. If it had been Sylvester out there, I would be dead.

Lassiter, then?

I almost wished it were. That would be easy. Have an argument, jump the offender in the dark: it sounded like Lassiter's kind of reaction. But unfortunately I had managed to see and feel just enough in the dark to know the man who tried to do me in had been wearing rough denim work pants and lace-up boots. Lassiter had been in uniform earlier when I saw him, and he liked fancy black cop-outfit cowboy boots, not lace-ups. I didn't think it had been him anyway; it didn't strike me as quite his style. He wouldn't have worried about my face.

Who, then?

No idea.

In the aftermath of the attack, even the first sip of whiskey hit me. I smoked a cigarette, feeling my head go around like a carousel in low gear. I was going to have a headache to end all headaches in the morning.

Minutes passed.

The slight scratching sound of footsteps outside was followed immediately by a light but urgent knock. I went to the door but left it bolted. "Yes?"

"It's me," Maryann's voice came through the thick planks.

I stuck the pistol in the back sweatband of my trousers and unlocked. She blew in all pink excitement, shaky, scared, and eyes like frisbees. "I told them I thought I saw a bear, just like you said. Then Ted Treacher wanted to walk me back to my room, and a couple of the others kept asking more questions, and I thought I was *never* going to get away from them!" She went on tiptoe and, frowning, cupped her hand under my chin to turn my head first to one side, then the other for inspection. "Are you all right?"

"I'm fine. Thanks for coming along when you did."

"That's a big lump back there. You need some ice for it."

"I've got some in this drink."

"You know what I mean. Can I have a drink too? I was scared half to death! Who *was* it?"

"The bottle is on the sinkboard over there, ice in the fridge, I've got no decent mix. And I don't know who it was."

"He could have killed you. What are you going to do now? Are you going to call the police?"

"No." I didn't try to explain that the last thing I needed right now was another visit from Lassiter.

"No?" she repeated, surprised. She poured herself a big, shaky drink.

Watching her, I realized for the first time that I was going to have trouble getting her out of here. "No, no police. The resort doesn't need any more notoriety right now, and I'm okay anyway."

"But you should call the police!"

"Why? So Lassiter can come back out here and strut around and find nothing, then make me go all the way into town to fill out one of his incident reports? Forget it, Maryann. I mean that. I'm okay. And I want your assurance that you aren't going to mention any of this to anyone."

She plopped leggily onto the couch beside me. "My gosh! Do you really expect me not to tell people?"

"Not *anyone*," I repeated.

Suddenly moody, she swirled the ice cubes in her glass. "I was so scared."

"Me too. But no bad harm done, right?"

She looked at me with dilated pupils. "If something had happened to you right after I just met you, I—I don't know what I would have done."

"Well, it's done with," I told her, as if it was.

"And you really are going to be all right?"

"Yep."

"You don't think you ought to see a doctor? I could drive you."

"No."

"Are you dizzy? Sleepy?"

"A little of both, but I'm going to turn in soon."

"You shouldn't be alone," she said firmly. "I'll stay." Then she raised her eyebrows like she had frightened herself. "In case you get complications in the night. Or sick, or passed out. Or something."

"No, Maryann," I told her gently. "That's not necessary."

"I want to," she said firmly, her chin showing her stubborn streak. "Didn't it occur to you to wonder what I was doing, coming down that path behind you in the dark? Well, I'll tell you." She heaved a breath for courage. "I was . . . coming down here . . . following you. I . . . wanted to spend more time with you tonight." She paused and her little tongue darted nervously over her lips, and she gasped for air again. "But then," she rushed on faster, "you got hurt, so now there's really a practical *reason* for me to stay."

"No, Maryann."

"I'll be good. I'll stay out here—nap on the couch. Brad! Give me a break, all right? It's no big deal for me to play Florence Nightingale, is it?"

"But not necessary," I told her.

"I won't take no for an answer. I'm staying."

"I'm in no shape for fun and games, Maryann."

"I know that!" she said, mightily offended.

I got up and limped to the table and came back. "Cigarette?"

"I quit years ago," she said, and took one.

Leaning back on the couch, I watched her inhale smoke, the voluptuous inhalation of a reformed smoker, fallen again. Fresh nausea began to coil in my belly. I hoped I was not going to disgrace myself with more retching.

She could, I decided, stay if it made her feel better. Nothing was going to happen. Not that I am noted for my nobility and restraint, even with Beth trusting me—of all things!—out there in California. *Maybe* I would have felt this sure of my fidelity if I had been well. But it was moot because I was feeling considerably rockier again.

So she could stay, I thought, and curl on the couch, and listen to the sounds of whatever ugly reflex reactions my body had yet to go through in response to a beating that might have been much worse, but had been bad enough as it was. And I would be glad to know there was human company nearby.

He had messed it up this time, whoever he was. But he would be back. The attack had not been random. Somebody—not Sylvester this time—had targeted me. Who? Why?

Whoever it had been, he had been interrupted. He would be back; I was willing to bet on that. Perhaps next time he would bring help.

eleven

By morning—before dawn—my accumulated aches and pains had me out of bed. I hadn't slept much, had taken a couple more Tylenol, had decided I didn't have a cracked rib after all, but was not encouraged when my urine showed traces of pink. I had a fine collection of ugly red and purple bruises on my chest and sides, my lower abdomen, and the part of my back I could see in the little mirror. The swelling on the back and side of my head had discolored. I messed around with the hairbrush and partly concealed it. People might notice, but I wouldn't look all that bad unless I took my clothes off or started whining every time I moved. I decided I would live, even if I felt like hell.

Being very quiet, I dressed in the darkness, found my flashlight, and crept into the main room of the cabin. In the kitchen alcove I silently got some ice and wrapped it in a paper towel. Holding it against my egg, I looked around.

Maryann slept on the living room couch, curled in the fetal position under a down comforter. With the remains of eye makeup and lipstick blurred by the night, and her hair gone from fuzzy bouffant to shapeless unkempt, she looked neither as young nor as pinkly pretty as she had last night. Sleep is not kind to women for whom being youthfully pretty has become a serious job; they puff around the eyes, and the makeup smears, and the crow's-feet hike through the uncamouflaged territory; the mouth softens and betrays laugh lines that are no longer amused; and there is a sad little vulnerability that can be seen with the defensive muscles slack, the concealing chemical compounds smeared away or blurred. At such a time the lady in her thirties or forties is revealed in all her real transitional vulnerability, unmasked, neither the person she really is nor the person she is pretending still to be. I like makeup. But I like women without it, too. They shouldn't have to mask anything with goop. Those lines and places where the flesh has relaxed were hard-won, and they're signals that milady has spent enough time on this globe to have learned something more interesting than a giggle and Oh, wow! Looking at Maryann like this, I liked her better.

During the night, at all the times I had been awake with one pain or another, I had been excruciatingly quiet, and Maryann had either not heard me or had elected to abide by her promise to stay put on the couch. Now, getting ready to start my day, I was not especially eager to wake her and have a conversation.

The storm had come a little after three o'clock, first distant rolling thunder, then the sound of wind tossing the trees, then gathering lightning, louder thunder, more wind that made the roof beams groan, and finally rain. It only pattered lightly here on the cabin roof, but you could tell other areas not far away were getting a downpour. It lasted more than an hour.

I lay still in my bed until it abated, the storm moving off south. If Maryann was awake, she gave no sign. The storm made me remember a time in another A-frame, that on St. Maarten, when Beth had been with me and we had only begun our explorations of each other. The memory-pictures became vivid, as they will in the dead of night, and in the face of all logic and rationality, I got an aching erection. The body pulls funny tricks. Sometimes hellacious danger triggers the sex drive. I don't know why. It's a species survival reflex of some kind.

The storm abated, and the thunder moved off across the mountains somewhere, rumbling distantly like the sullen big guns of somebody else's war. That was when I slept fitfully for a while.

I hoped to get out of the cabin without any conversation. In this, however, I was disappointed. As I slunk toward the front door, Maryann sat up, clutching the blanket to herself, located me in the dimness, and sent a wan smile. "Zat you, Brad?"

"Looks like me," I said.

She rubbed her eyes with her knuckles. "Oof. With my contacts on the coffee table, I wouldn't know for sure. How are you this morning?"

"A little creaky, but okay."

She wrapped the comforter around her more securely and swung bare feet to the rug. "No more problems in the night?"

"Not a one," I lied.

She looked blearily around and collected a soft pile of clothes and underclothes from the table. "Guess I better get going, huh?"

"Take your time. I'm going on. I've got some things to check out."

"Okay."

Outside it was just getting light. The trees, walks, and undergrowth glistened under a covering of rain droplets. Near the cabin it was not too muddy. The combination of light rainfall in the immediate area, and the umbrella effect of the ponderosas, had left the earth only slightly muddy. If my man last night had left any clues, they might still be visible.

So I poked around. I found the spot where he had hidden behind some baby tamaracks. The soles of his boots had left some V-shaped patterns in the soft earth. There was a fresh cigarette butt, too, only slightly browned by the light rainfall.

I didn't find anything else in the immediate vicinity. I spread my search out in a slightly wider circle, thinking there might be something else. There was. But it was not anything I had expected.

In a shallow earthen depression about twenty feet behind my cabin—almost forty feet from where I had found the boot markings and cigarette butt, the grass was pressed down in a circle about three feet in diameter. No sign of fresh animal droppings, and no tracks of deer or other animals. In a splotch of soft dirt, a single faint shoeprint.

I looked closer. That was when I noticed the scuff-marks in the grass and dirt near the depression—and the length of old, fallen log lying across the front of the depression, as it faced my cabin.

Somebody else had been here last night, or very recently. He—or she—had dragged the length of rotted log into its present position.

With a prickling sensation deepening on the back of my neck, I continued studying the scene, thinking about it. Why move the length of log? To hide behind it? No need. A person hunkered down in that grassy depression would be out of sight after dark.

Why, then?

Then I got it.

It was a shooting stand.

Nerves twitching, I got my pants and shirt damp by lying down in the grass behind the log. For a rifle, the log made a perfect rest. I extended my arm as if holding a handgun. Just right to steady that kind of shot, too.

I got back to my feet and walked around some more. I didn't find anything else. I don't think I expected to.

This was the kind of setup Sylvester would have had.

Last night? Maybe. Possibly my other attacker had struck first, aborting Sylvester's plan. Or maybe it had been some time earlier. I got ice in my gut, remembering how I had come out here and stood behind the cabin when I saw the distant lights.

Skurlock needed to know. I started up toward the lodge and the pay phone in the lobby. Probably no lines tapped, but a tap on the pay phone seemed less likely than one on my cabin line. Like the man said, I'm paranoid but they really are out to get me.

Partway up the path, I saw the familiar figure in the side parking lot, just dragging a suitcase out of the trunk of her rental car. It was another surprise, the only nice one I had had lately.

"Karyn!" I called.

She turned, saw me, grinned hugely, and waved. I hurried up toward her.

Karyn Wechsting was 24 now, and they didn't call her "America's next young superstar" anymore. You've got to be 15 or 16 to qualify as young in today's tennis world. But she might have been the best the U.S. had until a torn rotator cuff required surgery. I was glad to see her. Wearing baggy dungaree pants and a black smokejumper T-shirt and dirty Reeboks, she looked great.

She had never been considered a great beauty. A few idiot sportswriters—if that combination of words is not redundant—had even made pissy comments about how "plain" she was—her complexion a little too sun-battered, her hair too weather-bleached, her mouth too wide, her arms too sinewy, her legs too strong, with muscles that showed. Sort of like Martina or Steffi, Karyn was too perfectly suited to tennis, too athletic to be . . . well, cute.

But she had a grand and ready smile, and if she didn't meet some high-schoolish writer's "classic" definition of what made a woman pretty, so what? Some of us liked her strong arms and legs, her careless straw-colored hair, her what-you-see-is-what-you-get honesty. She was a great lady, for my money, and a great friend, and *I* thought she was wonderful-looking.

She held our her arms and I grabbed her in a bear hug.

"Oof," she chuckled. "Break my ribs!"

Mine too. The pain made me release her fast. "Ted didn't tell me you were coming!"

"Ted didn't know I was coming."

"So what brings you?"

"Hey." She grinned. "Maybe I ought to ask you the same question."

"Well, Ted's an old pal. And I sure owe him one. I thought I could help."

She nodded, sun-bleached tresses bobbing. "Me too."

"He invite you, too?"

"Heck no," she said, grimacing. "You think our Ted would ask a mere mortal *woman* for help?"

"So he really doesn't know to expect you this morning?"

"Thought I'd surprise him."

"This is great. This will cheer him up. Let's go find him."

We started across the vast asphalt lot.

"Does he," Karyn asked, "need a lot of cheering up?"

"Did I imply that?"

"Yep."

"Well, yes. There are problems."

She frowned, readjusting a thousand pale freckles. "Money?"

"Money, also local opposition from mossbacks who apparently don't want the area to change, also local suppliers who can't get anything delivered right or on time, also problems getting the existence of the place known to enough tourists and tennis nuts to bring in the income, also debts to fix things that ran down or broke during the long time the complex was closed."

"Is he going to make it?"

"He's counting on a celebrity tournament I'm helping him set up. The only problem with *that* is, we don't have enough players lined up yet. I'm making progress on finding guys, but it's tougher than hell, and we're running out of time."

She sighed as we neared the broad steps of the lobby entryway. "Might have known. I haven't had a letter for a while—despite the fact that I sent the dopus several—and then comes this little note, all forced, strained good cheer and a joke, and I thought, 'Oh-oh, he's in trouble.' So here I am."

"You're a good friend, Karyn."

She made one of her faces again. "You know how we traveled together. How we were in Belgrade, when we did that little thing to help you and Danisa."

"It was no 'little' thing."

She shrugged that off. "Whatever. My point is, as far as the way I feel about the big, awkward goon—we were together *a lot*. Best of friends? You know?"

I knew. Ted was a lucky man. I wondered if he had enough sense to know that.

We entered the lodge and started looking for him. There were workmen all over the place, making it spic and span for the visit by Allen Industries. I felt a slight apprehension. Karyn was almost too bright, on edge, anxiously cheerful. She loved him; it was as clear and simple as that. How was Ted going to react, especially with the lovely Sally around?

I didn't have to wait long to find out.

We found him in the back garden area with three workmen. As we approached from behind him, I heard enough to learn that the storm had hit the far end of the golf course hard. Until repair work could be done around a couple of the new greens, the men were to move the tees back to the old areas. He would go out later and inspect the damage in detail.

"Ted," I said.

He turned, saw us, and did a double take.

"Hi, guy," Karyn said, her smile betraying her uncertainty.

Ted hugged her, held her at arm's length, kissed her on the nose, hugged her again. His grin broke right through all his now-customary tension. "This is wonderful! When did you arrive?"

"I just drove in and ran into Brad in the parking lot—"

Ted eyed me. "Looks like maybe you mean you literally ran into him. What's up, sport? Where did you get the bump on the back of the head?"

"I hit a door."

He accepted it and turned back to Karyn. "It's great to see you. How long can you stay? A long time, right? Right! Say, I can't wait to show you everything. Let's have coffee out on the deck. You're here just in time for a very important meeting we're having here this weekend."

He seemed really delighted. It was fun to watch her light up in the brightness of his enthusiasm. We headed for the deck, he talking a mile a minute, telling her how wonderfully everything was going, how grand it was to own a place like this, how he was doing far better than he could ever have expected so early in his term of ownership. I think he had practiced optimism so long that he believed it.

I was struck again by his intensity. Bitterroot Valley meant everything to him. Karyn's rapt attention struck me too. She stared at his face as if every word—every expression—was priceless. I had never seen love so clear and vulnerable in the eyes of a woman.

We found a round parasol table on the uncrowded deck and ordered coffee.

"How did you get here, Kar?"

"Flew into Missoula last night. Rented a car. Got an early start this morning. What a nice drive down!"

"Listen, there's so much to show you around here. You're going to love it."

She smiled fondly. "Whatever you say."

The frown touched his face. "I'm going to be a little busy. Those people coming in. *Nothing* can be allowed to spoil that. Then this rain. It hardly sprinkled here at the lodge, and a mile away it was a downpour. I've got to get out there in a cart after a while and see what's happened. But later today, maybe we can take a drive?"

Karyn's smile broadened. "Whatever you say," she repeated.

"You'll like the tennis complex."

"I've just started working out oncourt again. The surgery was rougher than I expected."

"It always is. Our pool is nice. You can do some useful exercising there."

I soaked up the thin sun and let them talk. Ted didn't ask enough about Karyn. That was selfish: not like him. But he was not himself in a lot of ways these days. I wished he weren't quite so obsessed. It made him seem slightly crazy.

"I've really been busy the last few months, Karyn."

"I know," Karyn said, and her expression was so loving and vulnerable it was painful to behold. "I've missed you. A lot."

He lit a cigarette with shaky hands. "Of course it's all coming together now. Our room utilization rate is up . . . once we get over this next financial hump . . ."

Ted, I thought, *you dumb bastard!*

We were on our second cup of coffee when Sally Wallis strode out of the lodge, long bare legs purring, clipboard and file folder in hand. In lavender shorts and shell, with ankle-strap sandals and her wonderful dark hair loose, she looked like ten million dollars.

"Sally!" Ted looked startled. For all the world like a man caught by his wife in a compromising position with another woman. "Uh . . . Sally, I want you to meet Karyn Wechsting. Karyn is, ah, we've played tennis together."

Sally Wallis looked down at Karyn. The contrast between them was striking: the tall, classic, beauty and the thin, stringy, straw-haired Karyn. "I think you might have mentioned Karyn once, Ted. How very nice to meet you, Karyn. I'm Sally Wallis."

Ted stammered, "Karyn, uh, Sally is my business manager. Uh, we were just having some coffee here, Sally. Karyn is going to be a guest here for a day or two."

Sally looked down at Karyn with great, ironic eyes. "How very nice. We have a special rate for weekends."

Ted, looking dazed, did not contradict her.

"It's too bad this is going to be such a busy business weekend for us," Sally went on in the same saccharine tone. "Ted and I have worked closely in preparation for weeks now. But possibly Sunday night we can spend some time together."

"Yes," was all Karyn said. Her freckles stood out in chalky pallor.

Sally put crimson-tipped fingers on Ted's arm. "I'm so sorry to interrupt your reunion, darling, but we have some details that simply must be attended to at once."

Ted flushed and jumped to his feet. "Sure. Right." He gave us a stricken expression. "I'll—uh—see you later." He hurried off after Sally, who was already halfway to the back doors of the lodge.

Karyn had shrunk a little. She had no color. Staring into her coffee cup, she had gone from happy and vivacious to sunken devastation.

"She's a big help to him on the business side," I said. "Seems to be fairly good manager."

Karyn, white-lipped, smiled the thin, unassailable smile she smiled after losing a close, hard match. I had seen it often enough, and knew that the more it hurt, the more sternly controlled the smile.

This one was very controlled indeed.

"Sure," she said.

The porcelain sky didn't look quite as blue suddenly, in the storm's aftermath, and the air wasn't as fragrant or the trees as handsome against the distant hilltops. And Karyn sat there, very still, her tight little smile firmly in place. I babbled, foolish remarks about vacation spots, pretending I was too stupid to know how much she had just been disappointed, how much she had been hurt.

I put off calling Skurlock to show Karyn around. There was nothing he could do about what had happened anyhow, and she needed the attention. A little later Ted drove off from the lodge in his electric golf cart. We were still looking around an hour or so later when he came back, the cart and his feet and legs covered with mud.

"How does it look?" I asked.

His eyes snapped. He looked drained—dazed. "Lot of damage." He turned to Karyn. "Let me go change," he suggested. "Then what say we take a tour?"

She looked dubious. "I think Brad has shown me most everything, Ted."

"Well." He thought about it. "Probably just as well. Sally and I have to go to town. Date with the poster printer. Then we must confer with the laundry facility people. Some kind of problem with the billing. If it isn't one thing, it's another." He turned to me. "We'll have dinner late. Until then, you can take care of Karyn, can't you, Brad? Be a good fellow?"

Karyn bit off, "I don't require a caretaker, Ted."

He blinked. "Oh. Right. Of course." He grinned a ghastly grin and patted her on the shoulder the way a man might pat his hunting dog. "You're a dear. See you later." And he hurried off with that long, loping stride.

I looked down at Karyn. She pursed her lips as people do sometimes when they're struggling not to cry.

"He's not himself," I told her lamely.

She shook herself and came up with a moxie smile. "About those players you need for the tournament. Why don't you give me your list and let me help by making a few calls?"

"You would do that?" I asked in some surprise.

"I think," she said with a rueful tone, "I'm going to have some time on my hands anyway."

"I want to see you," Skurlock said when I finally got him on the phone in the middle of the afternoon and told him what had happened.

"Why?"

"Not on the phone."

I looked at my watch. "I've got to make sure some reports have been duplicated and the courts are ready for these visitors tomorrow."

"Smith, you've almost had your head taken off. Pay attention, here!"

"Listen, Skurlock. I came here to track somebody down. But I accepted Ted's invitation to help him, too. He's an old friend and he's in deep crud here. I can't let him go down the tubes."

He digested that in silence. Then, with heavy sarcasm: "Is there any time within the next few weeks or months when it might be convenient for you to meet me at the Dirty Cup Café here in town? I promise I won't take more than a few minutes of your valuable time."

I calculated the amount of crap I had to do and balanced that against the late dinner time Ted had announced. "Six o'clock?"

"Fine." He hung up.

* * *

Ted Treacher, more strung out than I had ever seen him, made life miserable for everybody all afternoon, sending people off on cleanup and food missions, jumping on the smallest detail one minute and then vanishing to his room the next like Achilles sulking in his tent. Karyn Wechsting seemed dazed. I tried to mollify the staff and handle some of the details he should have had ready a week earlier. Sally Wallis messed up most of what she touched, and made one woman on the housekeeping staff so angry that she quit on the spot. The result: I left the lodge a few minutes late for my meeting with Skurlock. My real business in Elk City had been screwed up again by my cover job with Ted.

By the time I reached town and parked beside the café, a cold wind was blowing hard out of a clear, arctic sky. Shivering, I hurried inside. *Snow for our nice tournament*, I thought. Then I dismissed all that, focusing on the business at hand.

I spotted Skurlock at once, hunkered at a corner table with an empty coffee mug and an ashtray full of cigarette butts. He looked about as happy as a kid with a broken stereo. There were about a dozen other people in the place, every one of them men. It was a good evening for coffee.

I went to Skurlock's table and sat down opposite him. "Sorry. Everything got screwed up out there today—"

"That makes it a perfect world, then," Skurlock growled. "Everything screwed up everyplace."

"Sorry."

His smoke-reddened eyes sagged in his tired cheeks. "When they suggested interagency cooperation, I told them it wouldn't work. But did they listen? No. You had experience, they said. You came highly recommended, they said. You would be a real asset, they told me."

"Did you want to meet to tell me something, Fred, or is my assignment at the moment just to sit here and listen to you bitch?"

The owner came over, bringing a cup for me and a refill for Skurlock. We fumed while he served us. He went on around the room, refilling other coffee cups.

Skurlock drew my attention back. "Just a couple of things. Number one, we now have taps on all the staff phones at the lab. A computer will copy and print out every phone number dialed out. So

I want from you all the lodge and resort numbers and the numbers of everybody else who's contacted you, even that chick from the newspaper."

"Lynette? Surely you don't think—"

"Do it."

"Yes, sir."

"I want those numbers tomorrow morning. Written out."

"Okay. Do I deliver, or—"

"I'll get them. I plan to be out there anyway."

"Is that a good idea, Fred? If you're seen too frequently—"

"I won't be seen," he told me, and his lip turned down in an angrier grimace. "Since somebody tried to take you out, and you think Sylvester was on the scene, my assignment has been modified. I'm to camp in the bushes out there the next couple of nights."

"That isn't necessary."

"I know it isn't necessary," he shot back sullenly. "But I follow orders."

I saw now why he was so angry. From being a potential asset, I had become a liability—another drain on his overextended time. "Fred, I don't need any watching. I'll be more careful."

"I've got my orders. Let me suggest, Smith, you just do what I do. Try to act professional. Do what you're told."

I didn't answer him.

"Understood?" he prodded.

"Understood," I repeated.

"If nothing further develops by the first of the week—after your precious visit by those big dogs out there this weekend—there's going to be another change in tactics. I can't babysit you forever. The new test series is going to be complete out at the lab within the next week or ten days, and that makes it a crucial time—a time when any espionage attempt is sure to be intensified. So that's why we change our approach, unless we get lucky and our man tries to take you out in the next night or two."

I ignored the sarcasm. "Change in what way?"

"Next week, if we're status quo, you visit the lab."

"On what pretext?"

"I haven't been told that yet. I've got an idea they don't care what fucking pretext it is—maybe the thinner the better. The idea is to try to panic somebody."

"That doesn't sound like it has a very high probability of success."

Skurlock drained his coffee cup and stubbed out his latest cigarette. "Smith, ours is not to reason why. The boys up top are getting restless. Maybe they know more than we do. I always try to assume that. It makes me feel better. Anyway, you have that list ready. And if you walk around outside in the next couple of nights, and you happen to spot me, just keep right on going. And for Christ sake, don't mistake me for our friend and start shooting. All right? Do you think you can do that?"

"Yes," I said. My face was hot. He knew how to hit dirty.

He stood. "In the morning, then."

He got up and walked out. Leaving the check for me to pay.

I stirred some sweetener into my coffee. It was good coffee, but right now it tasted bitter, like almost everything else.

Like most people, I don't take that kind of criticism well. I was not sure what Skurlock thought my opinion of myself was, and maybe he figured me for one of those dilettantes who sometimes spook around the edges of law enforcement, getting off on thinking they're "detecting" or "supporting" somebody. The truth was far different in my case, of course, and I wouldn't have been here if I hadn't felt pressure from Collie and the boys. But if anything, my knowledge that I was not professionally trained made Skurlock's antagonism bite deeper. *Had* I made matters worse? Would a better man have gotten more done?

I raised my coffee cup to my mouth again. Looking over its top, I glanced toward the door at the sound of chill wind rushing in.

The man entering was of medium height, painfully lank, with a dark beard that made his sickly-skinny face look even paler. He was wearing jeans and a wool shirt, work boots, a windbreaker, a navy stocking cap. He swept the room with his eyes as if he were looking for someone. His gaze stopped for just an instant on me—flickered—then moved on.

The owner walked over to where he was standing and said something. The man shook his head and replied. The owner got in the glass case supporting the cash register and handed him a package of cigars. The man paid quickly and went back out.

For that period of time I sat in shock, frozen.

I could not be one hundred percent sure. His face was entirely different, and I had not heard his voice, which would have been a surer tip. But it could be. I thought it was. The way his eyes had flickered across my face said something. Recognition—then almost instant professional reaction, continuing to move his gaze, as if no recognition had taken place.

The air in the café was still again after the door had closed behind him.

It was him, all right, I thought. I could hardly believe it. *Him.*

Now what?

Skurlock was long gone. I couldn't yell for a cop. Even if by a miracle I happened to get one, it would be Lassiter, worse than no cop at all.

What? Sit tight?

That was the safe and maybe the sane thing to do. But right now, while I sat listening to my gallbladder pucker with indecision, he was getting away.

I had to do something. Remembered my .38 in the glovebox on my car.

Got up, hurried to the counter, tossed a five beside the cash register, hurried out into the biting north wind.

It was fully dark now, grit in the air. I looked around and couldn't see hide nor hair of my prey. I didn't think he had had time to drive off. Hurrying to the Bronco, I dug out the .38 and went around the other side, the driver's side, headed for the front of the café, streetside.

There he was, obscure in the dark, just walking toward a pickup truck angle-parked beside a public telephone hung on a steel pole. He was still on the sidewalk, just at the other end of the building.

I took two long strides forward. Somehow, even with the wind, he heard—or sensed—me. He turned, saw me.

I went to one knee, holding the .38 out with both hands just like the real pros had tried to teach me in Virginia. "Sylvester!" I yelled. "Hold it right there!"

What did I expect? I don't know to this day.

What I did *not* expect was the incredible speed with which he moved. Not toward the pickup truck which I had assumed was his destination, but *the other way*. Toward the corner of the building.

And behind it. Out of sight. So fast I didn't even get a shot.

Now what? I didn't think. I ran to the corner and looked around, realizing after I had done it that I was asking for brains-on-the-pavement time.

But there wasn't anyone at all: just a little walkway between the building and a high board fence, distinguishable in the feeble illumination of a security light hanging from the back eave of the café building.

I hesitated again, but not long. I may be ignorant, but I am not entirely stupid. I would not have gone down that alley for a million dollars.

Turning, I headed back the other way. This time, approaching the far end of the café, I thought twice and swung wide, going off the sidewalk and into the street, going behind a parked Buick. I wished to hell Elk City had more streetlights. The nearest one was a half-block away and I couldn't see worth a damn.

Just as I moved around the Buick to a position where I could look down the far side of the café building, an engine roared to life. Something—a dark pickup—backed up wildly from the side lot, headlights coming around on me, the brights on and blinding. Tires screamed and gravel battered the side of the building like a fusillade of bullets. And here came the pickup. Right at me. Closing the gap instantaneously.

I didn't think of anything but self-preservation. I dove behind the back end of the Buick, sprawling on my chest in the pebbly asphalt. The truck screamed past me, the back wheels missing my legs, but coming so close I felt the wind. I rolled over and retrieved my revolver, which had gotten dropped in my unholy haste to avert being run down. But by then the truck was forty yards up the street. No lights on now, so no look at the license tag. No streetlamps to give me a decent look at what kind of pickup it was.

It reached the next corner and turned right, going around on two wheels, and was gone.

The door of the café banged open and the owner and a couple of patrons spilled out. They spotted me. "What happened, buddy?"

I managed to get my .38 hidden in my back pocket. "Reckless driver. Almost ran me down." I walked unsteadily toward them, brushing dirt from my front.

"You hurt?" one of the men asked solicitously.

"No," I told him. "I'm fine."

Great lies of the Twentieth Century.

It was true I was unhurt, except for my pride. But this time I had really and royally screwed up. I had *had* him. And I had let him get away. My disappointment and disgust were so intense I felt like throwing up.

twelve

On Saturday morning, I checked first with Karyn Wechsting. She was in her room and said she was making more calls, trying to round up players for our tournament. She had located a couple, and was now through my list and working from one of her own. I almost felt guilty about making her work so hard. Almost, not quite. I had too much else on my mind.

Downstairs, the way Ted Treacher had people doing last-minute waxing of floors and sweeping of carpets, you might have thought we were about to entertain the President of the United States.

Ted was tight, pale, turned in on himself, irritable with everyone, really unlike himself in every regard. I tried to talk to him but he couldn't seem to concentrate, kept drifting off into some interior never-never land. He was acting really crazy.

Perhaps if I had had less on my own mind I might have realized that there must be more going on with him than the visit from Allen Industries, as almighty important as he seemed to think that was. I didn't take the time to think about it.

Events following my screwup last night with Sylvester had not been all that pleasant either. It had to be reported, of course, and I had bitten my tongue and forced myself to call Fred Skurlock promptly from a pay booth in town. I caught him just walking into his rented office from our meeting at the café; he picked up when I started to leave an ambiguous-sounding need-to-talk-immediately message on the machine.

"You *what*?" he grated when I told him straight out.

I repeated the key gruesome details. He then treated me to a fine, three-minute monologue of largely unrelated profanities and obscenities, with a choice scatological paragraph in the middle and a footnote suggesting that I had again achieved an anatomical impossibility. I had it coming, and I listened to all of it without argument.

Finally he began to calm down. "You got no tag number?"

"It was too dark and he moved too fast."

"Description?"

"A pickup. Quarter-ton, I think. Dark color. Maybe brown. I'm almost sure it was a Dodge."

"That's great work, pal. That narrows it down to about ten thousand vehicles in this county."

I didn't say anything to that, either.

Skurlock added, "I'm going to get a composite artist in here. Might take a day or two, we want a good one of our own. You can give him your best shot at an up-to-date description of the guy's new look. We can post it at the lab and around town. They might even want to bring in another man or two to carry it up and down Main Street."

"I just got one good look, but I'll do my best."

The sound of his irritated sigh was audible. "I guess we have to look at the bright side. Number one, we now know for sure—for the first time—that he *is* here. I've just got an idea that will get us some more help. Number two, we have the start of a description. Does he look a lot different?"

I remembered. "A lot different. Yes."

"Okay. Go about your business for right now. More than ever I think I need to babysit you a little, so I'll be around as we discussed at the café."

"Whatever you say."

"Hey."

"Yes?"

There was a pause. Then, softer: "Take care of yourself."

After that, still shaken, I called the long-distance number for Collie Davis. Usually this was a good time of night to catch him, and I did. Using no names and awkwardly talking around some of the events, I briefed him.

"You messed up," he told me matter-of-factly.

"Right, Collie. Thanks, Collie."

"You sound strung out."

"Some."

"You're not dead. Congratulate yourself."

"I haven't been any help out here. Ted's situation has hogged my time. Do you have any idea of how bad a financial mess he's in out here?"

"We have an idea," Collie's voice replied coolly.

"Why haven't you guys helped him out? Damn it, after everything he did for you, why haven't you given him some financial help? You owe him!"

"Smith," and now Collie's voice was flat with bitterness, "I just read a memo telling us to cut back on our consumption of ballpoints and Post-It pads. Even if we thought we could launder money and get it to him—which would make us look *real* good to Congress if we were ever caught—we don't *have* any extra goddamn funds right now. Just because a man did something for us in the past, that doesn't mean we have to break laws and sell furniture to help him out when he later screws up his life."

"Collie, as usual your compassion touches me."

"Maybe I would make policy sound nicer for you if you hadn't just blown a golden opportunity for us."

"Do you think I don't know I screwed up?"

"Calm down."

"'Calm down'? How am I supposed to calm down?"

"You lived through it. And nobody ever expected you to be entirely competent."

"Thanks!"

"I'm going to do some checking, fast. Actually, this might not be the worst thing that could have happened. He tried to kill you, right?"

"I got that distinct impression."

"Great."

"*Great*? I—"

"See, now we know he's there, and we can say the life of one of our contract employees is in imminent danger." He paused a beat. "Do you see what I mean?"

It dawned on me. Now the Company had a thin justification for sending in one of their own. "Yes."

"Sit tight and help Ted and try to stay alive until I can get there," Collie said. "Is that asking too much?"

"I'll try," I replied.

So I had returned to the lodge and had a sad, crazy late dinner with Ted, Karyn Wechsting, and Sally Wallis. Ted twitched and went off into his private, worried world and Sally stroked his arm and called him darling and made sure Karyn got the message. Karyn looked pale under her freckles and gamely smiled now and then. I should have been more consoling or something, but I got sick of the batch of them and headed for my cabin at a relatively early hour. Maryann called me the moment I got there and said hopefully that she had a bottle of wine. I pleaded a headache. She sounded hurt. I locked up and listened to the mounting cold wind and then went to sleep wondering where poor Skurlock was staked out nearby and how miserable he was.

When the Allen Industries motorcade blasted up our long, treed driveway a little after lunchtime, you might have thought the President was arriving.

They pulled up in front: two full-size cars, a Lincoln Town Car and a Fairlane, and a Toyota Tercel bringing up the rear. A couple of young male executive types hopped out to open doors. A couple of other men climbed out, carrying attaché cases. Then came two women: a rather tall, slender, elegantly beautiful woman of indeterminate forties, wearing a silver silk suit, and a younger woman with tight-cut dark hair, a rumpled beige dress, and owlish, red-framed eyeglasses. The driver of the Lincoln sprinted to the lodge entrance to open our doors for the lady in the silver silk suit. She swept in with her entourage trailing behind her. Ted Treacher, looking strained and uncomfortable in a dark suit being worn for the first time, met her. I stayed a step or two behind him.

"Mrs. Allen?" he asked, extending his hand. "I'm Ted Treacher. This is a great pleasure."

Ardis Allen stopped and gave him a smile that would have chilled a snowman. "Hello, Mr. Treacher." She shook hands. "I'm glad to be here."

"I hope you had a pleasant drive down from Missoula?"

"Not particularly."

"I meant . . . uh, there's some pretty scenery."

"I didn't notice. Can we get right to work, Mr. Treacher?"

"Of course. Whatever you say. I thought we could—"

"This is Miss Cline, my personal secretary. Miss Cline will require the use of a personal computer with a graphics interface card and a modem to allow her to access our mainframe in Chicago. Miss Cline's room is to adjoin mine. This is Mr. Herndon, my chief accountant. He will need access to your financial records, of course, and a small office near your bookkeeping department where he can set up the computer and calculating equipment he brought with him. This is Mr. Tinkle, Mr. Herndon's assistant. These two gentlemen are Messers Ross and Housemueller, who are attorneys associated with my firm. And this is Mr. Lyle, who assists me directly. This is Mr. Eastman. If you can show us to our rooms, please, I suggest we reassemble in thirty minutes in your meeting room to outline the way I want to proceed on this visit."

Sweat gleamed on Ted's forehead. "That will be fine. I think you'll find we have everything in good order for you. I hope we've anticipated every question you might have."

"I doubt it. Most people haven't the foggiest idea of how to run a business with maximum efficiency. However, we shall see. That's why we're here, is it not so?"

Ted made some weak reply. Score the first points for Mrs. Allen. My first instinct was not to like her very much. Formidable, yes. Human, perhaps not.

Ted signaled to me and Sally Wallis. "This is my business manager, Mrs. Wallis, and this is one of my associates, Brad Smith."

Ardis Allen didn't give Sally a glance. Her remarkable chill eyes swiveled toward me. She walked over, graceful hand extended, and the glacial smile became almost genuine. "Brad Smith. Of course. I've seen you play often. How nice."

"Hello, Mrs. Allen."

"Mr. Treacher called you an 'associate.' Tell me: are you a part owner-investor in Bitterroot Valley?"

"Not exactly. I'm helping with promotion, and a small tournament—"

"I see. Of course. I hope you and I can have a good talk later in the day, Brad. I'm very enthusiastic about tennis. Keeps one fit. We might even play?"

"As you wish."

"Then we will." She turned. "Mr. Treacher, those rooms. . . ?"

The first meeting did not go very well. Ardis Allen opened by noting that a faucet dripped in her guestroom bath, there was an odor of tobacco which she could not abide, the draperies were dusty, and the windows streaked. She said she had imagined every forward-looking lodge in the world by now had segregated smokers, or had learned how to banish stale odors. It seemed an odd complaint, because she smoked as she said it.

Ted, sitting uneasily at the head of the long walnut table in the dimly draped conference room, smiled nervously and tapped his ballpoint. "We're still working on some things, Mrs. Allen. Obviously. But I think you'll find we're already top drawer in most aspects—"

"Really?" she cut in coolly. "There was not an adequate sign on the highway to guide visitors in. The grounds need mowing and general maintenance. There was no doorman to greet us in the parking lot, and you say your bellmen are off for the day due to some unfortunate mixup in scheduling. Your plumbing leaks, your rooms smell, your windows and draperies are dirty, and this coffee you've just served us tastes rancid. Our preliminary inquiries show late payments to suppliers and an average occupancy rate last month of less than thirty percent. I like this location, Mr. Treacher. I like the idea of moving my company into the recreation-housing-resort business. Let's not, however, pretend things here are any better than they are. I can assure you, my team will learn the truth whatever it may be, so pretense is silly. And I only hope your bookkeeping is better than your cook. These finger sandwiches are abominable."

Ted held his smile. It looked like a death skull. "We're solid," was all he said.

Ardis Allen opened the cover of her thin, letter-sized leather notebook. The first page, which I could see across the table at an angle, was crammed with times and schedule notations.

"Here," she said coldly, "is how we will proceed."

The next few hours were blitzkrieg. Ardis Allen, her secretary in tow and making notes of every observation, went with Ted on a tour of the lodge, the cottages and condos, the courts, and even the outbuildings. Then, while Ted was called into a closed-door head-knocking with her lawyers, she went on a chauffeur-driven tour of Elk City and the area as far north as the competing resort, driving past Elkhorn Lodge. Through all of the time, the Allen Industries number-crunchers were closeted with Sally Wallis and a local accountant who helped with the resort books on a part-time basis. I was assigned to take the mysterious assistant named Lyle around the resort to meet and visit with guests.

Lyle was a short, bloodless man with straw hair and marble eyes. He had small, soft hands and a feminine voice. He smiled a lot, but the smile reminded me of Peter Lorre in the old movies. Most of the guests took him at face value. On his orders, I introduced him as "a guest of ours." He visited casually with everybody we could get close to, talking about the weather, the mountains, the lodge, and tennis. It seemed obvious to me that he had perhaps never had a tennis racket in his hands. But he had done some homework, and seemed to convince most people of his sincere interest in the game, and in taking a more extended vacation here. What he was really doing was getting a good, solid feel for how well Bitterroot Valley was doing with its paying customers.

It was well past six o'clock when the accountants came out for a break and Ardis Allen showed up after her tour. She walked into the meeting between Ted and the lawyers, but wasn't inside long. She came straight up to me. "They're going to be a while. This might be a good chance for you to give me a quick look at the golf course. And then, if there's light enough, we might test the courts."

I located the lodge golf cart. As I walked out to it with the lady, Maryann came across the deck with a couple of other guests and gave me a sunny wave. I waved back and helped Ardis into the cart.

"A little friend of yours?" she asked as we started down the path toward the pro shop in the ravine.

"A guest," I said.

"Such a smile for you," she observed coolly. "And she looks so *sweet*, too." She made "sweet" sound like "mindless." She paused a beat, then added, "Not much of a challenge, however, I should imagine."

I didn't reply.

"Chivalry. How quaint."

We drove past the pro shop and down to the first tee. Following cart paths, I showed her the vantage points from which most of the course could be seen. The rainstorm had done more damage near the new No. 15 green than Ted had hinted. Part of the berms and the buildup area on one side had been washed out by a flash flood in the creek which formed the lateral hazard. Some heavy bulldozer work would be necessary to rebuild all of it properly. It was a good thing the old green and fairway landing area were still being used.

During the tour the sun continued lowering behind the western mountains and a chill began to sink in. Some clouds to the north made it look like there could be a repeat of last night's storms. Ardis Allen asked some questions about the course and cost of maintenance. I told her I was no expert, and hadn't seen the books.

"A course out here could never pay for itself," she said.

"It might surprise you once the resort was better established."

"But it will always be just a cost-intensive added attraction. The tennis must be the thing here."

"Maybe," I conceded.

"You think the course could be cost-effective?" she asked with a hint of rancor that I would dare to question her judgment.

"With the lodge better established, it can easily play thirty thousand rounds, even assuming four full months of snow cover. Even if every round were by a guest, counting cart rentals and equipment we should gross well over a quarter of a million. Add the pro shop and everything else and an income of seven hundred thousand is not unrealistic. That's from the golf course alone."

"But golf course maintenance costs are high," she said mildly.

Sensing homework on her part and a possible trap, I went conservative. "Break even at the level of play I'm suggesting, then start making money about the third year."

"It costs thirty thousand dollars a year, per green, to maintain a course."

"We can cut that. For one thing, we don't have year-around maintenance. For another, these greens are never going to be expected to equal a southern country club. Sand top-layering, aeration, fertilization, rollering, cutting. That's all. Small staff at minimum wage except for the greenskeeper, and we have a man who's retired to this area because he loves it, and he's working cheap."

Her eyes studied me. For the first time I saw something that might have been respect. "You talk a good game."

"It would take three years. You might have to eat a loss to get established."

"Over-optimistic," she said.

"I don't think so."

She was silent a minute, then abruptly changed the subject. "Why is he having so much trouble with local suppliers and an extended line of credit?"

"I suggest you ask him that—assuming what you say is true."

"You're loyal," she said.

I didn't answer.

"You also have a head on your shoulders," she went on. "You know, I could use a man like you in my organization."

Startled, I glanced at her, saw the surprising warmth along with the cool appraisal and irony in her eyes. Again I didn't answer her. We drove back up the path toward the lodge.

After another check with her team of experts, Ardis announced that it was time for a few minutes' relaxation. She decreed that I would meet her on the No. 1 court. Which, being a good boy, I did.

The lights were on by the time she showed up in royal-blue velvet warmups, her hair tied with a white sweatband, and an oversized Head racket in hand. She danced around gracefully while I courtesy-served her some balls to put away with a strong, much-coached forehand and a backhand that undercut every ball and made it bounce funny. After that she insisted we play a few "easy games."

The lady did not know how to play an "easy" game any more, I guessed, than she knew how to do anything by half-measures. I moved her around and didn't get much involved while she sprinted after every ball with grim determination, drilling them back at me down the lines with the fluid, artificial, pro-taught motion she was surely capable of repeating all day, every day.

It took me almost forty minutes to take some of the edge off her pent-up tightness. By that time she was streaming sweat and shaking a little, which made her altogether more attractive as far as I was concerned.

Unfortunately, when we met again in the dining room for dinner with one of her lawyers, Ted, Karyn, and Sally at nine o'clock, she had showered and changed and was the ice queen once more. She peppered everyone with quick, hostile, probing questions from the aperitif wine to the cherries jubilee and brandy finale. After that, she announced that she would have a session alone with Ted to discuss matters further.

"Godamighty," Karyn Wechsting breathed after the party had broken up and just the two of us left the dining room together. "The woman is a fiend!"

"She's tough. But Ted is hoping to get a lot of money out of her, and if this is what it takes, there's no help for it."

"Lunch with a barricuda!"

"Yep."

Karyn yawned in the lobby. "I'm tired."

"You okay?"

She looked at me. "I guess."

"He was just preoccupied today, babe."

She looked distant and sad. "Sally is very pretty, isn't she."

"If you like 'em sort of chubby."

She grinned and gave me a fierce hug, then jumped into the elevator.

Without asking anyone, I took the golf cart down the path to my cabin. Drove fast and parked it in front with the headlights on while I hurried to my door, got it unlocked, went in and got my pistol, and spooked back outside just long enough to douse the lights. I felt like yelling to see if Skurlock was witnessing my cowardice. Instead I just hurried back inside and locked up.

After a drink and a cigarette, the call to the West Coast went right through. Beth was sympathetic. I told her only about the lodge problems, nothing of Sylvester or the lab or any of that, since I had lied and hidden that side from the start.

We talked for a long time. She said she was getting stronger every day. All her law cases had been reassigned when she was hurt so badly, and she felt like she was starting over. I could hear the frustration in her voice. But she said she would get it going again.

The more we talked, the more I wanted her here.

Toward the end she said, "Get some sleep. Talk to you tomorrow. I love you."

"I love you too," I said. Then, unbidden: "Beth, won't you come out here?"

"Brad, you know I can't."

"Okay," I said, tasting the disappointment—in her, for refusing, in me, for allowing myself to ask again.

"I really can't, honey," she said.

"Okay."

After a silence she said, "Brad?"

"Um?"

"I really, really can't."

"I know, babe."

We hung up after that. It was unsatisfactory.

In the morning: more blitzkrieg. Ardis Allen's accountant-types were closeted with Ted Treacher's bookkeeper from town by the time I showed up in the lodge at 8 A.M. The lady herself was closeted with Sally Wallis. A couple of her other aides poked around in storerooms, empty condo units and even the heating plant, and made phone calls back to Chicago, talking to mainframe computers with laptops. Ted nervously paced the floor, muttering about how things looked good. His color was like waxed paper.

"Are you sure you're all right?" I demanded at one point.

"Of course! Why shouldn't I be? I'm just tense, that's all. Getting these people to invest in the operation here can make all the difference in our cash flow. You know that."

"I know that," I told him.

"Then don't start on me again, Brad."

"I'm not starting on you, Ted. You just act like a man on the edge. I'm worried about you."

"I'm fine. I'm just fine."

I shrugged and shut up.

A little after ten o'clock, Ardis Allen huddled with her group of helpers. The meeting lasted almost an hour. When they broke up, most of the party headed for their own rooms, Ardis announcing they were leaving soon for the drive back to Missoula, and her corporate jet. Ted palely offered lunch. She accepted hot tea.

"It's time," she told him, "for serious discussion."

"I'm for that." Ted's grin was ghastly.

We went to the small dining room we had used for earlier larger sessions. Ardis Allen brought one of her lawyers and an aide whose function had never been made clear to me. Ted brought Sally Wallis and me.

The door shut. Ardis Allen, at the head of the long table, opened the dark leather cover of her thin, legal-sized notebook.

"Ted," she began, using his first name for the first time I was aware of it, "you and your staff have been most accommodating, and we appreciate that."

"My pleasure," Ted said, spots of color touching his face.

"Unfortunately," she went on with the warmth of a robot, "our findings prove conclusively that there is a disastrous gap between reality and the claims and representations made by you and your counsel—both in correspondence and preliminary conversations with Allen Industries as well as in what I consider a most unfortunate stock issue prospectus." She paused and looked directly at Ted with ice eyes. "Not only have you misrepresented the financial health of the resort, you have misstated fundamental financial considerations in the stock prospectus, which in our view opens you to possible legal action by the Securities and Exchange Commission."

Ted stared, sheet-white again. The room fell silent.

"Not true," he croaked.

Ardis flipped a page of her notes. "The lodge building still requires major structural repair. The plumbing is probably beyond help, short of total replacement. The heating is inadequate and antiquated. The latest rainstorm caused serious leakage in the basement, which caused related damage. Despite the best efforts by Brad Smith, here, to put a happy face on it, the golf course needs considerably more tile and creek location work, and you're losing three more greens to weeds and root-borers. Your lodge occupancy is thirty-three percent. You've sold exactly four of eighteen completed condominium units. Twelve of your cabins are empty. As to your cash position—"

"Look at how much we've accomplished!" Ted cut in. "We're

open! We're getting more business every day! Granted, we have a long way to go. But we're making progress. We're making a go of it."

Ardis did not so much as look up at him, her hooded gaze remaining on her notebook. With a long, crimson fingernail she flipped another page. "When you bid successfully for this property, you guaranteed payment in ten years of one-point-eight million, with a good-faith down payment of two hundred thousand, and a balloon payment of another two hundred thousand dollars no later than eighteen months from closing. You plowed in about one hundred and fifty thousand dollars of your savings—leaving you, as best as we can determine, less than seventy thousand remaining in your other accounts. You borrowed another hundred and fifty thousand initially on a two-year single-pay note, and then took a second mortgage on the lodge and land for another ninety thousand, evidently as a way of finding initial operating capital."

As she spoke, Ted seemed to shrink lower and lower in his chair. Now she raised her head to stare at him. "Am I substantially correct so far?"

"You make it sound worse than it is," he told her. His voice sounded strangled.

"I could go on. I know our figures are accurate. Allen Industries did not reach its present size and success by being casual about large-scale investments, Mr. Treacher."

"It's not that bad," Ted insisted hoarsely. "We're going to make it work—"

"I believe that," Ardis said at once, surprising me as much as anyone. "With sufficient investment, this *can* work. It's a good area, undeveloped. I see the potential."

"Then," Ted said, his expression almost hopeful, "your decision to buy into our operation—"

The notebook snapped closed. "We have no interest in 'buying into' your operation."

"Then—"

"This resort needs new management, new vision. I am prepared to order my legal staff to draw up a complete sales contract—Bitterroot Valley, lock, stock, and barrel, for a price that will allow you to recoup all your personal losses, pay off every obligation, and take away a personal profit of between one hundred and eighty and two hundred and fifty thousand dollars."

Ted's eyes bulged. "Buy me out? Is that what you're saying? You want to buy me out?"

"That's what I'm saying."

"But I don't want to sell out. I'm looking for just a little financial help, just enough to get us over the hump—"

"That so-called hump is a mountain, and you can't climb it. You lack the financial base. You lack the business acumen, the support staff, the advertising budget, everything you need. I like the area. I like new challenge. We can diversify into this kind of operation. We can make it go. You can't. It's as simple as that."

"But—"

"There *is* no 'but,'" she insisted, flinty, inexorable. "*You have already failed.* It's just a question of time."

Her words drove Ted deeper into his chair. He seemed to shrink before my eyes. *Enough!* I thought.

He said quietly, "We weren't looking to sell. We just needed some help."

"You're finished," she told him with flinty directness. "Our formal offer will be in your hands by next Tuesday. You will be given seventy-two hours to respond. Please don't waste our time by making a counter-offer. I do not negotiate on matters like this. You can take our offer or leave it. I strongly advise you to take it. You're fortunate to have a chance to get out short of complete ruin."

Ted studied her with ravaged eyes. "Brad is helping," he said like a man repeating a litany. "I've got Sally."

Ardis's control slipped just a tad, and I saw the momentary curl of her lip. "Your people have no expertise, no business sense. Any more than you do."

Sally Wallis sat up straighter, eyes shooting sparks of outrage. "Whereas," she snapped, "you qualified yourself by becoming a widow."

It hit home, and deep. Ardis's eyes narrowed and she went just a little pale. She stood quickly, gathering up her notebook. "The meeting is over."

There were chill, polite words in the lobby, but within twenty minutes they had gone, the big cars gunning out of the driveway and vanishing into the trees that screened the resort from the highway. Sally Wallis made some bright, artificial, hopeful talk. Karyn had come down, and linked her arm through Ted's, trying to be encouraging.

"They'll bargain," Sally said.

"She said they wouldn't," I pointed out.

"They will. You can get more out of them, Ted."

"But I don't want to *sell*," Ted told her.

"I can see why," Sally said. "I didn't like her either. But maybe you should."

She looked at me. "What do you think, Brad?"

"I thought it was stupid of you to antagonize her the way you did at the end."

"She infuriated me."

"And you popped off, and probably ended any possibility of the negotiation that you're now saying might work."

Her face stiffened and her chin went up. "You don't understand these things."

"And you do. Right."

"Don't fight, don't fight," Ted said distractedly.

He went to his small back office. We trailed him. He paced the floor. "I was so sure they would buy in! Now what am I going to do? Where is the support going to come from?"

"Christ, Ted," I argued. "It can't be that bad."

"You don't know," he said. He seemed upset out of all proportion to anything that had happened. "I've got to have help. *Now*."

"Well," I said, baffled, "wait till you see her formal offer. It might be great. You might be able to get even again, and try somewhere—"

"You don't *understand*!"

After a while I went outside with Karyn. In the sunlight beyond the lobby, I saw that she had tears in her eyes.

"I'd do anything to help."

"He'll calm down," I said with more confidence than I felt. "He's just disappointed right now. He'll bounce back and then we'll have to take a hard look at what it's going to take to keep this place afloat."

"Even with all his debt?"

"Sure," I said, hugging her shoulders. "What more could happen?"

It was three hours after I asked the question that I got the answer. It was then that they found the body.

thirteen

Elsewhere

Elk City

"Mrs. Hill?" Sylvester said when she answered her telephone.

"Yes? Oh! Hello! I recognize your voice!"

Sylvester hiked his boots onto the edge of the cabin cot and touched a match to his cigar. "I'm very sorry, Mrs. Hill, but I am forced to cancel our planned meeting for coffee later today. Perhaps we can reschedule later in the week?"

Her voice took on her favorite whining sound. "Oh, that's all right, sir. One of my kids is feeling a little poorly, and I'm always so tired myself, being alone and all. Honestly, sometimes life is just so hard."

Sylvester thought the miserable woman would probably live to be 90, and complain that she was at death's door every day of her life. He swallowed the impulse to suggest suicide. Women who fulfilled themselves by being victims had always been among his most useful pawns.

He got to the business at hand: "From our last conversation I understood the full-power testing apparently has begun?"

"Yes . . . yes, I don't know anything much about it, of course, being just a salaried employee. You know, they treat me like dirt out there. Like dirt! Those air force people think they're so smart and great. It's enough to make you sick. I just hate it. If I hadn't always had bad luck, maybe *I* would be in charge of something and could show people how an office is supposed to be run. I—"

"Mrs. Hill, pardon me, but I'm on a pay telephone here and someone is waiting."

"Oh, *I'm* sorry! I'm so dumb, I—"

"Mrs. Hill, my organization, and all environmentalists around the world, are terribly concerned. If we could just know when the next battery of tests are to be run, we could put a thousand demonstrators around the fencing out there. If you could *possibly* help us obtain any scrap of information about exactly what is being tested, and how—"

"Well, I'll do all I can. You know that. It's just so hard, you know, with my health the way it is, and having to work all day and then come home and have sick tykes, and the money is so scarce since my husband ran out on us—"

"Mrs. Hill, we deeply appreciate your devotion to our cause. Please watch your mail. We will be sending you another small amount to help you defray expenses of helping us."

"Oh! You don't have to do that, sir! But I *am* so in need, they're so unfair in what they pay us out there, and the bills—people take advantage of a poor, sick woman living alone with just her kids—"

"Think nothing of it, Mrs. Hill. We value you. Truly! Now do call my number if you have anything to report."

Hanging up, Sylvester got up and allowed himself two fingers of good Canadian whiskey in a jelly glass. Dealing with his inept informer was almost as irritating as everything else that had happened lately.

The chance encounter with Smith at the café had nearly been a disaster. Even in getting away, Sylvester had been compromised, and he knew it. Smith had recognized him and could now describe him for others. Sylvester now had to stay much more out of sight. Worse, if a composite sketch was produced and shown to the local officer, Lassiter, he might recognize his cabin renter at once. In which case Sylvester could be blown entirely.

OVERHEAD

It would take a couple of days for any artwork to be produced and circulated. By that time, Sylvester needed to be out of this cabin and in some new hiding place.

The entire situation was galling. First Sylvester had been ready to take Smith out the other night—had been in position with a rigged gun-rest and good cover. Then he had seen the other man lumbering awkwardly through the brush, taking a position closer to the cabin. Sylvester had waited, teeth grating in frustration, until the other man started his attack. Then the woman had come along instantly, screaming, and Sylvester had had no choice but to get out of there.

That had been the right time to kill Smith.

The chance meeting at the café had been a second chance.

Both were now gone, wasted.

Sylvester had driven more than thirty miles this morning to find a pay telephone far from local observation. His call to his control had not been pleasant. He had been able to report that his colleague inside the lab, "O'Connor," now had one specification sheet for one of several electronic boards involved in the EMP transmitter. O'Connor thought he could get two more early in the week, when all the diagrams were laid out for circuit testing on a component-by-component basis. A full-scale test firing meant total concentration on operation of the equipment itself, and if Sylvester could get a hint on the timing of that from Mrs. Hill, with possible verification by O'Connor, then there might be a chance to get the rest of the plans while lab personnel were preoccupied with the actual "shoot."

This meant a clock was ticking. Success or failure of the operation inside the lab might well be decided within the next week.

Sylvester had also had to report the brush with Smith, however, and his certainty about Skurlock's real identity and the likelihood of one or more additional FBI agents inside the lab itself.

As a result, his new instructions were to restrict his own movements and hope Mrs. Hill and "O'Connor" could take the next necessary steps.

"And Smith?" Sylvester asked, bitterly knowing the answer already.

"You have standing instructions in that regard."

"Yes, sir."

Missoula

It was quiet in the neat Missoula airport. One of Ardis Allen's executives brought a plastic cup of coffee to the small VIP lounge where she was waiting.

She looked up from her notebook and accepted the cup with a thin smile. "Thank you, Barry."

"The pilot says they'll be ready for takeoff as soon as we're on board, Mrs. Allen."

"The rest of you go on out, Rex. Betty is in the phone booth over there, and I want to complete the call she's placing for me before we leave."

Rex hesitated a moment, perhaps thinking of the onboard radiotelephone system. He had long since learned, however, not to question the boss-lady's decisions. He merely nodded and hurried into the main lobby area to collect the rest of the group and their luggage and equipment.

Ardis looked again toward the booth where her secretary was holding. It was imperative, from Ardis's point of view, to complete the call *now*. It was not a matter to which she wanted to trust the Learjet radio link, no matter how secure AT&T insisted such technology was.

The formal offer for Bitterroot Valley would be prepared and sent as promised, but Ardis was convinced that Ted Treacher had no intention of accepting it. He had to accept it. Ardis had no alternatives.

The screws must be tightened.

She sipped her coffee, wondering why airport brew had to taste like battery acid. She tried to concentrate on her notes. She seldom had trouble concentrating on a serious task at hand, no matter what the distractions. Her mental discipline was the awe of all who knew her. But she was having difficulty concentrating now. She was angry and frustrated. She *had to have* Bitterroot Valley; without it, everything could collapse. Ted Treacher, with his sad-faced, blindly loyal cadre of fools, was incredibly impractical not to accept her offer at once. If so much had not been riding on it, the idiot would have been presented an offer light-years less generous.

Ardis could not fathom such stupidity. It crossed her mind that Treacher was being sentimental, but she automatically rejected the idea. She had never been sentimental about anything, and could not imagine anyone else being so when so much money was involved.

"Mrs. Allen?"

Ardis turned to see Betty anxiously leaning out of the telephone booth. Carrying her notebook and coffee, Ardis hurried over, took the telephone, and slid into the booth. "Thank you, Betty. Board the plane and wait."

Ardis closed the door. The telephone had the hiss of long-distance on the receiver. "Hello, Senator?"

The reedy old voice came back filled with bogus enthusiasm: "Ardis? Is that you, my dear? How grand it is to hear from you!"

"Senator, I know it's Sunday, but—"

"No problem, Ardis! No problem at all! Hearing from you is always a joy! Your voice brightens my day! Where are you? To what do I owe the pleasure of this call?"

Ardis imagined the bony octogenarian in his Georgetown living room, his lank, ailing old body swathed in a warm flannel robe, the light of his reading lamp bright on his bald head with its constellations of ugly liver spots. What kind of a political system was it, she had often asked herself in dismay, that invested such awesome power in a senile old man whose only real accomplishment was in fooling voters often enough to become one of the oldest legislators in America?

No matter how, she reminded herself, Senator Henthorne had the power. And she had Senator Henthorne.

"Senator," she said easily, "I've seen no results from that investigation we've discussed on several occasions, and I am deeply concerned."

There was a pause while—probably, she thought cynically—the old brain cells fired and misfired, trying to remember what in the hell she was talking about.

"The SEC," she prompted, fighting to hold her temper.

"Oh, yes, of course! The SEC . . . Ardis, my dear, I have been assured by the highest level of management over there that the investigation is ongoing, proceeding nicely . . . results will be forthcoming soon . . . As you know, my dear, the other line of inquiry you suggested has resulted in a rare—I might even say almost *unique*—interagency cooperation, and as I have assured you in our prior conversations, everyone is deeply motivated to get to the bottom of this nasty matter . . . bring the culprit to justice, especially in view of the loyalty question, and—"

"Senator," Ardis cut in, trying to avoid a filibuster, "I am deeply concerned. Do you understand me? I am *deeply* concerned and troubled."

"Yes . . ." He sounded befuddled. "Deeply concerned, yes . . . but progress is being made, and they have assured me—"

"Senator," Ardis cut in again, "this disgraceful situation *must* be brought to a head. I cannot emphasize to you, Senator, how strongly I feel this. I must tell you that I have been in touch with a number of other members of the Citizens for A Better Era, and I think it's safe to say that everyone in CABE is impatient."

The silence on the line was profound. CABE was the senator's political action committee, source of his campaign funding. Despite his age, Henthorne soon would be running for reelection again. "I see . . ." he said finally.

"Senator," Ardis went on, "it would be a tragedy for all of America if circumstances forced CABE to withdraw its support. We don't want that, do we?"

"Oh, my dear!" His alarm made his voice shriller. "Surely it isn't as serious as—"

"You *must* get action on the investigation, Senator, and now. For your own future." Ardis paused. "I am calling as a loyal supporter. I am very, very concerned, Senator, about what can go wrong if you are unable to spur this investigation into action now." She paused again, then added, "Do you see what I mean, Senator?"

"I believe I do," the old voice quavered. Then it strengthened, the strength of fear. "Yes. I do see, Ardis. I appreciate your call. Yes. I see that stern action must be taken now. At once. It has taken far too long, this probe. I share your sense of outrage. Justice delayed is justice denied. In view of the loyalty question, this should have been settled long ago . . . long ago! Yes . . ."

"Thank you, Senator," Ardis said. "I plan to call tomorrow to hear what progress has been made."

Perhaps the old man in Georgetown started a fumbling, gasping reply. Ardis would never know because she had already hung up the telephone and started across the mini-lobby, high heels clicking, headed for her jet.

Seattle

It was mid-afternoon on the west coast, and David Maxwell, a supervisor for the Securities and Exchange Commission, had gotten in only recently from the golf course. He was working on his second Harvey Wallbanger and thinking about shortening his backswing when the telephone rang.

"I'll get it," he called to his wife in the next room, and picked it up. "Hello?"

"Max?" the familiar male voice said.

Recognizing the caller at once, Maxwell straightened to attention. "Yes sir."

"Max, the decision has been made to move on that Montana case."

Maxwell knew at once what case his supervisor meant, but he was surprised and puzzled. "We've been moving along well on that, sir, but as our last report indicated, there are a number of loose ends—witnesses to interview, plus some more checking on cash reserve accounts—"

"The decision," his boss cut in tightly, "has been made. You and Critenden and Schultz get on it now. The U.S. marshals in Helena will be notified to provide all necessary assistance. Required court orders will be issued by as soon as possible this week in Denver, and taken to Missoula by courier. You can pick them up there. I want action now. This week."

"Christ," Maxwell said involuntarily, thinking aloud. "I'm not sure we're ready. We—"

"*Get* ready, Max. I mean it. Do it. Period."

Elk City

The air force research station high on the side of Grumpy Mountain ordinarily was quiet on Sundays.

This was no ordinary Sunday.

Cars filled the small asphalt parking lot just beyond the security gate in the lab's double twelve-foot cyclone fence. Three small dish antennas rotated swiftly on top of the long, flat, featureless main building. Two extra guards manned the front gate, and red domelights flashed continuously at the doors of the main building, signaling TEST IN PROGRESS.

Inside the building, Sylvester's colleague, using the name O'Connor, stood beside his electronics test bench in one of the quality-control rooms just off the primary experimental-section control center. Smaller red lights blinked at both of these interior doors, too, and an air force MP stood by each. There was no glass in the doors. From O'Connor's side one could see nothing.

O'Connor had to feign unconcern. In truth he was so frustrated he felt like yelling.

He turned from the guarded doors and pretended to make some routine VOM continuity checks on a large, solid-state power supply that had gone intermittent in one of the standby computers. It was hack work, idiot stuff. The kind he was allowed to do. He had to stay occupied or he might yell yet.

There was a sudden new stillness in the workroom. For a second O'Connor did not realize what had happened, but then he did: the central heating and air filtration system fans had shut down. Then the lights went on dim.

All but the most necessary power to every part of the lab complex had been shut off or reduced to a minimum. The complex had thirty times the power it might ever use, high-voltage lines snaking along the side of the mountain to the complex's own transformer station nearby. There were backups to the backups, and emergency alternators behind those. But when a major test was being run, due to the enormous amounts of energy drawn by the EMP equipment, everything possible was done to assure maximum standby current.

There was a sudden new change: an eerie, almost subliminal tone—a near-painful vibration beyond the normal threshold of human hearing. O'Connor looked around and placed it. The ceiling light fixtures were *throbbing* in tune with some great disturbance otherwise not detected.

After a few more seconds, as suddenly as the sound had started, it stopped.

The test was over, O'Connor thought. His sense of failure

heightened. There had to be a way to get inside the control room and at least see the actual equipment! Once in, he had to find a way to copy the crucial circuits. But he was no nearer than he had been weeks ago.

Patience . . . patience! he lectured himself. But it was impossible. These could be the ultimate tests. The entire weapons package, transmitter, computer control devices and antennas, might be shipped out of here tomorrow. Then what would he have? Nothing!

One of the metal doors to the control center swung open sharply. Dr. Jacobson, assistant project director, strode out with an angry and worried-looking air force colonel at his heels.

"The entire goddamned test can't be shut down because a two-thousand-dollar computer shut off!" the colonel rasped.

Jacobson, a short, slender man with a perpetual look of harassment, scanned the workroom. Except for a maintenance man pushing a broom at the far end, O'Connor was the only person there.

"O'Connor," Jacobson called.

"Yes, sir?"

"What do you know about PCs?"

Damned little, if the truth were known. But O'Connor saw a glimmer. "I've worked on the electronics of just about all of them, Mr. Jacobson."

"Come with me." Jacobson started back toward the sanctum sanctorum.

Elation burst through O'Connor's veins. He left his bench.

"Wait a minute!" the air force colonel bawled. "Is this man cleared?"

"He works here, doesn't he?" Jacobson shot back. "Everybody is cleared."

"I mean the special clearance procedure for"—the colonel pointed—"in there."

"No," Jacobson replied testily. "But do you want to try to complete this test sequence today or not? We've brought half the staff in for it, and unless that backup computer signals it's ready, we'll have automatic shutoffs until hell freezes over."

The colonel paced back and forth, fuming. Then he stopped. "All right. I'll accept the responsibility." He jerked a thumb in O'Connor's direction. "Go with him. Do what he tells you."

Fighting to hide his feelings, O'Connor walked into the secret lab. The moment he entered, his amazement overcame him. Power cables as thick as a man's arm snaked across the immaculate tile floor, centering on a bank of electrical and electronic equipment mostly hidden by plain aluminum rack paneling. Along one wall, power lights on a bevy of large and small computers, from lowly PCs to powerful gigabyte processors, glowed at the ready. On tall racks near the back wall of the chill, windowless room, the central transmitting equipment—tiers of chassis packed with circuit boards and heat sinks—stood idle, status meters in the green.

Most of this O'Connor could identify in an instant, thanks to his months of the most rigorous specialized training in the institute near Moscow. He was also able to identify at once the piece of equipment on the racks which was *not* familiar to him: the central transmitter module, heart of the system, the part on which U.S. research had leapfrogged ahead of the Soviet Union.

More amazing to O'Connor than anything, however, was the fact that only two other men in the room, aside from himself and Dr. Jacobson, were civilians. O'Connor recognized both of them by job if not by name. One was a specialist in radio frequency beam theory, the other a simple technician who knew little more than how to plug in cords and operate power switches.

O'Connor understood at once. In their arrogant sureness of their own technical competence, they had failed to bring in a single nuts-and-bolts *worker* for the tests. In their paranoid worry about secrecy, they had not even considered the possibility that a simple device like a personal computer might fail.

The men in the room might hold the highest college degrees and have impeccable research credentials. But no one here had much practical knowledge beyond how to change a lightbulb. They had more schematic diagrams and work manuals than O'Connor had ever seen in one place, all spread out on a center worktable. But they didn't have a clue on something this basic.

"Here's the problem, O'Connor," Jacobson said, leading O'Connor to the wall of computers. "This backup machine has gone down. Do you think you can fix it?"

"Let me take a look," O'Connor said with more confidence than he felt.

Everyone stood around in vast and gloomy silence as he pulled a yellow-handled screwdriver out of his small tool kit and removed the cover of the recalcitrant PC. The moment he got the lid free, he began to feel better. He saw instantly that the fuse block on the rear of the power supply compartment at the back of the machine had overheated and broken loose. It was a common failing of some early IBM models in their latest series.

"I can fix it," he announced. "I need some wire and a soldering pencil."

Removing the burned-out parts required only a few minutes. Then, announcing he needed a part, O'Connor left the room and hurried down metal corridors to Supply for a new fuse holder.

While in Supply, he went to a storage cabinet where stacks of old, unclassified equipment diagrams and operating manuals were held pending routine document disposal. Pulling three sheets out of an old manual for the emergency shutdown boards in an emergency-power generation unit, he took them along with the fuse holder, in its small gray cardboard carton, back to the control center.

Everyone was standing around, with plastic coffee cups in hand. Somebody had made fresh coffee. O'Connor saw a couple of men empty their cups and toss them into a tall trashcan beside the work table where all the manuals and schematics were scattered in apparent confusion.

It took less than thirty minutes to get the PC repaired and operating again. O'Connor buttoned it up and told them to turn it on. It whirred to life and obeyed the checkout commands.

"O'Connor," Dr. Jacobson said with a grim smile, "if I can swing it, there will be a hundred-dollar bonus in this for you."

O'Connor chuckled like the rube he was supposed to be, then hauled the discarded fuse holder carton, his little toolkit and sheaf of useless diagrams to the center of the room—the table with the precious plans. He put his toolkit on the table atop some of the plans, sandwiching his supply room plans underneath the kit and on top of a wad of the schematics he wanted so badly. He wadded up the fuse holder box and pitched it into the trashcan. "Do you suppose I could have a cup of that coffee?"

A grinning air force major poured it for him. Everyone else had turned to his assigned duties to power up the experiment again. In their anxiety to see if they were going to get it to work this time, they paid no attention to O'Connor.

The result, when he walked out of the control center three minutes later, was that he did not just have a cup of coffee and his tools. When he picked up his diagrams under the toolkit, he also managed to get three or four pages of diagrams for what he hoped was the central transmitter unit.

Once out of the control center, alone again, he moved fast.

Amazingly, no one noticed the absence of plan pages for quite some time. O'Connor was shocked by how long it took.

"O'Connor! Wait right there!"

The shout came almost three hours later as O'Connor had finished his shift and was getting into his Chevrolet in the employee parking lot. He turned and saw an air force captain and two MPs hurrying across the pavement in his direction.

"I'm sorry, sir," the captain snapped. "We'll have to ask you to come back inside with us."

"Gosh! What's going on? Another breakdown?"

"Please come along, sir."

O'Connor went in, flanked by the MPs. Inside it was grim. He was taken to his work station and the questions started.

—Had O'Connor possibly picked up some extra papers by mistake?

—Gosh! He would look.

—No, here were the schematics he had carried in with him, along with his toolkit. Nothing else here. Take a look for yourself.

The toolkit was examined and so were the diagrams. Then his locker was opened and searched, "just in case you got them in there by mistake, don't you see." Then, when nothing showed up at that point, there was a hasty whispered consultation and Dr. Jacobson apologetically explained to O'Connor that he would have to be searched. "Just a formality, of course. To clear you, you understand."

The personal search in the men's locker room turned up nothing, of course, after which O'Connor waited again, acting worried and upset, while more meetings took place.

He could imagine some of the content: *"He doesn't have them. Something else must have happened to them. We can't hold him indefinitely without a shred of evidence. As long as we're absolutely sure he isn't carrying them out of the lab, we have to let him go."*

Finally it was Dr. Jacobson who came back again. "I'm terribly sorry, O'Connor. There's been a little confusion we had to clear up. Hope it hasn't been too inconvenient. Of course you're now free to go."

O'Connor drove out. He knew he might be followed. He went directly to his little apartment on the edge of town, and stayed there. Notifying Sylvester would have to wait indefinitely. He must do nothing out of the ordinary now, in case their surveillance was heavy.

He had not gotten all the plans. But the briefest glance had suggested that he might well have gotten enough to suggest the entire diagramatic flow to an expert electronics designer. Success of the entire mission was now a distinct possibility.

He could bide his time for a while, and think about when and how he would actually retrieve the plan pages from the spot where he had stuffed them behind the bulletin board in the employee lounge—then get them out of the complex.

fourteen

The body had been wrapped in the kind of thick plastic sheeting they use in construction projects, then put in a shallow grave in the fresh, raw earth that formed a berm beside the new No. 15 green. The rainstorm Friday morning evidently had caused part of the berm to collapse, leaving the body close enough to the surface for some animal to dig part of it out. The plastic wrapping was heavily smeared with mud. One booted foot and a chalk-colored bare hand stuck out from the places where the animal had worried the plastic, then fled before making an even worse mess.

The plastic-wrapped corpse was only half exposed. I was glad for that. It was ghastly enough as it was. The protruding hand had been gnawed a bit, but still had a thick nugget-type ring on the third finger. The hand was curled the way a man will close his fingers to cup a match for a light, or shield a cigarette from the wind. Despite the hand's awful color, I almost expected to see the fingers move, produce the cigarette, dig at the enclosing plastic to get free.

The boots were hobnail worker's boots, the pants faded Levi's. Nothing moved. A distinct, sickening-sweet odor of decay clung to the wet ruined earth near the creek, now back in its banks. The cool evening dark sank in around us and we stood there: Ted, Karyn, me.

"It must have been right near the surface after the flooding," Karyn said hoarsely. "Then it got dug out just last night—or even today."

"You wouldn't see it from the fairway or the old green over there," I agreed. "Ted, it wasn't exposed when you made your inspection the other day, right?"

He started to say something but Karyn cut in: "Who is it?"

Ted stared gauntly at the plastic-wrapped corpse. His ashen face looked like he might be very close to being sick. "It's Clarke Higgins. The missing construction foreman."

"How can you know?" I asked.

"I know the ring. If you lean close, you can kind of see through the plastic—see his face pressed up against it."

"Ugh," Karyn shuddered. "I don't want to!"

Through the woods from the direction of the lodge came the sound of sirens. We looked up and saw two police cars coming hell-bent down an adjacent fairway, tires throwing precious sod, gumball-machine toplights flashing.

It had been Max, our golf pro, who located us in the lodge a few minutes earlier. He was shaky. He reported that a guest couple named Riffe had just driven their cart back to the clubhouse, the wife hysterical and the husband not far from it.

"They knocked a ball way the hell over the green toward the creek, out there in the construction area, and then went looking for it. They swear they found a dead body half-buried in some of the new green earthwork."

"Let's go, Ted," I said at once.

His eyes dilated like he was dazed. "Where?"

"To go see what they found."

"Maybe we should . . . think it over."

"Think *what* over?" I demanded. "Come on, goddamn it. Find Sally. Have her call the police. Max, keep the Riffes down at the pro shop until we get some of this sorted out. Tell them police orders. Ted?" He still stood like a statue. "Come *on*, Ted!"

He finally moved. We started out the door.

"I'm coming too," Karyn said, running to keep up.

"It's not pretty," Ted grated.

"I didn't think it would be."

We piled three in the lodge cart and headed out. It didn't take us long to find the spot. We could follow the Riffe couple's deep cart tracks through the soaked, newly planted grass the last thirty or forty yards, around the side of the high berm that still looked good from the fairway side. Now, as short a time as we had been here, the police were already joining us.

"I wish they wouldn't use their lights and sirens," Ted said. "We really need to keep this quiet."

"Keep it quiet?" Karyn echoed, puzzled.

"Something like this can kill a business."

"Ted, my God!"

We stood near the grisly discovery and watched the two cruisers drive down and through the narrow creek, then up the 15 fairway, streaming mud and water, to rock to a halt near our golf cart, parked fifty yards away to avoid the risk of bogging down. The flashers went out and the sirens ran down, and Lassiter lumbered out of one car and a plump little man wearing bib overalls and a sweatshirt hopped out of the other. He was bald, with a little mustache, and he had a large gold badge stuck on his bib. I noticed that Lassiter let him lead the way, and he was out of breath by the time he reached us.

He looked down at our discovery.

"Jesus God."

Lassiter, all scowls, looked the ground over carefully between himself and the wrapped figure, then moved with surprising gentleness across the bare earth, his boots making only light impressions in the wet surface. He bent and very gingerly touched the fingers of his right hand to the plastic, pressing it more firmly against the face beneath. He bent closer, squinting. Then he stood up with a violent exhalation.

"It's him all right," he said. "Higgins."

The little man looked worriedly at each of us. "Mr. Treacher, how did this happen? Who found this body? How did you get informed?" He frowned at Karyn and me again. "I'm Chief Manley Hamm. Chief of police, Elk City. Who are you people and what are you doing here?"

Ted, forming his words with the dead precision of a robot, introduced us.

"Okay, and this is Officer Lassiter. Now. Ted, what happened here?"

Ted told him in a few words what had happened—the Riffes, our notification by Max, how we had come down and found this.

"Where are these witnesses now?"

"We asked them to wait in the pro shop."

"Okay." Hamm frowned fiercely as he made decisions. Then he turned to Lassiter. "Jack, get on the radio. We'll need an ambulance here. Call and make sure the county is sending somebody. Tell them we need the coroner, too. Call the paper, have them locate that asshole photographer of theirs. I want him out here pronto, meaning five minutes ago. Tell the county to notify the district attorney we got a murder, a buried murdered body. Sheriff's got a report on Higgins being missing, so tell them that's who it is."

Lassiter lumbered off toward his patrol car. Hamm blew his nose and walked around the periphery of the scene, moving daintily on tiptoe in brightly polished little black shoes. He pulled a flashlight out of his back pocket and started shining it around on the ground even though it didn't seem quite dark enough to require that. Having nothing else we could do, we waited.

It was getting chilly. Karyn stood hugging her bare arms around herself. I kept my hands in my pocket and wished for a jacket. Ted, his graying hair on end, stood like a scarecrow, his eyes bleak as a whore's smile. He was trembling noticeably from head to foot.

Hamm finished poking all around the area. He pocketed the flashlight and dug out a notebook and started jotting things down, pausing every few words to lick at the stub of pencil. I thought he was a real rube until he started speaking some of his notes as he wrote them.

"Higgins, all right . . . No obvious signs of cause of death . . . maybe wounds on other side of body from what can observe before moving body. Have to wait for the medical examination. Dead a few days, judging by the state of decomposition. Real unpleasant, isn't it? . . . Let's see . . . footprints around on this other side. Did your couple at the pro shop drive up on this in their cart?"

Ted seemed in a trance, so I answered. "It looks like they parked over where we did. They would do better walking through here; they were looking for a ball."

"Hmm. But *somebody* drove a cart in here. Tracks all over on this other side. Almost got stuck, looks like. Deer tracks on top of the cart wheel marks. So not last night . . . earlier . . . but gotta be since

Thursday night–Friday morning rain. Friday night or Saturday night, then. Probably Friday . . . ground's begun to dry enough that the tires wouldn't have sunk in this deep Saturday . . ."

Hamm walked around some more with his curious, tiptoe stride, looking at the ground. "Don't think the person in this other cart buried the body here. More likely he found it, though, washed out by the creek. Say, *this* is interesting. See here? Shovel marks! Why, it looks like this body was washed out and then somebody tried to cover it back up again, and then a critter spoiled the fun by digging it up another time. Interesting! Real interesting!"

Ted still stood transfixed, his face like death.

"Chief," I said, "you're about two light-years ahead of me."

Hamm nodded, continuing to mince around carefully in his little patent-leather shoes. "Shouldn't be too hard to match tires from these impressions, figure out which cart was used. See some footprints, too, a couple, over on this side. Look like athletic shoes. He sunk in pretty deep in the goo, doing his shoveling to re-hide the evidence. With luck, might even get a match on the shoes."

That was when it hit me like lightning: *Ted. Coming back to the lodge from course inspection. Muddy shoes, mud-clogged cart.*

And acting like a zombie.

I swung around to stare at him.

His face looked like a skull.

"Next thing, I figure," Hamm was going on in his misleadingly quiet, bemused way, "is start a search to see if we can find that muddy cart or them muddy shoes, or maybe the shovel. Might help a lot. Shouldn't be too hard. Ought to inspect all your carts at the lodge right away, eh, Mr. Treacher? And talk to the couple that found this first, of course."

Ted stared, eyes bulging. We could hear Lassiter coming back behind us, walking heavily in the muck.

"Sound right to you, Mr. Treacher?" Hamm repeated mildly.

Whatever Hamm expected or was fishing for—and maybe he was just thinking out loud and expecting *nothing*—there could be no doubt he was as shocked as Karyn or I by what he got—what happened next.

"That won't be necessary, Chief," Ted told him in a voice absolutely lacking intonation.

Hamm stopped pacing around and cocked his head to study Ted. "What say? How come?"

"It was me," Ted said. "I found the body. I tried to cover it up again."

Karyn made a little moaning sound. I didn't believe it.

Hamm walked toward Ted, studying him intently with those deceptive, dumb-and-lazy-looking eyes. "Well is that right, now?"

"I panicked," Ted said. "I had important people coming—an investor. I couldn't allow a scandal on the very day they were arriving."

"So you killed him? Put him in here?"

"No! I just found him and buried him again. I didn't kill him! My God, what kind of a person do you think I am?"

No one said anything right away. I felt like someone had hit me in the stomach with a sledgehammer. Karyn put a hand to her face and staggered. I grabbed her, preventing a fall. Ted just stood there, looking dazed. For a few moments the only sound was Lassiter's clomping footsteps in the mud and his heavy breathing.

Hamm looked at Ted with a slack, thoughtful expression. "Well, now," he said. "Well, now, my goodness, Mr. Treacher."

"I came down to inspect the course for damage," Ted said.

"Ted," I said, "shut up. Don't say another word."

He acted like he hadn't heard me. "The rain had collapsed the berm—partly uncovered him. I knew right away it was Higgins."

"And why," Hamm asked in the same quiet, deadly voice, "didn't you call my office right then?"

"I told you. We had this important visitor. I . . . thought about calling you. But then we would have had a big mess—police cars, ambulances, all the guests gossiping. I— Well, my decision was to delay all that. I was going to call you today."

"Today," Hamm repeated.

"Ted," I repeated, "shut the hell *up*!"

Hamm said, "I think it's kind of late for that, Mr. Smith."

Ted stared at me. "How much chance do you think we would have had of getting Ardis Allen interested in investing here if we had a *body* on the golf course? If the guests had all been hysterical?" He pointed at the plastic-sheathed corpse. "Look at him! He had been dead for days already! Was another day or two going to matter?"

Lassiter hove up beside us. "What's this all about?"

"Well," Hamm sighed. "It seems like Mr. Treacher, here, just admitted finding this body the other day, and reburying it."

Lassiter's eyes bulged. "Is this some kind of joke?"

"No, Jack, it's no joke, I'm sorry to say."

Ted kept staring at me and Karyn. "You don't understand how it was. I had to make a snap decision. I panicked. Maybe I did wrong. But by the time I thought of *that*, I had already done it."

"Oh, Ted," Karyn said. "Were you that desperate?"

He just looked at her, his havoc-ridden eyes begging for understanding—and showing the despair that comes when you know what you've done is beyond understanding.

In that instant, God help me, I didn't understand what his thoughts had been, but I understood the kind of crazy desperation that could make a man do something no one in his right mind would do. I had been that way for weeks at a time in Vietnam, and I had been that way for longer after Danisa died. After a great enough shock—under sufficient pressure—the mind simply does not work right. The personality disintegrates. Only time—and luck—ever help someone get back together. Ted, under pressure I could only dimly imagine, had simply *acted*. That his actions had been crazy—unexplainable in normal terms—was beside the point. He had found the body and he had panicked, just as he said, and nothing about his reactions in the next few minutes had been remotely connected to rationality. So even as I despaired at his stupidity, I almost understood. I had been there.

In the distance came the sound of more sirens. It stirred everybody out of a moment of dumb-show inaction.

"Mr. Treacher," Hamm said, "I guess you know what happens next. You are under arrest. We'll be taking you into town to jail pending orders from the district attorney over at Tripptown. I guess we're going to have a lot more questions we have to ask you."

"On what charge?" Ted demanded blankly.

"On what charge?" Hamm took a half-step backward in surprise. "On what *charge*? Well, sir. For a start, I guess we can say obstruction of justice. I guess we can say accessory to murder after the fact. I guess we can say suspicion of murder."

"I didn't kill him! I just found the body! I told you that."

Hamm shook his head. "Well, now. I guess you should have thought, before you did this, how it would look. You *can* see how it sort of looks, can't you? I mean, here is the body, and here you are, and you're the only one so far we got linked to it in any way."

Ted's face went blank. Karyn, still in the curve of my supporting arm, began to shake and then cry without sound. Lassiter, with maybe more gusto than absolutely necessary, went up to Ted and grabbed his arms and put them behind his back. On went handcuffs. Lassiter started roughly patting him down.

"You just take him on back to town, Jack," Hamm said. "Then you stay there with him until I get back. I'll stick around here until they get their pictures and all, and load the body, and then I figure we'll be talking to these folks that found the body a while ago. Might be the sheriff will want me to do something else. But I'll be back to the office as soon as possible."

"Let's go," Lassiter told Ted, and shoved him in the direction of the car. He took out his .357. The way he did it gave me another chill. If Ted so much as stumbled on the way to the car, I thought, Lassiter would like nothing better than to shoot him.

That didn't happen. We stood silent and watched him march Ted to the cruiser, put him inside, and reattach the handcuffs to a security bar in the back seat.

More flashing lights appeared in the distance through the trees.

"That will be the ambulance, I reckon," Hamm said. "And the sheriff, too, unless I miss my guess. The sheriff is going to be pleased. He's up for reelection before long."

Karyn, huddled in my arms, looked up at me with tear-streaked incredulity. "Brad, how could he *be* so dumb?"

I didn't say anything. The shock was still too great.

Lassiter started his car engine and pulled away, lights flashing again.

Hamm exchanged looks with me. "Life," he said, "is sure strange."

fifteen

By nine o'clock the pictures of the scene had been taken, yellow plastic police tape had been strung around to tell people to stay away, the body had been removed by the funeral home to be held for autopsy, our guests who found the thing had been interviewed, I had closed the pro shop, and everybody around the lodge was talking about the excitement. Ted Treacher's arrest was—so far—still secret.

The excitement brought Fred Skurlock out of the woodwork—or, I should say, the woods.

"God damn it, Smith, *everything* is screwing up this investigation! Maybe it's time you just dumped the cover thing entirely and moved into town. That way—"

"Forget it, Fred. This guy is my friend."

"You won't cooperate?"

"Not if it means dumping Ted when he's in *this* kind of a mess."

Skurlock went off again, muttering about a report to Washington.

In the chill dark, Karyn returned from town, where she had gone to the jail with Ted's local attorney, a man named Jennings. Jennings came back with her. We met—Karyn, Jennings, Sally Wallis, and myself—in Ted's private office.

Jennings was a tall, bone-thin man of about sixty with a few gray hairs remaining on top of his head. He wore a faded gray suit of some kind of synthetic that had once been shiny. Now it was tired and wrinkled. He chain-smoked and had false teeth that clicked when he spoke.

"Ted's in a cell," Karyn reported. "They wouldn't let me see him, but Mr. Jennings was in with him for a few minutes."

"Are they questioning him?" I asked.

"They have asked a few questions, and plan to continue tomorrow when a representative from the district attorney's office comes to town," Jennings said, lighting one Marlboro off another. "I advised him to say nothing at all, at least until he has a lawyer."

"I thought you were his lawyer."

"You must understand that this is not my line of work. My association with Ted Treacher has been routine work: checking out the deed, approving title, examining loan papers—that sort of thing. Criminal law is not my bag." *Click*.

He had the sickly smell of defeat about him. I didn't do a very good job of concealing my irritation. "Did you find out what their plans are for him? Or is asking questions too stressful for you?"

Jennings flushed, but did not rise to the bait. Maybe he hadn't risen in years. "The sheriff was there. His jail in Tripptown is overcrowded. The plan is to keep Mr. Treacher in Elk City overnight, then transport him to the courthouse in Tripptown in the morning for arraignment."

"On what charges?"

"I did not talk to the district attorney. Therefore I did not determine that." *Click*.

I turned to Sally. "In the morning, early, you'd better get over to Tripptown and find a criminal lawyer. A good one."

"He'll want a retainer fee," Sally said.

"Right. Take it out of the lodge operating account."

"Our account balances are non-existent."

"*All* of them?"

"Yes."

"I've got some money," Karyn said.

"So do I," I said. I removed my billfold and dug out ten hundreds, which came close to wiping me out of cash money, and handed them to Sally. "If he wants to know who's hiring him, say I am. If he acts skittish, tell him there's a lot more where that came from. I don't want some ambulance-chaser, Sally. If Tripptown is the county seat, there ought to be a good criminal lawyer around. I want the best."

She put the money in her purse. "I'll find someone."

"If I may say so," Jennings said, getting to his feet, "Mr. Treacher did not make it easy on himself by concealing the corpus delicti."

"Thank you, counselor," I said. "And thanks for going in to see him."

For the first time, the man showed a flicker of fire in his eyes. "My wife died two years ago. My own health is not good. I did not come to the mountains to play Perry Mason."

Karyn was nicer than I was. "We understand, Mr. Jennings."

He gave me a resentful look and walked out.

I repeated to Sally, "The *best* lawyer, right?"

"I understand, Brad," she said sharply, as if offended by my insistence.

I asked, "Are *all* the accounts really depleted?"

Sighing, she went into her adjoining office for a moment and came back with a large, gray-covered ledger book. She put it on Ted's desk and opened it with a thump. "Mack Redman is our part-time bookkeeper, but on a routine, day-to-day level, I maintain the books. I'd like to be on a computer but we can't afford one. As you can see, I track our checking accounts, accounts payable, and accounts receivable. Please. Help yourself if you doubt my word."

I sat down and started through the pages. Karyn sat beside me, frowning at the columns of figures. It was a very simple and straightforward bookkeeping system. Even I could understand it.

Sally Wallis silently left the office.

Two hours later, I had a fresh headache and the feeling I had just looked into a tomb.

We were broke.

"My God," Karyn moaned. "And I was thinking I'd solved the worst problem when I got most of the players lined up for the tournament."

Despite my gloom I looked up sharply. "You found more players?"

"I was saving it for a nice surprise," she said ruefully, and slid a sheet of paper across the surface at me.

I scanned it. "Connors? You got Jimmy out of semi-retirement? Mayotte? How the hell did you get Tim Mayotte?"

Her grin peeped through. "My sheer wonderful personality."

"Karyn, this is great. Some of this paperwork we've done with to-be-announced slots—now we've got some real headliners to go with Lendl."

She nodded. "I've already done a little pre-publicity, sorta on my own."

"You're fantastic."

She beamed, and then began to frown again as her eyes returned to some of the financial papers strewn all over the place. "I don't see how it's going to be enough. How could someone as smart as Ted get himself into this big a mess?"

"He wanted this place badly," I told her. "Too badly. Sometimes 'smart' doesn't apply when a person wants something too much. From all I can tell, he just kept getting in deeper and deeper, like a gambler on a run of bad luck. 'I'll just borrow a little bit more and my luck will start to change and I'll get it all back,' he tells himself."

"Does that ever work?"

"No."

"Then why—"

"Karyn, how should I know? I guess he just kept deluding himself. At some point he *couldn't* turn back because he was already in too deep."

Karyn paced back and forth in the small office. "Damn it! He saved so much of his tournament winnings. He had it made! Now he's put it all down this rathole. How could he delude himself *this* long?"

I didn't answer her. I had done crazy things myself. Maybe in retrospect some of my "clever" investments in Texas oil and gas would look as stupid and self-deluding as Ted Treacher's pouring of more and more money into the pit. I had almost lost everything when the bottom fell out of the oil business. God knows I lost enough. I can still remember the investments people who told me to transfer just a little more money into the oil exploration accounts, give this little dip in the business time to bottom out. I almost did it, sending in more money to try to save what was already vanishing. I ignored their advice at the last minute and saved a lot. But I can still remember the feeling of panic, the urge to try *anything* they recommended to recoup earlier losses. If I had followed the advice of those geniuses, I would be in worse shape now than Ted was.

And his condition was pretty bad.

As nearly as I could estimate, Bitterroot Valley owed contractors, repairmen, maintenance workers, and the like about $60,000. There was the little matter of a balloon payment on the mortgage and a single-pay note, both due late in the year. The page showing payments due for food, supplies, laundry, telephone, electric power, and similar regular costs was a sea of red ink. There was enough in one account to meet employee salaries once more, at the end of the month. Many of the other bills were already past due, and I couldn't find any hint of a way to pay any of them.

"It looks," I said, "like we would need over a hundred thousand just to get the yapping creditors off our backs temporarily, and win enough confidence to run up some new bills."

"I just don't get it," Karyn said.

"Look at this place," I told her. "Look at the valley and the mountains. Hell, it's beautiful. Couldn't *you* start believing a dream here?"

"But it's so off the beaten track—"

"Is that necessarily bad? You can argue that it isn't likely to get much traffic because the area is undeveloped. But you can just as easily argue that it's a potential gold mine because there's virtually no competition yet, and you're in on the ground floor."

She threw up her hands. "Well, none of this matters anyhow. Not right now, with him in jail. What are we going to do, Brad?"

"About Ted? About the bills? About the tournament date we've got breathing down our necks? About the body? About Lassiter? About the local opposition? About the customers who will rush out of here when word gets out that the owner is in the hoosegow?"

"You don't have to get mad at *me*."

"Sorry," I said. "I'm a little mad at the world."

"I want to go to town and see Ted."

"Right. Let me get a couple of things straight with Sally first. Then I'll go with you."

"I'll be in the lobby. Don't be long."

I found Sally Wallis in the kitchen area, evidently having an argument with the cooks. Asked her to join me back in the office as soon as she could. She complied in about five minutes.

"What was that all about in the kitchen?" I asked.

"Peter is a prima donna," she said. Her face was still pink with anger. "It seems some food he ordered was not delivered because the earlier bills haven't been paid. He threatened to quit. I convinced him to bear with us a while longer yet."

"Sally, does Ted fully realize how bad this all is?"

"Of course." She stiffened, offended again. "I keep him fully apprised. I *beg* him to go over the accounts with me."

"Then how the hell does he think this place can even keep its doors open past the end of this month, much less put on a small tennis tournament?"

"I've warned him and warned him. The deeper we get, the more he deludes himself."

"Do you have any bright ideas?"

"No."

I stared at the desk and the damning ledger book.

"How are we going to pay for those tournament ads I asked you to place in all the newspapers?"

"I don't know. That's why I haven't sent them in yet."

I rubbed my aching head.

She said, "No one would blame you, Brad."

"For what?"

"If you just got out."

"I don't have any money invested."

"But your name—and your reputation—are on the line with the tournament. No one could blame you if you called everyone and told them you were just getting out while the getting is still good."

This was interesting. "Is that what you're going to do, Sally?"

She stiffened. "Of course not. I'm loyal."

"So loyal that you suggest I abandon ship."

"It's a *sinking* ship, Brad, and we both know it."

I studied her. Facing me, with one fist on a shapely hip, she gave the impression of great strength underlying that sleek, sensuous beauty. Not for the first time, I was struck deeply by an erotic undertone. There are beautiful women who remain somehow almost abstract: interesting but nothing more. There are others with a physical quality that leaps out at you.

She sensed—as such women always do—my reaction to her. She came across the little office and moved discreetly into my space, putting fingertips lightly on my upper arm. "I can cover for you, Brad. If you decide to go, I mean."

"Why would you do that?" I asked.

She held my eyes with hers. "I think you know I like you, Brad."

"I think *you* know that Ted is in love with you."

She sighed. "He thinks he is, yes. That's a problem. He's a dear. But I don't love him. I think I've made that clear. I'll help him all I can. But that's all. And there's no reason for anyone else to go down with the ship."

"Let's just keep things running for the next day or two," I suggested, "while we try to sort some of this out."

She removed her hand. She looked cool. "As you wish."

"Have we made any progress on bleachers?"

She flared. "How can you talk about *bleachers* at a time like this?"

"Pardon me, Sally. Whatever the hell else is going on, we've still got those pros coming in, thinking they're playing in a tournament. We've also got reservations, and Ted also advertised the tournament in his stock prospectus. We can't just let everything sink into the ground. As hellacious as things look, we've got to try to keep the resort going . . . get the tournament on."

She stared thoughtfully up at me for a moment, then relented a little. "All right. I see. It's maddening . . . but I guess you're right."

"So," I insisted. "Bleachers?"

"I haven't located any yet."

"Concessions?"

"I'm having trouble finding people who don't know about our current bad credit standing."

She said it so calmly, and with such beaten acceptance, that I almost yelled, or shook her. Instead I started for the door. "We'll talk again in the morning."

Karyn was pacing back and forth in the lobby. "Damn, it's about time!"

"Ted isn't going anywhere."

"I'll drive."

I followed her out to her car. She drove hard and well. I leaned back in the contour seat and watched the headlights spray over the narrow valley road on the way to town, and wondered how much of the resort's financial problem might have been eased if someone more resourceful than Sally Wallis had been handling the business end of things. Even in a quick run-through I had seen duplicate charges in the books, entered in different accounts, and placement of new funds in bank accounts where they couldn't draw even the slightest interest.

It seemed clear to me now that her management had been routine at best. Ted had trusted her and let her go, and she had not always made wise decisions. Of course an Einstein could not have put the resort in the black at this time. But Sally's nonchalant management style had not helped. It was almost as if she *wanted* him to fail.

One day, I thought, Ted would realize this. He would also have to face the fact that the lady did not love him, and never would. Women like Sally Wallis define love as a pleasant fluttering in the glands, something that happens, sweeping one off her feet. The idea that love might require an effort is quite beyond them.

When Ted finally saw her for what she was, it was going to hurt. Badly. Of course that didn't seem very significant at the moment. But betrayal can linger after other kinds of pain have been forgotten.

I know. Whenever I think of Elizabeth, my first wife, it is still with anger. I wish it were not so. It's been a long time now, more than twenty years, since I came back from Vietnam with a mortar fragment souvenir or two, and she divorced me. She deluded me and deprecated me, and I tried to ignore it, so that now, looking back, I hate not only her but myself, for my stupidity. Her contempt for me was boundless, I think, but at the time I tried to rationalize, and so made matters much worse by stringing them out. The fact that I was only 20 and a little crazy from Vietnam does not excuse me. And so I remember her with hate for what she did to me, and also for what I—for a while—in my denial of reality, became.

Ted, I thought, had also deluded himself. About Sally. About money. About everything. I would be justified in running off and leaving him right now. But there was that problem: how he had saved my and Danisa's lives in Belgrade; how he was a friend.

We drove into Elk City, past the feed barn, the abandoned railroad station, the all-dark Sonic Drive-In, the city building with its hail-battered F–80 on a brick pedestal. Everything was dark and shut down. I realized it was the middle of the night.

We found the jail behind the city building, a squat sandstone block with a radio tower sticking out the top and a police car parked in the drab illumination of the side-lot security light. Karyn parked and marched ahead of me to the door.

Inside, behind a brown plastic counter, a portable black and white TV set made noise on one of three aged metal desks. There were filing cabinets and chairs and a coffee maker and table with some old Motorola radio equipment on it, calendars and maps on the wall, junk. A movement at a desk behind the counter brought my attention to the only person around, a brush-bearded hulk wearing a flannel shirt and jeans. The movement that had caught my eye was when he removed his boots from the top of the desk and sat up straighter in the battered wood swivel chair.

He looked a little like Jack Lassiter, but younger. His eyes and mouth tightened in seeming recognition when he stared directly at me for an instant. In my own sharp, cool wash of memory, his response hardly surprised me.

He recovered. "Can I he'p you folks?" he asked, acting sleepy.

"We want to see a prisoner," Karyn snapped. "I was here earlier. Now I'm back and I want to see him. Ted Treacher."

The jailer blinked. "Not here."

"What do you mean, he's not here? Of course he's here!"

"No 'um."

"Where is he?"

"They taken him to Missoula an hour ago."

I asked, "What the hell for, in the middle of the night?"

"He had an accident. They taken him to the hospital."

sixteen

We barreled north on highway 93, headed for Missoula, headlights flashing on curving pavement, an occasional house or gas station dark off the edge of the road, patches of meadow, occasional stands of pine and fir, the humpy bulk of mountains black against a vast, cold, starry sky.

Karyn pounded the flat of her palm against the steering wheel. "Damn it, damn it, damn it! What did they do? What have they done to him? Why wouldn't that man back there tell us anything? Why won't this goddamned car *go* any faster?"

"I think a hundred and ten is fast enough on the straights, Karyn."

She shot me a bitter look. "Do you think you could do any better?"

"Absolutely not. You're doing great."

She groaned. "Sorry. Why pick on you? I'm *scared*."

"So am I. It won't be long now. We'll find out what's going on."

"But why wouldn't that man at the jail tell us anything?"

"Cops are like that. I imagine he was told to keep his mouth shut."

"Jewel. What a misnomer."

"What?"

"That was his name, according to the name tag," Karyn told me. "J–E–double U–E–L–L. Jewell. Jewell Lassiter. Didn't you notice his name tag?"

A new freshet of understanding trickled through me. "No."

She pounded the steering wheel again. "How much *farther*?"

"Not far now. Through this pass up ahead and I think we'll see the lights."

She lapsed into silence. I absorbed the new data.

Jewell Lassiter. Town cop Jack Lassiter's brother? Cousin? A relative, precise kind immaterial. He had not been in uniform. Probably not a payroll cop. Probably an occasional helper-outer.

It tied some things together.

In the moment when Jewell Lassiter had moved his feet off the desk, I had gotten a good look at his footgear, and it had sent sharp, chill daggers of recognition through me. No cowboy boots like Cop Jack for brother (cousin?) Jewell. For him, black knee-high boots, crosslaced all the way up, with small metal plates on the heels to keep them from wearing down too fast.

I knew those boots. I had gotten intimately acquainted with them when they hammered my body.

A while later we roared out of the pass and into Missoula. At an all-night gas station beside a salvage yard I asked directions to the hospital. The attendant asked which one. I spent fifteen minutes in the open-air telephone stand at curbside while Karyn paced around the car like a tigress. I finally got the right patient information desk at the right hospital.

"This way," I told Karyn, hopping back into the car with her. "About a mile, a big intersection, turn left. The lady said there are signs after that."

We got mildly turned around once in trying to negotiate one of the Mickey Mouse mazes that the fine city of Missoula calls a major intersection, and Karyn taught me a couple of new cussword combinations. It was almost four A.M. when we screeched to a halt in the medical complex emergency area.

We went inside, into eye-stinging, sterile brightness. A tired nurse stared at us over clipboarded forms at the counter. Mr.

Treacher? Yes. He had been admitted. Please check with Admitting, down this corridor.

At Admitting we found an elderly volunteer who seemed nice. She told us we wanted the second floor. We started to turn away.

"Did you know," the lady chirped, "that the patient is under police guard?"

"Sure," I said. "As a matter of fact, I'm FBI. This lady is Metro-pol."

Karyn hissed in the elevator, "Why in heavens name did you say that?"

"I was stupid," I told her. "I do stupid things like that when I'm upset."

"What did they *do* to him?" she repeated.

"We'll soon find out."

The elevator doors slid open on a waiting area facing a nursing station. There was no one in the waiting area. We walked to the nursing station. Lots of white, lots of glass, lots of telephone-monitor-chart-Formica-stainless-steel stuff. One of the nurses gave us a dirty look. God, I love nurses. They seem to divide into two chasm categories: some of the finest, most caring people in the world, and super-bitch.

This one didn't even condescend to speak. We had drawn the queen bitch herself.

"Pardon me," I said to her stiff, starched white back. "We're looking for Ted Treacher, admitted about—"

"No visitors," she snapped without turning.

"Room number," I snapped back.

She wheeled around in her chair, revealing an amazing length of legs that resembled pale sausages. "I said, no visitors, no admittance."

"And I said, please give me the goddamned room number, nurse."

She glared. They're not used to someone talking back. Meanwhile, Karyn had turned to a display card file on the counter. She nudged me. "It's two-twenty-four."

"Great." I glanced at the numeral signs on the wall intersection and took her by the elbow, propelling her away from the desk. We hurried to the next hall corner and turned right and saw the blue-uniformed city cop in the chair outside a closed room.

"Shit," Karyn murmured.

"To be expected," I said, sounding calmer than I felt. "Come on."

The cop looked up at us as we approached, and slowly got to his feet with that deceptive lazy look some of the very best ones have. He looked thirtyish, vigilant, and relatively intelligent.

I said, "Is this Mr. Treacher's room?"

"Yes, sir, it is." His name tag said MERKLE. "No admittance. Sorry."

"But I'm his brother," I said.

"Sir, sorry, but Lieutenant Green is inside with him right now."

"How can we get some information?"

"Sir, I suggest if you want to wait in the waiting room down there, I can tell the lieutenant—"

He got no further. The door behind him swung open and a rumpled, balding man in faded blue sweats and dirty Converse All Stars came out. I got a glimpse of a sterile-looking private room and the end of a bed beyond the door before it closed again.

The uniformed officer turned. "Lieutenant, this is the subject's brother and—"

The detective's sleepy eyes raked over us in swift, weary appraisal. "If you'll come this way with me. . . ?"

He led us down the hall to another deserted waiting room. Cardboard pictures of buffalo and elk looked down on brown plastic chairs and couches. The area smelled of stale cigarette smoke. The detective rummaged in his pockets and got out a pack of Marlboros and started adding to the stink. He studied us again. "I'm Abe Green. Missoula police. "You're. . . ?"

"Brad Smith," I told him. "And this is Karyn Wechsting."

Mild recognition scuttled behind the eyes, and he studied Karyn more closely. "I've seen you on TV."

"How is he?" Karyn demanded. "What happened to him?"

Green ignored that and turned back to me. "I thought Merkle said you were Treacher's brother."

"That's what I told him."

"You aren't his brother."

"Right. I lied."

"Why?"

"I wanted to get in."

"Lying to the police isn't going to get you very far, Smith."

"Thanks, Lieutenant, I'll remember that."

"What *is* your relationship to the subject?"

"Business associate. Old friend."

Karyn, with an edge in her tone, insisted, "How is he, and what happened to him?"

Green sat down. As he dragged on his cigarette, I noticed the slight tremor in his hands and the dirt under his fingernails. He had been hauled out of bed in the middle of the night. He needed a shower and a shave. He appeared to be the kind of man who seldom looked neat, but didn't usually look this grubby.

In a tone of infinite weariness, he said, "The subject was transported here in an ambulance from Elk City. Prisoner. Unspecified charges, none formally filed—"

"We know that," Karyn cut in impatiently. "What *happened*?"

"The report states he had an accident in his city jail cell in Elk City. Fell from his bunk or tripped and hit against the plumbing fixture in the cell. Brought here, emergency treatment, X-rays, surgical procedure—"

"Surgery!"

Green looked at her a bit like a scientist might look at a bug under his microscope. There was a tightly controlled anger in him just under the surface. I got the impression that he might be a very good cop, operating under the most trying circumstances.

He said slowly, "The subject suffered bruises, minor scalp lacerations, two cracked ribs, a broken arm and possible undetermined internal injuries. He—"

"Jesus Christ," I said.

The eyes flicked over my face. "As I was saying, he is now resting comfortably and remains under medical observation. He is under protective custody by my department pending medical re-examination in the morning—which is damned near here, I guess—and determination of charges to be filed in Tripptown on information to be filed by the Elk City PD."

"Oh, the bastards," Karyn said. Then she started to cry without sound, the tears rolling down her cheeks. "That dirty son of a bitching Lassiter—"

"Well, now," Green cut in quietly, "that kind of talk isn't going to help anybody, is it?"

"Did the Elk City cops come with the ambulance?" I asked.

"Officer Lassiter, I believe his name is, and Chief Hamm were here earlier. I believe the officer returned to Elk City. I think the chief might still be in the cafeteria downstairs, where he was conferring with my chief here."

"We want to see Treacher," I said.

"The prisoner is not to have visitors."

"We want to see him now," I repeated.

"I told you my orders, Mr. Smith."

"We're his best friends, Green, and the only question is whether we're going to see him right now, or in a few hours after we've had our attorney file about six lawsuits guaranteed to allege you're conspiring to cover up police brutality in Elk City."

Green stood, bristling. "We don't take kindly to threats."

"Then consider this friendly advice. You'll get clearance for us to have a few minutes with Ted now, or you'll find yourself in the middle of such a shitstorm of bad publicity that you might never have credibility around here again."

He studied me. "You mean it."

"Lieutenant, I am awfully, awfully mad right now."

He stabbed his cigarette into the ashstand. "Will you wait here, please?"

He was gone about ten minutes. When he came back, he had Hamm with him, along with another taller and bulkier man, introduced as the Missoula police chief.

"I've authorized you to visit the prisoner for no more than ten minutes," the Missoula chief told me. "That's what the physician in charge has recommended at this time. When the physician authorizes longer visits, I'll put both of you on the acceptable list, assuming the prisoner okays both of you. That ought to be tomorrow sometime unless there are unexpected complications. Any objection to that?"

Karyn said, "We both want to see him."

"One of you can see him now, one in the morning when the doctor says it's okay."

Karyn looked at me. "All right," she said finally. "I'll wait."

I turned back to the Missoula chief. "Thanks."

"No problem."

"One more question. Is Officer Lassiter from Elk City going to be authorized to see him?"

The chief's eyes narrowed. "Why do you ask?"

"Because if he's to be on your approved list, I need to know it so I can be at the courthouse when it opens in the morning to ask for a restraining order."

He was good. His slab face showed nothing. "Officer Lassiter is not on the list."

Hamm fumbled around with the stub of a cigar. He looked chalky. "Officer Lassiter has been suspended pending an investigation." He paused, looked at his shoes, then added, "Normal procedure in such cases."

"Right," I said.

"Look," Hamm said abruptly. "I can assure you, we're all embarrassed about this."

"Embarrassed?" I repeated. "*Embarrassed?*"

Karyn put her hand on my arm. "Take it easy, Brad."

"Embarrassed?" I repeated again. "My friend down the hall made a stupid mistake. You took him to your pissant jail for questioning—*no charges filed*. The next thing we know, he's 'fallen off his bunk' and had bones broken."

"Calm down, calm down," Hamm muttered.

"How high are the bunks in that jailhouse of yours, Hamm? Twenty feet? Did he happen to hit a cop's flashlight on the way down, or fall on a cop's blackjack that just happened to be lying on the floor where he hit? Did he just happen to bounce off three or four walls and maybe get slammed into a toilet bowl too? I can see how you might be 'embarrassed.' Do prisoners often have this kind of strange accident when they're in your jail for questioning? Does it always just happen to happen when you've left them alone in the building with Lassiter?"

Hamm nervously licked his lips. "I told you the action we've taken. I don't know what else can be said."

So disgusted I could hardly see straight, I turned to Green. "Can we go see Ted now?"

* * *

When we reached the door, Green started to enter with me.

"I want to talk to him alone," I told him.

Green calmly studied me a moment. Then he stepped back. "Ten minutes, max."

I went in. The door closed behind me.

It was still. Bright light over the bed shining up and across a white acoustical tile ceiling. No machines or gadgets, just a beige metal dresser and washbasin and closed closet and the bed, with Ted lying in it, eyes closed, bandages around his head, some rapidly discoloring stitches in his face, a heavily cast arm—his right—resting at an angle over his chest on top of the sheet.

I walked to the side of the bed. His eyes opened. For an instant there was fear and shock.

"Hey, pal," I said.

He recognized me. His intense relief made him flush. "Hey," he croaked.

"How do you feel?"

"Bad."

"What happened?"

"Lassiter. Hamm went home so he started asking me a lot more questions. He . . . wanted me to sign a confession. I told him to stow it. He . . . came in the cell." Ted's color started going splotchy and his chest began to heave in agitation.

"Take it easy," I soothed.

Ted reached out and grabbed me with his good left hand. His fingers closed on my hand like chill mechanical bands. "Don't let him get at me again."

"He won't, Ted."

"You mustn't let the son of a bitch get *in here* with me!"

"He won't. I promise."

Tears slid down his cheeks. "He . . . beat shit out of me."

"I know," I said, feeling totally incompetent to help him with this pain.

"Then he got me down and kicked on me a while. I peed a while ago. I've got blood in my pee. The nurse said they would check it, but it'll probably clear up. He said to confess killing Higgins. I told him to go shit in his hat. He left. I thought it was done with. I was puking and bleeding on the floor. Then he came back and he had this . . . cinder block . . ." The tears flowed harder, the body shook as if a galvanic current were being shot through it. "And he said, 'You won't talk, you rich bastard, you'll regret it the rest of your life, you'll never play tennis right again,' and then he . . . he put my hand in the cinder block and he held my arm there in the air and *jumped on it* with his foot—" Ted was sobbing now, trembling all over, and I had to lean over his quaking body to pull the words out of the sobs. "He jumped on my arm . . . it was like you would lean a piece of kindling up against something to snap it off, and when he came down, the *sound of it*—" He went to pieces.

I bent over him, grabbing him in my arms, hugging him, trying to make some of the convulsions lessen. It was futile. He sobbed uncontrollably.

"It's all right now," I said inanely. "It's going to be all right, pal. It's done with now. We're going to handle it . . . we're going to handle it."

By the time the uniformed cop opened the door and said my time was up, Ted had started to calm down a little. I think they must have given him some kind of a sedative earlier, because he seemed to just slide off a cliff of agony into the beginnings of a drugged, dreamless sleep. I managed to disengage from him. He stared at me and then he closed his eyes.

"Thanks," he murmured.

Thanks? I thought, leaving the room. *Thanks?* I was so angry at him for his stupidity—for his wishful thinking and dumb-ass actions—I wanted to hit him myself. I definitely wanted to hit somebody.

But it was Karyn standing in the hall just outside the door, every freckle looking like a penny against her worried pallor.

"How is he?"

"Better than I expected."

"Tell me."

So I lied. He was comfortable, I told her. He didn't remember what had happened, I said. He ought to be okay by morning.

We reached the dingy little waiting room and no one else was there.

"What now?" she asked wanly.

"I," I told her, "intend to pile up on this sofa and try to get a couple hours' sleep. Then we can see what the doctor says . . . what the police say."

She looked bleakly at the couch I had indicated, and another one like it across the tight little room. Then she squared her thin shoulders. "All right, then, Brad." She walked to the other couch and tugged off her shoes and half stretched out. She was not a small girl and she didn't fit very well. But she looked as determined as she often did in a tough match.

I pulled off my own shoes and stretched out on the facing couch. She stared unblinkingly at me. So I closed my eyelids and let the thoughts swirl around chaotically, and the fatigue was just crushing. I dozed.

At about six A.M., light at the windows and renewed activity in the hospital awoke me. I staggered to the washroom and splashed water on my face, and finger-combed my hair. When I got back to the waiting room, Karyn was just returning from her own restroom visit. The bitch goddess was gone from the nursing station. Her replacement, a human being, said Ted's condition had been upgraded to good. We went to the cafeteria and had coffee. When we got back to the second floor, the doctor in charge pronounced Ted out of danger and able to see any visitors the police okayed.

Karyn went in right away. Evidently Ted didn't tell her the worst, the part about his arm and the cinder block. She came out crying quietly, but far from the basket case I felt inside.

A little later, back in the cafeteria again, we were approached by a slender, red-haired man with an expensive dark suit, an attaché case, and some freckles. He was pink, freshly scrubbed and earnest, and he looked about sixteen.

"Allow me to introduce myself," he said. "I am Francis Peehoff. Your attorney of record in the matter of the state versus T. Treacher, charges unspecified. I was retained by telephone last night by your Mrs. Wallis at the resort in Elk City. When she informed me that my client had been brought here, naturally I came at once."

He was so very young and so very well-meaning. I exchanged looks with Karyn, then asked, "You have a lot of experience in criminal cases of this type, Mr. Peehoff?"

"Actually, not a great deal yet. But I was in the top ten percent of my law school graduating class last year, and I won top honors in moot court."

"Has Mrs. Wallis paid you a retainer yet?"

"She said that would be taken care of later today, actually."

I dug out my checkbook. "What is your usual retainer?"

"Well, five hundred dollars should be a beginning."

I wrote a check and handed it over.

"But this is for seven-fifty!" he protested.

"Correct. I want to pay you for your travel and time this morning."

"But that is hardly necessary as yet, is it?"

"Yes, it is. This is payment in full. Thank you, Mr. Peehoff. You're off the case. Have a nice day."

His feelings were hurt. He left looking downcast. I almost felt sorry for him.

Karyn was indignant. "How could Sally Wallis hire somebody like that over the telephone, sight unseen? Didn't you tell her to get the best?"

"I did."

"Everybody seems to be against us. I don't get it. It's insane. It's like even Sally was against us!"

"Yes, it is, isn't it," I said. "Look. I'm going to haul it back to the resort. Will you stay here, keep an eye on Ted, and find the best lawyer you can to take this mess over?"

"With pleasure," she snapped.

A little later, having found a rental car, I prepared to head south for Elk City and the mess I knew was there. A last look-in on Ted found his color better, his nerves not quite so bad.

"What are you going to do now?" he asked.

"Fight the bastards," I told him.

"How?"

"I don't know. I'll think of something."

He looked away, and there were tears in his eyes again. "Maybe . . . it's . . . time to give up. I've hosed everything up."

Many men think tears always mean weakness. A part of me started to be angry at his willingness to surrender—at *his* weakness—but then I knew better and caught myself. He was down. He had every reason and right to be down. He had been maimed, physically and spiritually.

But I couldn't entirely let him get away with it. "Bullshit," I said, and left him lying there.

At the corner, I used a booth to call California, where I managed to track Beth down in the courthouse law library. She sounded glad to hear from me until I started filling her in on some of what had happened.

"You sound awful," she said finally. "Everything sounds awful. But you sound like death warmed over. What are you going to do now?"

"Find lawyers. Check books. Get some resort checking accounts solvent. File lawsuits. Reorganize a business. Transfer some money of my own to make sure we can keep going temporarily. Pay some bills. Try to get Ted out of jail. Prepare for a tennis tournament we have no right to be trying to put on. Try to figure out what the hell has been going on here, and why everybody seems to want us to go under."

"Brad. You don't sound like yourself."

"Sorry. I'm mad."

"You're going to put *your own* money into this thing?"

"Yes."

"Is that wise?"

"I don't know about wise. Right now I don't care a lot about wise."

There was a long pause, and long-distance circuits chirped and whispered.

Finally: "Brad. Is there anything I can do to help?"

I wanted to scream and yell at her. "No. Obviously not."

"I'm worried about you—how you sound."

"I'm going to be as busy as a one-armed paperhanger, Beth. Don't be concerned if you don't hear from me for a few days. So long." And without waiting to hear her reply, I hung up.

Back in the car, I headed for the highway. Even with the rage, it was going to be hard, fighting the need to sleep.

You were a dumb-ass, Ted, I thought. A *real dumb-ass*.

You were dumb to bid for a failed resort in the first place, dumb to stick with it, dumb to delude yourself, dumb to run up more bills, sending good money after bad, dumb about everything. How you could be so dumb—and desperate—as to rebury that body is beyond my comprehension. You thought you could "rediscover" it and notify the cops after Ardis Allen's crew left, but that was the dumbest trick of all.

But there is nowhere written a rule that says, just because you're dumb and desperate and scared, you should be beaten by a puke like Lassiter, or even that all the cards should be stacked against you for reasons unknown, the way they have been at Bitterroot Valley. And maybe once I would have just thrown up my hands and said you were such a dummy that you deserved most of what you got, Ted, before last night and what he did to you in that crummy jail.

But you didn't deserve that. Nobody deserves that. Maybe you didn't deserve any of it. They shouldn't have driven you so far that you became so desperate and reckless that something like that beating could happen. And if there is a way, somebody is going to be taught that: that this time they went too far.

Fred Skurlock would not approve, I thought, driving south into the mountains. Too bad.

seventeen

Elsewhere

Chicago

Tense but satisfied, Ardis Allen closed the cover of the secret technical report on the Montana project. Her closest staff members had worked all night, giving it the finishing touches after their return from the west. Their covert field inspection during her time at Bitterroot Valley had confirmed earlier reports.

Moving the remaining materials out of the mine would require a massive effort. Secrecy must be maintained. But it had to be done. Public disclosure now, in view of the medical problems in Elk City, could ravage Allen Industries for allowing the original problem—and for the concealment effort Ardis had spearheaded. EPA fines alone could devastate the company. The publicity could be more ruinous.

Ardis turned to the computer workstation on the credenza behind her sprawling desk and opened a message file to her chief of Montana operations, Dr. Hawks:

TO: Hawks, Dept. 11
FROM: A. Allen
SUBJECT: Field report

1. Your report and plans approved.

2. Initiate stage 1, page 5, at once.

3. Stage 2, utilizing more personnel and heavy equipment, cannot be approved at this time due to presence of unauthorized persons near the site. Stage 2 will be approved for action as soon as land surrounding the site has been obtained, thus assuring control by company security personnel. We anticipate completion of negotiations for purchase of adjacent land parcels within thirty days.

4. Please note that stage 1 requires maximum security. Minimum staffing is mandatory to maintain confidentiality and reduce chances for accidental observation by outsiders. Only the most trusted technical staff personnel (list, page 11) are to be employed in this effort. No more than six staff workers are to be onsite at any time, with separate offsite quarters and ID credentials listing a fictitious employer and workplace.

5. Polygraph testing of stage 1 team members will be conducted on a weekly basis.

6. Both security and hazardous materials bonuses (page 14) are authorized.

7. No copy of this memorandum is to be archived to disk or preserved in any other way.

With a touch of a key, Ardis automatically encrypted the message and sent it electronically to the Technology/Research complex sixteen miles away. She then turned to her telephone and touched a button.

The small conference speaker on the instrument responded almost at once with the familiar crisp male voice: *"Yes, Mrs. Allen?"*

"Frank, please contact our people in Elk City."

"Yes. Instructions?"

Ardis briefly gave them and broke the connection.

It never hurt to hedge your bets when the stakes were this high.

Leaning back briefly in her swivel chair, Ardis looked out through the wall of glass at the city towers around her. It might have been considerably easier, she thought, if her offer to buy Bitterroot Valley had been accepted at once. Given the domino effects of her angry telephone calls yesterday, and the incredible turn of events in Montana last night, she had no doubt that the complex and its precious surrounding—and insulating—land would fall into her hands soon.

If financial factors alone had not been enough, the closeness of a crackdown and onsite investigation by the Securities and Exchange Commission should have pushed Ted Treacher over the edge. Now the news that he had been arrested—the strong possibility that he could be charged with something catastrophic like murder—had provided Ardis with her final reassurance.

Her memorandum estimate of control of the resort land within thirty days, she thought with satisfaction, could be viewed as wildly pessimistic. It was all working out at last.

Elk City

Jack Lassiter knew he should have expected it.

"Come again?" he mumbled.

Chief Hamm folded pudgy hands on his desktop. He looked infinitely sad and tired. "You're suspended, Jack, until we get a complete formal investigation on this Treacher thing. That's standard operating procedure, even in a little department like this one."

"He fell!" Lassiter protested. "I had nothing to do with it!"

"Sorry, Jack. You know, his ending up in the hospital like that has already got the rumors flying up and down the street. The DA says he won't file any charges against Treacher until we get an autopsy on Higgins's body. He also says this thing that happened in our jail, here, is going to make prosecution of any charges against Treacher harder."

Hamm sighed and raised thick arms above his head in a stretch. "This is for your own protection too, Jack. We'll talk to everybody, have a private hearing, file a report. Then I'll talk to the mayor and the DA and we'll see what shakes down."

"What am I supposed to do in the meantime?" Lassiter demanded, shaking.

"If I was you, Jack, I'd go home." Hamm thought about it. "Yes sir, that's what I'd do. I'd go home and get some rest. You've been awful edgy lately."

For Sylvester, some good news could scarcely have come at a more opportune time. He had been pleased to hear about the new trouble at the resort, but only on general principles. *This* news, on the other hand, meant everything.

His colleague, O'Connor, had waited before risking even so much as a trip to a public telephone booth. Now, however, Sylvester knew about the great breakthrough at the lab.

"You *must* wait for the next step until we can be sure there is no likelihood of being stopped and searched," Sylvester told him. "Until then, the papers must remain where they are inside."

"Understood," O'Connor replied. "However, there is the question of balancing threats. It appears certain they will run a new security investigation into my background. If they were to locate any weak spot in my credentials, it could go very badly for me."

"Yes," Sylvester agreed. "For the time being, however, no more contacts between us, nothing more in your activities which could in any way raise suspicion."

"Understood."

Now, Sylvester thought, a painful waiting game would begin. O'Connor had performed brilliantly, ad libbing a solution on a moment's notice, and under great pressure. The Soviet Union desperately needed the plans to understand—and to counteract—the American missile defense effort based on EMP radiation. Otherwise, this new technology could destabilize the new superpower cooperation. But as long as the plans remained inside the lab where O'Connor had secreted them, everything was left uncertain.

The time immediately ahead, Sylvester thought, was going to be maddening. Every impulse said to hurry. But for the moment all they could do was await their opportunity—which surely would come soon.

eighteen

It was a bleak, chilly day in Elk City when I got back, and then I had to wait for another funeral procession. Judging by the number of kids in passing cars, it was another child's funeral. I was depressed and more tired than I liked to admit, even to myself. Nothing was going right.

Back at the lodge, things got no better. I looked for Sally Wallis but she was not around. Somebody said she had gone to town for an appointment. Staff people asked anxiously about Ted, and I put the best face on it that I could. Apparently no one realized the scope of the legal problems he might be facing.

Mrs. Tanshita, the little Asian woman who ran our registration desk and supervised room preparations, was among those most concerned. She told me she needed guidance on planning for our little tournament, which—I now remembered—was less than two weeks away.

"Maybe I can help," I told her. "What's the problem?"

She gave me a desperate smile. "Ploblem is, what am I supposed to do? When am I supposed to stalt doing something?"

I didn't get it. "Well, you've been given instructions already, right?"

She looked painfully embarrassed. "I am solwy. No."

"Mrs. Wallis hasn't issued detailed instructions?"

"No sir, I—"

Christ. "I'll get back to you on this, Mrs. Tanshita."

I went to the kitchens. There I located Wayne Persuitt, the resort chef and supply master. When I asked about ordering extra supplies and contacting additional food service people, I drew the same kind of blank stare.

Ted's office was my next stop. I got an outside line and held it, and started making calls.

Forty minutes later, the scope of our unreadiness had begun to emerge more clearly. If anyone had been contacted about outside concessions for the tournament, I couldn't find them. The companies I could locate within a two-hundred-mile radius who handled such things as tents, crowd control, signs, and bleacher assembly had never heard of us either.

For all I could tell, nothing had been done to get ready for the tournament. Sally Wallis had done nothing on her own, and had not followed any of my instructions.

My patience snapped. Getting the start of a mega-headache, I went from Ted's office into the smaller business area next door where Sally kept shop. She was still not back. I closed her office door from the inside to prevent unduly nasty surprises, and investigated.

In the filing cabinet I found my Xeroxed tourney releases and envelopes, unmailed. Also my hand-scrawled list of preparation instructions, evidently untouched. I then went through Sally's desk and found only the usual clutter. The bottom drawer, however, was locked.

After prying futilely at the drawer for a minute or two, I left the office and went into the bowels of the building, to maintenance. The custodian looked surprised when I borrowed his big pipewrench and a short-handled eight-pound sledge.

Locked in Sally Wallis's office again, I proceeded on the theory that the desk might be easier to repair if I went through the side panel to get into the locked drawer. Even so, by the time I was through the panel and inside the desk, the place looked like a wrecking crew had run amok.

Kneeling in the wood splinters and broken paneling, I hauled the broken drawer out onto the floor and examined its contents. I found some cards—that funny, loving kind—addressed to her and signed by Ted. I also found a couple of magazines, some area maps and brochures, a scattering of cosmetics, and a small metal lockbox. Locked.

Tough box. I was not sure whether I would get it open before I had smashed it into a nugget with the sledge. But finally the little lid broke off.

Inside were a Missoula bank deposit book and an envelope containing a number of deposit slips. They were neatly filled out with the name of the agency writing the check, the payee, and the amount. Sally had on several occasions made personal deposits larger than her paycheck. Some of the other deposits, made with checks written by Barnwell Mining Co., were even more interesting. I studied them briefly and made some notes. By this point I was not really very surprised. I put two of the deposit slip copies and my notes in my pocket, unlocked the office door, and went out.

When Sally Wallis got back a little later, I was sitting on her shipwrecked desk with a cardboard carton containing all her personal items beside me. Her eyes flared wide and she stopped in the doorway.

"What *is* this?"

"It's the day you move out, Sally. Your stuff is in this box. Leave."

"What have you *done*?" She came in and saw the way the desk had been brutalized. She swung outraged eyes to me. "How *dare* you!"

"Get out," I told her.

"You had no right to intrude into my personal things! I can have you charged in court for this!"

I almost enjoyed it. "Maybe I won't file charges against you for embezzlement or conspiracy to defraud—based on the deposit records now in my possession—if you just keep quiet and get your ass out of here within the next sixty seconds."

For a moment she didn't back down. I could see her mind going Mach 3. She knew I had her cold.

"You skimmed our accounts," I told her. "In addition, there are these deposit slips showing checks from Cliffton and Wells, the law firm in town. Who's behind those checks, Sally? Would I be wildly wrong if I guessed Allen Industries, paying you to help make sure we go down the toilet so Ardis Allen can buy at her price?"

She had gone sickly pale. She looked a decade older, and decidedly unattractive. "You can't prove a thing."

"Get your fat ass *out*. Now."

She did.

I asked Mrs. Tanshita to assemble the key staff people in the deserted banquet room. There, under the dusty chandeliers, standing among the naked tables and chairs, I told them Ted was in the hospital, Mrs. Wallis was no longer employed here, and I was taking over temporarily as manager. They seemed only mildly surprised; maybe some of them had started to guess how Sally Wallis was skimming off, or maybe they had worked at this God-forsaken place long enough that nothing surprised them any more.

Anyway, winging it, I gave them lots of explicit orders. They left the banquet room with the serious expressions of people who intended to do what they had been told.

I went back to the office and called a couple of my bankers in Dallas. They didn't approve. I told them to do what I ordered. I then called a bank in Denver and one in Missoula and told them what I was up to. They thought setting up accounts by telephone like this was out of the ordinary, but the mention of amounts did a lot to cool their irritation about deviation from normal protocols. When I made my third call, to the little bank in Elk City, they were ecstatic; they had already received the electronic order from my people in Dallas, refueling the anemic Bitterroot Valley Resort accounts.

All that taken care of, I swallowed four Tylenols and considered my next step. I needed help now, and badly. So I took the only additional step I could think of.

Thirty minutes later, I was in the Bronco and on the road. A slip of paper beside me on the seat spelled out my road directions.

Avery Whitney's place was one of those factory-built log homes, two stories, with a stone chimney on the side, dormer windows on top and a broad covered porch that went all the way around. A large satellite dish sat clear of the scattered pines in the broad, neatly mowed acreage out front. As I pulled up in the gravel driveway, I spotted two vehicles in the nearby barnlike garage: his Cadillac pickup and a spotless Mercedes.

I expected Whitney to answer the door but instead I got Miss Teenage America: perhaps 19, dark hair loose on her shoulders, the prettiest hazel eyes in the world, a quick, winsome smile. She wore minuscule denim shorts, a sleeveless pink cotton top, and tennis shoes, no socks. The outfit displayed a lot of her honey-colored tan. Tiny-waisted, she had sweet hips and wonderful bare legs.

"Hi," she said. "You must be Mr. Smith."

"I believe I am."

"Come in!"

The living room, with a raftered ceiling and miles of gleaming hardwood floors accented by small rugs, was a combination of Western and American Indian. Somehow I had expected it to be cluttered, but it wasn't. A giant-screen TV-stereo center dominated one wall, the fireplace another. The furniture was dark, mildly contemporary. In a far corner was a big walk-around bar. Avery Whitney stood behind it.

"Come in this house," he rumbled. "Have any trouble finding us?"

"Your instructions were good," I told him.

"Brad Smith, meet Melody Ryan. Melody, this is the famous feller I was telling you about."

She beamed and offered her hand. I shook it, getting soft tingles. "Gosh!" she said in a voice that matched her name. "I saw you on TV just the other night! On one of those old-time sports shows!"

"It's amazing, how the film holds up from the olden days," I said.

"Gee, yes, but you're a lot younger than I thought you'd be!"

"Melody, honey," Whitney said, "why don't you run on outside now and see if you can't finish mowing out front. Brad and me want to have a confab."

"Yes, Avery," the little vision said happily, and tripped out the door.

Whitney plunked ice cubes into two stout tumblers and applied four fingers of Windsor Canadian to each. "Sit down, sit down, take a load off." He brought the tumblers around the end of the bar and thrust one at me. "You don't look too good, son. You're moving kind of stiff, and the side of your face there is all swole up like a frog. I heard Treacher killed somebody and got thrown into the jailhouse."

I sat down in one of the small, deep leather chairs flanking the long pale sofa. "He found his construction foreman's body and moved it. They've jumped to a lot of conclusions."

"How about your face?"

"I ran into a door."

"Right." Whitney plopped onto the couch, hiking one booted foot up onto the cushions and ignoring the flakes of dried mud that scattered around as he did so. "Seems like your friend has done one real stupid thing right after another."

"He had 'an accident' in the jail last night. Had you heard that, too?"

Whitney's bushy eyebrows went up and down and his mouth tightened. "Guess I hadn't heard that part yet. Melody and I slept in. I'll tell you what, that girl is almost too much for me. I'd marry her, but goddam. If she was around *all* the time, I think I'd be a dead man inside six months. What kind of an accident? As if I didn't know."

I told him. He listened carefully, scowling, tugging at his whiskey once in a while, and I went ahead and told him about Sally Wallis, the failure to do anything to prepare for the tournament, and some of the deposit slips I had found.

"So the little tart was skimming," he said when I had finished. "Damn Sam! I feel bad about that. She probably did it to me, too. And I recommended her to Treacher. Although I dunno why I should be surprised about anything, come to think of it. How much do you reckon she'd got?"

"I don't know. Plenty. There were also deposit slips showing she was being paid about a thousand a month by Barnwell Mining."

He sat up a little straighter. "That so!"

"What do you make of that?"

Whitney chuckled, but there wasn't much amusement in it. "Well, sir, I don't reckon she was digging mineral for them."

"No, I didn't assume so."

"Matter of fact, I don't know *what* she might have been doing. As far as I know, that company has been all but dead for a long time—a paper company only."

"They're the ones that own the mine adjacent to our golf course."

"Yep, but they just keep it fenced to keep people out that might get hurt. They don't do nothing there."

"Are you sure of that?"

He raised an eyebrow. "Of course I'm sure! You don't operate a mine without all kinds of obvious activity: lots of workers, digging machines, big trucks going in and out all the time. Why? You think otherwise?"

I shrugged. "I'm just checking."

"Besides, that old mine is too dangerous. Over the years, couple of people have clumb the fence or wandered in somehow and gotten themselves killed."

"How?"

"One fell down a vertical shaft. Another, a snotnose kid maybe fifteen, was found just inside the fence, beside an old gravel conveyor. It looked like the top rotating platform fell off and crushed him."

"None of that explains why the company would be paying Sally Wallis a retainer."

"No, it sure don't, does it."

"I intend to find out why. Any ideas?"

"No, sir."

I sipped the whiskey. "I'll find out."

"Hope you don't get hurt."

"Why should I get hurt?"

It was his turn to shrug. "Funny doings around here. People like their secrets kept. Don't like outsiders nosing around."

"Well, that's tough."

He grinned slowly. "You're a stubborn, mean mother, ain't you."

"Stubborn, yes. And right now, a little chapped."

He tossed back the last of his whiskey and climbed stiffly to his feet. "Ready for another?"

I showed him my glass, which still had over half the first portion in it.

"For a mean guy," he observed philosophically, limping to the bar, "you ain't much of a drinker."

"I fired Sally," I said.

"Well, sure." He poured again.

"So," I went on, feeling goaded and angry, "Ted is in the hospital, and from there he might very well go to jail, and I don't see another manager candidate out there at the resort, and I don't have time to advertise, even locally. That tournament is staring me right in the face."

Whitney smiled beatifically. "Deep shit."

"Very deep."

"What did you come to me for?"

With the feeling of going off the high dive, I went ahead. "I've come to ask if you'll help me."

He was halfway back from the bar, and he stopped in stride. "Me?" He looked genuinely surprised. "*Me?*"

"You know the resort," I said doggedly. "You know how to run it."

"Yeah! I ran it right into failure!"

"I don't believe for a minute that was your fault, Avery."

"Whose fault do you figure it was, then?"

"I figure the same people who have screwed Ted—the same ones in the conspiracy with Barnwell Mining, Cliffton and Wells, and I don't know who else yet—dragged you down with the same kind of sabotage that's plagued Ted. So I figure you know damned well how to run the resort, and you might even save the bacon on the tournament preparations."

Whitney stared at me in silence from his resumed position on the couch. Outside somewhere a riding mower engine fired and accelerated under load. Melody was following orders.

Finally Whitney said, "I don't see what's in it for me."

I was ready for that. "To get us set up and through the tournament, a fee of five thousand dollars. Payable half now, half after it's over. If we break even on the week, another five. If we make any money, the additional five thousand plus five percent of the profit."

He studied me soberly. "All payable, I reckon, in more of Treacher's hot checks?"

"The accounts are solvent now. We have reserve funds."

"From *where*?"

"I've plowed in some money of my own."

"You figure that was smart?"

"Screw smart."

He shook his head. "You really are some kind of mean sumbitch, ain't you!"

"Or a fool," I said.

He chuckled. "Yes, sir! Or a fool!" His body shook as the laugh swelled and spread through him. "Or a fool! Yes, sir! Oh, have you ever got that right! Or a fool! That's a good one, all right!"

"Plus," I told him, "we're going to beat these people. I'm going to find out who all of them are, and the resort is going to succeed, and they're going to sweat bullets, watching that. After what they did to you, I thought you'd enjoy being part of the fight."

He looked at me awhile. Then he got up and started walking up and down the long room. "Oh, you're a mean one. Yes, you are! But you don't know some of the mean sumbitches you might be up against around these parts . . . no sir, you sure don't . . . Might be kind of fun, but might be sad, too, seeing you go down that same toilet I went down . . ." He turned and fixed me with his good eye. "What do you figure are some of the things you need done first?"

I told him: room preparation; screening of reservations; cleanup; food supplies; linens and extra help; calls to every radio and TV outlet in a five-hundred-mile radius, plugging the thing; concessions; tents; signs; bleachers.

He listened to the end of my recital. "Lot of work."

"Yes."

He resumed pacing. "You got your checkbook?"

I took it out of my jacket pocket.

He glared. "The checks will be good?"

"Absolutely."

"You pay me twenty-five hundred now?"

"Yes."

He scowled. "Melody comes with me. I ain't hiding her. That little bunny rabbit is the finest kind, the best thing that's happened to me in thirty years. If people don't like seeing an old fart like me hugging around on Miss America, then the deal is off."

"Melody comes with you. Agreed."

"I'll probably need about ten thousand in expense money to get started." He watched me with the keenest interest.

I wrote his advance paycheck on my personal account and handed it to him. "I'll call the bank in town and tell them you're authorized to write checks. I have to go in and sign a signature card. You'll have to do that too."

He studied the check, folded it, and put it in the top left pocket of his buckskin vest. "Trusting soul, ain't you?"

"Avery, I've got to trust somebody. You're the one."

The eyebrows canted. "Might be wrong."

"Don't think I am."

He nodded. "Ain't."

I stood and we shook hands. "I need you to get right on this."

"Okey dokey," he said cheerfully, pausing to wipe his nose on a blue bandanna. "I'll just collect a few things and get over there."

If I had misjudged Avery Whitney, I thought, it might turn out to be one of the biggest mistakes of my life. *Avery*, I thought, watching him pitch some papers into a cardboard box, *you'd better be straight. And you'd better be a miracle man.*

It didn't seem too much to ask.

When I got back to the lodge, Fred Skurlock was waiting in the lobby.

"Christ," I said. "Isn't this a little obvious?"

"I think," he said dourly, "we're at the point where it just doesn't matter."

Reading his face, I knew it was more bad news. "Come on back to the office."

Skurlock didn't want any coffee. He didn't even comment on the wreckage of a desk I still had back there. He paced up and down. "New development. It seems they've 'lost' part of their most critical engineering papers out at the lab."

"Lost?" I repeated, feeling stupid.

"They were running a test. Lot of confusion. They had some trouble and the graybeards had all the diagrams and stuff spread all over the place. When they got to a breaking-off point, they started putting things in the right folders again, and that was when they noticed some of the schematic drawings and specifications not where they were supposed to be."

"My God, how long had they been missing?"

"The engineers swear the papers were all there earlier in the day."

"They weren't just misplaced?"

Skurlock looked at me like I was an idiot. "You think they haven't checked everything four hundred times?"

"Then the plans were gotten out of the lab? They're *gone*?"

"They swear they can't be gone. Everybody was body-searched.

Every locker and desk is being gone over. Whatever happened, the papers have to still be inside the complex someplace."

"What now?" was the only question I could think to ask.

"We have got to find Sylvester," Skurlock told me. "It's no longer a matter of if or when. We have got to locate him now. If we can find him before they figure out a way to get those plans out of the lab, we can still recoup. Otherwise, if they get the papers out . . ." He threw up his hands.

"How do we do that?"

"You drop this silly shit out here at this lodge. You come to town and meet my sketch artist. You help me start asking everybody in Elk City for a lead. You make yourself highly visible, and we hope we either get a lead or he comes after you."

I studied his expression again. My stomach felt like somebody had poured lead in it.

He was right. It had been made clear from the start that I was here primarily to help against the spy threat to the lab. That it was important was proven by Sylvester's presence. I hadn't accomplished anything of significant help. Ted might be in terminal trouble with the resort, and I might be savagely upset by the beating he had taken at the hands of Jack Lassiter. But I had to set some priorities, and now.

"Give me until morning," I said. "It's too late to accomplish anything yet today anyhow."

Skurlock nodded. "Fine. The same café. Nine o'clock." He turned and walked out.

Almost since my arrival in Montana, the idea had been brewing. Skurlock's ultimatum meant I didn't have any more time. I reexamined my logic. Local opposition to the resort, some of it at least funneled through the law firm in town. Sally Wallis, hired by the same outfit to snoop and sabotage things. The funerals in town, and all the weird security around the old mine site, and the lights I had seen. Allen Industries' unholy intensity in wanting to buy us out.

I decided it all tracked.

Also, I had no more time to mess around. I either had to take drastic steps or forget it.

"Hi!" Lynette Jordan chirped when I got through to her. "I

haven't heard from you guys for a few days! I've been trying to catch you. This thing with the body out there and everything. They won't let me write any of the story. They say I'm too young. But if you could just—"

"Lynette," I cut in, "would you like an even bigger story?"

I heard her intake of breath. "Like. . . ?"

"Get Bobby Winkleman and his camera. Come out here right after dark. Don't tell anyone."

"Wow! Real cloak and dagger, huh? What's it all about? You're not spoofing me, are you? I—"

"Hey, I couldn't be more serious. Keep this under your hat. And come. Okay?"

If she had said no, I don't know what alternative I would have turned to. But the hint of secrecy and a big story were too much for her. And in our earlier driving around, she had started to trust and maybe even like me.

"I'll be there," she said.

nineteen

Elsewhere

Elk City

Sylvester made the telephone call routinely.

"Yes?" Sally Wallis's voice answered.

Sylvester hesitated. She did not sound like herself. Her voice had a choked-up tone. Like a woman who had been crying.

Finally he said, "Mrs. Wallis?"

"Oh," she said. She sounded disappointed, petulant. "It's you."

"I'm calling as usual, Mrs. Wallis, to see if you have any information for me."

Silence on the other end. This was alarming.

"Mrs. Wallis?"

"I can't help you anymore."

"Mrs. Wallis," Sylvester said quickly, "I'm sure you remember our original conversation. As a divorce investigator looking into Mr. Smith's activities, it is vitally important for me to keep tabs on his financial and other involvements. As I explained to you at the outset, Mr. Smith's estranged wife believes she is being seriously wronged, and that he is in the process of reinvesting large sums of of their joint financial holdings without her knowledge or consent. Therefore, any information you can provide about his activities will possibly prevent a terrible wrong being done to a fine woman. Your reports to me so far have been useful. Now, if the fee system we agreed upon earlier is no longer satisfactory—"

"You don't understand," Sally Wallis's voice cut in bitterly. "I won't help you anymore because I *can't*. I've been . . . discharged."

"Discharged? Who discharged you?"

"*He* did! Brad Smith!"

"On what grounds, Mrs. Wallis? If he learned you were providing us with information about his activities—"

"What difference does it make?" Her voice rose to a hysterical pitch. "He broke into my desk—found everything! He fired me on the spot and now I don't know what I'm going to do—he even threatened legal action against me!"

Sylvester put his cigar in the ashtray on the cabin table. His hand shook. This was much worse than he could have imagined. How had the idiot woman given herself away? *How much did Smith now know?*

He made his voice sound calm, unctuous. "Mrs. Wallis, I am sure something can be worked out to compensate you. This is a terrible thing. I assure you—"

"Just leave me alone!" she screamed over the telephone. "I intend to get even with that bastard, and nothing else matters!"

And she hung up.

Sylvester stood holding the telephone, listening to the whine of the dial tone. When the tone clicked off and a recorded voice started saying an instrument was off the hook, he came to his senses and hung it up.

With a flick of his Zippo lighter he refired his cigar. But there was no pleasure left in it.

The woman had been caught. Smith had figured it out, and that was the only thing that was significant. No charges had been filed yet, and Sylvester could not think of any that might be lodged. But Smith could harass the woman, threaten or even file a civil lawsuit of some kind, bring in experts to pump her for additional information.

She did not know where Sylvester was staying. But when he first met her—the only time they had met face-to-face—she might have noticed his pickup truck. She might have noticed other things, too

. . . his fishing hat that day, perhaps some other hint he could no longer remember.

She was a link to him and therefore a threat. And now, with success so close at the lab, additional threats could not be tolerated.

The more Sylvester thought about it, the surer he became that Sally Wallis was simply an unacceptable added complication.

Night wind had begun to sound against the wood shakes of the cabin. It was getting colder. Ordinarily Sylvester might have put logs on the fire and settled back to listen to his radio. But now he was decided. After quickly changing to dark woolen clothing and a pea jacket, he got his automatic out of its hiding place. He carefully screwed on the silencer tube, wrapped the weapon in an oily cloth, and carried it with him out to his truck.

Less than thirty minutes later he had parked well off the road on the west edge of Elk City, selecting a brushy area downhill from the pavement and well hidden by high brush. Turning his collar up against the wind, he started across the fields on foot, moving slowly to conserve his meager reserves of energy.

It took twenty minutes or so to reach the edge of town, and the little cottage where she lived. In the house a hundred yards across the road, lights blazed in all the windows, and Sylvester could hear the sounds of a TV set turned up very loud. Only one dim light shone from Sally Wallis's house, that in a back room, probably a bedroom. Her car sat at the side, on a gravel driveway in the deepest shadows. All to the good.

Removing his gun from under his coat, Sylvester walked up on the small wooden front porch and banged his fist loudly on the door. Having done so, he reached up inside the porchlight receptacle and turned the bulb a full turn to the left so it could not be turned on from inside.

There was a delay of a few moments. He pounded again. Hid the gun behind his back.

A light sprang on inside the house beyond the small windows in the top section of the door. Another delay: she trying the switch for the porchlight. Then the rattling of a security chain, and the door opened a few inches.

Sally Wallis peered out of the dim interior light. Her face looked puffy, as if she had been crying. She recognized Sylvester in the light spilling out. "Go away!"

"Please, Mrs. Wallis!" he pleaded quickly. "We feel terrible about your misfortune, and want to help you!"

She hesitated in the act of closing the door. "Help? How could anyone help?" Her voice was slurry. She had been drinking. That was a plus. "Just leave me alone!"

"But I have something for you!" Sylvester wheedled. "We want to compensate you!"

Her eyes widened. "Compensate?"

"In a small way, pay you for all your trouble. Please let me in."

She thought about it, then swung the door closed, but only enough to allow the security chain to be loosened. The door swung wide.

"Come in, then," she said thickly, stepping back in the little living room as Sylvester entered. "What do you have—oh!"

Her voice failed and her expression changed to twisted shock as Sylvester brought the Makarov around to level on her. She threw up her hands. The pistol made its nasty little chuffing sound, rocking in his hand. Sally Wallis was hurled backward in a spray of blood and brain tissue.

Sylvester scarcely gave her a glance. Stepping over her body, he tipped a chair in the living room and knocked over a lamp. He hurried into the kitchen and jerked out drawers, throwing the contents on the floor. In the bedroom he pulled the mattress off the bed, hauled out all the drawers, tossed clothing from the closet all over the room, knocked pictures off the wall.

He was so deft in his quick imitation of the actions of a burglar that he found her envelope of cash hidden in the bottom of the last dresser drawer. Six hundred dollars, more or less.

He pocketed the bills, and then, to make it look even better, removed the cheap jewelry from her musicbox and pocketed that, too. Then he broke a corner out of a bedroom window, made sure the latch was open and that the window could be raised, and left the house the way he had come, through the front door.

Forty minutes later he was back in his truck and back on the road, headed for his mountain cabin once more.

twenty

Getting ready for Lynette Jordan and photographer Bobby Winkleman, I went to our maintenance building and found a set of three-foot bolt cutters, some heavy pliers, and a good utility light. Leaving these in the office after sneaking them in there, I walked down to my cabin and got the .38, which I carried back up hidden under my jacket. I made sure the batteries were charged on the lodge building's courtesy golfcart, and then settled in to wait for my helpers from the press.

While waiting, I got to accomplish one other thing.

"How's he doing?" I asked Karyn Wechsting when I tracked her down through the switchboard at the hospital in Missoula.

"Oh, hell, Brad, I don't know. He's a little better, physically, I think. The doctor says everything will heal. Except maybe the arm. It was so badly shattered. There was nerve damage. Muscles torn and all. They repaired everything they could. Ted says his fingers feel numb. The doctor says the feeling ought to come back, and everything be fine. If not, he says there are microsurgery techniques . . ." Her voice trailed off. She sounded bone-tired and depressed.

"It'll be okay," I told her with more conviction than I felt.

"But what if it *isn't*? That's one of the things that has him so low.

I mean, it would be all right if he weren't still an athlete—if it weren't his racket hand. If he ends up with weakness in that arm, or numbness in the fingers, how is he ever going to hit a ball worth a damn again?"

A non-player might have pointed out that he was lucky to be alive and more or less in one piece, with his brains unscrambled. But even as decrepit as I was in this young person's game, my remaining skills were inordinately important to me. Like Ted, I had taken years out of my life to become as good as I once had been. You don't pay that kind of price for a skill and then become indifferent to it. Ted Treacher might never again win a big tournament, but his ability with a tennis racket was vital to his persona, a big chunk of his heart, central to where he lived emotionally.

Lassiter, I thought, had known this through some primitive intuition. When he had shattered Ted's arm, he had gone at a crucially vulnerable part of Ted's whole existence just as surely as if he had crushed his nuts. Now, if the arm and hand refused to heal perfectly, Ted would feel himself as much a cripple as a man with a wooden leg, a woman in the early days after a mastectomy. This was part of the reason why Ted had been so broken when I saw him in his hospital room. Lassiter had succeeded where time and bad luck and all the local chicanery had failed: he had cut Ted's spirit out by the roots.

"Look," I told Karyn now. "This is going to take time. He'll heal in time. Right now, the important thing is to make sure he knows we're standing with him all the way, and get him the best possible legal representation."

"He knows we're with him, Brad. He frets that you're getting yourself in over your head, just like he did."

"That's neither here nor there."

"I know. As to the lawyer, I've interviewed a couple and gotten some opinions around town, and I've retained someone."

"A good lawyer?"

"There are two opinions. Some of the local law enforcement people and hangers-on around the judges at the courthouse think he's the worst bastard who ever lived. A few other people, including the courthouse reporter for *The Missoulian*, think he's just about as diabolically clever and hard-working as anybody they ever met. When I went to see him, he ushered me into this great, cigar-stinky office with saddles and bridles and pictures of John Wayne and antlers and rifles all over the walls, and told me he's the meanest sonofabitch in the valley. Then he went on to show me a map of prehistoric times in this region. Did you know there used to be a prehistoric Lake Missoula that stretched from around here to halfway across the universe? Mr. Tuhey said he's the meanest sonofabitch in *that* valley, the old one."

"Tuhey? That's his name?"

"Jefferson Tuhey. Wait till you meet him, Brad. He's as big as those elk he says he hunts every fall, and he's got muscles like a weightlifter—which he is, incidentally—and the mildest little blue eyes and goatee."

"Well, he sounds wonderful. But the question is, can he get Ted out of these charges?"

"He hasn't seen Ted or the DA or anybody else yet, but he's looking into it right now. I'm convinced that he can do it if anyone can."

"Good." I started feeling a little better. "About his fee—"

"He asked for ten thousand dollars up front, and I told him that was fine."

I hesitated an instant. *At this rate I'll be bankrupt by nightfall.* "Okay, Karyn. I'll have a check for him when I come up."

"Brad, I already paid him."

"You didn't have to—"

"I know that." She sounded calm and firm. "I wanted to. Also, I intend to put additional money into these accounts you're fixing up. I think they can use another transfusion."

"Karyn, that's not necessary—!"

"I know it's not necessary, damn it. But I want to do it and I'm going to." She paused, and the fire suddenly left her voice and she sounded like a little girl again. "And if I go bankrupt in the process—"

"Then I'll say welcome to the club."

It was good and dark when Lynette and Winkleman arrived. Winkleman looked bored and irritated, but he had two cameras around his neck and a gadget bag stuffed with strobes and related equipment. I took them to the office.

"What are we going to shoot?" Winkleman asked irritably. "I don't do architectural interiors!"

"We've got a story here that's going to make you a lot of money and a lot more prestige," I told him. "All you're going to have to do is keep your eyes open and start shooting when the pictures come."

"Right, right," Winkleman said disgustedly, rolling his eyes. "Big deal. Celebrity shots, right?"

"Bobby," Lynette said, "I told you this might be something really big for both of us. Now please just shut up and let the man talk. Go ahead, Brad."

I explained briefly.

"Oh, no!" Winkleman said, rolling his eyes.

"What?" I said.

"You're not getting *me* into no illegal entry!" He jumped to his feet, rattling multiple cameras. "I'm getting outta here!"

"Bobby," Lynette groaned.

But he wouldn't listen. He started for the door, barged out of there. Lynette rushed out after him. I heard their voices. But in a couple of minutes she was back again, alone, toting one of the cameras.

"The idiot," she fumed, red-faced with anger. "The asshole! —I got one of his cameras, anyway, and I've got a Polaroid in the back of my car."

Despite the complication of having two helpers along, I had wanted as many witnesses as I dared take. Winkleman's bug-out had left me only Lynette. But judging by the determined glare on her face, she was a good one.

"Can you operate that thing?" I asked, indicating the camera.

"I can do it as well as Bobby can!"

I doubted that, but we weren't looking for studio quality here. "Let's go," was all I said.

My little .38 hidden in my pocket, I led the way out in the darkness to the cart.

"Boy, all the comforts," Lynette said nervously.

"Yep."

We set out. Lynette was quiet, tense, a little puzzled. I certainly hadn't explained everything. My stomach felt like it had a boat anchor in it. I did not know exactly what we were likely to encounter in the way of resistance. I hoped the element of surprise would carry us through. You could never be sure about these things. As committed as I was, I also recognized that we were—if you wanted to get sticky about it—getting ready to break a couple of laws that people often took very seriously indeed.

We drove down the paved path toward the golf course, going the back way in case Fred Skurlock still had my cabin staked out, running in the dark with only the tree-filtered starlight to guide us. It crossed my mind that Sylvester could hardly ever hope to find me in a more vulnerable position than this. But that was a passing thought built on a habit of worry, and it went on through my mind and was gone. First things first, I told myself: deal with this and then you can get back to being scared of Sylvester.

At the bottom of the asphalt path I turned onto the newly sodded lawns of the unsold condos, slowing to avoid undue jolting as we went on downhill, staying well clear of the golf pro shop. Once we had crossed north of the No. 1 tee and had driven out onto the first fairway, heading generally west, the terrain rose beneath us and we drove into brighter illumination coming from the bright sliver of moon that had been concealed by the trees and rise of hills. We purred across the fairway, going as fast as the silent electric cart would haul two on the flat. The wind cut through my dark jacket, biting in.

We reached the trees on the far side, and I slowed as we drove into their darkness. My eyes did not adjust at once and I had to go slowly. Even so, we spooked a large animal—almost certainly a deer—which exploded into violent motion just ahead of us, then went crashing off into the underbrush in flight. When we came out onto the next fairway it was brighter again, and now we were getting close.

Ordinarily I would never have tried this. I could only hope Lassiter or some other crazy man was not walking the fence tonight. I didn't see that I had any choice. Still, a small voice (maybe sanity) in a corner of my mind whispered, *This is crazy, Smith. No one in his right mind would take this chance.* I told the little voice to hush.

We drove through the narrow band of woods on the far side of the 15 fairway, climbing the ridgeline. At the top I stopped long enough to haul out the binoculars and scan the fence and compound.

The pale light from the sky made the hillside milky-clear. I saw no vehicles, no movement of a watchman. Stowing the glasses in the forward shelf of the cart, I drove slowly down the hill, riding the brake. The cart made almost no sound at all. At the bottom I parked.

The world seemed utterly still. Every pebble and piece of junk inside the fencing stood out in bold relief. Long shadows slanted away from the moonlight. My skin prickled with the feeling we were being observed. I devoutly doubted the wisdom of doing this, and thought momentarily about turning back. In tennis I've often gone after shots that I knew were impossible, just because my pride wouldn't let me do otherwise. My pride kept me from turning back.

I got out of the cart, hefted my blanket-wrapped tools, and signaled Lynette to follow me. She did so soundlessly, needing no instructions to be still. Kneeling at the corner of the fence, I unwrapped the big boltcutters and applied them to the fence. The jaws bit through and the parting wires made a bright spanging sound. With a couple of shoulder-crunching heaves I pulled the wire mesh open enough to let somebody crawl through.

I looked at Lynette. Her eyes looked like pie plates, and I saw the circuits going inside her head at about the speed of light. I could tell she was making connections and guesses. She was a game young woman.

Kneeling, I whispered, "Think about it. Kids dying of leukemia. A company like Allen Industries pressuring us to sell. *This* place next door. Heavy fence for a mine that's *abandoned*?"

Lynette's eyes got even wider. She tumbled at once.

"What say?" I prodded.

"Let's go," she whispered.

That was neat. I climbed through the hole in the fence and held the wire apart for her to follow. She scrambled through.

I led the way down the fenceline. An owl called in the nearby trees, startling me. You have crazy thoughts at times like this. I wondered if an owl was a good or bad omen in native American superstition.

We moved on. The camera gear made chittering metal and plastic noises. The moonlight here made the night seem about as dark as a major city intersection.

We climbed up the gentle, rock-scrabble slope toward the

jumbled wreckage around the mouth of the old mineshaft. Gravel scraped under our feet. I began to breathe hard. Adrenaline.

We started past the wreckage of a conveyor of some kind, passing between it and the hulking black of a half-collapsed storage shed. As we moved by, my eye caught the tiny wink of ruby red. I grabbed Lynette's arm, holding her back just long enough to lean over and verify what I thought. There was a small, bright, malevolent pinpoint of ruby-colored light inside a hole in the old shed: intruder alarm.

No more time for caution, not that we had ever exercised much. I pushed past Lynette and retook the lead, hurrying up the hardscrabble dirt and rock at the mouth of the old shaft. Dragging out my mini-flashlight with my left hand, I got it turned on and sprayed its cone of startlingly bright, penetrating illumination into the darkness under the old beams ahead of us. Couldn't see a thing, only more dark and timbers.

Dank stale air rushed up out of the earth as we moved deeper. The shaft turned abruptly and I followed it around. Distantly came the sound of an electronic bell hammering. The light of my flashlight sprayed across the unexpected brilliance of metalwork in the tunnel just ahead.

Our way was completely blocked by a metal partition bolted into heavy girderwork that penetrated ceiling and floor of the shaft. There was a door in the steel wall that looked like something you might find in a bank vault. Three small amber lights glowed on a control panel beside the door.

"*Now what?*" Lynette whispered, her eyes huge in the dark.

Suddenly the amber lights turned red. I heard the door groan. Turning, I shoved Lynette roughly back against the wall behind me.

Just in time.

The door slid open, revealing a brilliantly lighted earthen tunnel beyond. The light hurt my eyes. Silhouetted against the brightness, a short, bald man wearing blue coveralls and carrying a flashlight and a handi-talkie walked cautiously out into the shaft ten feet from where we hid.

The man raised the handi-talkie and spoke into it. He had a dry, raspy voice that told me he was no longer young. "I'm on the outside now, no sign of anything. Proceeding to the shed."

The little radio squawked back with a calm, tinny voice: "*Probably another coyote, Sam.*"

"Ten-four."

He took a couple of slow, shuffling steps in our direction. I snapped my mini-light back on, hitting him squarely in the eyes with the beam, and closed the space between us in two big steps. He made a terrified involuntary sound, sort of a choke, and went stiff. Having the muzzle of a revolver jammed into the side of your neck will do that to you.

"Don't yell," I whispered. "Don't move. I can blow your head off."

He obeyed. I grabbed the radio and handed it back to Lynette. Then I turned him around, being rougher than I had to be, to make sure he stayed scared, and shoved him toward the open doorway.

He stumbled through ahead of us. I kept the gun pressed painfully into his spine to discourage any thought of funny stuff.

Squinting in the brilliance, I saw a downsloping main tunnel, maybe ten feet in diameter, with new raftering reinforcing old. Other shafts slanted off the main one in several directions. While I was still making up my mind about what to do next, Lynette's reporter curiosity overcame her fright and she darted into one of the tunnels on our right.

A second or two later, her voice came back sharply: "*My gosh! Will you look in here, Brad? Wow!*" The mouth of the tunnel she had entered lit up brighter with repeated strobelight flashes.

I held our prisoner against the wall. He was well into his fifties, a soft, small man who smelled of beans and cigars. His eyes looked so scared I almost felt sorry for him.

"You can't get away with this," he choked.

Lynette's voice sang out again, urgently this time: "*Brad! Come in here!*"

I pushed the little guy ahead of me. The tunnel opened immediately into a much broader cavern. The ceiling lights sharply illuminated everything.

The room carved out of earth and solid rock was forty feet tall, at least twice as long and wide. It was packed. From floor to ceiling, it was tightly stacked with fifty-gallon barrels and large, white, plastic-enshrouded crates.

Just what I had expected—except for one thing.

The cavern was immaculate. Every container looked as intact

and solid as the day it was made. No signs of leakage . . . contamination . . . pollution of any kind. *What the hell?*

Lynette's strobe kept going off as she hopped around from here to there, aiming the camera like an old pro, shooting pictures as fast as the strobe would recharge. "Look at this one!" she gasped. "Wow! Let's try to find one that's leaking!"

All of them had stickers or painted labels on them: DANGER: *Toxic Waste.* But this place looked like the cleanest operation I had ever seen.

Before I could figure anything out, or even start absorbing my disappointment, a new sound—a siren alarm—started deafeningly in the shaft behind us. I heard doors slamming, footsteps running on dirt and rock. I shoved my scared, middle-aged prisoner away from me, and he darted for the doorway and was gone, his voice echoing back as he yelled for help. I shoved my .38 into my hip pocket and waited.

There was no chance to escape now, but I wondered what they thought they were going to do with two prisoners—one of them a reporter.

I also wondered what *I* was going to do to explain breaking into what looked like a model waste storage facility with not a trace of the toxic leakage I had been so sure I would find.

twenty-one

Elsewhere

New York City

Ardis Allen returned to the Plaza well after midnight to find five telephone messages, all from her vice president, Eric Rose, in Chicago. All five asked her to return the call at once. All five had "urgent" notations.

Ardis was irritated.

Her trip to the city for the international exposition on petrochemical support systems had started well. The day's meetings promised expanded business. The theater revival had been amusing, and dinner impeccable at the Italian restaurant off Madison near 60th. She had enjoyed the flirtation with her escort, and thought it might go further during her trip to London next month.

She was irritated because all the "urgent" messages were likely to be nothing more than panic by one of her executives back home, afraid to handle the most minor problem without first consulting her. She would never understand why she could not find men with the intelligence and courage to take action of their own, without constantly nagging her for approval of every little decision. The rate of turnover among executives in Allen Industries was 43 percent above industry norms. Ardis was convinced she had to fire so many executives because promising people so often turned out to be cowards and weaklings.

Carrying the message slips to the bedroom telephone in her suite, Ardis removed her gray satin heels and earrings, gratefully eased the zipper at the side of her Erickson gown, and stretched out on fluffed-up pillows before placing the return call.

The telephone out in Chicago—her executive's home number—rang once and was immediately answered. "Rose," his voice barked harshly.

"Eric. Ardis. I have some urgent message—"

"Mrs. Allen! Thank God we've located you at last!" It sounded like Rose put his hand over the mouthpiece, but she could hear him calling nervously, "She's on the line. You can stop trying those other numbers." Then his voice came back clearer: "I've got Finnerty, Judson, and Eastman here."

Ardis began to feel faint alarm. "All of you? At this hour? Eric, what's going on out there?"

"It's in Montana. At the Barnwell facility. There's been a break-in."

Ardis's feet hit the floor. "A *break-in*! How could *that* happen?"

"We don't know all the details yet. Two people got inside—"

"Inside? Inside the fence? Surely not inside the—"

"Inside! Inside! All the way inside! They saw everything and one of them had cameras—"

"Shit!" Ardis fumbled through things on the side table, looking for a cigarette. "Who was it? Where are they now? No, wait a minute, wait a minute—where are the intruders now? Did they get away?"

"The team at the cleanup test site called the local police. The two intruders have been taken to the jail in Elk City."

Mistake, Ardis thought, closing her eyes. "That was stupid! We should have kept them prisoner and not notified the law, at least until we could sort things out."

"I know, I know, that's what I told Heppley out there, but they were in a panic and somebody had already called the police chief out there. Our man—the one the lawyers hired to work the fence part-time—has been suspended in another deal. So the chief himself went out, along with a part-timer and a deputy-sheriff."

Ardis's stomach had begun to hurt. "He arrested them?"

"Yes. They're now in the Elk City jail."

"On what charges?"

"No charges yet. The police chief wants to charge them with breaking and entering, and I don't know what else, probably first-degree burglary. I talked to Heppley about that and told him not to sign a complaint for anything until we had instructions from you."

Ardis lit one cigarette off the other. "That's something, anyway." She rubbed her eyes, getting mascara on her fingers, while her mind raced. She could hardly believe how bad this might be. "Let me think a minute . . . Who *are* these people?"

"I'm afraid one of them was a young female reporter—"

"A reporter! God!" It was getting worse by the minute. "How did it *happen*?"

"Okay. Apparently they cut a hole in the security perimeter fence after dark tonight. The television surveillance system was down for maintenance."

"Why didn't the motion detectors pick them up?"

"They did. One of the site team—I think it was Allison, he's the chemist we—"

"Go on, go on."

There was loud, excited talking behind Rose's voice. Ardis could imagine her executives milling around, yelling at each other. Probably contradicting each other in their panic. At least this time the panic was justified.

Rose told her, "Allison went out, thinking it was probably an animal or something, as it always has been before. The intruders overpowered him, got through the security door, into Level One, Primary Holding."

Ardis groaned.

"That's where the rest of the site team captured them. The woman struggled and suffered a slight blow on the head. She's okay. I made sure of that. She's *okay*. She had been taking pictures, but our people took her cameras and smashed them. That was when they panicked about the young woman, who was bleeding, and decided they had to notify the law."

"That was stupid! The worst thing they could have done!"

"Well, Mrs. Allen, I agree with you. But I guess . . . you know how paranoid they all are about secrecy, and to have people walk right in that way . . . Well, they panicked."

"Let me get a few things straight, Eric. Is our site secure at this time?"

"It's locked, we have extra people on watch, and the police have left the scene. However, the police chief there, and the sheriff, both say they must visit the scene again in order to write their reports."

"Christ. And describe everything they see, I suppose?"

"I don't know." Rose sounded miserable.

"Get Cliffton on the phone out there," Ardis ordered. "We are not going to press charges. Our position is that it was all some kind of mistake. Tell him to do what he has to do to keep the law—and everybody else—off the property."

"Mrs. Allen—what if he can't?"

"God damn it, he's got to!"

"Okay . . . okay . . ." Rose sounded confused and uncertain.

"No one is to say anything to the press if some of this starts to get out," Ardis added, beginning to think of things that had to be done to contain the damage—if possible. "No one says *anything*. Understood, Eric?"

"Yes, Mrs. Allen."

"All right. Tell Cliffton to talk to those people before they're released from jail. He is to emphasize that what they saw was a *clean* dumpsite, a perfect one. He is to do everything in his power to convince that reporter that she has no story—there's no pollution. Understood?"

"I understand, Mrs. Allen. But if she's smart enough to suspect that we've been trying to cover up an unauthorized dumpsite while we secretly clean it out—"

"God damn it, it's his business to make sure she doesn't think of anything like that!"

"But what if she understands a little about EPA regulations? What if she figures out that we've never filed a report on this site, and we're liable for federal penalties that could amount to—"

"Eric, all that is precisely what we have to keep from happening! Damn it, it might have been simpler if they just hadn't called the police! And why in the *hell* hadn't Cliffton and Wells found new part-time fence guards? Is everybody out there an idiot?"

"Mrs. Allen, all I know is what I've told you."

"Tell Cliffton he is to use his own judgment on this part, because I know a lot of reporters who are too stupid to be swayed by money. It makes them practically impossible to deal with. But if he sees a chance to, ah, compensate that reporter for loss of a possible story, then that's authorized. Just make sure he understands how careful he has to be in that regard. All we would need at this point is for the little twit to be able to write that we tried to buy her off!"

"Mrs. Allen." Rose sounded frightened. "Pardon me. But if one of them is a reporter, she was out there looking for a story. And you know how the press are. She *got* a story, even if it's not exactly the one she probably thought she would find. It might be real hard—if not impossible—to keep both those people quiet."

"That's bullshit," Ardis snapped. "Anybody can be bought if the offer is presented right. It's just a question of subtlety, and how much it takes. Get Cliffton on it. And I want you out there, Eric. Now. You're listed as operations manager in all the Barnwell papers. Nobody will automatically link you to us. If they do, later, maybe by then you'll have controlled all the damage. Take the Lear. Call Slade. You can leave within an hour."

"Are you coming out, Mrs.—"

"No. That wouldn't look good. You're to lay low as much as you can. If I showed up, it would definitely tip the Allen Industries tie-in. I'm going to—" Ardis paused, rubbing her forehead in thought of the alternatives. "I'm going to stay right here with the exposition at this time. But I want regular reports, Eric. You ought to be in Elk City before daylight. As soon as you know anything further, you're to call me here. I'll activate the satellite pager so you can get me anywhere, any time. Understood?"

"Yes, Mrs. Allen."

"Is there anything else you can tell me at this time?"

"Just the names of both people who broke in. The woman is named Lynette Jordan—"

"I remember her. She's the little snip I assumed was guilty. She thought I would drop everything for an interview with her when I was out there. Damn! And the other name?"

"Smith, first name Brad."

Ardis Allen went cold from head to toe. The only explanation for

Smith's involvement was that he had already figured out the Allen–Barnwell connection—some hint of why she wanted the resort land. Now, in his break-in, he had confirmed at least part of what previously must have been only clever suspicion.

Good God! If he had gotten this far, how many more deductions might he make?

Ardis swayed. She began to see the real dimensions of the disaster. How was she going to keep the lid on all of this?

Chicago

It was past three A.M. when Theodore Judson left the corporate headquarters of Allen Industries and made his way to his car in the underground parking. Judson, fifty, was brutally tired. But his vindictive excitement made the fatigue only a druggy backdrop to the energy flowing out of his glandular system.

It took Judson almost forty minutes to drive the empty streets to his apartment. While driving, he joyfully, repeatedly, reviewed everything he had heard tonight, along with what he was going to do about it.

A single lamp burned in the living room of his silent apartment. He did not so much as bother to light more lights before going to the telephone. He looked up the number he wanted in his Rolodex and started punching it in. *You passed me over twice, Ardis,* he thought. *You viciously terminated Paul Dominick, the best man our company ever had. Now let's see how you like being screwed, you bitch.*

The telephone at the other end of the line rang repeatedly. *Come on, come on!* Judson thought fiercely.

Finally a voice answered: husky, unfirm, elderly. "Yes? Who is it?" Jeremy Jeffries, vice-chairman of the board, was 70, and at this hour he sounded every year of it.

"Mr. Jeffries," Judson said, "this is Theodore Judson. I feel compelled to report to you that Mrs. Allen has been keeping a terrible secret from the board of directors. Now, the secret is coming out. Out of loyalty to the firm, sir, I beg you to listen to what I have to tell you."

twenty-two

Chief Manley Hamm came back to the cell with a breakfast tray for me a little past eight o'clock the next morning. He looked worse than I felt.

"Morning," he grunted. He shoved the tray under the old-fashioned bars. "Flapjacks and java. Good enough?"

I discovered the pancakes were still hot. "If these are from the cafe down the street, I think I'm beginning to feel better."

Hamm shifted his weight from one foot to the other. "You want to tell me what this is all about?"

"What did the people at the old mine say it was about?"

The chief's face formed a million wrinkles. "They're acting weird. Not saying anything."

"Well, then, for the time being maybe I'll just act weird too. How is Lynette feeling this morning?"

"She's fine. Right now she's taking a shower, and my wife is standing outside the door." Hamm looked hard at me. "What in the hell *is* that stuff out there in that old mineshaft?"

"You were in there, chief. What did it look like to you?"

Hamm's facial furrows deepened. "Looked like waste stuff. Stuff that hadn't ought to be in there. Aren't they supposed to have signs up and all, for a toxic waste dump? Isn't there regulations and all?"

"Go back east and ask them those questions at Love Canal," I suggested.

Now his face really fell. "Shit oh dear," he muttered.

Some kind of door chime sounded down the hall, in the outer office. He turned and waddled out of the cell area.

I attacked the breakfast. It was good. Even the lukewarm coffee hit the spot. The fact that I had an appetite surprised me. Nothing had gone quite as I had expected.

Hamm was gone a long time.

When he came back, he had his big keyring in his hand. "Well, this is your lucky day." He shoved a key in the cell door lock and turned it. "They say they don't want to press charges against you."

"You mean we're free to go?"

"That's what it looks like," Hamm replied glumly.

"Who told you that?"

"Company lawyer. He's out front. He wants to talk to you and Lynette before you go. You can use my extra office."

"I don't get it."

"Brother, that makes two of us. Follow me."

I followed the little man through the corridor and into the front office. There we found Lynette already waiting beside the gray-haired, freckled Mrs. Hamm. Lynette looked pale and shaky.

"You all right?" I asked.

"Sure," she said with a game little smile. "But damn. Did your cell have as many bugs as mine did?"

"I didn't know if some of those were bugs or ponies."

She shuddered. "They're letting us out."

"So I hear."

"All right, all right," Hamm muttered, producing big brown envelopes with our personal things in them. "Please make sure everything on the inventory sheet is in the envelope, then sign here that you got everything."

We obeyed.

"My cameras were broken," Lynette said.

"Sue," Hamm snapped. He pointed to the closed door to an adjacent office. "In there, if you please?"

We obeyed again. As we entered the tiny, musty office, a thickset man in a rumpled gray business suit rose from behind the barren desk at the far wall.

"Mr. Cliffton?" Lynette burst out in surprise.

Cliffton—I assumed of the sign I had seen on a small building on Main Street. CLIFFTON AND WELLS, ATTYS AT LAW—came around the desk and gave her a brief, phony paternal hug. "Lynette, I'm certainly sorry we've had all this unpleasantness." He extended his hand to me. "And you must be Brad Smith, sir. Hello."

Lynette demanded, "You represent Barnwell Mining?"

Cliffton went back behind the old desk and sat down, motioning us to the three straight chairs arranged in front of us. "Yes, Lynette. Our firm has watched after the company's local interests for a long time. No great secret about that."

Lynette wasn't having any. "You could have fooled me!"

"Well." Cliffton avoided eye contact and looked uncomfortable. He took a cigar from his inside coat pocket. "Anyone mind if I smoke?"

"Yes," Lynette said.

Face coloring, Cliffton put the cigar away again. "To get right to the point here, folks, what we have is an embarrassing situation. But one that I think can be easily resolved. You see, my client has been renting its old mine facility to another company for temporary storage of certain, ah, caustic materials. As each of you saw for yourselves, the storage is clean and secure. All perfectly proper. The materials are in the process of being moved out of the site, and in another few months it will be pristine again. Just like nothing ever happened.

"However, to avoid unnecessary public concern, the local temporary storage has been kept confidential. All perfectly legal. So there's no cause for concern on any of that." He eyed Lynette. "No story, either, as you can see."

Lynette glared at him and didn't fall for the lawyerly ruse of getting her to nod or agree.

Discomfited, Cliffton took out his cigar again, put it back away again. "Well. The company doesn't want any publicity, obviously. People would misunderstand, don't you see. So after serious consultations, it has been decided that the best thing for everyone is simply to let bygones be bygones. A quid pro quo, as it were. My client will overlook your breaking and entering, and press no charges whatsoever. In exchange, you will understand my client's position and make no public disclosure of this temporary—and completely harmless—storage arrangement."

Lynette's chin jutted combatively. "I'm not sure everything you say is completely accurate, Mr. Cliffton. I happen to know that companies maintaining toxic-waste dump sites are required by law to file regular reports with the EPA. Have those reports been filed?"

"Of course!"

"Well, if that's true, then how do you explain the fact that nobody around here knew anything at all about the site?"

Cliffton spread his hands. "There are thousands of those reports filed every year! They're routine! And you yourself saw that this site is harmless, perfectly maintained! Why should there be any publicity?"

"I guess we'll see about that," Lynette bit off. Then she sprang a question that showed how sharp she really was: "Who's the parent company, incidentally?"

Like most "incidental" statements, this one wasn't incidental at all. It was the one I had been waiting to ask. Cliffton turned the color of old underwear.

"I am not at liberty to divulge," he said thickly.

"Well," Lynette said, sticking her chin out again, "I can't speak for Brad, but I'm a *reporter*. If the deal is no charges for silence, I guess I'm just going to have to go back to jail."

"No, no," Cliffton said hurriedly, sweat appearing on his forehead. "None of that is necessary, not necessary at all! Look, people. I'm only trying to make clear to you that no harm has been done here. No crime. Therefore, no story." He spread his hands again. "No story. But of course you are free at any rate. I have only been trying to talk sense, here."

Lynette stood. "Well, I guess we're free to go, then?"

"Of course! I—"

She turned to me. "Hey, Brad. I'll call you at the resort later, right? I've got a lot of checking up to do."

She turned and steamed out of there. Cliffton stood as still as a man who had seen a ghost. I went into the outer office, expecting to see Chief Hamm. He was there, all right, and so was his wife. But the other person in the office surprised me a little.

"Hello, pal," he said with his crooked grin. "I'm told they're granting amnesty to the burglars, and you're free to go."

"Collie," I told him, "you always show up at the times I least expect you."

"Be glad it's not Fred."

"Oh, yes, Fred. I assume he's too busy boiling the oil?"

Collie put an arm over my shoulder. "I've got a rental car outside. He's free to go, Chief Hamm? Thanks a million. So long!"

I gave him directions for the resort. We drove out of town. The cold front had blown through and we had a brilliant, sunny day with the temperature around 45 and the snow on the mountains looking blinding-white from a thin recoating that must have fallen at higher altitude in the night. Collie, wearing dense wool slacks and a pullover, drove hard and well, as he always did. He seemed to enjoy the mountain road.

"I know what you're thinking," I said.

"What?" he asked.

"There's been a breach of security at the air force lab, Sylvester is somewhere in the area, and instead of attending to business I've been out playing cops and robbers."

He glanced at me, then turned his eyes back to the twisting road. "You said that, not me."

"Fine. It's all true. Right now, however, I'm not sure that's the point."

"What is the point, then? And what are you so steamed up about?"

"I figured Ted Treacher's troubles must stem at least in part from pressure being exerted by Allen Industries. Then I got thinking about that old mineshaft, the high incidence of deaths from things like leukemia and lymphoma around here, and I put two and two together. What I came up with was the theory that Allen Industries must have some bad shit stored in that mine."

"Which they do, right? You proved that with your Dick Tracy act last night."

"Collie. The site is *clean*."

He didn't say anything to that; kept driving.

"Clean," I repeated.

"So?"

"I think it's always been clean. I think they were the source of the pressure on Ted, because it's an illegal dumpsite they want to clean out in secrecy. *But that site is not the cause of the illnesses around here.*"

"I think," Collie replied after a long silence, "that what you're trying to get into here is irrelevant."

"That was a shock last night, Collie, to walk in expecting to see crap leaking into the ground—into the aquifer for Elk City—and instead see what looks like a textbook, clean operation. I did a lot of thinking about that in jail last night. Jail is a great place to think."

"Is this conversation necessary? You're out now and we still have a problem on our hands—"

"It was the lab, wasn't it." I made it a statement, not a question.

"I don't know what you're talking about."

"It was the lab."

"It was the lab *what*? Look, Brad. We've known each other a long time. Don't talk riddles to me."

"It's no riddle to you, Collie. They're doing EMP research out there. Electromagnetic pulse radiation. High-power stuff. Anti-satellite technology. You aim the dish and you send up a pulse of radiofrequency energy that blows the circuits in the enemy satellite. Or you hit an incoming ICBM with it and wreck its computerized trajectory."

He didn't say anything. I waited, but he refused to respond.

Goaded, I went on. "There's controversy about EMP. I read about the Boeing lawsuits. The contention is that workers were exposed to EMP, and later developed various forms of cancer. *Just like in Elk City.*"

"Nothing is proven," he replied. "There are lawsuits about all kinds of things all the time. Don't jump to conclusions."

"I'm not, on that case. I have no idea where the truth lies. But this is different. Here, the EMP radiation is focused in a very narrow beam, and at very high power. *If* EMP can cause cancer, and *if* at some time in the past the lab out there had a malfunction, and sprayed all or part of Elk City with a full-power burst—"

"You have no evidence of that," he said quickly. "You're leaping to crazy, unsupported conclusions."

"One of the first things I heard about when I got here, Collie, was a mention of the day a few years ago when a lot of townspeople were irritated because their TV sets blacked out during the Super Bowl. I didn't think much about it at the time, but I sure had time to remember it and think about it last night. Was that the day? Did an antenna malfunction and send the pulse along the earth instead of into the sky? Have there been other days? If I ask around, will I maybe start hearing about the day all the automatic garage door openers lifted doors without being told? Or refused to work at all? Or maybe microwave ovens malfunctioned. Or electric clocks went haywire. Or VCRs—"

"God damn it, Brad, enough!"

In my rage I was not going to accept that. "How many test failures were there? How many times has Elk City been sprayed with EMP—"

"Just once," Collie cut in, his voice flat with frustrated anger at me. "Just that one failure. A long time ago. A computer aiming device misreported elevation of the dish. But nobody can prove any connection between that incident and any illness!"

I leaned back in the Ford's front seat and took a deep, bitter breath. "So all this time people have been dying. And we've kept it a secret, and kept right on testing."

"There's no way it could happen again. The entire basis of the testing is different now. That's the truth!"

I thought about it. "I'm going to believe that. But what I can't understand, Collie, is why you couldn't tell me some of this at the start. You guys lied to me again."

"I didn't know it then."

I did not reply. My sense of betrayal was intense.

After a while Collie asked, "So are you still onboard?"

"I don't know," I said. "Am I?"

"I'm going to drop you off at the resort. Then I have to get back to Missoula. I'm meeting Skurlock and a couple of other people there. We have to reevaluate. I'll let you know."

I didn't answer that, either.

He dropped me off and drove away. I walked into the lodge and found myself right back in Ted Treacher's world, humming right along on the road to disaster, as if nothing had happened. They didn't even know what had happened last night.

"Some kind of disturbance over at the old mine last night,"

Avery Whitney told me when we met. He cocked his good eye at me. "You know anything about it?"

"Nope," I said.

"You weren't in your cabin last night."

"Nope."

"Nowhere around here."

"Nope."

He pushed me into the chair of the office desk. "I've got requisitions to sign, here. I need some accounts paid, pronto. Then I want you outside to approve the plans I got for setting up the tournament bleachers and all."

It was like going through the looking glass, but I forced myself to pay attention to the vouchers and invoices while he blustered around, making threatening phone calls to suppliers and repairmen. I tried not to make mental calculations of how fast the money was running through our accounts. After that, I went with him outside. On our walk to the courts, he pointed out where the food concession tents were going to go, and how ropes would be set up for crowd control. He had done a lot very quickly, and I was grateful. I resisted the impulse to ask if he was sure there would be a crowd to control.

When we got to the courts we found guests playing on several of them, but we walked around behind the south end lines, between the retaining fence and the row of permanent bleachers along that side, reaching the center few courts that were not occupied.

"What I figure," Whitney told me, "is this. We already got these stands on the west side. But we need a lot more seating, right?"

"Right," I said.

"Are you paying attention? You look like you're thinking about something else."

"I'm paying attention. Go ahead." I concentrated.

He pointed. "What we do is, we create a center court. We put roofing paper all over courts eight and ten, and Visqueen plastic on top of the roofing paper. Then we erect the temporary wood bleachers there on eight and ten, facing in, making nine our center court. Behind these bleachers we can stand a couple, three rows of other bleacher seats facing out, so we create other watching areas for courts one to seven and eleven to sixteen. You run the main match of the time on nine, with other matches as necessary on the outer courts."

"Sounds great. How do you stand the bleachers up?"

He gave me a sarcastic look. "With our hands."

"You know what I mean, dammit. Do you bolt them down, or—"

"Yep, you do. We'll have to drill us some holes along the edges of the side courts. It won't be too bad, not too destructive."

I decided to ask the hard question. "Have you found any bleachers yet?"

"I'll need another twelve thousand, five hundred dollars," he answered.

"What? For what, for Christ sake?"

"Seven thousand and five hundred to rent the bleachers, five thousand to move 'em in here and pay the people to erect 'em."

"Have you *found* bleachers yet?"

"Why, hell yes, you blamed fool. Do you think I would be making all these plans if I hadn't? I'm renting them from the high school."

"If bleachers were available locally, why didn't we know about it earlier? Sally Wallis said she couldn't find any. Oh. Of course. She didn't look."

"Well, I did."

"And the school said okay?"

"At these rates they were thrilled outta their minds when I asked."

I walked back to the lodge noticing some of the other details: the fresh paint, the markers for power that would be fed to concession stands, the new signs standing behind a storage building, waiting for the paint to dry. Again I had the feeling of never-never land. Getting Avery Whitney's help was the best thing I had done. He was going to make the tournament *happen*.

Darkness had long since come when I got to Missoula that night. Little house and street lights, white and amber, twinkled on the lower mountain slope on the east side. That part of the city looked like a Christmas tree tumbled onto its side. Stars blazed in the cool night sky, limning the lumpy shape of nearby Blue Mountain to the west, and a few high clouds partly obscured a spooky gibbous moon. I had had to come see Ted tonight, but I felt paralyzed for want of sleep. I stopped at a convenience store for another plastic cup of coffee, then headed on to the hospital.

I had not heard from Collie Davis or Fred Skurlock. Lynette Jordan had called with some very interesting news.

"They won't print it," she started out, huffy.

"Who won't?" I demanded.

"These damn guys here in Elk City. So I'm taking Bobby Winkleman with me as we're heading for Salt Lake City. I bet we can get somebody *there* interested!"

"Why are you taking Bobby, after he chickened out on us?"

"Because he developed the film and made the prints."

"*What* film?" I asked, startled.

"I had changed out one roll before those goons grabbed us and mussed us up," she said blithely. "I managed to get that roll in my pants before they tied us up. Bobby made some dynamite prints, and I'm taking him along to vouch for their authenticity."

"Lynette," I said admiringly, "you are a wonder."

"Sure, I know that!" she said cheerfully.

"Just be careful, all right?"

"My gosh! What could happen?"

"Did you ever hear of Karen Silkwood?"

"Oh. Wow. You're right. We'll be careful. But I still think we've got a story here, and I'm going to try to pursue it."

I wished her luck, then found myself sucked back into the vortex of the resort mess. Tournament preparations—brackets, confirming phone calls, talks with agents and sponsors—filled up most of the rest of the afternoon. Calls to the media in several cities, including Salt Lake and Denver, finally got the ball rolling on badly needed publicity. I also made reservations for either Karyn or myself to make a big looping trip around the major cities in a four-state area next week to publicize the tournament. If we ever got that far.

There was also just time for a brief meeting with our part-time accountant, Mack Redman. He gave me a preliminary report on some of the financial records Ted Treacher had hidden from him. There was a short-term, one-pay note that Ted had taken out personally. It was overdue. That was when I knew I had to get to Missoula.

Now, with the drive behind me, I parked in the hospital lot and made my way up to Ted's room. There was a new cop on duty. While he was making a telephone call to make sure I was okay, I went in anyway.

Ted sat propped up in the bed, his white head bandages and the cast on his arm bright under the ceiling lights. Karyn Wechsting, in the blue plastic chair beside his bed, looked up from her magazine.

"Tennis, anyone?" I said, and quite properly felt like an idiot.

Ted managed what was supposed to be a smile. "Hello."

I gave Karyn a brief hug and awkwardly patted Ted's good shoulder. Karyn looked worn out and pale, and he looked like he had been through a cement mixer: pasty, drawn, dry-lipped, skeletal in the harsh light. I pulled up the other chair. "Thought I'd run by and see how you're doing."

He nodded, the ghastly smile holding. "Okay."

"Hurting?"

"Not much. They give me pills."

Karyn volunteered, "He's refusing the pills now."

He said, "You can become a dope addict in one of these places."

The cop opened the door and glared in at me and closed the door again.

"I didn't wait for his ID check," I explained.

Karyn said, "You look tired."

I grinned at her. "You don't look too good yourself."

Ted said, "You're both doing too much—you ought to get out of here." For an instant his eyes looked like he was going to cry.

I gave them the condensed version of hiring Avery Whitney and getting ready for the tournament, and left out everything about Sally Wallis and the other fun things that had been taking place.

Ted asked, "How can we pay Whitney?"

"I put a little money in."

He sat up straighter, making his IV apparatus jingle. "You mustn't do that!"

"Too late. I already did." Then, seeing his anguished expression, I added, "I've been looking around for a little investment. I figure we can work out the details on profit-sharing later."

"But you know by now what a mess we're in! And with Allen Industries not coming in, I've *failed*. We can never pay—"

"Bullshit, *kimosabe*. The tournament will put Bitterroot Valley on the map. I've got a lot of other ideas, too. I've always wanted to own a piece of something like this. By the time you're on your feet again we'll be ready to make a fight of it side-by-side. So just cool it and concentrate on healing, okay?"

Now his eyes did fill, the kind of sudden, shocking flood that hits people sometimes after they have been desperately hurt. "You're crazy." His voice was so hoarse I could scarcely understand him. "I refused to face the facts. I made mistake after mistake. Even getting you up here was a selfish, desperate gamble, hoping you would salvage the tournament—impress Ardis Allen. But I've failed."

"That's what you say," I told him, making my voice gruff. "After you're better, we'll argue it out and you'll see how wrong you are."

He sat there looking at me and the tears ran down his cheeks and splashed off his chin onto his chest, making big gray splotches on the hospital linen.

Not knowing what to do or say, I turned to Karyn. "So you found us a good lawyer?"

She grinned. "Oh, my, did I."

We talked about that a while, ignoring Ted's tears. Then Karyn mentioned meeting a local tennis pro who idolized Steffi Graf. So we talked about Steffi in an aimless, gossipy way, and then gossiped about Martina and the size of her entourage these days, and I launched into a long and excruciatingly boring tale of how we had traveled in the olden days, alone, carrying our own suitcase and rackets. About that time Ted rallied a little and said some of us had been born twenty years too soon, and I said if we had been born later, we would have missed some of the good stuff like Vietnam.

"I never think about Nam," he told us. "That's all behind me."

I didn't challenge him. But I didn't believe him, either. I had heard him protest in the same words before. Men and women who saw combat in that war will often say such things—repeatedly. I think I came out of it better than most, but it will never be entirely "behind me." I still catch myself going back there in my mind, and it usually takes me by surprise and I am simply *there again* for an instant or an hour, sent by some sight or sound or smell. I didn't like it then and I don't like it now. I saw too many things and was too scared, and I wish I could forget some of the things I saw, but I never will, and the smells will be with me always.

I don't know if we should have been there. I suspect it was all a waste of time and life and money. I went. I got back. That's all I know. Leave the platitudes to the hawks who stayed home and did National Guard duty. They can talk enthusiastically about fighting because they never did any. People like that are good at being certain about most things anyway. I never was, and after Vietnam I am much worse at it.

"It's a funny thing," Ted mused now. "I didn't get a scratch over there. Now I'm back where it's supposed to be safe, and . . . this." He looked at his cast.

"Well, we'll get you a medal anyway," I told him. "I can't promise a pension, though. I guess we'll just have to get rich off the resort."

"Is Avery really helping?"

"Oh, yes."

"I can't imagine that."

"He's good help."

"I know that . . . I know that. I just . . . can't imagine it."

I changed the subject. "Are they feeding you in here? You look skinny."

He nodded. "I've started holding down food now."

"You want anything from outside when I come back?"

"I can't . . . think of it."

I got up. I had had all I could take right now. "Okay, Ted. Get better. Everything is in good hands in the meantime."

I got out of there.

Karyn followed me into the hall moments later and we went to the lounge. I lit a cigarette and wished I could inhale two at once.

"God damn it," I said.

"He's better, though, Brad. He really is."

I didn't think so, but I didn't say anything. There are blows that deck a man permanently.

Karyn went on, "And I'm going to make Lassiter pay for this. If the police don't file charges, I'll sign a complaint and *make* them do it. Maybe our lawyer can file civil charges, too."

"You've done a lot already, Karyn."

She opened her little purse and took out a small piece of paper and handed it over. "Take this."

It was a check. Her personal account. I read the amount. "You can't afford this!"

"Don't tell me what I can or can't afford, you dummy. Take it. Put it in the operating account, or wherever it's most needed."

"You could lose every bit of it!"

"You put money in, didn't you?" she shot back.

"Well . . . sure. But that's different."

"The hell it is, cowboy. Take the check."

With a deep breath I put it in my shirt pocket. "He doesn't deserve you."

"Right, right," she said, the sarcasm heavy in her tone.

"You look beat," I insisted, all my mother-hen flags waving. "You have to get some rest."

"I want to be here with him."

"You don't have to be here all the time."

"I love him, you jackass! Where else would I be?"

So I left her there in the lounge and went downstairs, passing some happy people chattering about a new baby and how cute she was, how like her daddy, and returned to the Bronco. I headed south into the mountains, going home.

Home. That sounded funny. I didn't feel like I knew where home was anymore. Physically, emotionally—any way at all.

I told myself my feeling of failure and lostness was just fatigue.

God knows I was tired enough. I did not have the stamina I once had. Which brought me face-to-face once more with the growing knowledge of my own aging, my own irreparable calendar losses. And so I mentally slunk into self-pity.

Middle age—ghastly term—had begun to slip up on me, arriving long before I had anticipated it: the creaky back in the morning, an occasional preoccupation with what is politely referred to as regularity, the failure of my knee to come back after the last surgery, shorter breath and slower reflexes and thoughts about my smoking and cancer, and the unrecognized habit of scanning the obituaries for the name of a friend. And when there was no friend listed, glancing down the ages of the newly dead, feeling vaguely reassured when they were in their 70s or 80s (hell, I've got almost half my life left!), and ignoring the tiny tug of worry when they were 40 (a fluke; I'm in good shape).

OVERHEAD

Once you are truly young, and life goes by like a videocassette in rapid search forward. Then—maybe, just maybe—the best part is over, but you're still agile, still optimistic, still with not many losses. And then one day it has been five years since you were on center court, and then it has been ten, and a writer refers to you as a senior. And the tiny voice tries to cry out: *It's getting away from me! Where did it go? How much time can there be left?*

I had a friend when I was a kid whose name was Harrigan. He lifted weights and worked out regularly long, long before that was accepted behavior. He played for USC and later in the NFL, and we exchanged notes once in a while and in 1978 had a memorable afternoon and evening together in San Francisco. Harrigan in those days was like my friend Barney in Wyoming and my parents and my sister and a tennis coach I had in college: perhaps I didn't see them often, but they were *there* somewhere, invisible in the dimness around me on the highwire up near the dim top of the circus tent, a mile above the tent floor, subtly helping me control the sway of the wire, the precision of my next steps. Just knowing they were there made me surer-footed.

Then I read about Harrigan in a short at the back of *Sports Illustrated.* Jerry (Beeswax) Harrigan, former wide receiver for the Cincinnati Bengals, buried last week in Napa. Harrigan was on an escalator in a department store in San Francisco when the tread broke away and he fell into the machinery and was crushed. Harrigan was 36.

My God. Eaten by an escalator! Is that supposed to be funny, or what, Beeswax? Isn't it bad enough that you can walk out your front door and be slashed by a kid crazy on dope? Or run down by a sweet suburban housewife intent for just the wrong few seconds on reversing the Huey Lewis tape in her Ciera's dashboard unit? Or poisoned by something that got into your can of tuna halfway around the world? Or done in by some unfilterable rogue virus that wanders by and takes up residence in your lymph system? Or suddenly become rapidly cooling meat on a golf course because a heart muscle or a blood vessel in the brain has been quietly working along for forty or fifty years, waiting for just the right moment to prove it has been defective since birth? Quote Pete Maravich during a pickup game: "I feel really good." Ten seconds later, dead.

I missed Harrigan. I missed a lot of people. I missed my parents most of all. The vacancies in my life grew and grew, and with each new loss I crept deeper into the middle—or perhaps the ending—of my life.

We walk along, balancing with our pole, like the Wallendas. We have our family and friends there on the wire with us, helping us balance under the umbrella of their nearness. The farther out from the safety of the platform we go, the higher is the precipice below, the more blinding the smoky spotlight glare, and the wire swings with a gentle, deadly rhythm. We feel good at first, and move with confidence. But then we begin to realize how precarious our position really is, how far the fall.

Still, we move on because that is what we do. Slower, with legs that have begun to shake. The wire trembles. Behind us, someone cries out, and their voice fades away. We look back. They are gone. We resteady the pole, lick our lips, put one resin-coated slipper ahead of the other, take another step. But as we go deeper into the vast black obscurity, the spotlight from far below harsher in our eyes, we feel the wire swaying more dangerously, and we hear other cries, and we dare not turn to look back again because we know others have gone, and maybe already we are out here entirely alone. We are not as strong, each loss diminishes us, we need the others more than we ever did before.

Another cry, another loss. Why not give up and fall? *There might be a net*. But we do not think there is a net. We begin to realize more clearly that there isn't a far end of the wire, either, and our turn is coming. But we press on, secretly more frightened and unsure, more lonely and alone. The wire sways and cuts into the soles of our feet. We tremble, take still another step, smile for the audience impossibly far away. *Don't fall, anyone. Please, don't anyone else fall. It's getting scary up here. I can't do this alone.*

Maybe some of the fright and the sense of diminishing years had been factors in making me react so conservatively when the oil bust took so much of my savings. Maybe without thinking about it I had been hedging my bets, calculating for my old age.

The realization added to my anger. I told myself I was not old yet. I could always make a modest but decent living as a club pro or college coach. And I hadn't had a major magazine article turned down in over three years . . . I was getting *good* at writing about tennis for a national audience.

And I hadn't been *that* bad on this assignment, I tried to tell myself. Ted and the resort could still be salvaged. The security breach at the air force lab could still be sealed. We might still find Sylvester—and hope it wasn't the other way around.

My sense of disillusionment about the lab, and the old accident, was still intense. I did not know what I was going to do about that. But for right now I had to shelve it.

Right now I had to stay awake and get back to Elk City.

It seemed enough. I stopped at a little café in the country, a pool of light alongside the mountain road, and bought fresh coffee. Then, fighting sleep, I drove on.

twenty-three

Elsewhere

Elk City, Montana

Morning. Ten o'clock and cloudly, so it seemed earlier. Jack Lassiter drove his pickup through the weeds toward the old house.

The family house . . .

Purvis Lassiter had moved his bride to the house in the canyon four miles east of Elk City on the eighteenth day of March, 1946. It was a new house then. A lowering sky spat bitter snowflakes driven by a harsh, high north wind. The house, raw and largely unfinished inside, felt even colder than the wintry day beyond the bare-stud walls, but Purvis Lassiter had high hopes.

He carried in some of the freshly chopped firewood he had stacked along the west side a few days earlier, and soon had a fire roaring in the big stone fireplace. After the room had begun to warm, he made love to his wife on coats spread on the floor in front of the fire.

Purvis Lassiter said it was going to be a great and happy home.

For a while it was. Eleanor Lassiter was a big woman who appeared as strong as her husband. In reality she was not nearly that sturdy. But she held up her end of the hard work in making the house a home, and in 1947 she delivered her first son after a difficult and complicated labor. The boy was named Purvis Jack. A second son was born six years later, and he was christened Jewell, after Eleanor's brother. From the start everyone called the child Buster.

His birthing, too, was long and difficult, and some people said Eleanor never fully regained her health after that.

In 1959, Purvis Lassiter fell from the barn roof he was repairing. When his boys got to him, he said he could not move. He was never able to move again. He lived another four years.

Eleanor stayed on the farm, cash-rented the land to a rancher, and got a job in town to make ends meet. Continual stress further weakened her. In 1966 she caught a cold, which turned into influenza, which turned into pneumonia, and died.

The oldest boy, Jack, was 19 then. Not three months after his mother's death, he was drafted. Buster, 13, lived with his namesake uncle for a few years and the farmhouse was rented. Then he too was drafted. By the time he was released from the service, his older brother Jack was back on the homestead, living alone, acting crazy sometimes. Buster moved back in too, intent on helping Jack—fulfilling what he saw as family responsibility.

They had lived together in the house since that time. They didn't bother much about keeping things up, so the ramshackle old farmhouse had lost its gutters and most of its paint and a couple of windows on the west side, which had been replaced by pieces of plywood. One side of the front porch sort of leaned to the south. A few firs had volunteered here and there, and the weeds stood up five feet high, making the place look abandoned, except at night when the lights were sometimes on.

Despite its rundown state, the old house was important to Buster Lassiter. Buster was sentimental. Jack was not. He would have insured the place and then burned it for the money long ago except that Buster, on being told of the scheme, became very upset and swore he would turn Jack in if he ever carried out the plan.

Jack had never quite forgiven Buster for that. Jack was good at holding grudges.

Now, pulling along the pressed-down path through the high weeds that led to the front of the house, Jack pulled up behind

Buster's ancient Buick, turned the motor off, and went onto the front porch. He was bone-tired and bitter.

He turned the front doorknob and went into the house. The paper curtains had been drawn and it was really dark inside. His footsteps scraped softly on the bare wood floor.

"Jack?" a voice sang out from the dark living room to the right through double doors. "Izzat you?"

"It's me," Jack said, furious that he hadn't gotten in without having to talk to his stupid brother.

A light flashed on in the living room, revealing aged overstuffed furniture with clothing and coats piled on it and lamps with broken paper shades and little landslides of newspapers and magazines everywhere. Buster Lassiter rolled off the sofa where he had been sleeping and lumbered across the room, rubbing puffy eyes. He wore grayish long underwear, red wool socks.

"Go back to sleep," Jack told him. "I just came by for some stuff."

"Where you been?" Buster asked, his forehead wrinkling like it always did when he was worried.

"Around," Jack told him.

"I was worried, Jack. You been gone a long time. After you had that big commotion with Chief Hamm—"

"I can take care of myself," Jack cut in angrily. "I don't need no nursemaid."

"I know that, Jack. But where have you been?"

"Out looking for a job, what the hell do you think?"

Buster blinked stupidly. "Around town, you mean?"

"Where the hell do you think a man would get a job around this gawd-forsaken place? Hell no! I've been to Arvada and Tripptown, places like that."

Buster's shoulders sloped in visible relief. "You find something?"

"Not yet, but I'm still looking."

"Oh, Jack," Buster said. "I am real relieved, boy. I tell you true. I known how mad you was. I was real worried you might . . . you know—go after them fellers out at the resort, or something."

"Why would I do that?" Jack demanded. "Now, that would be real stupid, wouldn't it?"

"Well, yes, it would, Jack. But I know how you get mad . . . how you like to get even."

"Go back to sleep," Jack said. "I just came to get some fresh clothes and all. I've got me about four job interviews Saturday morning."

"Whew," Buster breathed, his boyish, stupid smile spreading. "I guess I worried for nothing, huh!"

Jack didn't answer him. He turned and went straight up the stairs to the second floor. A mouse scurried, startled, as he turned on the light in his bedroom. He grabbed the clothes he wanted and tossed them into a sack. Then he put his revolver and ammo in the sack with the clothes, and took his beautiful, customized Mauser rifle off the rack over the bed. He went downstairs.

"What are you doing with the rifle, Jack?" Buster called in alarm from the living room as Jack passed the door.

"I might get in some hunting," Jack called over his shoulder, and went on outside.

He was tossing the stuff in the pickup when Buster, looking scared again, appeared on the porch behind him. "Jack? You're not planning anything crazy, are you?"

"Not unless finding a new job is crazy," Jack flung back.

Buster frowned sadly, swaying forward and back like he always did when he was worried, baffled. "Jack?"

"What?" Jack yelled back angrily.

"Jack . . . There's something I got to know."

"What is it, meathead?"

"That night back a ways ago. The night you come in muddy and all. You said you'd got stuck in a crick."

Jack knew what was coming. He braced for it, feeling his anger swell. "So? Do you want to talk about the time I fell through the ice, too?"

His brother stared forlornly at him with those big, stupid eyes. "Jack, that was the night that there construction guy come up missing."

"I don't know what you're talking about." Jack started to climb into his truck.

"The construction guy! The one they found his body the other day! Higgins! That one!"

"What about him, Buster? Don't you even know they arrested Treacher for that? He's in the hospital up in Missoula, and when he's good enough to get out, they'll be slinging his ass in jail again and charging him with murder."

"Jack, it happened over there by the old mine. You work security over there. I hate to ask this of my own brother. But I need to know, Jack! What *really* happened to that man? What do you know about it?"

"Don't know anything."

"Jack!"

"You've got a hell of a nerve, Buster, thinking I had anything to do with that deal."

"Jack! I've got a right to know! You know I would go to my grave before I ever told a soul. But I got a right to know, Jack! I'm your brother! *What happened to that man?*"

Jack Lassiter studied this big, dumb, unlovely hunk who was his nearest blood kin. Jack was very, very tired and strung out. For reasons he did not understand, and didn't much care about understanding, he felt the urge to hurt Buster. He knew the secret would be safe, and he also knew it would hurt.

He stepped back away from the pickup truck. "Okay, Buster. I was on duty that night. When I got there, I found the gate had been left open. I went in and looked around. They have some people working in there. Secret. I walked up to the old shaft opening and found three, four of them standing around, scared shitless. One of them was wearing this big white suit, like you see them on TV wearing to fight fires or something. He'd even had a white hood on, but he'd taken that off, had it under his arm."

Jack paused, drawing breath, remembering.

"On the ground was this man," he went on. "Higgins."

"Oh, no," Buster moaned.

"He was dead. Not a mark on him. But he was dead, no doubt about that. And they was in a panic. Well, I could report it. And probably lose my job with them. Or I could help them out. So I decided to help them out. I took the body back to my jeep, drove over onto the golf course, found one of them places where they'd moved a lot of fresh dirt first, dug me a hole, put him in."

"Oh, no," Buster groaned again. "They killed him and you hid him!"

"They didn't kill him. He walked in there and turned and seen this man in the big white suit, and it scared the liver out of him. He just keeled over. Don't look at me like that, damn you! All I done was did them a favor!"

"You hid the body," Buster said, wringing his hands. "And now that other feller is going to be charged for it. Oh, Jack, this is terrible!"

"You just keep your yap shut, see?" Jack told him. "You asked, I told you. So now you can just keep your yap shut. I'm going to look for a new job again. So shut up about it!"

"Oh, Jack, oh my gracious, Jack—"

Jack Lassiter got in the truck and slammed the door. He started the engine and drove out through the weeds, letting them blot out the rearview picture of his stupid slob brother, still standing there with his weakling worried look on his ugly puss.

Well, you asked. Now you know.

The bitterness and rage pulsed in Jack's head, making it hurt. There were little lightning-flash pulses along the edges of his vision. The pulses were always high and to the right in the visual field. They signaled one of the headaches coming on. Jack had had the headaches for years now.

He felt disoriented and crazy. He did not know if all crazy people *knew* when they were being crazy, but he did. But being crazy was okay. You were what you were, and he had learned to live with it. All he had to do when he was in a crazy streak was be more careful about people watching him.

People watched him a lot. They talked about him. Sometimes, through an agency he did not understand, he could hear them talking about him: urgent voices, angry and hurried, whispering swift accusations in his left ear. He could never quite make out what they were saying but he knew it was bad stuff, all of it being said about him.

He reached the dirt road that led back to the highway, then turned onto it. He thought about being fired. *What am I going to do?* he wondered, and the thought carried with it an avalanche of desperation.

It was Smith, the other tennis player—the one still loose—who had caused all this, Jack Lassiter thought. Treacher couldn't have brought a complaint; nobody would believe a murderer. And nobody else would have had the nerve. But Lassiter knew Smith would not leave it alone. He would make it come out in the official probe that Lassiter had to have broken Treacher's arm. And then the chief would fire him for good—maybe even bring criminal charges.

Lassiter had treasured the police job, the power and closeness to big people in town. He had loved his night watchman job, too, because he knew funny, secret stuff went on out there sometimes, and he—*he!*—was important enough and trustworthy enough to be allowed to safeguard it and keep his mouth shut.

But now he didn't have the night watchman job at the mine, either.

All Smith's fault.

Lassiter hated Smith's kind anyway: smooth, always neat, wealthy, probably from a country club family. Never a problem in his life, a bastard that it was always easy for. Looking down on people like us, thinking we're scum. Making us lose our jobs.

Lassiter had felt this kind of rage in Vietnam. But he had never gotten to kill many people in Nam. They had killed a lot of his friends and he had never gotten sufficient revenge. The one time he had made the gooks pay, his own country had given him a court martial instead of the medal he had expected. Now he had to figure the best way to make Smith pay, once and for all.

Tripptown, Montana

"Shit!"

District Attorney L. L. Llewellen slammed his palm on the copy of the autopsy report lying on the desk in front of him. "This *can't* be right!"

Dr. Matt Simonds, the county's part-time official coroner, removed his pipe from between his bearded lips and nodded sadly. "It's right, Lew."

Llewellen slammed the report again, this time with the angry back of his hand. "The man was out there for days! You can't be sure! The mud and decomposition could mask anything!"

Simonds exhaled a cloud of aromatic smoke. "The Higgins corpse, just as it states there in my report, did suffer decomposition. And it was a hard, tough case. Why else would I ask the judge to approve bringing in a forensic specialist all the way from Minneapolis? That hurt my pride some. But I had to be *sure*."

"And now," Llewellen said bitterly, "you are?"

"Yes. There was sufficient tissue integrity to allow discovery of major trauma of any kind. And even if that were not so, examination of the contents of the skull resulted in indisputable evidence."

Llewellen stared at the disastrous report. His stomach sent out a sharp stab of pain, eating itself in anguish.

"We'll get another report," the district attorney said. "A second opinion."

It didn't faze Simonds, who had expected argument. "All organs have been preserved. The torso is on ice. But I've told you: the findings here are certain. Once we began careful examination of the contents of the skull, we agreed immediately. Get ten more consults, and I'm afraid you'll just be disappointed ten more times."

Llewellen held his head in his hands. "You're that sure?"

"The medical evidence is incontrovertible. Higgins died as the result of a congenital aneurysm at the base of the brain."

"Which just happened," Llewellen said with savage sarcasm, "to burst at the wrong moment."

Simonds stayed calm. He was a man whose sideline working for the county did not allow emotional involvement. "The aneurysm was weak from birth. It's not uncommon. Remember that famous basketball player who scored all the points? A health nut. Still young. Playing in a pickup game in a gym somewhere with friends. He had always had something like this, too. Some heart vessel, I think. It held up through all the stress of all those NBA games, all those miles of running under pressure and stress, on the verge of exhaustion. Didn't hold up that day. Burst. He died instantly. Nobody could have predicted it."

"So Higgins just happened to walk out there and have an aneurysm and drop dead—and then bury himself?" Llewellen said, sneering.

"Not saying there wasn't some kind of confrontation. Maybe something made his blood pressure jump: a fight, a scare, something. But he died of natural causes. You simply can't make murder stick on this one, Lew. Sorry."

"Manslaughter, then."

The doctor raised his shaggy eyebrows. "I'm no lawyer, but it doesn't sound very good to me. This is *an act of nature*, Lew. An *accident*. QED. Good defense lawyer can get in a dozen medical witnesses all to say that. And from what I hear, this man Treacher has got a good lawyer."

"Jefferson Tuhey," Llewellen said. "God! I hate that bastard!"

Simonds did not respond to that. "Sorry," he said wearily, and walked out of the office.

Llewellen sat still for a long time, looking at the wreckage of his case against Ted Treacher.

twenty-four

When I awoke the next morning and walked up toward the lodge, I saw a gantry truck out near the pool, and workers erecting the first concession tent. Avery Whitney was right there supervising, the lovely Melody alongside him. They waved. I waved back, and walked on to the main building. That was where I found Collie Davis, hunkered up defiantly against the cold north breeze, having coffee on the patio.

"It's too cold out here," I told him.

"I know," he said. "Sit down."

I sat.

"We're sort of at a crossroads here," he told me after I had signaled for my own coffee.

"Explain," I suggested.

He gave me a gimlet-eyed inspection. "Are you going to continue to try to assist?"

"Of course," I told him, surprised. "Why wouldn't I?"

"Because you figured out about the old lab accident, et cetera."

"You told me the tests are now being run differently, and are really safe."

"Yes."

"Is that the truth, Collie?"

He gave me a look. "Yes."

I waited while my waiter brought the pot and cup. He went away and I poured. "I have this urge to try to find out if the government has any plans whatsoever to offer restitution to the families of people who have died."

"Don't ask, Smith. I'm not a big dog in Washington and I can't give you any answers and that's not what I'm here for."

"And maybe a restitution program would blow the secrecy of the project, and, in today's political climate, cause it to be canceled?"

"You know as much about that as I do."

"I don't like it," I told him. "Furthermore, I don't think we've heard the last of the dump site out there. When Lynette Jordan's stories start seeing the light of day, the EPA is going to be in here. When they declare the site clean—as I feel sure they will—then it's going to raise questions all over again about why the cancer rates are higher than average. I think the lab's mistake is going to come out, Collie, sooner or later."

"You may be right," he said dourly. "In the meantime, we've got a security breach out there, and Sylvester spooking around. That's my business. I can try to do something about that, just like Skurlock. Now are you in or out?"

I met his eyes. It was not his fault. Maybe, ultimately, it was nobody's fault. Or maybe it was the fault of the goddamned endless competition between us and several other nations of the world. But he certainly couldn't stop that, any more than I could.

Maybe nobody could. Once the runners leave the blocks and the batons have already been passed through the first two relays, maybe all anyone can do is run as fast as they can, run until their heart bursts.

I told him, "I'm in."

He nodded. Then: "Your woman Sally Wallis is dead."

I spilled some of my coffee down the front of my warmup. "When? How?"

"They found her in her house last night. Neighbors noticed her car hadn't been moved for a day or two and called Hamm. He went out, found a broken window, the house rifled and all torn to shit. She was in the front hall by the living room. Shot once in the face."

"A burglary?" I said, shocked. "That's too coincidental."

Collie nodded morosely. "Bullet is an international load. Nobody heard a shot. I'm thinking the shooter used a silencer. In fast, out fast, make a mess to confuse the issue." He studied my face.

I said, "Sylvester?"

"That's what I'm betting."

"*Why?*"

"You said she was skimming and sabotaging, and her checkbook showed deposits paid out of that law firm in town. Maybe she had another source of income, too. Maybe she was willing to sell information."

"Information? About—?"

"Who knows?"

I thought about it. "You think Sylvester or one of his chums might have been paying her?"

"I think it's possible. Then you fired her. They might not have known why. Might have worried she could tell us something. So she had to be terminated."

"God almighty. I find that hard to believe. She was a minor-leaguer."

Collie shrugged. "Anyway. It makes us feel pretty sure Sylvester is still around. And we haven't found anything at the lab yet. We're circulating your description of him all over town, even at the high school. Maybe we'll turn something up. Also, Skurlock's people are going back into the background on all the civilian employees out there. Especially a guy named O'Connor, the electronics man who was on duty and helped them out. So far, nothing. Every telephone line in the place now has a tap on it. Everybody leaving the facility daily is being searched head to foot. They've shortened the work day one hour to provide time, and air force security is handling it. Everybody is pretty pissed about it and they don't think that kind of extreme precaution can be continued very long."

Collie paused and sipped his coffee, then put the cup in his saucer with a little *chink*! "We have got to fish or cut bait."

"How?"

"Skurlock's agent inside the lab, Manning, is tailing this O'Connor character on a full-time basis. The FBI is going to bring in four more men as soon as they can get here, either late today or tomorrow.

As soon as they're in place, interviews start at the lab. Every person out there, starting with the civilians but overlooking nobody. With polygraph."

"I remember just a couple of weeks ago, Collie, when it was going to be fairly simple. I was going to come here and Sylvester was going to react, and you guys were going to catch him."

Collie finished his coffee. "Yeah. Well. Live and learn. You just stick close to home until either Skurlock or I get back to you this evening, right?"

"That I can do."

He reached for his wallet.

"Hey," I said. "Coffee's on the house."

"Much obliged." He left.

The news about Sally Wallis hit me fairly hard. I hadn't liked her. But I hadn't wanted her dead. There is nothing gratifying about a beautiful, vibrant woman suddenly becoming a corpse.

Mulling it over, I went down to the courts.

I found Avery Whitney there. He had had workmen set up some sawhorses, barricading off the middle three courts. Guests were playing on numbers 1, 2, 3, and 14. Whitney prowled around the middle courts, watching workmen with long orange extension cords attached to heavy-duty electric drills. They already had several big-bore anchor holes drilled in our pretty green court surface.

"How's it look?" he demanded as I walked up to join him.

"Like a disaster area," I replied.

He chuckled, *basso profundo* snuffling sounds from deep in his chest. "Give us more good weather and we'll get the whole dadblamed business installed this weekend."

"You've found enough workers?"

"No problem!"

"The signs look good. Now about the rest of the tents—"

"No problem!"

"What's the latest on the concession companies?"

"No problem!"

"Ted," I told him, "might cheer up when they let him out of the hospital, if his lawyer can get him free on bond."

"Jefferson Tuhey is his lawyer?"

"Right."

"No need to worry, then. I always said, if I ever got in bad trouble with the law, Jefferson Tuhey would be the man I'd hire right away. That sucker is *mean*."

"I like hearing it. Karyn called this morning and said she was on the way to Tripptown with him to file some motions, and ask for bail to be set. But they haven't even filed formal charges yet. They haven't released the autopsy report. Nobody can figure out what kind of game that DA is playing."

"If I know Lacey Llewellen," Whitney rumbled, "it's pocket pool. That man is one of the sorriest, most worthless no-good excuses for a lawyer I *ever* encountered. The only way he ever got elected was his Democrat opponent fell in a river and drowned himself three days before the election."

Talking to Whitney was like wrestling with an automatic carwash. I asked him a few questions about preparations, got four more "no problem!'s" for answers, and headed back for the lodge.

When I walked up to Mrs. Tanshita at the front desk, she told me someone was waiting for me in the office.

"Who?" I groaned. "What now?"

"Sir," Mrs. Tanshita chirped happily, "she would not give her name."

I steamed back there, intent on finding new trouble.

Which was certainly not what I got.

She stood from the desk chair when I walked into the doorway, and she looked so pretty and so nice and so unexpected that I just stood there.

"Hi," she said with an uncertain smile. She was wearing a peach-colored business suit that did wonders for her wondrous figure, and her hair had a swirl in it that was new and just right. "Surprised?"

"*Beth?*" I said, gawking in disbelief as she came toward me.

"Is it okay I just came?" she asked, nesting in my arms. "I thought—you sounded so awful on the phone the last time—maybe I can help?"

At some point in the afternoon—after I had begun to recover from my happy shock that she was really here, in Montana, *with me*, *now*—Beth commandeered one of our telephone lines from the cabin and began trying to track down information in Tripptown about the autopsy report. She didn't do any good. At which point we looked at each other and—logic and responsibility and all that good stuff to the contrary—I told her we had business that could only be discussed in bed.

She frowned, using a crimson fingertip to brush back a strand of rebellious blond hair from her forehead. "Brad. We have too much serious business to talk about, here."

Then, despite her yips of protest and my stern Calvinist left hemisphere saying it was disgraceful, and I should be Responsible and Serious, Etc., I took her directly to the A-frame under the big ponderosa pine, unloaded her bags, locked the door with her safely inside, and forcefully initiated strenuous lollygagging.

We hadn't been together for a long time. Beth was a little tired and I was strung out. But after a few minutes all that became secondary—or thousandary—for a little while.

Considerably later we sat in the big rumpled bed and smoked and talked more serious business. Beth could not entirely hide the fact that she found my recitation of developments alarming.

"My God, Brad. You transferred *everything*?"

"Well, almost everything," I admitted. "But we can make this work."

"If you don't, then what happens?"

"I guess I play more exhibitions and teach more lessons and write more articles, babe."

She sighed, pretty naked breasts bobbing over the coverlet. "All to help a friend?"

"A very special friend. Besides, this is a business investment."

She sighed a second time, with equally interesting results. "You're risking a lot."

Wondering what she would say if I told her the CIA part, I merely nodded.

"We'd both better get to work," she added. "I'll try Tripptown again for that report."

"Right now?" I asked. "This minute?"

She swung a beautiful bare leg out from under the covers. "Sure, right now. Why wait? Hey! What—? Brad—? *Again?* . . . Oh, my

. . . I guess you mean again . . . You sex maniac . . . What are you—? What do you think you're— Oh . . . Yes. Do that. Yes. Do that. Please. Oh God . . ."

Her promised phone calls were delayed a while.

After that we really did get up, and then the late afternoon fled by in a welter of details. Beth talked to our lawyer, Jefferson Tuhey, on the telephone. She reported that she hated Tuhey. "He's just right for the case," she added. "He would sell his mother down the river if it helped his paying client."

I waited with growing impatience for the promised return visit by Collie or Fred Skurlock. Six o'clock passed, and then the clock showed seven. It was almost eight before I finally began to suspect that plans had changed and they might have decided they didn't need me anymore.

Leaving Beth at the dinner table in the lodge, I strolled out into the gathering darkness to make sure the emergency lights had been set around the court construction area. We didn't need somebody falling over something and suing us.

But lawsuits were not very high on my mental priority list at the moment. I was still processing Sally Wallis, Beth's wondrous arrival, and about ten other things. I had my .38, but it was shoved deep into an inside pocket of my jacket. I was just not very alert at all.

So by the time the figure loomed out of the dark and came at me—and I recognized the other Lassiter, the big moose who had had his feet up on the desk at the jail that night—he was right on top of me.

Cold slashed through my nervous system and I moved instinctively. My first two steps were *away from him*, spasm-steps toward the fence.

"Hey," he said. The single word was an odd, muted rumble, the voice of a sleepy giant. "Wait."

I kept moving to my left, half-blind in the dimness. My shoulder hit hard against the chain-link fencing. I came off it in the other direction. I banged my knee against the bottom row of the permanent bleacher seats, the bright pain making my leg almost collapse. Internal alarms howling, I groped around for my gun, started to pull it out—and dropped the damned thing. It fell through a chink in the bleachers, out of reach.

Trying to get it, I brushed my hand over a discarded empty soft drink bottle, knocking it off the seat. It hit the pavement with a cheap plinking sound and skittered underneath somewhere, out of sight and equally out of reach. I couldn't see anything else.

Lassiter's slope-shouldered enormity moved a ponderous step toward me. "Mr. Smith?" he said.

"I've got a gun," I said. My voice cracked, sounding shrill with fright in my own ears. "You'd better hold it right there."

The shadowy figure stopped advancing instantly—stood there, swaying like someone who might be drunk. He said in the same curious, cavernously gentle voice, "I ain't here for no trouble, Mr. Smith."

I looked around. I still didn't have sight of anything I might use. He just stood there, moving side-to-side like a great old tree in a wind. I was five or six feet from him. I backed up two steps, increasing the gap, and started calculating my chances of doing a scared rabbit act.

"You just hold it right there," I said, bluffing again.

"I need to talk to you, Mr. Smith, real bad."

"About what?"

"It's my brother. It's Jack."

What the hell? "I'll tell you what. You turn around and walk back up that way toward the lodge. If you want to talk, we can talk in the lodge."

He hesitated, and then amazingly took one step back. But he stopped again. "I can't."

"What?"

"I can't go up there. I can't go in the light. He might be out here someplace. Watching."

I was totally baffled. "*Who* might be out here?"

"Jack!" Suddenly he sounded on the verge of tears. "My brother. He's . . . not right."

"I don't know what you're talking about."

He moved again, but not threateningly. To my new surprise, his bulky shadow slumped down—sat on the bottom tier of the permanent bleachers. I could see well enough to make out his gesture of defeat as he slumped forward, locked hands between his knees. It began to dawn on me that he wasn't about to attack anybody.

"You know me," he said huskily, like a man just beaten badly in a fight. "I was in the jail when you and the lady come in. I was . . . settin' the jail. They taken your friend to Missoula."

"I remember you." My nerves began to ease slightly but I was still baffled and fidgety. "You're Jack Lassiter's brother."

"Yessir. Buster Lassiter."

"What are you doing here?"

"He beat on your friend."

"Your brother Jack? Yes. And you helped him, right?"

"No! I never!"

I stood there, trying to get it sorted out. The first adrenaline rush had begun to ease off, leaving me hot and weak in the knees. "What are you doing here?"

"It's him."

"Jack, you mean?"

"Yessir."

"What about him?"

"He done a bad thing. A terrible thing! He hadn't ought to have did that. I dunno what gets into him sometimes. It's like he gets crazy. He's not that bad a guy, sometimes. But then he gets mad. He gets all sorta crazy and he does stuff. And now the chief has told him he can't work for the town anymore, and he told me how he buried that body of that construction guy, and he's mad—crazy mad, and there's no telling what he might do sometimes when he gets like this."

He fell silent.

"What do you mean, he buried somebody?" I demanded, incredulous.

"The construction guy! He didn't kill him! The guy was already dead—he just died! But Jack buried him, and then I guess the body washed out and *your* friend tried to hide him again."

"Good Christ, Lassiter. Do you realize what you're telling me?"

"I know . . . I know." He twisted big hands together miserably, rocking forward and back in his anguish. "I just don't want him to do nothing even worse. He's not a bad man. He's just . . . sick."

My eyes were more accustomed to the light now. I could see that he was wearing battered jeans with the right knee torn open and a white or gray T-shirt with some kind of faded, once-colorful sunburst logo on the front. The shirt sagged over his great, sagging belly and protuberant breasts. His bare arms looked huge in the pale dimness;

his neck was as big as a man's thigh, his blunt-shaped skull sitting on it like a rock on a stump.

He hadn't made a hostile move, and his words and tone continued to sink in for me, forming a pattern. The slow, steady *sadness* in him hit hardest. But I was still totally off-balance. I didn't speak. Didn't know what in the hell to say.

He added, "He might do . . . violence."

I said, "And you don't hold with violence, I suppose."

The heavy head slowly shook from side to side. "I don't fight."

"What did you call it that night you jumped me down near my cabin?"

From his chest came a long, low, mournful groan. "I never."

"I didn't see much, but I saw your boots."

"Come again?"

"Your boots. Your boots. The same ones you were wearing at the jail office the other night. A man recognizes boots when he's seen them coming at his face."

He groaned again. "Jack and me live together. He always takes my stuff. He always has some of my stuff in his car."

Came the dawn. "Are you trying to tell me your brother wore your clothes and boots—and he was the one who tried to kick my insides out?"

"I dunno. I dunno what you're talking about." He raised his head to look up at me. "*I* didn't do it!"

"Did you *know* he borrowed some of your clothing that night?"

He hung his head. "He does it all the time. He takes whatever he wants. He don't care what I think."

"And you just let him?"

"What else could I do?"

"You could stop him."

"Stop him?"

"Stop him," I repeated. "He might have killed me. What if someone had seen him running off, and recognized your clothes, and you ended up in jail, charged with assault or even something worse?"

He seemed to think about it a long time. Finally he said, "Well, he's done stuff like that. But nobody ever thought it was me, or leastwise they couldn't prove it."

"And you just let him keep on doing it?" I demanded, incredulous. "You don't at least get mad at him?"

"You don't get mad," he told me quietly, with grave patience.

"You don't?"

"No. You can't."

"Why *can't* you?"

"Because you're big."

I began to feel like Alice on the wrong side of the looking glass. "Because you're *big*?"

"See, when you're big, you can't afford to get mad. Like, see, if you get mad, and you get in a fight, you might really hurt somebody, for one thing. And also, if you get in a fight, people are always going to say, like, they'll go, '*That* guy must of started it, because he's big.' So you can't get mad because it'll always have been your fault, people will say. Momma taught us that a long time ago. We was always big for our age."

I tried to see my way through the maze. I felt like I was seeing inside someone from outer space or the Creature from the Black Lagoon. "So you always get run over," I summarized. "Because otherwise, since you're so big, people would always assume the trouble started with you."

"Right! And besides that, you go in a saloon or a pool hall, and there's always cowboys in there, truckers, motorcycle guys, you know. They see you, they think, 'I got to put this guy down.' They go, 'I haf to try this big blubber out, so I can say I whupped him.' So *you just can't go in places like that,* see? Because you can't get mad." He paused and seemed to think about it. "And I *sure* can't get mad at Jack. I mean, it's the war. That did it. It ain't his fault. He's a nice guy, basically."

Nothing about him said deceit or violence. He reminded me of one or two other big, powerful, stupid men I had known, men whose size was a red flag to drunks and superstuds looking for a cheap victory. Given his kind of size and obvious power, Lassiter was a trophy animal to a certain kind of bully. You either fought a lot or you shunned certain places and situations, and learned to back down and accept sneering taunts and comments.

This Lassiter, I thought, was one of those who had learned to back down, or avoid even that pain by staying deep in the brush, where the trophy-hunters seldom spotted him. It was a paradox, but his very size and strength had made him a gentle giant.

I crossed from my defensive posture by the fencing and sat down beside him. He dwarfed me. His smells—rank animal sweat, tobacco, a feral odor of brush and earth—enclosed us both.

I said, "You don't know where he is now?"

"He said he was going off to look for a new job. Maybe he did. I just got worried. I know how he can get. He might try to hurt you worse. He's desperate. We needed the money for them jobs he had. All we got coming in now is the little he's getting from that man renting our fishing cabin, and he's so sickly looking, he might leave any time."

"Sickly looking?" I repeated.

"Pale. Skinny."

"Wait a minute." My pulse had started to thump. "Where is this fishing cabin? On your land someplace? Off the beaten path?"

"Oh, yeah, it's *way* back up the mountain. You only get up there on the one little gravel path, and even that's hard to drive sometimes. Poor feller. He said he'd been so sick—heart attack. I guess he must of been. Even his voice sounds sick. Real weak . . . high . . . almost like a woman's voice, you might say."

"Lassiter, listen to me. This might be important. You think that man is still using the cabin?"

He looked surprised. "Why, sure. I seen smoke in the woods from his fireplace not long before dark, before I got so worried and decided I had to come over here and tell you."

I grabbed his arm. It was like grabbing a tree limb. "You can show me how to get there?"

"Yes, sir, but—"

"I want you to wait right here. This man you just told me about might be a very important person, and I might need to see him very, *very* badly. Do you get what I'm saying?"

I stood and pressed down on his bulky shoulder. "Wait right here. This is really important. Wait. Will you do that?"

"Well," he said soberly, puzzled, "I guess if it will help you any—sure."

I left him and ran for the lodge, mentally rehearsing Skurlock's telephone number. *Skurlock*, I thought fervently, *you'd better be there!*

twenty-five

Elsewhere

Chicago

Traffic had thinned in the street canyon in front of the Allen Building. Lights shone inside the vast, empty lobby. A gleaming black limousine pulled up to the curb. Ardis Allen, furious, hopped out before her driver could rush around to assist her.

A worried-looking executive, Eric Rose, had been standing on the sidewalk in front of the lobby windows, waiting for her. He nervously tossed his cigarette away and hurried to intercept her.

"You made good time—"

"Don't give me small talk, Eric, God damn it. Unlock this door!"

He did. Ardis swept past him and inside, long spring coat billowing, heels clacking on the lobby tiles. She headed straight for the express elevator. Bracelets jangling, she pressed the call button and the doors sprang open for her. She stepped inside. Rose had to make a frantic leap to get between the fast-closing doors.

The two of them whisked up in a distant whisper of air and whine of motors. Ardis, her hair piled atop her head, beautiful in full evening makeup, scowled at the floor indicator lights over the doors.

"They'll regret this," she clipped. "I'll have the head of every man on the board."

"They're in a panic," Rose said nervously. "It's the only explanation. They've never even *considered* holding a meeting without—"

Ardis turned on him viciously. "Damn their panic! I run this company. If there was ever a time for discipline in the ranks, it's now. What good can be accomplished by a meeting of three-fourths of the board? Word will get out and the press will make something of it!"

"It might be innocent," Rose suggested, grasping at straws. "They might simply seek reassurance from each other—"

"I'll show them 'reassurance'!"

The lift doors hissed open on the executive floor. Ardis swept past the empty reception desk and into the office area for the Allen board of directors. A gray-haired woman named Spang, recorder and stenographer for the board for many years, got nervously to her feet as Ardis and Rose entered.

"Mrs. Allen! I hope I did the right thing, letting you know—!"

"You'll get a bonus," Ardis snapped, starting past the woman's large desk, headed for a pair of closed, massive, dark oak doors. "They're still inside?"

"Yes—"

"How long have they been meeting?"

"Over an hour now. I didn't know where to start looking for you—"

Ardis pushed the heavy doors open and burst into the meeting room.

Tobacco smoke blued the air. Seven of her board directors—a quorum—sat around the great conference table. The table was littered with newspapers, report files, memoranda, yellow legal tablets, dirty ashtrays. All of them looked up, startled. Ardis registered some of the frightened eyes.

She strode past the side of the table, heels digging into the thick carpet, and made for the head chair. Jeremy Jeffries, vice-chairman of the board, had just risen from it.

"I'll take the chair," Ardis said with icy rage.

Jeffries, seventy, stood his ground. White-haired, pink-faced, he had removed his coat, and wet rings encircled his armpits. He looked scared, but he did not move.

"Get out of my way, Jeremy."

"No, Ardis," Jeffries said quietly, sad but firm.

For a moment Ardis Allen could not believe what she had heard. "You old fool! I will take the chair! This meeting is uncalled and unauthorized. I demand an explanation."

Silence in the room was total. Every eye was on them.

"I called the meeting," Jeffries said. "I am in the chair, and will remain in the chair."

"How dare you! This will be the last Allen meeting you ever attend, Jeremy! As for the rest of you—"

"No, Ardis," Jeffries cut in with the same deadly quiet. "You're the one who is through, I am sorry to say."

Ardis stared at him. The rage rushed out of her as if a valve had been opened. Suddenly she began to understand.

"You can't," she said.

But she knew they could. It had never crossed her mind that they even might. But they could. They *could.*

Jeffries was still talking in that slight, deadly tone. "—already clear that you unilaterally set up, and then concealed from this board, an unauthorized toxic waste dump in Montana. Once you realized the site's secrecy could not be maintained forever, you compounded the evil by failing to file the proper reports with the Environmental Protection Agency—or with this board of directors. This secret has now started to come out. We have seen the first reports from a reporter in Denver. There is sure to be an investigation. In all likelihood we will now face disastrous penalties and potential lawsuits in addition to the cost of cleanup. This policy should never have been pursued. In acting outside the knowledge of this board, you have grossly exceeded your authority and imperiled the very life of Allen Industries."

Ardis tried to speak. Her throat stuck closed. She swallowed sandpaper and found her voice. "Speculation. Sheer speculation. If some small division ran away out of control on its own, we can locate the guilty parties and let *them* face any charges or recriminations—"

"No, Ardis," the old man said softly. "This was your doing."

"That's absurd! You have no proof!"

"Your conduct has been inexcusable. The only possible chance this company has to survive is by total reorganization—new leadership that might have a scintilla of hope to regain public trust some day—"

"You're insane! I built this company to what it is today!"

Jeffries's eyes drooped with sadness. "Yes, Ardis. You performed miracles. But you went too far. You told none of us. You became a dictator. You exceeded your authority. You violated our trust."

"If you had a shred of proof of these wild charges you're tossing around so recklessly—"

The sound of a door opening behind her—and the swiveling of every set of eyes to that door—stopped Ardis in mid-sentence. She whirled to see who had had the temerity to interrupt.

The man who entered the room was broadly muscular, handsome in his severe dark suit, his hair mostly gray. His eyes looked like forged steel, and he had a thick leather folder under his arm.

Paul Dominick? "What are you doing here?" Ardis demanded.

"I've brought some more interesting reading material for the board, Ardis," Dominick said with a chill smile. "Almost all your confidential memos."

"You were told to destroy those after reading them! God damn you, I *trusted* you! You were the one person I—"

Dominick's widening grin of revenge silenced her.

He said, "It's a little late to think about that, isn't it? Just like it's a little late to be thinking about changing the office locks that day." Dominick strode to the table and put down the heavy folder. Memo slips and letters cascaded across the smooth wood surface. "Gentlemen, I think these will answer any questions you still may have."

There was no recourse, and Ardis knew it. Her sense of defeat was devastating. She was finished.

Washington, D.C.

Within two hours of the Allen Industries' board action, a telephone rang in the Washington home of Evan Patterson, a commissioner of the Securities and Exchange Commission. Patterson had already been asleep. The voice on the other end of his line awakened him fast.

"Mr. Patterson? This is Senator Henthorne."

Patterson cleared his throat. *Now what?* "Yes, Senator. How good to hear from you again."

"About this case involving Treacher Resorts and Investments in Montana."

Shit. "Yes, Senator. As I explained in our conversation just the other day, we are moving with all possible speed on that. We have two deputies in Missoula, and another in Helena, checking incorporation papers and other documents. We fully expect to move before the middle of next week at the latest. We will get a court order to seize all the company's files, and charges—"

"Is it a good case, Patterson?" the senator's reedy old voice broke in.

Patterson paused, considered his options, and decided to be blunt. "Senator, despite your keen interest, I am forced to tell you it is *not* a good case. Very small sums are involved, and we'll be stretching it to prove conspiracy. False advertising may be the best we can make stick. However—"

"In that case," the senator's voice cut in brittlely, "maybe you ought to drop it."

After seven inquiries and as many phone calls, Patterson thought he must have heard wrong. "What?"

"I said, if it isn't a good case and you don't like it, maybe you ought to forget the whole thing, Patterson. Would you like to do that?"

"I— Yes, Senator. I would."

"Then do it! You'll hear no more from me about it! Good night!"

Patterson stood with a dead instrument in his hand, stunned.

At the other end of the line, Senator Henthorne shuffled to the bar in the corner of the living room. He chuckled to himself. So Ardis was done for! he thought merrily. No more Ardis, badgering him for power plays. No more veiled threats through his PAC.

Wonderful.

The senator poured himself a brandy and toasted the portrait over the fireplace. It was his favorite picture. Of himself.

twenty-six

"How much farther to the turnoff?" Collie Davis, behind the wheel, asked.

Buster Lassiter, crammed in the front seat between Collie and me, peered out through the windshield at the dense woods lining the country road. "Two miles, about."

Collie reached forward and pulled a knob. The headlights went out and we were running in the sudden dark of only the parking lights. Behind us, Skurlock's headlights instantly vanished in our rear window.

Collie slowed. The sedan pitched and wobbled through the holes and ruts of the dirt road. In the closed car, the smell of Buster Lassiter's sweat was overpowering.

Nobody said anything. Occasionally the trees overhead parted enough to let us see the partial moon through broken clouds. Skurlock's parking lights gleamed close behind, amber in the mirror on my side. They had gotten to the lodge in well under an hour: Skurlock and his associate who was working inside the air force lab, Manning, and Collie. A half-dozen brisk questions had elicited enough from the frightened younger Lassiter to confirm for them what I had said on the telephone. A few more questions determined the general lay of the land and we had set out.

We drove on, pitching and rolling, a wheel occasionally dropping into a deeper hole that tossed us roughly against each other and the side doors. We made a couple of sharp, steep turns, then crossed a wood-plank bridge.

"It's right up ahead," Lassiter grunted.

Collie slowed. In the faint yellow light I saw a side road forking off to the right, going sharply up the side of the steep dirt hill.

"That's it?" Collie asked.

"Yessir. Right up there. Ain't nothing else up there. You come out in some tamaracks and a few old ponderosas, and there it is, right on the knoll."

Collie stopped the car, dousing the parking lights. Reaching back, he flipped the dome-light switch to avoid a flash as he opened the door. We got out, then, and met in the near-total dark between the cars, Skurlock and the beefy Manning coming up from the back. Both FBI agents had their arms full of guns—a couple of what looked like AR-15s, a shotgun, some handguns. Even in the dark I could see Buster Lassiter's eyes bulge.

Skurlock put a friendly, reassuring hand on his shoulder. "Mr. Lassiter. You can hike across the pasture and get home from here?"

"Yessir. It's just right down yonder less than a mile."

"All right. You go on, then. You say nothing about any of this to anybody, right?"

"Right. Yes sir. Whatever you say, sir."

"Go on, then. I'll be in touch with you tomorrow. Remember: don't say anything to *anyone*. Have you got that?"

"My bud didn't know that man was a bad man! You got to believe that—"

"We believe you, sir." Skurlock amazed me; his voice was warm and reassuring. "You just go on home and rest easy. You've done a good thing. All right?"

Lassiter swayed in the dark, digesting everything. He finally said, "All right, then, sir. I go now?"

"Go now, sir. Yes. Please."

With a final frightened glance at the firepower, Lassiter turned and headed off into the murk.

Skurlock breathed a heavy sigh. "All right, then. I think we can go in one car from here, Collie. You figure we can see enough to poke up that path in the dark?"

Collie nodded. "There's enough moonlight, I think. My eyes are adjusting."

Skurlock grunted. "Should have had some night glasses. Okay. Let's go."

We got back in Collie's car, me in the back with Manning. Collie eased the car up the dirt incline and we started to climb, poking along in low range without lights. Skurlock and Manning started messing with the AR-15s. There was a lot of metallic clattering and crunching.

"You prefer your Browning?" Skurlock asked Collie.

"It's enough."

Skurlock hooked a thumb back at me. "What about him?"

"He's had our course, but he's not current."

Skurlock grunted again and handed me back the shotgun, a pretty Remington pump. I took it. He handed back a box of shells. "You know how to load it?"

"I can manage."

"Load it, then. But don't work the action to put one in the chamber until we're out of the car."

It occurred to me to tell him I wasn't an idiot, but I was too tense, and my recent track record wasn't good enough to support the argument anyway. Beside me, Manning expertly worked the action of his automatic, chambering a round, and flicked the safety on.

The smell of Lassiter's sweat still filled the car, but by now I was sweating as profusely. It was all nerves. Collie drove slowly, expertly, and we climbed. Some kind of animal peered at us from the side of the road and then, startled at last, bounded away. Skurlock rolled his window down. We made a couple of sharp turns. It was an abominable road, pitching us around constantly.

If Buster Lassiter hadn't been lying—and there was no reason in the world he might have been—Sylvester was on top of this little mountain. My guts were strung so tight I could hardly swallow. We were going to get him. Finally, I thought, we were going to get him.

It may have taken ten minutes or it might have been closer to the hour that it felt like. We finally came over a little hump and around a rock outcropping, and we were on the top.

Collie stopped at once.

It was still. Very still.

Collie pointed. "From what he said, it's through those trees."

Skurlock popped his door, then paused. He pointed toward the left. "Manning, around there. Collie, how about you going around this side? I'll go through the middle. Brad, you stick with me. Close. Get in position, wait for my move. Got it?"

"Got it," Collie said. He sounded mild and amused.

We piled out of the car. Manning melted into the brush on the far side of the car and Collie went ahead, staying close to the embankment, approaching along the right-hand side. Skurlock, rifle at the ready, signaled me to follow him. He started toward the trees at a lope. Remembering to chamber a round, I followed him.

Despite his bulk, Skurlock went through the knee-high prairie grass like a running elk. The grass tugged and whisked around my legs as I ran bent-over, finding to my surprise that I had to work hard to keep up. By the time we had crossed the uphill, open field and reached the denser darkness of the big trees, I was mildly out of breath. Skurlock, however, gave me a glance to make sure I had stayed close, then signaled with his rifle for me to move to his right. I obeyed and he promptly started ahead again, bent low, on the move like a combat infantryman.

We went through the stand of trees and came to the clearing on the far side. There, perhaps thirty yards from where we crouched, stood the cabin. Moonlight made it distinct. An electrical line, with a telephone wire piggyback, strung out of the woods to our right and drooped across the open to a corner of the log structure. I didn't see a car or truck, but a light shone from the front window. A wisp of smoke curled from the stone chimney. I could smell it.

Crouching, Skurlock peered hard at the cabin, then off to our left. I tried to follow his sightlines and spotted the quick, furtive movement in a dense stand of weeds slightly downhill and on the far side of the cabin. Skurlock's head pivoted to the right and I followed again. First: nothing. We waited. I could practically feel Skurlock mentally raging at Collie to catch up. Then we both spotted the figure dart out of the stand of lodgepole pines and go down flat behind some brush.

Skurlock stepped into the clear and made wide, looping signals with his right hand. Then, regripping his automatic rifle, he glanced at me. I almost missed his whisper: "Stay behind me, be ready to cover."

With that he straightened up and ran for the front of the cabin. He moved so swiftly that I was left several steps behind. I sprinted to try to catch up. To my right and left I caught peripheral glimpses of Manning and Collie Davis rushing from the sides, going toward the rear. I was still several paces behind when Skurlock reached the front door and kicked it open, going inside and vanishing to the left of the door opening in a single, violent movement. I waited a beat—heard and saw nothing—and went in behind him.

The front room stood empty, fire in the fireplace, the smell of cigar smoke in the air. As I entered, Skurlock had already crossed the square room to hurl open the door to the bathroom. He went in fast, gun ready, and came right back out again. Glancing at the open rafters over our heads, he grunted an obscenity and came close to knocking me down on the way back out through the front door.

Not knowing what the hell to do, I stayed right where I was. Looked around. Noted tables, chairs, corner bed, kitchenette with a refrigerator and butane stove, teapot on the stove. I went over and touched the teapot. It was still warm. I felt weak-kneed in the letdown after such high expectations.

Voices sounded outside: Skurlock's, then Collie's. They came back into the cabin, eyes at pinpoints against the glare of the overhead light.

"Missed him," Skurlock muttered.

"Truck's gone," Collie said, looking around. "Could somebody have tipped him?"

"More likely he caught sight of us before we doused our lights." Skurlock went to the door, peered out, pointed. "Jesus Christ, will you look at this view? You can see for forty fucking miles."

Manning finally came in, flashlight in one hand and assault rifle in the other. "Deep tire tracks out there. You can still get a whiff of the exhaust. He must have spotted somebody coming and got out of here in one hell of a hurry, digging up dirt with both back tires."

"Why didn't we meet him on the road, then?"

"Looks like he took off to the north, right down the side of the hill."

"Shit."

That seemed to say it. Skurlock put his safetied rifle on the table. I remembered to slide the safety of my shotgun back on. Manning went back outside again. Collie shoved his Browning into the shoulder holster.

"The teapot is still hot," I pointed out.

"Yeah," Skurlock said disgustedly. "We didn't miss him by much."

"Couple of numbers on this scratchpad," Collie said. He had gone to the little table where the telephone was, and was shuffling through the junk on it.

"We'll check those out," Skurlock said. He looked around. "We'll check every damn thing in here. Damn! So close and yet so far."

"It would be nice if we could lift a decent set of fingerprints off something in here. This is the first time we've ever been absolutely sure we found a place where he had just spent considerable time."

Skurlock nodded. "Well, don't touch anything that might carry them. When my other guys get here tomorrow we'll go over this bastard with a fine-tooth comb. We might have missed him again this time, but we'll get *something* out of it."

Manning came back in again, out of breath. "Saw some headlights way the hell off to the north. Look like they were already on the road over in that direction. Want me to call the sheriff?"

Skurlock glumly thought about it. "No," he said finally. "By the time they could get anybody in the vicinity, he could be in Butte. And we don't know what kind of truck to tell them to watch for."

We stood around in silence. Manning poked through some old newspapers and flipped back the covers on the bed. He found a suitcase under the bed and pulled it out. Opening it, he found some clothing—flannels shirts and Levi's, mostly—and riffled through them. While he did that, Skurlock shuffled through some coats and shirts hanging in an alcove beside the bathroom door. Collie went through kitchen drawers and cabinets, just idly poking in. Trying to make myself useful, I pulled drawers open on the old dresser.

"You want to look at this?" I asked.

All three came over. In the bottom drawer, neatly folded under a fresh box of 9mm Lugar ammunition, were some papers. Skurlock took them out. The biggest paper was a state road map, much used.

When Skurlock unfolded it, two Polaroid photographs fell to the floor. I retrieved them. They were views of the air force station, taken at long range from the access road.

Skurlock spread the map, briefly studied it, and pointed. "See the X? That's the mark for the location of the lab." He flipped the map to the other side, then back. "Nothing else I can see."

We looked at each other. We had finished what we could do without equipment or tearing the place apart.

Skurlock made some decisions. "Ride back down the hill with these guys," he told Manning. "Take the car and find the sheriff. Tell him enough to get his attention, no more. I want a couple of deputies up here to help me seal this place off and stake it out. Call Archibald and tell him we've *got* to have the extras in here by noon tomorrow, latest, and we need forensic equipment and an operator. I'll stay here until you get back with the deputies. Then we'll talk about what else you need to do."

He turned to Collie and me. "That's all I know to do tonight. You're going back to the resort? I suggest maybe you'd both stay out there tonight. You can give Collie a room, right? Okay. That way I'll know where to reach both of you if anything happens before morning. Otherwise I'll be in touch then."

"Sounds fine," Collie said. He swept the room with his eyes again. His disappointment made his eyes sag. "Mighty near thing."

"'Mighty near' only counts in horseshoes," Skurlock told him.

Leaving Skurlock, we trooped down the hill through the trees, carrying our guns. My knee hurt. We didn't talk until Collie had turned the car around and we had started down, with the benefit of headlights this time.

"What now, do you think?" I asked him.

"I don't know," he admitted.

"Do you think this near miss might run him clear out of the area? Make it too hot for him?"

He glanced at me in surprise. "You know Sylvester better than I do, pal. Do *you* think he'll bug out?"

"He could," I said. "But . . ."

He waited, then prodded me. "But what?"

"But I don't think so."

twenty-seven

"*He's* here?" Beth hissed in surprise when she spotted Collie the next morning.

"I forgot to mention that," I said lamely. "He arrived while you were holed up with the telephone, finding out what you had to do to be recognized by the courts in Montana, and trying to track down the mortgages and other papers for us."

She looked at me with shock dilating her pretty pale eyes. "You had plenty of chance to tell me."

"Well, I know," I said weakly.

We had walked up from our cabin and had almost reached the lodge. Collie was out on the deck with coffee. Beth had stopped when she spied him, and she still stood there on the path, hands on her hips, glaring at me with shocked dismay. She just stared—didn't say a word.

"I was going to explain the whole thing to you," I told her. "It just didn't seem like the right time."

"Brad, is this entire thing here some kind of undercover operation?"

"No! That is to say, uh . . ."

"Damn you! And to think I dropped everything and flew up here to help you with your Ted Treacher troubles! And all the time you were holding back on me again. I've got half a mind not to present myself to the court, and just go back home."

I had never seen her so mad. "Okay," I said. "There's . . . a little . . . operation here. But the other trouble is real. You can see that. Do you think I made up that pile of unpaid debts or the charges against Ted?"

She thought about it and shook her head. "I don't know what to think right now. I'm really disappointed. I feel . . . betrayed."

"It's just two things going at once," I said, knowing how slippery *that* sounded. "Everything I told you is true. You've already been a tremendous help. Just having you here has made everything better." I reached for her. "Hey. Come on. Let's go on up and see Collie. He's a good guy."

She eluded my grasp. "Does this mean . . . that other man . . . is here?"

I played dumb. "Who?"

She pressed her spread fingers across her chest. "The one who *shot* me?"

"No," I lied instantly. "Of course not."

She studied my face. I saw she was very close to tears.

Finally she said, "You go ahead. I've got to think about this." And turned and hurried back down the path toward the cabin.

I walked on to the lodge and went out on the deck to join Collie. The wind was brisk but the wind was down and it would be warmer today.

My face must have showed how I was feeling.

"Lovers' quarrel?" Collie asked with mild irony.

"She didn't know you were here. She didn't know I was operational."

He sipped his coffee. "Um. Sad."

"She's got every right to be pissed," I fired back. "What kind of an asshole *am* I, encouraging her to come here when Sylvester is poking around?"

Collie studied me. "Well, yes," he said after a while. "You wanted the woman you love here with you, rather than in California, having martinis with some other man. You got lonesome. I guess that does make you a very bad person."

"Collie, you know what I mean."

"Yes, I suppose I do, but I've already heard from Skurlock and he wants us both in town by eight-thirty, latest. So what do you say we save the breast-beating for later and get the show on the road?"

Fuming, I went into Elk City with him. Skurlock was set up in an office above a little grocery store. He had a sign on the door, MONTANA GEM COLLECTORS. One of his new men, name of Mims, was with him.

There had been no sign of Sylvester, he reported, and nothing new at the lab. He had interviewed Buster Lassiter again but hadn't gotten anything more that was really helpful. Jack Lassiter was nowhere to be found, and Buster thought his older brother must be off on another job-hunting trip. As a sidelight, Skurlock said he understood we would be seeing inspectors from the Environmental Protection Agency, visiting the old mine site, in about a week. There would be no publicity because the agency preferred to work that way whenever possible.

"I wonder what people will think when they report the site is perfectly clean," I said. "Do you suppose anybody will ask if the air force station is equally clean?"

Skurlock looked at me like he might a termite he had just found in his woodwork. "That's a political concern. Our concern is espionage."

With its enhanced manpower, the local FBI contingent was going to start its polygraph tests at the lab in the morning, finish sweeping and testing the mountain cabin, get out more circulars showing the artist's sketch of Sylvester made from my description, and—when they found him—talk to Jack Lassiter.

Collie was going inside the lab for a day or two, unless something new broke. I was to go back to the resort and stay out of trouble.

"We don't see Sylvester or anybody else coming after you now," Skurlock told me. "He's in deep hiding or he's bugged out. So for right now you can tend to your knitting out there."

When I drove back to the resort, I had to look twice to make sure I had come to the same place. A lot of Avery Whitney's plans and work had all come together at once in a single morning.

A larger, lighted sign stood at the intersection of our road and the highway. Rows of small triangular plastic flags—red, white, and blue—lined the entrance area. As I approached the front parking area I saw a colorful city of tents and banners moving gaily in the gentle breeze. Somehow or other, Avery had gotten three flagpoles erected. The American flag waved from the peak of the tallest one. One of the others displayed the state flag, while on the third hung a white banner with a circular pattern of blue letters on it. I had to get closer before I could see the crossed tennis rackets in the middle, surrounded by the words *Bitterroot Valley Resort*.

The tops of more tents stuck up through the trees nearer the courts. I could see the highest rows of the bleachers that formed a small stadium around our designated center court. A Coors beer truck, a Coca-Cola truck, and two smaller vehicles with the names of vending companies on them were parked in a row behind our kitchen loading dock. There were more cars than I was accustomed to seeing in the parking lot, and a crew of several men out back swarmed around a crane truck with portable lights on top.

Some of my morning moroseness faded. We were actually going to have a tournament.

I parked in front and went in through the front lobby. Beth popped up out of a lobby chair and hurried to meet me. She didn't look like she was spoiling for a fight, and her first words confirmed it: "Karyn called from Missoula."

"Did she have some news?"

"Yes. The court in Tripptown ordered Ted released on bail."

"Great! How much bail?"

"I don't know. She didn't say. But she's already sent that lawyer—what's his name?"

"Tuhey. Jefferson Tuhey."

"Yes. She's already sent him over there with the money. And since Ted is well enough to leave the hospital now, and doesn't have to go to jail right away, they'll be out and on the way back here sometime after lunch."

"That's good news."

She watched my face for a moment. "I'm still really, really disappointed and angry, Brad."

"I was going to tell you when the time was right. In the meantime, as far as Bitterroot Valley is concerned—"

She cut in, "In the meantime there's still the fact that you've plunged your life savings—everything you have—into Bitterroot Valley. Ted Treacher could still go to jail for a long time. The publicity might undo anything you can accomplish with this tournament. People might stay away in droves after a scandal. Then there's the SEC thing. And all those long-term debts. Brad, you could lose *everything*."

"Does this mean you only wanted me for my money?"

She was so intent and serious that for an instant she didn't realize I was kidding. Then she did, with a visible start. She took a comic swing at me.

I ducked. "Can I ask you a legal question?"

"About what?"

"About Barnwell Mining."

"I meant to mention that myself. The only reason I didn't tell you last night was I was so tired. Then, this morning . . ."

"What is it?"

"I asked the clerk in Helena about old incorporation papers. Your guess was right. Barnwell is a wholly owned subsidiary of Allen Industries."

"I knew that," I said.

"How?"

"It had to be. Listen. Tell me this. Outfits like Barnwell, that muck around in the ground and take out minerals, and so forth, probably have to file something annually with the Environmental Protection Agency, don't they?"

"Sure. Assuming they have any impact on the environment."

"What happens to the report they have to file?"

"From what I've read, there are millions of reports filed each year. Some get scanned. A lot don't."

"You mean," I said, "some just go into a cabinet somewhere?"

"Sure," she repeated matter-of-factly. "It's not a very good system. In the past eight or nine years, it's been allowed to get a lot worse. Unless a company is very big, and they report very, *very* big pollution they're involved in, the report just gets filed and forgotten."

"You mean a company would *report itself*?" I asked, feeling like Alice again.

"You report, you check the boxes that show 'progress,' and keep right on about your business," Beth told me. "Brad, there are so many polluters in this country you couldn't track all of them down and make them clean up their act if you did nothing else. Besides, this administration doesn't give a damn. Remember what Reagan said? Trees pollute more than people. George Bush is no better. The White House attitude—if a complaint ever got that far—would probably be, 'Oh, well, so we've killed some fish and birds, and maybe destroyed the atmosphere, but so what, we're creating new jobs.' Given that attitude at the top, and shrunken agency budgets, what would you do?"

"How the hell does anybody *ever* get caught and forced to clean up their act?"

She smiled ruefully. "Well, sometimes it gets so bad that the government can't keep its head in the sand anymore. Like when the Cuyahoga River caught fire in Cleveland a long time ago. Or Love Canal."

"So even if a company reported itself, it's likely nothing much would be done."

"Unfortunately, right."

"Then why wouldn't a company file reports?"

"The only reason I can think of would be that they don't want the existence of the site to be known to anyone. Which would imply that it was set up illegally in the first place, and the perpetrators either hope to let it secretly molder forever, or one day clean it out without anyone ever finding out about it."

"How much trouble do you get in, if you're supposed to file reports and don't?"

"The government takes a dim view of people who don't file at all."

"I see." Ardis Allen, I thought, might be in very deep trouble. I had been far too busy to pay close attention, but I knew Lynette Jordan had published some bylined pieces in the *Rocky Mountain News* about the dumpsite here. They hadn't gotten widespread coverage yet, and didn't make sensational copy, since she had made clear that it looked like a sanitary dump. But unless I missed my guess, the EPA would be chapped to have to read a newspaper to learn about the existence of the place.

"So what now?" Beth asked me.

"Try to get this tournament in high gear," I told her. "Avery has done a lot, but now I've got to pitch in, too."

She accepted that.

I watched her, and then I had to ask. "And what about you?"

"What about your spy stuff?" she countered.

"What about it?"

"Damn it, Brad! What can you tell me? Don't I have a right to know?"

"Come on into the office and I'll tell you what I can."

So we went back there, and I told a little of it, as much as I thought I really could. She listened, asking no questions.

"So they think you're out of danger?"

"Yes."

"But he's still spooking around."

"I'm betting he's gone."

She thought about it.

"So?" I asked finally.

"I'll stay," she said. "For now."

"Beth, that's great. I—"

"After going this far with you," she cut in, "I want to see if this tournament does get off the ground, or if you go bankrupt."

In the lodge office, telephone memos had stacked up. Our tourney players were sending in their arrival confirmations, and all those were piled up, too.

One of the telephone memos was in response to one of the first groping, desperate feelers I had put out after it became apparent we had to try to carry the tournament forward. The memo slip was from Barney Hilgenberg at ESPN.

I returned the call. The secretary at ESPN finally let me through.

"Brad?" Hilgenberg's familiar nasal voice intoned. "You win, buddy."

"How so?" I asked, pulse stirring faster.

"We've looked everything over, and the decision is to do something with your tournament out there after all."

"You mean you're going to shoot some tape on it?"

"Better than that. The Taledega stockers have to postpone because they had a hell of a fire in pit row, wiped out almost all the cars, got into the stadium seats and made everything unsafe until they've done major repairs. That gives us a five-man crew available.

So what we want to do is get them out there as soon as possible, set up right away, do some interviews, and shoot a promo. We'll get that on as soon as it can be sent back by satellite. Then we'll plan to shoot four hours of tape next Friday for broadcast late Friday night, and four hours live both Saturday and Sunday. You think you can accommodate us on all that?"

Accommodate them? *Accommodate* a TV crew that would put Bitterroot Valley into a few million living rooms during weekend prime time? I said, "I think we can handle it, Barney. Sure."

"Okay, buddy. Our technical support staff will be in touch. I'll be back to you next week. Hang in there!"

Later in the day, Karyn Wechsting came back with a pale and shaky Ted Treacher in the car with her. Karyn did not look a lot better than Ted did, physically. Her freckles stood out like crayon marks on chalk-colored paper, and there were new worry-lines around her tired eyes and mouth. Her hair had the dried consistency of hay.

I hugged her and reached out to shake hands with Ted, forgetting his cast. He awkwardly gave me his left hand. He had lost more weight, which he couldn't afford, and his eyes had a numbed, eggshell look about them.

Mrs. Tanshita and some of the other lodge staff came into the lobby and greeted Ted with sincere concern and gladness. Whatever else might be said about the way he had run things, he was much loved around the place. The quiet intensity of the greetings and questions about his injuries added a pathos to his return.

Avery Whitney bowled in, Melody in tow, and launched into a world-class bragging performance about how we were doing. I protested his insistence that Ted immediately see how the courts were rigged, and the way tents and other facilities had been prepared, but there was nothing for it but that Ted and Karyn had to be ushered around immediately. I went with them, and thought the tour, brief and optimistic as it was, seemed almost too much for Ted.

"My lord," he said later, when we were safely ensconced in the downstairs hospitality suite, the door locked on everybody but him, me, Karyn, and Beth. "You've been whirling dervishes around here." He dropped into one of the deep white plastic easy chairs and heaved a sigh that signalled how tired he really was. "Everything looks . . . wonderful."

"We manage," I said. "Not to worry about any of that. Now, suppose you guys tell me what happened with the bail and charges, et cetera."

"In the first place," Karyn said, sitting on the arm of the chair beside Ted like a protective angel, "Clarke Higgins was not murdered."

Beth, standing nearby, reacted faster than I did. "What do you mean? You mean the autopsy report has finally been released?"

"Yes. We think they've held it a couple of days."

"What did it show?" I demanded.

"There were no signs of violence on the body."

"No broken bones or signs of a beating?" Beth asked. "No gunshot wounds, anything like that?"

"None."

"Then—"

"Higgins died of an aneurysm. Carried since birth."

"So it couldn't be murder," I said, my dim brain catching up.

"But," Beth probed, "they clung to the other charges?"

"Yes." Karyn looked somber. "They haven't ruled out additional charges, either."

"Like what?"

"I don't know. But Jeff Tuhey says Llewellen is a crazy man on this case—is really embarrassed and vowing to press everything he can, any way he can."

Ted stirred. "He states that he must make an example of me. Citizens have an obligation to support law and order, he says, and my inaction may have allowed the scene to get so old that the whole truth of what happened may never be known."

"That's crap," I said.

Ted raised his face, his eyes widening in surprise. "But true, of course."

"No, it isn't," Karyn snapped at him. Then she turned back to us. "We have to be in court late Monday morning. The charges will at least be clear at that time. Ted has to plead to whatever additional stuff Llewellen may file by that time."

Ted absentmindedly moved his cast-shrouded right arm. The movement made him wince.

"Is that hurting?" Beth asked.

"Nothing much," he told her, and idly rubbed his good left hand over the stippled tan surface of the cast.

"Hell," I said, "you'll be as good as new before you know it."

He looked up sharply. Seemed to gather himself. He said, "Could Brad and I have a minute or two alone, please?"

Karyn and Beth looked equally surprised, but Karyn murmured "Sure" and they left us in the suite. I sat down facing my friend across an oval glass coffee table. I didn't like the feel of this.

"When he jumped on my arm," Ted said calmly enough, "he broke both bones in the forearm. The radius and the ulna." He raised the cast slightly and looked at it thoughtfully. "I have a curved metal plate around each broken area, and eight stainless steel screws into the bone, attaching each plate. I've seen the X-rays. I insisted, you see. They took some bone out of my hip and transplanted it in there, to replace some of the fragments of the radius they couldn't piece back in. They assure me it will all grow back together all right."

"Sure—" I began.

"Eventually," he went right on, "the screws will have to come out. Perhaps months—perhaps years from now. The reinforcing plates are scheduled to stay. They're very cheerful, the doctors, don't you know. They enjoyed the challenge of such a severe bollixing-up as I got. They say I'll be fine. With enough physical therapy I can have . . . normal . . . sedentary use . . . of the right hand and arm again."

"Sedentary use?"

He gave me a death's head grin. "Possibly even play tennis again. In a slight, casual, non-competitive way."

"You'll do better than that!" I protested instantly. "You can—"

"They were very clear about it," he cut in again, with the same eerie, defeated calm. "I am finished as a quality tennis player, Brad. Forever."

It made me feel kind of sick. "Doctors don't know everything."

"Part of the idea for Bitterroot Valley," he said, as if I hadn't spoken, "was that players like you would visit—provide an ambience. And *I* would be here all the time, sort of the resident old pro, with a bar lined with old action shots from tournaments, a prominent glass case displaying trophies, all of that rot. Selling the resort by using me as the drawing card. 'Play with a former world champion and enjoy his hospitality,' all that.

"But none of that is going to work anymore, Brad, do you see?"

"You're still a former champion, damn it!"

His eyes flared with pain. "But *I'm a cripple*! And who in bloody blue blazes wants to muck about with a cripple?"

I left my chair and went around the coffee table and knelt beside him, seizing his shoulders. "I think you're full of it, pal. We can make this work!"

"You're a good friend," he said huskily. His eyes had gone wet. "But it *won't* work. You've already done far too much—you and the others. Even old Avery Whitney! Lord! But there won't be any more charity. After the tournament . . . I want all of you out."

"What if we won't go?" I asked with false cheer. "What if we like it here, and want to stay?"

"I'll get you back your money, Brad. Somehow. I'll pay you back every cent if I have to auction off every stick of furniture."

"Like hell you will!" I shook him none too gently.

He winced, forcing me to release him. "Don't you understand?" he cried. "I don't want to fight anymore. I've had it. I'm through."

Ted had never been a quitter.

Once in the French I had watched him play a match against one of the bigger guns, maybe Becker, maybe Connors, my memory is faulty on that score. But I remembered everything else: how Ted had been down two long sets, 4–6, 4–6, and trailed in the deciding third, 3–5, with his opponent serving for the match.

It was hot that day the way it can only be hot, it seems to me, in France: steamy hot, sticky hot, suffocating, so that the air feels like an itchy wet blanket around you, sucking out your strength. But Ted hung in there, taking the deciding game to deuce twelve times. Then he got an add, then he broke the other guy, and the match started to turn.

He was out there more than two more hours, skinny legs pumping, making impossible gets all over the court, staving off five more set points, getting behind again in the fourth set and rallying once more with a series of cleverly disguised lobs and drop shots that had the other guy talking to himself. When Ted finally won, in five hours and forty-six minutes, he went into the locker room and had muscle spasms and nausea that amounted to convulsions.

But he won because he would not quit.

He had never been willing to quit at anything.

Seeing him the way he was *now*, after being beaten and hurt so badly, made me want to throw up.

"I've got to find a way to make him keep fighting," I told Beth much later that night.

Beth, wrapped in a big white terrycloth robe, sat with her legs tucked beneath herself, facing me on the cabin couch. She swirled the ice cubes in her highball before answering.

I said, "The idea of getting him to go on bothers you?"

"I'm just wondering, Brad," she said reluctantly.

"About?"

She met my eyes. Her solemn intelligence shone. "Is there really a chance?"

"Sure," I said immediately.

She sipped her drink and didn't say anything. The late-night silence lay deep around the A-frame, enclosing us in its cocoon.

"You don't think so?" I prodded, a little irritated with her.

"I just don't know," she said. "I haven't looked at the books, and if I did, I probably wouldn't be able to get through all the bookkeeping complexities. But if what you've told me is accurate, you're facing a hell of a battle even if things go well from here on out."

"That's true," I said. "But this place does have the potential. Some good traffic, nice exposure on ESPN next weekend, a few condo sales, and we have enough cash flow to meet the first balloon payment and keep our heads above water."

"That's assuming, of course, that Ted's participation doesn't become a moot question."

"How could it become moot? Oh. You mean . . . if he ends up going to jail?"

"It could still happen, Brad. He was *so* dumb not to notify the authorities the instant that body washed into the open. And that district attorney must be obsessed with the idea of getting him on something—anything."

"But the autopsy was great," I pointed out stubbornly. "Even if they manage to stick him with something, it's practically a formality."

"A formality," she cut in sharply, "if the news carries the fact that the owner of Bitterroot Valley is a felon, in prison someplace? How is *that* going to fit into your ideas of getting a favorable press to bring in buyers and resort clientele?"

I thought about it. "We just won't let that happen."

She reached across and put her fingertips on my arm. "Honey, you're a fighter and I love you for that. But all this is costing a fortune. I know you've put almost everything you have into trying to keep things running. But wishing doesn't make it so. Mr. Whitney was done in. The odds are stacked against Ted. Just because you've gambled everything you ever worked for, that doesn't mean you can hold back an avalanche."

I got up and padded barefooted to the bar, where I freshened my drink. My nerves were getting bad. I reminded myself to keep the freshener a short one.

Walking back to the couch, I told her, "Tuhey is a good lawyer. He'll protect Ted in the criminal proceedings. We've got Allen Industries off our backs. We'll make it."

"I hope so," she said solemnly.

Despite my best intentions, I chugalugged the rest of my whiskey. "Ted's the problem. I've got to get him motivated again. He's never been a quitter."

"Maybe . . . he just *can't* struggle any more."

I accepted that by not replying. Hemingway liked to talk about how life sometimes bent people, sometimes in such a way that they healed and then went on, stronger because of the hurt. He said life sometimes broke people, too. But he never really came to terms with that. Maybe he couldn't. Maybe at the very end Hemingway understood being truly broken, beyond healing, and that was why he went down to the hallway that fine sunny morning outside of Ketchum and put both barrels of the shotgun to his forehead, just above the eyes, and pulled both triggers.

I had to face it too. I *wanted* Ted to mend. The constant worry and financial battering—the betrayals he could not predict or comprehend—had made him vulnerable. Then in his thrashing around he had done something very stupid, and he was not the kind of man who easily forgave himself for stupidity or any other weakness. The brutality in the jail cell, courtesy of Jack Lassiter, had been the final blow.

A beating like that can be so unexpected, so shocking, that it violates your spirit at the same time it savages your body. The pain may go away. The memory of the violation never goes away. A psychologist once told me that the body never forgets what has been done to it; people are plunged into depression after major surgery, he said, because the brain *does remember* what happened, even though anesthetics turn off consciousness. For Ted it could be like that. The helplessness, the shock of violation in that kind of brutality—the mutilation—the terror—might never recede enough to allow him normalcy again. His arm might heal but the breaking might be forever.

Lassiter had been viciously clever in so carefully preparing, then breaking Ted's arm. *His tennis arm.* Once a bully cop had boasted to me in a bar about how he had castrated a suspected rapist, and gotten away with it. That cop too had known how to find the candle flame of a man's will to live, and snuff it.

The only clue to helping Ted that I could think about was the tournament. He had had the idea—had staked his hopes on it once. Now we were committed and it was almost on top of us. I had to make it work, and in the process pull Ted back from the abyss.

twenty-eight

Elsewhere

Elk City

Sylvester drove back in late at night, and avoided the main part of town. His vision seemed slightly blurry—the road was indistinct in the headlights—and his fatigue was so crushing that his heart flopped around in his chest like some wounded animal.

Since narrowly escaping entrapment at his cabin, he had been moving constantly. His thin reserve of stamina was long since depleted. Now he was running on nerves—and desperation.

His first act, after seeing the approaching lights and making good on his pell-mell, cross-country driving escape, had been to put seventy miles between himself and Elk City, then find a remote roadside public telephone.

"Yes?" the neutral voice answered on the second ring of the emergency telephone half a continent away.

"Sylvester here."

"Go ahead."

"The papers are not out. They are cross-checking all biographical statements and backgrounds. Total depth. Rumor has polygraph operators en route."

There was the slightest pause, probably while the contact signaled someone else to join him in monitoring the call. "Continue."

"Sketches of me have been made from an eyewitness and are in broad general circulation. Earlier tonight at least two vehicles of men approached my place. I narrowly got away. It appears they have called for additional assistance."

There was another pause, then a faint but distinct click on the line. A new voice said, "Sylvester?"

Sylvester recognized his voice. A man he had never met in person. But this voice was the highest authority; it had been on the line, giving orders, at the time of the St. Maarten episode, and before that the Lechova matter, and at earlier times when the stakes were this high.

"Yes," Sylvester said.

"Your assessment, please?"

"My associate is in the gravest danger. My effectiveness has been severely compromised."

"You have seen a copy of the sketch of you?"

"Yes. It is not a good likeness. However, it may be good enough. I am staying out of view at this time. In addition, three persons, including Smith, have seen me face-to-face."

"They could identify you."

"Yes."

Another pause.

Then: "Sylvester. The operation is to be terminated at this time. Notify our mutual friend. He is to activate his withdrawal plan immediately. You can notify him at once?"

"Within a few hours, yes."

"About these three persons who have seen your face . . ."

"Yes."

"If possible without incurring unacceptable risk to yourself, these three persons should be eliminated. Tell me your assessment of the situation. Can you undertake this assignment before withdrawing?"

It was not unexpected. Sylvester had already calculated the odds.

He knew the voice could send in another operative. But a delay of days might ensue. By that time, the three persons who posed a threat to him might have scattered.

And two of them, at least, he thought, would not be difficult.

He told the voice, "I can undertake the assignment."

"Good. Do so. Then you too withdraw."

"Understood."

Following that conversation, Sylvester had tried at once to contact his colleague, O'Connor. There was no answer. Sylvester then considered all his options concerning elimination of the three persons who knew his new face: where he was likely to find them, and in what circumstances.

At least two of the three might have to be confronted close to other people. Even the silencer-equipped Makarov might attract instant attention. Use of a knife or garrote was possible, of course, but in the one case it could cause undue struggle, and as Sylvester mentally inventoried his weakened condition, he did not like to take that chance.

Something else was needed: something silent and effective.

If he had had his full kit of tools, Sylvester would have had no problem. A puffer of the type he used to kill Dominic Partek would be ideal. But Sylvester had had no time to assemble a full kit before arriving in Montana, and he could hardly wait for one to be brought to him.

After thinking about it a while, he decided on an old-fashioned remedy.

That was when he drove more than seventy miles to reach Stirling, Montana, in the dead of night. Located the small pharmacy. Broke in, got what he needed, got away fast.

Then, driving the second leg of a ragged highway triangle, Sylvester had cut back through the mountains to reach the outskirts of Missoula before dawn. The sleepy motel clerk had scarcely given him a look when he rented the room for the day, saying he did not want to be disturbed after driving all night.

From the room, Sylvester had finally managed to get through to O'Connor.

"My friend?" Sylvester said. "The sky is very clear."

"Yes," the voice replied, instantly awake. "Water is clear, sky is clear, a good day for a game."

"You are to terminate and withdraw," Sylvester said. "Now. Quickly."

O'Connor paused a beat. Sylvester knew he was eating his disappointment at having been so close, and now being pulled out. It was a bitter pill for both of them.

"Understood," the voice said then. "I will comply. At once."

Sylvester broke the connection and could finally yield to the fatigue that was crushing him.

That had all been earlier. Now it was night again, and although he had slept fitfully through much of the day, Sylvester felt no more rested. He had drained too much energy out. There was nothing left to recharge the batteries.

But he could not rest. Not yet.

He drove to the area where he knew Mrs. Hill lived with her children. It was not a good place for killing: houses placed close together, windows facing windows. And the complication of the children in the house.

Sylvester mentally shrugged as he parked in the alley. Some risks had to be accepted in order to eliminate graver ones.

In the dark car he got out a faded red industrial towel and pulled the plastic bottle—his burglary booty—from the glovebox. He uncapped the bottle. The sharp stench of the anesthetic stung his nostrils. Quickly he doused the towel, recapped the bottle, and got out of the car.

He hurried up the alley toward the Hill house with the cloth bunched tightly in his fist.

twenty-nine

By Monday noon I was feeling considerably better about the tournament and not much better about anything else.

Melody's telephone calls to all of our professional entrants who I could track down had cheered them considerably; ESPN's plans for live coverage, with tape-delayed rebroadcasts, made my players' appearances in the tourney a lot more attractive to their sponsors. With TV, shirt patches would get always-welcome national exposure. The companies that paid big bucks to get their player to wear their logo patch would be happy, even if our tournament was minuscule. What made the sponsors happy tended to make the players happy. Now they weren't coming just as a personal favor to me and Karyn.

Our publicity efforts had also taken effect. ESPN was running promo spots. Nearer home, The Sunday *Missoulian* had gone ape in announcing our plans, running pictures of the headliners such as Lendl and Cash along with two pictures we had provided of the lodge, and even carrying our information on ticket prices and a map showing how to find us. The newspapers in Salt Lake City and Denver had not been so profoundly impressed, but both carried major stories about us inside their Sunday sports sections. Monday morning our reservation phones rang off the hook.

On the other hand, Ted Treacher was not off the legal hook. With Beth going along, he and Karyn had driven to Tripptown for his first appearance in court on the Higgins case. Jefferson Tuhey thought the DA might drop the whole thing, but Llewellen hung in there, pressing charges of obstruction of justice and felonious moving of a body. Tuhey pleaded Ted not guilty and the judge set bond at $5,000 on each charge, which Karyn posted. They were on the way back.

A little after lunch, Tuhey called for me. He said he was still in Tripptown, and it wasn't in his job description but he thought I ought to know that a Missoula company had just filed suit against us, alleging $23,000 in unpaid bills for roof repairs to the lodge. The lawyer for that company had told Tuhey he was also preparing a separate lawsuit on behalf of the construction firm that had built several of the cottages and six of the nine unsold condominium units. The suit was going to charge we had failed to "vigorously and expeditiously attempt" to sell said units. The lawsuit asked $600,000.

We did not need more bills or lawsuits, and it was sort of depressing.

Down at the courts, Avery Whitney had had the workmen set up sawhorses barricading off the middle courts, and the bleachers were going up.

"Well?" he demanded as I walked up. "How's it look?"

"Like a disaster area," I replied.

He chuckled, *basso profundo* snuffling sounds from deep in his chest. "We'll be finished by tomorrow morning."

"You've found enough workers?"

"No problem!"

"The signs look good. Now about the rest of the tents—"

"No problem!"

"What's the latest on the concession companies?"

"No problem!"

I started to turn away.

"I need some cash money to pay some of these truckers," he told me.

"How much?"

"Oh, nine thousand ought to do it."

"Avery, where in the hell do you think I'm going to get nine thousand in cash?"

"Write a check, man. I'll get Melody to drive into town with it. It's—"

"Don't tell me," I interrupted. "No problem, right?"

He rumbled again and spat. "That's my man!"

Collie Davis appeared soon thereafter. He didn't look happy either.

"What news?" I asked once we were closeted in the office.

"O'Connor didn't show up at work today. He's the electronics guy they let inside the test control room the other day when part of the plans disappeared."

"Have they looked for him?"

"Went to his apartment. Empty. Took most of his stuff. It looks like he's bugged out."

"Hell! Does that mean he got away with the stuff?"

Collie shook his head. "The boys out there say absolutely not. Even Skurlock doesn't think the man could have gotten out with anything, and Skurlock would be pessimistic if his L.A. Raiders were playing the Little Sisters of the Poor. The hell of it is, if there's somebody inside at the lab that we haven't fingered yet, they could carry the plans out at some later date. And we can't keep strip-searching everybody forever."

"How about the polygraphs?"

Collie winced. "So far we've discovered three unfaithful husbands, one theft of a roll of toilet paper, and two women from the office who got so hysterical that they jumped the needle off the chart when asked their name."

"You," I told him, "are a gold mine of happy news."

"One of the office employees is missing too," he added.

"Was he a suspect?"

"It's a she. And no. Woman named Hill, I think it is. Not important. Did scut work—routine typing of letters and unclassified memos, sometimes operated the front central phone during coffee breaks. She's lived around the area for a long time. The idea that she might be a mole is pretty unacceptable."

"But she's gone."

"Under funny circumstances. She put her kids to bed, said she was going to watch TV for a while. Kids woke up in the morning to find her missing. They figured she might have gone to the convenience store or something, and didn't call neighbors until several hours had passed."

I thought about it. "You think there's some kind of link?"

"Well, there could be, but we can't come up with a theory. The woman adored her kids. Everybody agrees on that. Even if you said she was working with O'Connor and they got orders to withdraw, it seems beyond the realm of possibility that she would bug out and abandon those kids."

I hesitated, then asked the question I had to ask: "Do you think Sylvester is gone too?"

Collie frowned and scratched his head. "Nobody's seen him."

"Do you think he's gone?"

"Why would he stay, if they've aborted the operation?"

"Because there might be somebody else inside, regardless of what Skurlock and everybody else thinks. And Sylvester might be hiding someplace close to take the plans from that agent once he—or she—can get them out of the compound."

"It's possible," Collie said, "but unlikely. However, on the chance that it *might* be something like that, I've been authorized to hang around a few more days."

"What are Skurlock's plans?"

"Help continue the search and investigation inside the lab. When that's done in another week or so, who knows?"

"What are my instructions?"

"Hey. Run your tournament. Try to help Treacher. On the assumption we *might* still have some further need of you, I'm not terminating your per diem. But I think you're home free, my friend. So enjoy."

I went back to work with a wary, puzzled feeling that I could not quite understand. We had been very close to meeting again, Sylvester and I. I hadn't wanted that, God knows, but I had been up for it. Now had he really fled?

The importance attached to the air force lab's research was made obvious by the fact that he had been sent here in the first place. But I thought he was too important to risk here now.

On a personal level it was a letdown. For a few months I had felt reasonably safe and secure; after all, even if he had survived St.

Maarten, he would take time to be treated and heal. Now, after assimilating the initial shock of finding that he was not only alive, but in Montana, a primitive part of me had been continually keyed up, waiting for something to happen. Hell, I had been sent here to *make* something happen. And now: nothing.

It didn't feel right.

Beth, Ted and Karyn drove back into the lodge lot a little later. Ted looked like hell—haggard, wrung out. Karyn couldn't quite muster her usual sunny smile, and even Beth looked glum.

"Hey, is it that bad?" I asked, vainly trying to cheer things up.

"I guess," Karyn said, "we got our hopes up about a dismissal."

Beth shook her head. "That district attorney is every bit the loser Avery said he was. I suppose technically you can support an obstruction charge, but who's going to vote for jail time when the autopsy report clearly states the man died of natural causes? And that stupid 'moving a body' count is a law that usually relates to funeral homes or cemetery operators! But Llewellen is going to press it all the way because he made some statements to the press about Ted's guilt, and now he can't back down without looking like an idiot."

I put an arm over Ted's shoulder, being careful to avoid the cast. "With Tuhey on your side, you'll probably get a complete acquittal."

Ted shrugged. "Tuhey says we may want to plea-bargain."

I looked at Beth. "Plea-bargain for what?"

She sighed. "Llewellen hinted he might go for a deal where Ted would plead guilty to a misdemeanor count of failure to report a death."

Looking at their glum expressions, I thought about it. "And drop the other charges? Is that so bad?"

"It is," Beth said, "when you add that Llewellen says he'll insist that Ted pay a five-thousand-dollar fine and do ninety to a hundred and twenty days in the county jail."

"That's ridiculous!"

"If we could just find out who buried that body in the first place . . ." Karyn said, and didn't complete the thought.

Ted mopped a moist handkerchief over his gray face. "I suppose it wouldn't be so bad. It's not like I'm going to have anything else to do. Well, I'm exhausted. I'm going to my room."

I took his arm. "I'll walk you."

"I say, Brad. I don't need a nurse!"

"I'll walk you, asshole." I grinned and went with him toward the elevators, leaving Karyn and Beth standing there.

We rode up in silence, and nothing was said while he dug out his room key and opened the door. He turned to me with a ghastly smile. "Well, the cripple has been delivered, so—"

"I'm coming in a minute," I told him, and went in ahead of him.

He closed the door behind us and followed me into the living room of the suite. It was nicely done in contemporary furniture, lots of books and magazines, a pretty view over the shed roof of the restaurant toward the courts. Out there the bleachers were going up at an astonishing pace.

Ted sank into a chair so weakly that I almost expected to hear bones rattle. "What do you want?" he asked, his face gaunt with fatigue.

"What was that crack about your having time to go to jail?"

"What did it sound like, sport? It's the truth."

"We've got a resort to get out of the red, here!"

He shook his head. "Oh, no. I've failed. I'm going to sell out."

I was stunned. "Do you have a buyer?"

"No. But I'll advertise. With Allen Industries out of the picture, I'll just have to find someone else."

"Ted! This tournament is beginning to look like a success. Just what you were counting on! We can turn this all around, and with Allen Industries out of the picture, I'll bet a lot of the local sabotage will end, too."

"You don't understand. I don't care anymore. After what happened to Sally—" He broke there and started to cry.

Oh hell. I went over and knelt beside his chair, grabbing his good arm. It felt string-thin, the skin dry and cold to my touch. "Ted, I know you feel like hell right now. But you'll feel different."

He shook his head. "No. No. I won't go on. I won't owe you. I won't drag you down too. I'll sell to the highest bidder—get enough to pay my debts, including what you've poured in. And pay back Karyn, too—let her get out of here—"

"You dumbass! Did it ever occur to you that *neither* of us might *want* to get out of here? That girl loves you. Don't ask me why. I agree with you. You're not worth a damn. But *she* doesn't feel that way. And as to me—well, I like it here. I like the open country and the idea of helping run a resort—all the tennis and golf I want. I'm not about to let you flush it, you idiot, and I don't think Karyn is either."

He had raised his face to stare at me during what was, for me, a very long speech. "Karyn?" he said softly. "*Me?*"

I sighed in exasperation. "Some women, you moron, don't sleep with a man unless they *do* care a hell of a lot about him."

He just stared at me.

I said, "Promise me this much. Promise you won't sign any sale papers with anyone until after you've talked to me about the deal."

"If someone came along and I had a chance to make—"

"Promise, asshole, or I break your other arm."

The threat so startled him that he actually smiled. "I promise."

"Good. Now take a nap. I want you at the head table tonight, being your most charming self. The first of our tournament guests are due to arrive and I don't intend to entertain them single-handed!"

"I guess I can see what you see in it," Beth sighed that night, very late, as we settled down in bed.

"See in what?" I asked, to be difficult.

She gestured, her tennis bracelet tinkling in the dark. "This. The lodge. The mountains. The people coming to have fun. The clean air. Everything."

"And half of my part can be all yours," I told her.

She didn't answer.

"I said—"

"I heard you, Brad."

"Want to say yes now, or think about it and keep me in suspense?"

Her tone in the dark was flat, refusing to play. "If those lawsuits against the resort are filed later this week, as indicated, I'll go over to Helena and file the necessary responding motions and pleadings. I don't know how fast they try civil suits. Maybe we can get some kind of settlement, or maybe we can get to trial in short order. If so, I might even be able to stay long enough to handle that for you."

Silence fell between us.

"You talk like you're leaving," I said.

"I never said I was going to stay."

"Oh," I said.

Then we lay there in the dark a long time, and she finally rubbed her wrist gently back and forth, up and down, on my forearm. I don't know what she expected from me. Whatever it was, her words had frozen me up and I did not respond at all.

A long time later she breathed deeply and turned over, putting her back to me, and rumpled her pillow to sleep. I still didn't move. A lot of feelings kept going through me, and none of them were pleasant.

thirty

Elsewhere

Elk City

In the abandoned tarpaper hunting shack deep in the woods about six miles north of the highway, Sylvester opened a can of pork and beans with his knife. Night wind stirred, blowing through invisible chinks in the walls. Shivering, Sylvester started to eat.

Suddenly the plank door flew open. Wind gusted in, making the stubby candle on the packing-box table flutter wildly. Sylvester swung around to face the intrusion. Jack Lassiter, hair wild and eyes crazy in the candlelight, filled the doorway.

"Mr. Lassiter!" Sylvester gasped. He put down the knife and can of beans. "You startled me! How did you ever find me, my friend!"

Lassiter lurched into the shack. Coat flapping open, stubble beard black on his face, he filled the small enclosure with crazy, electric energy. "You lied to me!"

Sylvester sank to the teetery chair and put his hands weakly on his hat and coat, spread neatly over a corner of the packing box. "What? What in the world do you mean?"

"I come back from job-hunting. I seen a poster. I talked to my bud. You're not a fisherman! You're a goddamned spy or something!"

"Oh, my friend! You've been misinformed! I—"

"Shut up!" Lassiter reached behind his belt and produced a .357 magnum police revolver. He leveled it unsteadily. "I ought to kill you here and now for the way you made a fool of me. But I ain't doing that. Oh, no. When I get you to town and turn you in, they'll have to give me my job back. They'll probably give me a medal."

Sylvester let his shoulders slump. He picked up his coat and started to put it on. "How did you find me?"

"I showed you this dump when I drove you up this way through the woods, remember? I thought, 'Where would he know to hide around here?' And right away I—"

Sylvester fired the Makarov twice through the folds of the coat. Both bullets hit Lassiter in the chest. The force of the shots slammed him backward against the wall. His revolver spun out of his hand. He crumpled sideways, hit the floor, and did not move.

Pistol alert, Sylvester moved cautiously near the body. *Arrogance*, he thought: the fool had made enough noise approaching the shack to alert a deaf man. But—

At that instant, the "body" erupted. Sylvester was bending over to assure himself that his shots had been lethal. Lassiter's eyes shocked open, his arms reached up and knocked the Makarov out of Sylvester's hand—grabbed his wrist and slammed him against the wall with shocking force.

Stunned, Sylvester rolled along the wall and tried to get to his pistol on the floor. Lassiter, blood-covered, terrifying, some kind of walking dead man out of a thousand nightmares, heaved himself to his feet, stumbled forward, got both arms around Sylvester, and drove him across the floor of the shack.

They hit the makeshift table. Tools, food, and clothing flew in all directions. The candle was knocked out. Sylvester crashed against the back wall of the shack with the madman pummeling him, trying to get hands around his throat. *This man is dead. How can he—?*

Trying to push the great weight off him, Sylvester had just gotten one hand against Lassiter's chest. And felt the stiff metal mesh of the police bulletproof vest.

But there was no time to think about it because Lassiter had succeeded, he had both big hands around Sylvester's throat, and he was choking off precious wind.

Writhing on the floor with Lassiter on top of him, Sylvester banged his free hand into the cold corner of the stove, tools out of the toolbox that had been on the table, slimy canned beans that had been thrown everywhere. He groped desperately for something to use as a weapon. His knife was down here somewhere.

His hand did not find it. Lassiter was screaming something, choking the life out of him and pounding his skull against the filthy floor, and Sylvester knew he could not last much longer. There was red around the black of his vision and the tendrils of oxygen-deprivation lassitude had begun to weaken his struggle.

His hand found something on the floor. Closed on it. The octagonal plastic handle of a screwdriver.

Hope flared weakly. He brought the screwdriver up and pounded it down on Lassiter's back with all the strength he had remaining. It punched through jacket and shirt and buried itself to the handle. Sylvester felt the hot spurt on his hand. Lassiter seemed to feel nothing.

Blackness was closing in fast now. There was no sense of pain in his neck any more, just the furry edges of unconsciousness, tightening like the petals of a black flower.

Sylvester wrenched the screwdriver loose from Lassiter's back and brought it down again, in one final convulsive effort. The blackness started to close the last glimmer of consciousness. A tremendous weight fell completely over him.

For a few seconds he did not comprehend. Then a spasm of air reached his lungs. He coughed, retched, and fought back to partial consciousness. The weight covering him was his attacker—inert.

Sylvester struggled, managing to push the weight partly off him. Then, strength flooding back with panic, he pushed Lassiter's body to the side and managed to reach a sitting position.

It was deathly still in the shack, and Lassiter did not move.

Almost two hours later, back in the brush-choked woods not far from the shack, he staggered the last necessary spadeful of dirt out of the hole. Clambering up on hands and knees, he got unsteadily to his feet and surveyed his work in the feeble light coming down through branches from a starry sky. He was exhausted, pain-filled, his throat swollen half-shut so that every breath required effort.

Putting the shovel aside, he bent to the body and with one more convulsion of effort rolled it into the shallow grave.

Thirty minutes after that, the grave covered over, he started back toward the shack. But he was too weak, he could not make it. Rest. He had to rest. He sat heavily in the thick brush, sweaty and shivering inside his coat.

Now only one person here had seen him with sufficient clarity and attention to make a positive identification, he thought. Only one.

He was far too exhausted to think much now, however. Even about that.

Tomorrow, he thought.

Tomorrow was soon enough.

Sylvester lay back, rolling onto his side and bunching his body up against the cold,and fell over the cliff to numbed sleep.

thirty-one

Ivan Lendl was the first of our pros to arrive, coming into Missoula on the early flight from Minneapolis Thursday. Melody Ryan, thrilled out of her mind, met him and brought him back to the resort in the courtesy van. Within thirty minutes of his arrival, Lendl was on the golf course with Avery Whitney. When they came back almost four hours later, Whitney looked glum and Lendl had the scorecard stuck in his shirt pocket.

"How was it?" I asked.

"Hard," Lendl said, stone-faced, and went alone to his room.

"God damn it," Whitney growled, "I thought you said he played to a twelve."

"Maybe I meant seven."

"Maybe you did. That sucker shot a seventy-nine!"

I grinned. "People improve. How much did he take you for?"

"Oh, I got to him for three dollars, but I had to leave my left testicle out there on the teebox to do it."

"Avery, I can't tell you how sorry I am about that."

He marched off, still growling, to see if the ESPN people needed anything at the moment. After a while he came back with a scrawled sheet of paper showing when they wanted to do some taped interviews that might be used for plug in case of rain delays. Two of them were with me, talking tennis talk, a couple were with the players, and two more were with Ted Treacher, one on his tennis career and one on the resort and the tournament.

"Have you seen Ted lately, Avery?"

Whitney snorted. "Haven't seen him yet today."

Carrying the paper, I went off looking. I found him in his room. Not dressed yet, and unshaven.

"You'd better get cracking," I told him, trying to hide my irritation. "There's too much to do for you to be lazing around, feeling sorry for yourself."

He studied the paper. "You're right." He stood. "This will be excellent free advertising to sell the place."

Into the dead silence I finally said, "It's going to be a nice little tournament. The only thing in the world that could mess us up now is rain, and the weather channel says warm and dry."

"How many rooms do we have occupied?"

"All of them."

That would have cheered a mummy, but he simply stared into space as if it didn't matter.

I added, "No more cabins, either. The guy from the real estate office is licking his chops. He expects to sell at least three of the condominium units this weekend."

Again I waited, and again Ted was silent, looking far away.

I was very close to shaking him like a recalcitrant kid. We were coming back. Every hope for the tournament was within reach. He simply would not respond. Even remembering my own recent craziness, I felt fed up with his seemingly insurmountable melancholy. Recent bad news aside, our situation had begun to look light-years better than it had only a few days ago. In my conversation with him, the orthopedist in Missoula had been encouraging about eventually rehabilitating Ted's arm entirely. We could beat the criminal charges somehow. But still Ted was like this, as if it were a matter of pride to be defeated.

I told him, "The interviews will help. But not to sell. I already told you that."

"I plan to start an ad in the back of *USA Today*. I have enough left personally to pay for that. With this success behind us, we'll get interested buyers."

"God damn it, Ted! I said no!"

"You've sunk a small fortune in trying to keep us afloat. You have to be repaid."

"Am I yelling about being repaid? I like it here!"

He shook his head. "It would take years to get out of debt."

"It won't take years to get a little ahead of it, and even eke out a decent living."

"No," he said. "I won't allow that. I know when I'm whipped. I'll find a buyer and I'll sell. And you'll get back every cent."

"Get shaved and dressed, and get ready for those interviews. If you say any more about quitting, I'm going to beat the hell out of you."

He looked at me with a wan, crooked grin. "Shouldn't be much of a challenge to a man with two arms."

He seemed hopeless. I left him there.

Downstairs I found Collie Davis.

"New information?" I asked, feeling my gut tighten.

He shook his head. "Status quo."

"Did they find that missing female employee?"

"No. And nothing at the lab, either. Skurlock is fit to be tied." He looked around the bustling lobby, out through the windows, over the pennant-decorated courtyard toward the flags rippling in the breeze over the courts, the banners around the bleachers, the tents. "Looks like you've got all you can say grace over."

"We're ready. If the crowds come to pay at the gate, we can show enough life to stave off the creditors."

"You worried?"

"Would you be, if you owed a million dollars?"

"Hell. I'm worried, and all I've got is a past due on my American Express card." He frowned. "You going to make it here?"

"Christ, Collie, ask me in a week. Or a month."

His frown deepened. "I won't be here that long, pal."

"They're pulling you out?"

"Not for a few days. There's still the off-chance Sylvester is hanging around. But I don't much think so, now. And as far as danger to you is concerned, I think we're past that."

"I'm glad to hear it. Want to share your reasoning with me?"

"Well, you're going to be here the next few days, right?"

"Right," I agreed. "So?"

"Nobody in his right mind would come here after you at this time, with thousands of people milling around. And whatever we've ever said about Sylvester, we've never said he was stupid."

We had the big staff meeting at four P.M. Ted sat dully, not taking part. Avery Whitney and I ran through all our checklists. The outside concessions were ready, all the extra reservation people and household staff were on hand, our kitchens bulged with food, and the main ballroom gleamed, awaiting the evening's festivities. I felt myself getting excited along with everybody else.

After the meeting, I did my taped interviews with the ESPN commentators, then stayed to watch. Lendl, back from a long workout oncourt, came in still wearing his sweats, and they interviewed him. Then it was Ted's turn.

To my surprise, he livened up when the cameras rolled. In the monitor he looked reasonably healthy and optimistic. The interviewer, Ed Edling, asked how he was enjoying life as a resort owner, and he hesitated only fractionally before launching into a smooth, dishonest reply that implied everything was wonderful.

Karyn, standing beside me in the office to watch a monitor, glowed with pride. "That's the way I want him to think!"

"If he's really thinking that way," I was forced to point out.

She frowned at me. "What do you mean?"

"It encouraged me for a minute, too. Then it occurred to me that he would put on this kind of act to make potential buyers more interested."

She slumped, crestfallen, but then straightened up again. "We'll make him believe his own sales talk, then."

My admiration for her intensified. "If anybody can do that, kid, you're the one."

The next hour for me was spent in a meeting with our three umpires and the volunteer linespeople we had been training. Our umpires were good ones, men who had worked open tournaments in such places as Los Angeles, Denver, Vail, Chicago, and Atlanta. Importing them had cost more than I might have liked, but a good person in the chair can make all the difference between a fine match and chaos. Our linespeople were mostly members of clubs in Missoula, Butte, Bozeman and Helena, here in response to flyers Ted Treacher had gotten put up on area bulletin boards very early on. I felt pretty good about them, too.

When I left that meeting, thinking I might actually sneak in an hour of practice, a familiar rotund figure greeted me in the lobby. Elk City Police Chief Manley Hamm looked nervous.

"Chief, what can we do for you?" I was already thinking that if he had been sent to arrest Ted again, somebody was going to pay.

Hamm peered around. "You're getting crowded. Going to be a big turnout."

"We hope so."

He fidgeted. "I've got a couple of volunteers lined up, and we're notifying both the sheriff's office and the highway patrol. So I think you can count on maximum cooperation. If you have any requests, just let me know."

"Cooperation?" I echoed. "Requests? For what?"

He gestured in the air. "Crowd control. Traffic. Anything else you might need. We aim to have people out on the highway to direct the traffic in case it gets snarled, and we can have somebody on the grounds here too, if you want. You just let us know."

"Kind of a change in policy, isn't it, Chief?"

Hamm colored. "It was never policy to impede progress out here."

"Just not to help, right?"

His jaw began to work. He was angry, but it wasn't all directed at me. "Everything we were told made us believe the whole area would be better off if there wasn't any resort out here."

"And Cliffton and Wells were persuasive, right?"

Hamm tugged at the wilted gray collar of his uniform. "We had enough trouble . . . all the sickness, too much traffic. We wanted everything to stay pretty—"

"Cliffton and Wells works for Allen Industries," I said, refusing to let up. "If they had their way, this area could become some kind of chemical plant putting out a lot of pretty green smoke and yellow stuff foaming up the river."

He winced. "Anything I ever heard about the quiet work being done at that old mine had to do with gold or silver. Or maybe copper.

And if they secured surrounding property—this was my guesswork—then they might be able to go ahead with all the mineral rights."

"Too bad that wasn't the case."

"You don't have to beat me over the head with it, Mr. Smith."

I changed tack. "Are you the one insisting charges be pressed against Ted Treacher?"

"No! I— Hell! The autopsy proved he didn't kill Higgins. I mean, it was stupid, he screwed up, throwing dirt back over the body. But is that something a man is supposed to go to *jail* for . . . especially after what Lassiter did—I mean—after what happened to him accidentally in our jail?"

"No, Chief. It isn't."

Hamm fretfully shook his head. "Have you seen him, by the way?"

"Ted?"

"Jack Lassiter. My ex-officer."

"Not lately. Why?"

"Just asking. Buster, his brother, is worried about him. Came in this morning and said he hasn't seen him, and he never stays away quite this long. I thought, in view of your previous, um, unpleasantness with him, you might have heard from him."

"I haven't seen or heard from him, Chief. Which makes me happy."

Hamm thought about it, sighed, and went away.

It was getting late in the day. I had run very early this morning, but needed a workout oncourt in the worst way. Karyn was willing to hit with me, so I ignored a few business telephone calls and changed into tennis clothes and met her on court 14. Ted, Beth and Collie came down and watched. I noted with some discomfiture that Beth frigidly ignored Collie, treating him like a pariah. I felt both bad for Collie and uneasy for myself about that. She would *not* completely forgive either of us for my original failure to give her all the facts about my motives for coming to Montana.

Karyn and I worked out for a little over ninety minutes, finishing under the lights, and I was atrocious. Stiff from court inactivity, I had no timing and had lost some of my wind. My bad knee hurt. Toward the end—tired, out of breath and sweat-soaked—I began hitting out a little better and getting a few of them in. But the way I had been forced to draw the brackets, I had to face Lendl tomorrow, and that was pretty sickening.

All I had hoped to do was avoid totally disgracing myself. But now, unless I did better than this, the customers might start demanding a refund on the basis of alleged fraud.

"You looked better toward the end," Karyn said.

"But better than what?" I countered disgustedly.

The time for the pre-tournament banquet loomed. All of us got ready. I dragged out my suit. When we started gathering for cocktails at 8:30, standing at one end of the big ballroom with its long, linen-white tables, I felt uneasy. Invitations had gone to lodge guests, of course. But we had also mailed them to all the important people in Elk City. The mailing had gone out with no RSVP, so we had no idea what the response might be. I wondered if anybody from town would show up.

At 8:45, I gently broke away from a group including Jimmy Connors and Tim Mayotte, and walked out into the lobby to smoke. I peered anxiously into the front parking area.

As I did so, I spotted some of the people just leaving their cars to our valet parking out there. I recognized the mayor and Chief Hamm and their wives, resplendent in best bib and tucker. Coming along close behind them was Bud Bavinger, editor of the paper. There were others.

They came into the lobby, looked slightly apprehensive when they saw me, and walked forward slowly.

I hurried to meet them with handshakes. "It's great to have you with us tonight. Come in. Let me show you back to the ballroom."

They relaxed a little.

"The place sure looks grand." Bavinger's wife smiled innocently, craning her neck at the chandeliers. "I'm *so* glad we have you people with us. You know, I never did believe some of those stories about a place like this bringing in dope and an undesirable element!"

"I certainly didn't either," Hamm's wife chirped. "Elk City *needs* a place like this. It will make us grow in the right way!" She looked up at me with a sunny, tremulous smile and patted my hand. "And I think it was just *wonderful* of you to get into that old mine and prove that those awful people from Chicago were secretly storing things that might have hurt us!"

Amazing, I thought, how the wind could change.

* * *

So the dinner went wonderfully. My players, a head or more taller than the local and guest crowd, and further distinguishable by their casual slacks and jackets, mingled, smiled, even signed a few autographs "not for me, you understand, but for my children!" Our locally hired five-piece combo played a few tunes that were recognizable. It went on very late.

After that, the four of us—Ted and Karyn, Beth and me—closed ourselves off in Ted's room for a nightcap and a post-mortem. Beth glared at me when I called to invite Collie to come up, too, but she didn't say anything.

"Hey, it's going to *work*," Karyn said, smiling sunnily. She looked cute in her ball gown. "The people in town have thought it over. They've decided to *like* us. It's going to be a great couple of days."

I rubbed my shoulder, which felt slightly sore, and looked around. I was on the couch beside Beth, and Karyn perched on the arm of Ted's easy chair across the coffee table from us. Collie, wearing jeans and a Georgetown sweatshirt, stretched out in the other chair off the corner of the table. The fire in the fireplace made it seem nice and cozy. Everybody seemed mellow. Except Ted. He paid little attention to what we were saying, instead staring into his own private space.

Which did not look like a happy place to be.

I tried to rouse him. "What think, Ted? You figure I'll beat Lendl tomorrow?"

He looked at me, surprised and unable to recognize a joke.

"Or," I added, "let me put it this way: do you think I can win *a game* against Lendl tomorrow?"

"Maybe," Karyn said with a grin, "if he gives you three chairs."

Even Collie got that reference to the old Bobby Riggs handicap system. But Ted just stared at us as if he didn't quite understand the gist of our conversation. In the old days he would have joked even if he didn't quite get it.

Karyn tried once more. "Oh, sure. You'll beat Lendl, and when Pam Shriver gets here Sunday for the exhibition, I'll beat her, too."

"Maybe we could get *her* to play Lendl."

"Maybe we should *all* get out there at the same time and try to play Lendl."

We waited for Ted. He didn't respond.

I gave it up, climbed out of the couch. "I'd better make sure all our celebrities are happy, and we don't have any guests with busted faucets or something. Beth?" And we got out of there.

Walking down the corridor with her silent at my side, I wondered if time would heal what she saw as my breach of trust in not telling her everything at the outset. I had lost a lady not all that long ago because I refused to violate secrecy in order to give her an ego stroke. The idea that it could happen again—that hurt.

My mind was filled with other worries, too. Was Sylvester a thousand or ten thousand miles away by now? Had he managed somehow to get the plans out of the lab, and we just hadn't been smart enough yet to realize how he might have accomplished it? And out at the lab, were they perhaps running another test? Was the EMP beam going into space, as scheduled, or were the bigdomes in error with all their protestations of perfecting the test procedures, and was another pulse slamming into some part of Elk City right now, tearing molecules off DNA chains, fiercely heating—and destroying—disease-fighting clusters in a fraction of a gigasecond, setting up little immune system chain reactions in the fastest-growing tissue, especially in children?

Maybe it was Ted's indomitable blackness of mood. Maybe it was fatigue and letdown. But suddenly, riding down to the first floor with Beth silent and glum at my side, I felt like I had stepped into some kind of other-dimensional bubble: my own optimism evaporated, any faint sense of accomplishment I had been nurturing about the operation vanished, and I realized that I hadn't done a damned thing worthwhile or even permanent—except perhaps alienate Beth and bet almost everything I had on an illusion.

thirty-two

Cars started rolling into the temporary parking lots well before eight o'clock Friday morning. Despite signs and ropes designed to channel fans directly to the stands, we got considerable traffic through the lobby, already crowded with excited guests. I saw people strolling down among the cabins and condominiums, too, and took that as a hopeful sign for sales.

"How's it going on tickets?" I asked Avery Whitney at 8:45.

"Smooth as cream, son, smooth as cream."

"How many have we sold this morning?"

"Couple thousand."

"That's great. Concessions? Parking? Ushers?"

"No problem!"

By nine, starting time for the Cash–Bell match, we had about 3,000 in the bleachers, and incoming cars were backed up all the way to the highway. We delayed the starting time fifteen minutes.

"Wonderful," the gray-haired Ted Bell muttered to me out of Pat Cash's hearing. "Now maybe I can extend the match till nine-thirty."

More fans piled in. We were almost out of daily tickets, pegged to bleacher capacity. I did some fervent mental arithmetic: four thousand fans at ten dollars each, plus our percentage on every cup of coffee, soft drink, hot dog, or kolache sold at the busy concession tents . . . we might not only put Bitterroot Valley Resort on the map with this tourney. We might even come out ahead financially.

With Whitney and Melody scurrying around, bossing a horde of temporary flunkies, the operation was slick. We had a wonderful break on the weather, the temperature already past 50, headed for a predicted high near 70, not a cloud in the sky. I spent a couple of hours putting out the few minor patron brushfires that did erupt, and worrying about Lendl.

Cash took out Bell, 6–2, 6–3, in a match that pleased the crowd because Bell was still in fine condition, a player who could scurry around and make a lot of difficult gets and return the ball to Pat with soft underspin and a variety of dinky cuts that prevented a forehand massacre. Our crowd had swelled to capacity and I had okayed selling some standing room. We had nearly five thousand jammed in by the time Jimmy Connors took the court with Aaron Krickstein a little after noon. I watched a few games. The way it started, it looked like it might be a long one. Finding Melody, I asked her to get the schedule signs changed to show me and Lendl starting at 3:30.

Then, already thinking ahead to my scheduled debacle, I went to the lodge dining room to stow in a few carbohydrates. Beth came along, but when Collie Davis hove into view she froze up and said she was going back courtside.

Collie stared sadly after her as she walked away, beautiful bare legs purring beneath the hem of her lavender shorts. "She's a great lady. I wish she didn't hate my ass."

"She doesn't just hate your ass, Collie. She hates all of you."

"Unfortunately, I think you're right."

"She'll get over it."

He studied my face. "You think she will?"

"Eventually."

"And how about this mad-on she's got at you, over your taking this assignment?"

"It'll be fine. Not to worry." I thought of Avery Whitney and added, "No problem."

He let that rest. A few minutes passed while I stowed in carbohydrates. Then he said, "You're going to stay up here, aren't you?"

"I'm not sure, Collie. I'm thinking about it."

"What does she think?"

"I think she's thinking about it."

"I hope so, Brad. She's a neat lady." He lit a cigarette and looked thoughtfully into the distance.

I pushed the rest of my sandwich aside and poured sugar into my iced tea. "What time is it?"

"Two."

I gulped part of the tea. "Gotta go."

He looked surprised. "Match time already?"

"Yep." I stood.

"Isn't this a little early?"

"Yes, but I've got to change and get my knee brace on, and then go to the bathroom fourteen times."

He grinned. "I've never seen you compete. As long as we've known each other. This ought to be great."

"Not very," I told him.

The imp tried to get out of his eyes. "Oh, no! You mean you don't think you'll beat Ivan Lendl?"

"Go to hell, Collie."

"I mean, it's not like he's universally considered the top player in the world. Some people rank—"

"Go to *hell*, Collie," I repeated, and left him there.

Down at the courts I checked progress of the Connors–Krickstein match and saw Connors had won the first set 7–5, and they were tied at 2–2 in the second. I watched a point or two through the fence, made sure from Avery Whitney that nothing complicated needed my attention, then went back through the canvas tunnel to the pro shop lockers.

It was quiet in there, cool and still and gray-white, with the rows of pale green metal lockers on both walls. You could smell showers and sweat, foot powder and somebody's lingering aftershave. As I entered, the sound of the crowd, yelling after a good point, penetrated the cinderblock walls with a sound like distant kettledrums.

The pro match would run at least another hour, and then the schedule called for club and open doubles play on all three stadium courts. I was in no hurry when I entered the locker room. I always got there far too early in the days when I was a real player. Few opponents ever beat me at getting ready, anyway.

Even so, when I turned the corner of the locker room and peered down its long, empty length, I saw another figure bent over the bench at the far end, lacing up his shoes in front of his locker: Lendl. He was already dressed in his white shorts and the trademark shirt. He looked up briefly, as unsmiling as a lizard.

"Hello," he said.

"Hello," I said.

Shit, I thought.

My locker was at this near end. I opened it and began changing. In the silence, the sound of my pants zipper sounded loud.

In the days when I had my reflexes and two sound knees, and my body would do exactly what I asked of it, the time before a hard match was the most exciting time there was. And pleasant. There was always a scare factor in the equation somewhere, but that only made it better, more intense. Then the stakes had been truly and frighteningly high, and I had loved it. Today, nothing was really involved except my stupid masculine pride, but I felt queasy with apprehension and I was not liking it at all.

My career at the very top of professional tennis was briefer than most, a meteor. I peaked very late, thanks to Vietnam and the injury I brought back with me from there. Then there were those two years when I *almost* won most of the tournaments, *almost* staged the miracle rally, *almost* got to face the crowd with the big silver cup held over my head. And then there were the four years when my body did everything I ever dreamed it could do, when my timing was perfect, when the fatigue and cramps and little injuries didn't make a damn, when all the shots went in.

A magic time.

Soon over.

My decline did not follow the usual course of advancing age, failing nerves and reflexes, faltering eyesight. It would have, of course, and I had begun to experience the middle-age yips on a few occasions. But what got me was the knee. That marked a neat and final chapter to my meteor-story, a little like Arthur Ashe's first heart attack.

Of course I was luckier than Arthur. My problem was not life-threatening. I had two operations and went through the rehabilitation program and tried to make a modest comeback. But it didn't take too many years of being battered from side to side oncourt, jerked around by kids literally half my age, to know it was almost time for me to hang them up as a touring pro. Then—when I blew the knee out again and had to go through it all another time—there was no more denying reality. I was through.

A long time ago now . . .

But I could still remember *how it had been*—how it had felt to be the best. That was why I didn't want to go out there today and look like a jackass, even against one of the truly great ones like Lendl. What I dreamed in my Walter Mitty mind was of his having an off-day, not caring a whole lot, playing casually, since it was after all practically an exhibition, as small as our purse was. And me finding myself absolutely on top of my game—or what was left of what I laughingly called my game—and me somehow actually taking him to a tiebreaker in the third set.

No, not even my Mitty-brain could imagine me as the eventual winner. No matter how casually he might start a piddling exhibition like ours, a player of Lendl's greatness has such discipline that he is constitutionally incapable of slopping around and losing to someone as far gone as I. But I wanted to play my best—prove I wasn't totally washed up and ready for the county old folks' home.

Maybe—*maybe*—I might steal a set from him. . . ?

Oh, boy.

I took my sweet time getting ready. Finally I got the knee brace out of my locker, wrapped it around my leg, and began lacing it in place. The brace is an unpretty thing, grayish canvas, with stiff plastic reinforcing ribs longitudinally, and a small steel hinge arrangement on the outside at the joint. It weighs less than a pound, but it feels much heavier when you're wearing it. It's similar to ones I've seen on football running backs who are trying to play while still rehabilitating a knee. It keeps the knee from stressing laterally when you plant your foot to stop a body that's intent on hurtling right on in the original direction. Or that's the theory.

I hate the ugly goddamned thing. I have never gotten used to wearing it. It doesn't feel good. It limits quick movement and cuts your speed, and it's an embarrassment. But there is no cartilage left in there, and fewer complete tendons, and not as much kneecap as there once was. For serious tennis it's the brace or wheelchair city. Given those choices, the brace I can live with.

With the thing finally strapped on and laced up and adjusted, I walked around the locker room a while, flexing it and making sure the hinge was set just right, so it wouldn't lock up. It seemed okay. Then I had to urinate about five times and then I sat on the bench, pretending to examine my rackets. Lendl, silent and remote at the far end of the room, did stretching exercises, and warmed up with some steps-in-place. Time dragged. I wondered how I had gotten myself into this. I mean, had I lost my mind? Didn't I have any pride left at all?

It crossed my Mitty-mind that maybe Ivan would pull a muscle as he stretched, and have to default. No such luck.

They came in at 3:05 and said Connors had just won his match in a tiebreaker, and we should get ready. Lendl, stone-faced, gathered rackets and towels, made sure he had a pocketful of sawdust, and came down the locker aisle past me. His icy features softened in the slightest, briefest grin. "Good luck."

"You too, Ivan."

He went out. I gathered my gear, took a deep breath of resignation, and followed him.

In the tunnel we met Connors and Krickstein coming the other way. Both were sweat-soaked, their hair matted to their skulls, their eyes glazed with the fatigue and disorientation that follows any match with any degree of seriousness. Then, in a sharp cloud of sweat-stink, they were past. I followed Lendl on out of the canvas tunnel into the makeshift center court stadium.

It wasn't Wimbledon or Flushing Meadow, but the roar of the crowd as we emerged was startling—waves of raw animal sound rolling over us, racketing back and forth, making my ears ache. I hadn't played in front of this many people since Belgrade.

I kept my head down as I walked toward the players' benches on either side of the umpire's chair, and didn't look up until I had taken out a racket, pranged it a few times on my palm, needlessly toweled the grip, and retied my shoes.

The glare of the sun on the court's surface made it hard to pick out faces in the bleachers, but I saw some individual faces: a kid gnawing on a hot dog, a pretty girl coolly returning my stare from behind her big, red-framed sunglasses, a brawny man leaning back, sucking on a Tootsie Roll. The childlike part of me felt a stab of resentment. Why should they be having fun—and be so casual—

when I was scared of being annihilated out here? *Had the gladiators felt like this?*

Calm down, Smith.

We took the court and warmed up. My adrenaline started pumping so fast I got out of breath. Lendl's warmups all came back low and hard and accurate. I dumped a couple of mine into the net. Then I tossed up some lobs, and Lendl—*Jesus Christ, it really was Lendl over there!*—blasted practice overheads back past me.

We had a coin flip. He won—naturally!—and went back to serve. The chair called for quiet, ladies and gentlemen, please, and they really were polite.

Up came the ball over there. Motion. Then it was *over here* much, much too fast, and past my frantically outflung racket. Ace. Wonderful way to start.

He held serve at love, and I struggled mightily before winning my first service game as well. Lendl was glacially calm as always, looking across the net at me between his serves as he rubbed pocket-sawdust into his grip, scattering flakes all over the service area. He hit another ace. I got a couple back. He hit one long. Alleluia. But he won that game at add-in on a volley I couldn't have reached with a bicycle.

In the next few games, he held serve easily and I struggled. But as I thoroughly warmed up and found myself not being blown entirely off the court, I relaxed. The fear of humiliation was gone, replaced by the pleasure of getting to compete against one of the world's finest athletes. It was something I had missed—would always miss, now that I was "old."

In the eighth game, up 4–3, he broke me, then served out the first set to win 6–3. Opening the second set, he promptly broke me again with two whistling crosscourt backhands and a forehand deep to my right that he came in behind for a winning volley. He was playing smoothly, perhaps not with total intensity, but marvelously well. The great ones have pride; they do not go out there, even in the most casual exhibition, and mess around. They understand that they owe something to their talent.

So it did not surprise me when he broke me again in the third game, then flawlessly held serve to go up 4–0.

He showed no emotion, of course. He seldom did in real

matches that meant something. The few thousand dollars in prize money at stake here probably could have been lost in one of his checkbook subtraction errors. He was simply doing what was expected of him.

Except for minor irritation with myself over some of my unforced errors, I didn't feel much either. We had now gotten completely into the rhythm and pattern of the match, and despite his lopsided lead I was not disgracing myself. There was no hostility, no histrionics. Only business as usual.

Some people, especially fans who don't know a lot about the game, are not overly fond of Ivan Lendl. As nearly as I have ever been able to figure out, they want him to make faces, throw fits (or extra denim shorts!), gesture at the sky, flirt, scream, berate the chair, or otherwise be "colorful." Desensitized to the etiquette and traditions of the game by spoiled teenagers and older neurotics, they expect scenes. Because Lendl does not provide them, he is said to be "cold."

He is not a barrel of laughs. That I grant. But I think also that he had been given a bum rap. He plays tennis and minds his own business. In addition to being one of the greatest and most disciplined athletes in the world, does he also *really* have to have a line of funny patter, a Robert Redford smile, and an occasional childish temper tantrum?

Tennis and golf are the only sports left where decorum and personal dignity count for much. Football and baseball can have their McMahons and Bosworths and Boggses. I'll take a Lendl or a Nicklaus any day and time. If Lendl is "cold," then power to him; he's maintaining the self-control tradition of our game.

So Lendl just kept pounding them back at me, neither overextending himself nor taking it easy on me. If he had started to coast, I would have felt insulted, and he understood that.

I rallied mildly and held serve in the fifth game, then took advantage of two double faults on his side to get him to deuce and 1–4. He netted a volley on the next point, and somehow I managed to get my racket on the add-out service and knock it down the line where his crosscourt had to be too severely angled, and went into the net. So I had broken him once. Which is more than a lot of far better players can say.

After I held my serve again to trim his lead to 4–3, the crowd sort of got into it, rooting openly for the old fart, me. Lendl rubbed sawdust into his grip, rolled a service ball around and around in his palm, got ready to serve, looked across the net at me with absolutely the same expression he had worn since the locker room, and jammed me with one I couldn't handle. Somehow I got him to deuce again, but he had lost patience with me and had cranked it up a notch. He blew me away, winning six of the next seven points to finish his service and then break mine at love.

We shook hands at net.

"Good match," he told me.

"Thanks. You too."

We both shook hands with the man in the chair, then went back down the canvas tunnel together. My legs felt like wood and my shoulder and elbow hurt. The knee sent up throbs of discomfort. The clock showed five P.M. That surprised me. My body knew we had been out there a long time, but in my mind it had been five minutes.

After a long, steamy shower and change into comfortable sweats, I went back out and watched a little of the Mayotte–Carpoman match with Beth and Collie. Terry Carpoman was putting on a show, waggling his butt and making faces, and the crowd loved it. He was one of our more curious youngsters and there was an element of craziness in him that made you feel almost like he might be dangerous, might really blow up and do something terrible out there.

Early in the second set, with the lights on against gathering darkness, he did blow up. The call might have been bad. His behavior was worse. After staring, screaming, walking around and cursing, he went back to the service line and, apparently totally out of control, smashed his racket over the railing. Our man in the chair promptly assessed a point penalty. When Carpoman kept storming around and kicked over a table of Cokes, our referee escalated it to a game forfeit.

That seemed to get Carpoman's attention. Steaming and stewing, he got a new racket and prepared to resume play.

Disgusted, I left my seat. "My knee hurts. I'm going to go get some Motrin at the cabin. You want anything?"

"I'm fine," Beth said with a little smile. She loved tennis and was really into the match below.

I left her there with Collie and walked behind the bleachers, down past the central courtyard, down the asphalt path. Guests and visitors strolled around nearby. We were going to sell some cabins and condos, I thought.

But most of my concentration was still completely involved in the Lendl match, replaying points, savoring angles and impacts and responses to instantaneous surprises. Walking carefully in the dark, I got to our cabin and unlocked the front door and stepped inside, fumbling with my hand along the wall, groping for the light switch.

I didn't get that far.

There was no warning, nothing. Suddenly an arm snaked around my neck and a cloth went firmly over my mouth and nose, pressing hard. I caught a whiff of the cloth. The smell made old synapses fire: *I was six years old and a couple of baby teeth had to come out, and the dentist put me in the chair and put a cloth like this—with this sharp, unpleasant smell—over my face.* To knock me out.

I had fought him then, but he had held me down and put me under anyway.

This time I gasped—got some of the damned foul stuff down in my lungs—but then held my breath. I tried to wrench loose from whoever had me, but his grip was some kind of judo trick or something and I was helpless in his leverage. My mind rocked and reeled. I kept holding my breath. Then—I think panic made me think of something bright—I let my legs go limp.

He let me slide to the floor of the cabin. But he kept the cloth over my face. I kept holding my breath, simulating unconsciousness. I was not going to be able to do this . . . much . . . longer.

Who the hell was this . . . What did he think he was doing . . . How long could I hold my breath . . . Why hadn't I been more careful . . . My lungs were on fire . . . Roaring in head . . . heartbeat—

Reflex took over and my lungs gasped in a tiny spasm for oxygen. The stinking fumes went in and then I regained control in an agony of revulsion. But it had been enough. I slid down a long black tunnel into a silvery world at the end, but the silver turned black as I reached it.

thirty-three

Elsewhere

Courtside

With the score tied at 3–3, Terry Carpoman dashed raggedly across the court, got his racket on the ball, and flipped a great sizzling backhand up the line, passing Tim Mayotte on his way to the net. The ball made a yellow blur under the artificial lights as it dove down at the intersection of the side and back lines.

"*Out!*" the man standing at the back of the court called instantly, and extended his arm to signify wide.

Carpoman, long sweaty hair straggling over his face, had started to turn away, fist upraised in triumph. He wheeled back and stared, slack-jawed.

A few whistles of disapproval echoed out of the bleachers. People stirred in uneasy excitement.

Collie Davis glanced at Beth, seated beside him. "What did you think?"

"It looked in," Beth said, watching the little drama oncourt.

"I couldn't tell," Collie admitted.

Below their position, Carpoman stormed to the net and slammed his racket on the cord. His face had reddened until it looked demonic. "Did you call that ball *out*?" he yelled.

The back judge stood still, his youthful face tight and strained. His arm was still extended to indicate wide.

"Did you," Carpoman yelled louder, "actually call that ball *wide?*"

More whistles shrilled, and now it was impossible to tell if a large segment of the crowd disapproved of the call, or of Carpoman.

Beth murmured, "He looks like a crazy man!"

Carpoman whirled and charged the man in the chair. "What's your call?" His voice carried far past the thronged bleachers, out into the night beyond the lights. "Are you going to overrule that stupid call?"

The man in the chair leaned over the side. His microphone carried his quiet reply, amplifying the dry, pressured sound of it: "The call was wide."

Carpoman threw his racket down. It shattered on the pavement. "How can you *make* so many stupid idiot calls! What's the *matter* with you people? This is supposed to be a nice little tournament, but does that give you an excuse for being blind assholes? That ball was inside the line two inches!"

"Please play, Mr. Carpoman."

"You fucker! I'm not playing another point until you correct some of these stupid goddamned calls! I—"

"Abuse of equipment, penalty of one point."

"*What?* Jesus Christ! I demand to see the tournament director! I want that blind bastard off that line back there! I am not going to continue!"

The man in the chair looked pale, but he was game. "Play."

Carpoman pointed. His eyes looked crazy in the lights. "That ball was well inside the line! You can't just call *every* one wrong! When are you going to make one right?"

"Play," the chair repeated.

Carpoman stamped his foot, looking for all the world like a three-year-old having a tantrum at his mother. "Bullshit! Bullshit! Did you even see the ball at all? Answer me that! Did you see the ball? Do you have *any idea* where the ball hit?"

The man in the chair adjusted his microphone. Collie Davis thought the man's hand shook a little.

"Penalty for delay, one additional game point. Score is now forty-fifteen, Mayotte."

Carpoman jerked like a man who had been shot. He appeared unable to believe it. The crowd rumbled. More whistling mixed with a smattering of applause and a few boos. Tim Mayotte stood at his service position, hands on hips, studiously looking at the ground.

Collie told Beth, "I don't know a lot about tennis, but it looks to me like our friend down there is about one 'hell' or 'damn' from disqualification."

Beth shook her head. "Poor Brad. This is all we need: a darned temperamental mess by somebody like Carpoman."

Below, Carpoman spun away from the net, picked up his latest broken racket, and stormed back to the end line. He stood there, hands on hips, elbows akimbo, back to the court, shaking his head. He looked up at the lights, then back at the pavement. Then he turned and strode over to the bench and tossed his racket down and pulled another new one out of his equipment bag. The crowd, enjoying it, continued whistling and making a lot of noise. Mayotte waited, intent on his fingernails.

"I'm sort of sorry Brad missed all this, myself," Collie told Beth. "This is a virtuoso performance."

She nodded and turned from the court action to look at him. "You're trying awfully hard, and I guess I should appreciate that."

"Trying?" Collie echoed, thinking what great eyes she had.

"Trying to be friendly—make me like you."

"I'd like us to be friends, Beth. You mean everything to Brad."

"No." Her pretty mouth sealed itself in a thin, bitter line. "I come second at best. You and what you stand for come first."

Oh hell, Collie thought with dismay.

Below, oncourt, Carpoman had inspected his latest racket, and now walked back onto the playing surface. Studying his strings, he started back toward the deuce court as if ready to resume play. Then he stopped and turned and started back toward the net again, raising his racket to point at the man in the chair again.

Collie Davis again wished Brad were seeing this. He had been gone a long time, hadn't he?

Collie glanced at his watch.

He had been gone far too long.

Something—a residue of training, bad experiences, or plain old intuition—suddenly tightened in his belly like a coiling snake. He felt feverish.

"Beth," he said as casually as possible, "this looks like it's going on a minute. I'll be right back."

She nodded, intent on what Carpoman was saying below now.

Collie hurried down the bleachers and then under them, stretching his long legs to go even faster, pressing between people around the concession stands, headed toward the lodge, a huge, indistinct ghost in the distant side-scatter of the court lights, and the cabins beyond.

Far too long for Brad to be gone. Far too long.

Maybe—just maybe—a false alarm. *God, let it be a false alarm.*

Once past the bleacher area and onto the sidewalk that led around the gardens, he ran. Through the utility area and down the path, and to the cabin. It was dark. But the front door stood ajar.

He stepped inside, flicked on the lights. Two impressions hit at the same time. One: the cabin was empty. Two: a faint, medicinal smell hung in the air.

He recognized it: chloroform. Or something very like it.

Collie hesitated about ten seconds, an avalanche of disastrous thoughts tumbling through his brain. He turned and started outside, running back up the path.

"Look out! Look out!" The voice came from a side pathway, and hit him at the same time two blinding little headlights startlingly half-blinded him. He jumped out of the way and a golf cart, headlights blazing, skidded into the brickwork beside the path, knocking over a clay pot.

"Watch the hell where you're going!" Brad's helper, the old man named Whitney, bawled at him.

"Have you seen Brad?" Collie panted.

"No, but I'm sure looking for him. Our golf pro just told me some asshole stole one of our carts a few minutes ago!"

Collie grabbed the front canopy brace of the cart. "Stole one of these? When? How? Where?"

"I don't know all the answers, you blamed fool! He said he seen this dude racketing away from the cabins in a cart not long after dark, not using the lights, going hell aplenty down the fairway and off over in that direction, north. There's nothing out there but a bunch of useless woods and ravines. He said there were two of them. Probably both drunk."

"Drunk?" Collie demanded. "Why do you say drunk?"

"Well, the one driving was weaving all over the place, and Rex says the other guy in the cart with him, the driver was practically having to hold him in there on the other seat, to keep him from dumping clean out of the thing. I guess I'll call the police. Damn, I—"

"Give me the cart," Collie snapped.

"What? Hey, you can kiss my ass. I—"

"Give me the cart, damn it!"

Avery Whitney's good eye suddenly widened in a spasm of recognition. The Browning Collie had leveled on him was a very impressive piece of artillery.

"No need to get excited, no need to get worked up," Whitney wheedled.

"Out of the cart!"

Whitney hopped down. Collie Davis shoved him aside, jumped into the thing, and pressed the little accelerator pedal to the floor. The cart almost leaped out from under him as he bounced it over the brickwork bordering the walk, turned it in a tight circle, and sent it whistling down the cart path as fast as it would go, heading in the direction Whitney had pointed.

thirty-four

It felt like the third instant replay of the same incident in a football game: I had been through this already, but it still didn't make sense. All I knew was confused pain, glimpses of near-reality and then plunges back into blackness, violent movement, vertigo, fear, an overwhelming nausea and weakness I had to overcome . . . could not beat.

Nothing made sense.

What I knew then was this: unconsciousness there on the floor, then a feeling like an explosion inside my head, and a great roaring; then hands shoving me around; the smell of fresh air; my lungs in spasms; then a blurred sight of flooring in motion and the door frame going past me and sounds of something being dragged on pavement—me—then a hell of a falling sensation and night-cool wind, and disorienting motion, and passing out again.

I think I know now how he did it. At some point he had been given a short course in investigative techniques that included material on methods used by burglars to break and enter. They teach you that kind of thing at Langley, and also in the big stone building in Moscow.

You see detectives or bad guys picking locks on TV all the time.

They shove a little tine, like a dentist's tool, into the lock to hold back the security mechanism. Then they insert a second thin tool in beside the first, and push the locking wafers into the open position. And then they turn the doorknob and *voila!*, open sesame.

I have it on good authority—a member of the club in Richardson who had a lock business—that such stuff can be done. Locksmiths also have gadgets that clamp onto locks or knobs and vibrate the living hell out of the innards until random selection "reads" the wafers open.

There are other tricks, too. Once upon a time, not so long ago, a well-known safe company manufactured a particular small model in which the locking bar was raised to open the door by manipulating a handle on the front. The locking bar fell into place, securing the door when it was closed, by the gravity system. My club member once was called to open such a safe, long locked and the combination forgotten. Since I had expressed interest in such matters, he asked me to go along with him on the call. When we got to the scene, he examined the safe, clucked as if perplexed, then ordered everyone from the room except me. Then he locked the room door. Then he sat down and smoked a cigar and drank a cup of coffee, not even looking at the safe.

Finally, after more than an hour, he told me, "That ought to be long enough to convince them this was hard."

Then he had me help him turn the old safe onto its side and then onto its top. Gravity dropped the locking bar into the open position. He swung the door back and we returned the safe to upright. When we let the customer back in, my friend was mopping his sweaty face and licking his fingertips as if he had had to sandpaper them to work that difficult combination.

I don't think my man had to be quite that smart. He might have picked the lock, but he didn't have to bother. What I think he did was more straightforward. As my locksmith friend also showed me once, there are a lot of strong locks. Most of them are not as strong as a big set of visegrips.

I don't know how long he had been waiting. Long enough. Collie Davis's assurance that *no one* would be reckless enough to try anything during the crowded days of the tournament had lulled me, and the attack might have come earlier if I had been alone earlier. Now my carelessness had gone overboard, and he had me—must have been watching somewhere, and saw me leave the courts, and then he must have hurried ahead of me to the cabin, applied visegrips to the side door or a wrecking bar to a window, and slipped inside quickly enough to be waiting for me. And I walked in fat and happy, and he had the anesthetic-soaked cloth ready and waiting.

The only smart thing I had done—primitive choking reflex as much as thought—had been to hold my breath. And go limp as if I had passed out.

The amount I did inhale was bad enough. I went in and out of consciousness like a yo-yo. I knew just enough to realize he had tossed me into some open vehicle—a golf cart—and was driving me fast, chaotically, through darkness. I jounced and bounced around, half on the floor of the cart, and went in and out of consciousness some more. He held me by the back of my shirt, enough to keep me from being pitching clear out. I couldn't get together enough to do or think anything.

At some point a few of the slivers of consciousness began to coalesce. The cart was stopped. I was no longer in the cart. Flashback to childhood . . . my father and one of my uncles standing close together, tossing me from one to the other, so that the sense my little-boy nervous system got was of being tossed *miles*, flying through vast space, almost getting killed. I must have giggled or shrieked in my terror; the men who played the game with me never understood I was terrorized. It was like that now. I was picked up, *tossed*. Hit the ground hard, face-first. That was when I blacked out again.

Time. How much I didn't know. Fragments of dreams and bad pictures swimming around. Sick. Partial consciousness again. A great, roaring pain, and chill, wet earth pressing against my face.

More confused unconsciousness. Then I sort of came back again. Further awake this time. Things sharper, my brain working.

Quiet. No motion, no pitching around. I was cold. Wet. Something cold and wet underneath my sprawled body. Wet earth. Yes. I remembered that.

Then my ears woke up. I heard *sluuping*, sliding sounds somewhere nearby. I opened my eyes. Darkness. Not quite total. Feeble light, like starlight, or a moon.

I tried to get my eyes to focus. In the center of my blurred field of vision, very close to my face, were two muddy rocks the size of footballs. The rocks were identical. I was seeing double.

More odd, wet, sliding, sucking noises. Crunching. The sound of stuff hitting other stuff, soft, padded. A sound of like . . . a sound of like something I knew . . . a sound of . . . sound of like . . .

Then it hit me.

Shoveling.

I snapped into clearer consciousness. My vision still doubled, but in an instant I had my mind back in place, functioning at a crazy, magnified, speeded-up pace. Sweat bolted out of every pore of my body and I almost retched. The roaring in my ears intensified. How had I heard the shoveling over this roaring sound?

I risked moving my head an inch, getting the right side of my face out of clammy mud. It gave me a view along the cloddy earth on which I had been tossed. I was on the ground beside a golf cart. In my blurry vision, one of its back wheels looked enormous.

More shoveling sounds. I moved another inch or so, expanding my field of vision past the cart. I couldn't see much but I saw enough: a pile of fresh dirt. Movement. A bulky figure that looked, from where I lay, about the size of Godzilla.

The figure moved with a jerky, repetitive rhythm: bend, scoop, swing; bend, scoop, swing.

Sylvester.

Digging a hole.

Slowly, painfully, with the deliberate steadiness of sheer mental discipline, sinking the shovel in the hole, lurching weight against the shovel to dig out a scoop, then bracing to lift the scoop out of the hole, toss it onto the wet pile. *Sluup!*

Jesus Christ.

Digging.

Digging *my grave.*

The shock of it started to swing me off the globe again, into some deep-space vacuum of unconsciousness. In unreasoning panic I fought the wave of confusion, swam frantically back up. Got in focus again, sick at my stomach, gripped by a terror that went to the bone marrow.

He was *in the hole,* out of sight to his hips. Almost finished.

Almost ready for me.

His back turned.

I felt a mad impulse to scramble up and try to run for it. Panic almost made me do it. I sent a tentative signal to my legs, ordering them to bunch their muscles. The message got scrambled or something. My legs did not respond correctly. My mind flashed back to my childhood experience with the dentist again. I had walked awkwardly, dizzily, almost falling down, after he woke me following the tooth extractions. My mother had helped support me to the family car.

I thought for a second I must be tied up. That made the panic climb to an even higher plateau. *Wait a minute, wait a minute, try to think*. I sent some more signals down and around my body. I could move a little. I could not feel any ropes or wire. Therefore I was not tied up. Therefore the problem was the aftermath of the gas: my brain just wasn't sending very good signals, or the lines were crossed.

The shadowy figure in the hole moved differently. Stood straighter. The arms swung. A shovel came up and was slung out of the hole to the top of the pile of wet earth beside it on my side. The shovel tumbled down the wet pile and hit me on the shoulder, splattering mud clods. Behind the pile, the shadowy figure climbed painfully out of the hole . . . rose to its full height beside my intended grave.

Stood there. I stopped breathing.

Moved only slightly, and then the hands and arms moved with quick precision. The sound that followed was of cold metal, a slide snapping, slamming again. I knew that sound, too: the sound of a gun being checked, a cartridge ejected, maybe, but with the certainty of another fed out of the magazine into the chamber.

God only knew where we were. I was functioning now, and knew he had taken me out of the cabin and somewhere in a golf cart. But the *where* didn't matter. What mattered were the hole and the gun.

And the fact that we were obviously in some isolated place. So there would be no cavalry to the rescue. If I wanted to live, I had to save myself. I had never wanted more to keep on living. But I didn't see how I had a chance.

The shadowy figure moved now, the feet and legs visible through my almost-closed eyelids as they came around the dirt pile, boots making scraping, sucking sounds in the mud. I lay still as death. He nudged me with a muddy boot. I didn't breathe.

He had experience at this, I thought. Maybe many times. A nice, quick incapacitating gas or drug injection, to assure complete silence in a crowded area, and then a trip to an isolated place, and then the silencer-equipped automatic to finish the job. Crowned by an unmarked grave. Neat.

He moved closer to me. He coughed. His lungs sounded bubbly, strained. Planting his feet, he reached down. He grabbed me by my left shoulder and tugged, starting to roll me over. Neater yet, to put the bullet in the front of the skull. Then it would be done, except for rolling me into the hole and shoveling the mud back in on top of me.

I had no plan yet, but panic took over. The fact that he was taken totally by surprise helped.

As I rolled over, I swung my good leg as hard as I could. His motion reinforced my levering action. My knee got him squarely in the groin. He made a sharp choking and let go of me. I rolled over, right on top of the shovel.

This time my legs obeyed. I scrambled dizzily to my feet, grabbing the shovel as I stood. He was *right there*, bent in pain. I swung the shovel with everything: a big, sloppy roundhouse swing, all the way over the top, a motion like an overhead shot. The flat bottom of the tool caught him flush on the forehead. The blow sizzled all the way up the handle and into my arms and shoulders, the solid, soft feel you get on a perfect serve or a long iron shot.

It should have put him down. All it did was stagger him backward, gun still in hand.

Enough. I turned and jumped the grave and ducked sharply sideways and plunged into the dense underbrush a few feet on the other side. I ran headlong into something—a slender young tree—and staggered sideways. Behind me came that sharp, ugly, unmistakable *phhhttt!* of a silencer-equipped weapon, and simultaneously the bright little metal sound of the action working. I dived to my right, then left again, running.

I couldn't see much. That didn't matter. Panic was in charge. When I plunged over the brink of a little embankment and sprawled into a freezing little rivulet of water, all I knew was that I had made too much noise, and I got up and out of there in seconds. I careened along the far side of the gully, saw starlight through some trees, and ran the other way, toward the deeper dark. Weeds and creepers and stinging tendrils lashed at me, tearing facial skin, but all I could think was that they were slowing me down.

Something whispered by my ear and hit a tree trunk with a nasty splatting sound. I dived to my left, found deeper cover, went over another unseen embankment and tumbled head over heels almost straight down, through flying rocks and mud and sliding dirt, bouncing off a rock or small stump, tumbling again at the bottom to hit and roll and stop, the breath half knocked out of me.

In the sudden quiet, punctuated only by the sifting and sliding of pebbles and dirt coming down in my wake, I heard him up above: the sound of a man moving through brush, kicking small rocks. He didn't have to be quiet. He had the gun. He could follow *my* noises and take his sweet time.

Rabbits must feel like this, I thought.

It made me mad. The anger flooded some new strength in, and with it came a jolt of clearer thinking. I rolled over and, instead of getting to my feet to run, started to ease along on my belly.

It took some willpower. Every instinct said to bolt for it. But he was up on top and I was down here and he couldn't see me. So I bit my tongue and crawled. Put each hand in front of me carefully, sliding along.

Time took on a new reality. Minutes went by, but I didn't know anything except the crawling, fighting to maintain quiet. But the trouble was that he had figured out my tactic now, and he was being quiet too.

And I had no idea, as a result, of where he was.

After a while I couldn't stand it any more. I got slowly to my feet. My legs shook so badly they would hardly support me. I moved forward at a faster, still-cautious pace. The ground started to rise under me. In another minute or two I was on all fours, crawling up a shale incline. Then the incline suddenly became vertical.

I stopped, gasping for breath, and tried to figure out what had happened. Then I understood. I had crawled up against a stone wall—literally. A little box canyon. And I had reached the far end of it. Only six or eight feet wide here, it simply . . . stopped. In an almost sheer rock face.

Behind me, perhaps thirty or forty yards distant, pebbles tumbled.

Panic gusting again, I got to my feet and felt above me for a projection that would help me start my climb out. My hands found the stubby root of an old tree or something. I grabbed it and heaved myself up, clawing at the rock for a foothold.

It wasn't as bad as it might have been. Not at first. Then it got steeper. With my toes dug into tiny indentations, I clung with one hand to a little rocky knob and felt around for my next hold. My fingers scrabbled over loose shale, it felt like, and sheer stone. My right hand, clutching the knob, cramped. The pain went down my arm like fire. *Come on, come on, you can't let him get you now.*

My frantic groping found another protruding root almost out of reach to my left. I caught it and hung on, pinioned against the face of the cliff, heart threatening to rip my chest open.

A voice racketed shockingly through the dark: *"Brad! Brad! Where are you?"*

Collie Davis's voice.

I hung on, swinging between surprised elation and fear. He didn't sound far away: off to the left somewhere, on higher ground. I wanted to yell. I needed help badly enough. And if I yelled, he could locate me. But so could Sylvester.

There came the sounds of a lot of thrashing around, somebody plowing through brush. It was pretty close to me on the left, across the ravine I had blundered into, the direction of Collie's voice.

"Brad!" his voice yelled again.

From behind me came the rapidfire chuffing of Sylvester's gun: three times, four times, close together. Then another sound blasted the dark, the unmuffled muzzle blast of somebody else's gun—four times, fast, then one more.

"Brad, god damn it, where are you?"

"Here!" I yelled, and found new strength to get another hold and swing myself higher on the wall.

Another chuffing sound came. Something spattered on the rocks about three feet over my head, showering me with painful little fragments of stone. Off to my left the bushes rattled and rustled, and the responding series of gun blasts was incredible—Collie probably emptying his Browning.

I found another good hold and pulled myself higher and got a choking faceful of weeds and grass hanging over the top lip of the wall. Grabbing both hands filled with the coarse vegetation, I heaved with both feet and managed to lift myself over the top and onto blessed flat grass.

I had just enough trembling energy left to crawl maybe ten feet and roll under some bushes with some kind of nasty little stickers all over them. I didn't care. They hid me.

A long time passed. I may have passed out for a while.

Finally I heard the sounds of movement. Close. Getting closer. A man walking through the heavy stuff. I moved my head fractionally and strained my eyes in the dark.

The figure emerged, staggering a little, from the obscurity of a thick stand of lodgepole pines. It came toward my hiding place.

"*Brad?*" its voice called. "*Where the fuck are you?*"

Collie's voice. Intense relief flooded through me like hot butter. "Here!" I croaked, and started to crawl out.

He bent and helped me. In the dim starlight I could see he was covered with dirt and rock dust, had a thin rivulet of blood streaming down the left side of his face, looked like he had torn his shirt half off.

"Are you okay, pardner?" he demanded worriedly, peering at me close up.

"Okay," I told him. "Did you get him? It was Sylvester—"

Collie spat. "He got away."

thirty-five

Collie was back at the lodge very early Saturday morning, just as the morning sun peered over the mountains to the east and bathed the valley in thin, pearlescent sunlight. We would have partial clouds today and the air felt distinctly chilly. Collie looked about as bad as I felt after three hours' sleep.

I had the waiter bring us coffee on the deck and we sat there together, bundled in our coats against the weather. Already a handful of guests were out and about, some of them heading for the courts for a workout before our tournament action drove them off again.

Collie, a dark bruise and some scratches adorning his face, looked me over. "You look about like I feel."

"Thanks, Collie. You're not the picture of happiness yourself."

He peered around. "Beth not up yet?"

"She's gone somewhere."

That surprised him. "Where?"

"I don't know. She said she had an errand."

"Active lady."

"Yes."

He tried the coffee. He had something fresh on his mind, but didn't seem ready to spring it. Aching in every bone and joint, I felt impatient with his everlasting goddamned reticence.

"Anything on Sylvester?" I asked finally.

He winced. "Sheriff's office in Missoula reports a brown Dodge abandoned on the road near the smokejumper base. Mud inside. Couple of uneaten sandwiches. Brown paper bag with a half-used bottle of chloroform or something similar under the front seat."

"Damn."

"My sentiments exactly."

"He changed cars."

"Or caught a bus."

I sat up straighter. "You weren't checking the bus station?"

His face colored with irritation. "*I* wasn't checking anything, Brad. That's not my job, remember? Skurlock and his people were supposed to be checking. So was the sheriff and so were the cops. Not just in Missoula but all over the place. But it took them a while to get everybody in place, remember? Hell, it took us a while to get back here and find Skurlock and let him know what had happened. Buses left before anybody got in place to watch. Planes left, for that matter."

"And maybe he stole or rented a car," I added.

"I think you're getting the picture now."

"Do you think he's really gone this time?" I asked after a pause.

"Yes. I really do."

"You thought that before."

"This time I'm surer."

"Any basis?"

He squinted his eyes, the way he sometimes did when he had to admit something painful or embarrassing. "The people at the bus station remembered a man. Fit the description. Bus to Bozeman."

"Well, dammit, meet the bus at Bozeman, and—"

"Somebody did. He'd gotten off along the way somewhere."

I thought about it. "Well, at least he's gone."

"Yes. Which means the lab is clear."

"So," I said, "they can go back to irradiating people."

"Will you get off that? It's *safe* now. It has been for a long time."

I let it go. Sipped my coffee, absorbed feelings and random thoughts.

Sylvester must have had his truck out in the boonies beyond our property last night. Collie and I hightailed it back to the resort in one of the golf carts, the one he had chased us with, and got messages to Chief Hamm, the sheriff, and Skurlock in pretty short order. The first cars were on the scene within forty minutes. They went all over the territory. The sheriff even got a helicopter out, and it puttered around most of the rest of the night with its searchlight poking down. About two A.M. somebody found a spot not far from my ravine where fresh tracks indicated a pickup recently parked, with deep dig marks indicating a fast getaway. We figured that had been Sylvester.

All our guests and players had been sound asleep when all this happened, and since the search had centered more than a mile from the lodge, and most consultations had been out on the highway, they remained blissfully ignorant. Which was the way we intended them to stay. Ted and Karyn had been up, of course, knowing something was up, and Avery Whitney and Melody also knew a little. They—along with Beth—had had a lot of worried questions when Collie and I reappeared much the worse for wear.

Neither of us was seriously hurt. Collie, despite his dirty, disheveled appearance, was marvelously reassuring. After a long time, he headed back for Elk City and I staggered to a shower and bed.

Beth was in her deepfreeze configuration. I tried to reassure her. She wouldn't talk much. She cried a little. It ended up a cooler replay of our last argument. I didn't know what the hell I could say or do. She had realized I was missing, Collie was missing, and something exceedingly bad might be happening. Her old terror of Sylvester had reactivated, in spades. Now she was blaming me, it seemed—or, at best, staying frozen as a self-defense against a bad case of yammering hysteria.

It hadn't helped matters before dawn today when I struggled out of exhausted sleep to find her silently dressing, getting ready to leave the cabin.

"Whassis?" I asked, sitting up in bed and becoming aware of pain thresholds.

"I've got to go somewhere," she said.

"*Now?*"

"Yes."

"Where?"

She didn't answer.

"Where?" I repeated.

"Tell you later." She came to the bed, whisked cool lips across my nose, and got out of there.

I had sworn to myself a hundred times that I would never, *ever*, try to invade her control of her own life. She was an independent lass, and treasured her autonomy. She had done stuff like this to me once or twice before. Correction: she had done stuff like this in my awareness before. I had to teach myself not to think of her independence as something *being done* to *me*.

But I was depressed about it. My disappearance last night, brief as it had been, had clearly shocked and dismayed her. I didn't know where she had gone, what she was doing now, and my insecurities about our relationship galloped.

The waiter came back with a fresh pot of coffee. A few more guests began to appear. Collie poured fresh cups for both of us.

"You might as well know," he said then. "Your cop friend's body has been found."

I jerked. "Lassiter?"

He nodded, morose. "Kids out camping found him. Got back to town two or three hours ago, reported it to Hamm. I went out. Looked like a wolf or a bear or something dug him out of a shallow grave. Lassiter, all right. Shot. Rifle or handgun. I'm betting handgun."

"Who?" I asked, assimilating the shock.

"Who else? It reeks of an execution-style murder. There were stab wounds in the back, and a lot of bleeding. But unless a post proves the aorta was severed or something, the gunshot wound was what finished him. Neat. One shot. Behind the ear."

"*Why?*"

"I've been thinking about that. Maybe Lassiter knew something. Or maybe Lassiter was one of the few people who had spent some time around the new, redesigned Sylvester face job."

I made a logical jump. "What about that woman at the lab? You don't suppose *she*—"

"If she was working with Sylvester, she might be in a shallow grave somewhere, too."

We looked at each other.

"So," Collie said, "two eyewitnesses cold. Which might have left only you."

"Hell! A lot of people must have seen him around!"

"Sure. But they might have been the only two who spent any

time with him—might really provide a better description to our artist. And you're a trained observer. Well, a somewhat trained observer, anyhow. At least somebody who could look at him in a lineup and say, 'Yep, that's him, that's definitely our guy.'"

I leaned back. "God. Lassiter. Dead."

Collie's eyes narrowed. "It's not like you loved the guy."

"I was thinking of his brother."

"Oh. Yeah. Hamm was going to look him up. Nice guy, at least compared to the dead one, according to Hamm. Dumb but okay."

"A nice, sort of dumb guy," I said sadly. "Right."

He lifted his coffee cup. "I'll make reports. I've got an idea they'll recall me."

For some reason the idea of his departure alarmed me. "You'll at least stay through the rest of the tournament."

He shrugged. "I'm not that big on tennis. And you're clear now."

"Hell. Hang around."

"Brad." He leaned forward. "Don't get addicted to Sylvester."

"What the hell do you mean by that?"

"He's gone. He's definitely gone. It's *over*. Get on with things. There's no need for me to stay and there's no reason you need me."

I studied his face. "Right."

"You've done some help for us here. You'll probably get a nice letter about it."

"Tell them to send money, Collie, okay?"

He turned. I followed his gaze and saw Beth coming out of the building. She looked pretty in her spring dress, and she was frowning with determination.

Collie stood. "Talk at you later."

"What's your hurry?"

"She doesn't like me, much. I can't blame her, but I'm not in the mood to be frowned at. See you." He left the table, giving Beth a big, phony grin and a jaunty wave.

She came over to the table and sat down, a small frown still knitting her eyebrows. "Is there coffee?"

"Sure." I handed her one of the extra cups, and poured for her.

She added some creamer, looked out across the deck toward the woods and mountains, touched fingertips through her hair. "I've made some decisions, Brad."

I think right then I knew what was coming. "Oh?" That was all I said.

She kept looking at the mountains. "It's beautiful here. You're going to stay, aren't you?"

"I want to, Beth. Yes."

She nodded. "I needed to be alone and think this morning. I've been driving around. It *is* beautiful. It's your kind of place. You should stay. The lawsuits can be worked out. With the tournament a big success, your creditors will back off and wait and see awhile. You'll have some breathing room."

"And with you in court for us—" I began.

"No," she said, and looked at me for the first time. The pain was clear in her bright eyes.

"Meaning what?" I asked. Not wanting to know.

"My work is in California. This whole thing here—your deceiving me about all the reasons you came here in the first place, and then Sylvester showing up—and last night, realizing you were missing and thinking you were dead—" She stopped, shuddering. "I can't do this, Brad."

"This was a once in a lifetime operation," I argued. "I'll probably never be asked to help out again. And Sylvester is gone—"

"No," she said, cutting me off. "I'm going home, Brad. Back to California. To my work."

We stared at each other.

"We can work something out," I said.

She smiled, but there was no humor in it whatsoever.

"We *can*," I insisted.

Her coffee cup rattled in the saucer. She got up abruptly. "We'll talk more later . . . okay?" Then she gave me a really brilliant smile, but her eyes glistened.

For the next couple of hours I attended to lodge and tournament business with all the concentration and feeling of a robot.

This could not be happening, I thought. I could not be losing Beth Miles. There had to be some way to work things out. She had to be made to understand my kind of life. Sure, she could work in California, but people conducted cross-country relationships, didn't they? If people wanted something badly enough they could find adequate compromises, couldn't they? We couldn't just . . . *lose each other* . . . could we?

The spectators started to arrive. Ted appeared with Karyn, and seemed better today, with a hint of the old glint in his eye. Avery told me everything was no problem. I was headed for the courts when a familiar but unexpected figure—large, lumbering, in sweatshirt and bib overalls—approached me.

"Buster," I said, surprised. "What are you doing here?"

Buster Lassiter swayed back and forth. His eyes were wet. "My bud. He's dead."

"Buster, I just heard. I'm really sorry."

"Somebody shot him!"

"I know. I heard that too."

"I know a lot of people didn't like him, but he wasn't that bad a man!"

"Sure, Buster." I pointed to a bench among the shrubbery. "Hey, let's sit down."

He started to cry. "It was the war. He wasn't all that bad before. They . . . done stuff to him. I've always tried to take care of him. Like Momma would want. I just couldn't do it good, like she could of."

"Buster, it wasn't your fault."

The tears dripped off his chin. I don't know why it is more affecting when a big, powerful man weeps. The fat on his arms and chest trembled and he started making snuffing noises through his nose. "He didn't deserve this. I mean, he didn't kill that foreman over here. All he done was bury the body—hide it. He told me that his own self."

Our tournament crowd was even bigger today. We got started a little late with Pat Cash playing Jimmy Connors on center court and the semis of the mixed doubles getting under way on 11. Avery Whitney, a sun-kissed, largely bare-skinned Melody with him, got me aside long enough to report that two of our major bank creditors were among the spectators.

"I gave them comp passes," Avery added, fixing me with his good eye as if daring me to criticize the decision.

"No problem," I shot back.

"They have a good time and see all this crowd," he told me, evidently assuming I had lost some brain cells during Sylvester's attack, "they'll go mighty slow on pressing us for payments on principal."

"We can hope," I agreed.

"Sure, boy. I figure we got a fighting chance now."

"We?" I echoed.

He rolled his cock-eye at me. "Well, you dang fool, you don't think after *this* experience that you can run this place without my help, do you?"

"Avery, I don't see how we can afford you."

"I'll tell you what. We can talk about that. For right now lemme put it to you this way. I would sure like to stick around awhile and help make sure you guys don't screw everything up around here, now that I got it on the road to recovery."

I grinned at him. "We'll take it under consideration."

He exhaled explosively through his nose. "You are some kind of goofus if you even *think* about trying to do without me." Shaking his head in disbelief, he looked at Melody and immediately brightened. Putting his arm around her slender waist, he gave her a friendly stroke on the flank. "Come on, sweetness. Let's check the parking lot and then disappear for an hour."

Melody blushed with furious pleasure "*Avery!*"

He shrugged and started to walk away. Melody paused perhaps two seconds. "Bye!" she murmured, and danced after him.

The day's matches were great. Cash finally bested Connors in three nice sets, 4–6, 7–5, 7–6 (19–17), and Tim Mayotte, who had taken Terry Carpoman to the cleaners the evening before, gave Ivan Lendl all he wanted before going down by identical scores of 6–4, 6–4. Some of the amateur and guest mixed doubles were still going on late in the day when Fred Skurlock appeared, scowling as usual.

"Still no sign of anything new at the lab," he told me. "I agree with your friend Davis. It looks like they've cleared out. Including Sylvester."

"We almost had him," I said. "Twice."

Skurlock cocked his head. "*He* almost had *you* the same number of times."

I ignored that. "Collie said Lassiter's death looked like an execution."

"I can't argue with that conclusion. Professional. We're all thinking Sylvester again, until something else is proved."

I waited while some guests strolled by our position on the brick walk between courts and lodge. Then I asked, "What now for you?"

"Stay around. Watch. Help with the interviews and search out there on the side of the mountain. If those lost papers are still inside someplace, we'll find them. Tomorrow or the day after, we start peeling off metal wall panels."

Skurlock rummaged around and found a thin cigar in the pocket of his nylon jacket. "I'm seeing the DA over in Tripptown tonight. After what that other Lassiter brother told you, and then what he gave Hamm in a sworn statement, it looks to me like they don't have an excuse in the world to badger your friend Treacher any more."

"Llewellen is trying to avoid political embarrassment, from what I heard."

Skurlock lit the cigar with a house match cupped in big, capable hands. Smoke billowed. "Yeah. Well. From what I've seen, he's suffered quite enough in this thing. Also, your friend Davis filled me in a little on what Treacher did for you over there in Yugoslavia a couple of years ago. I think it's time some people got off his back."

I studied Skurlock's craggy face. "A man could get himself in trouble, interfering in a local matter."

His eyebrows shot up in surprise. "No, all I'm going to do is share my viewpoint with him. I'm not going to suggest anything. I plan to be very careful about that, and"—he pulled a tiny microcassette tape machine from his pocket—"I'll have this going just to make sure nobody can ever allege I did more than have a nice, casual conversation with him."

"I'll be interested to know how it comes out."

"Um. Me too."

In the evening we had a dinner-dance in the ballroom, and Avery Whitney had managed to come up with a six-piece orchestra of college kids from Bozeman who not only could read music, but knew how to play the right notes. Not a keyboard in a carload. They were so good that even Ted Treacher seemed to perk up, dancing a few of the numbers with an obviously adoring Karyn.

"You're good for him," I told her once late in the evening when it was our turn together on the floor.

"If those charges can be dismissed—"

"I think they will be, Karyn."

"And all the lawsuits over money?"

"Karyn—oops, sorry—we've made a showing this weekend. The creditors can't be getting any more pressure from Allen Industries or anywhere else. We're behind. God, are we behind. But most creditors would rather wait awhile longer in hopes of full payment with interest, rather than pressing a lawsuit sure to guarantee our going into Chapter Eleven."

She nodded, her hair tickling my ear. "Will Ted have to be here for every bit of it in the next few weeks?"

That surprised me. "We'll have to know where he is, in case a question comes up that we can't answer."

"You say 'we.' You and Beth?"

I swallowed thickly. "I don't speak for Beth. I meant Avery and me."

"You're staying, then."

"Yes."

"Good," she said with genuine satisfaction. "Because I want to get Ted out of here for a few weeks."

"Where?"

"San Francisco for a start, I think. Then San Diego, and then maybe Hawaii. And hell, maybe Tahiti or someplace like that. Mostly warm places. Nice places. Beaches. Sun and sand and tequila sunrises. Where he can have his arm checked as necessary, and can be found by telephone if you have to talk to him. But where he isn't constantly reminded to worry about all this horseshit."

"Take him away from the horseshit. Right." I liked the idea.

"And *you* can worry about all the horseshit."

"It sounds good. Have you told him your plans yet?"

"Not yet. I thought I'd get all the tickets first and then just issue his traveling orders."

"You, lady, are a wonderment and a pleasure."

"Yeah. I sure am grand, all right. Let's stop, Brad. You're too good a dancer. I'm getting dizzy."

I danced with Beth for a while then. She was quiet, remote. I didn't force things. I had the sense of everything coming to a point of termination or change. My insides cramped with fear about which of these options was turning over in her head.

thirty-six

In the night I awoke from a bad dream and found Beth standing, a shadowy nude, in the middle of the living room. A cigarette glowed.

I put my arms around her from behind. "You don't smoke anymore, remember?"

"Oh, bullshit, Brad Smith, don't boss me around."

Although she felt sleek and firm and wonderful, I released her. "Still mad?"

"I'm not mad." She sounded very remote.

I turned her to face me. She looked so pretty and lithe and sexy she made my throat ache. "You could have fooled me," I told her.

She took a deep, ragged breath. "I was going to tell you in the morning. I'll just have to go ahead and tell you now."

"Tell me what?" I said. I knew. Everything about her had already told me. But a part of me hoped desperately that if I just played stupid enough—just absolutely refused to face reality—maybe something would change.

She said, "I'm leaving tomorrow."

"Oh, Beth."

She turned away from me again, an ivory statue in the dimness. "I've been away long enough. I have cases pending down there."

"Why can't you establish a practice in Missoula or Helena or someplace like that? You could commute to Denver and everything else."

"I just can't do it, Brad. I can't live in fear. I can share you with tennis and your writing and even with a resort like this. But I can't share you with . . . them."

I heard myself say, "I could quit. Once and for all." Only as I said it did I realize the extent of my despair at the prospect of losing her. "I *could*," I added, insisting.

She turned and put warm palms to my cheeks. "And be miserable? You can no more do that than I can change who I am."

"We'll work it out some other way, then," I said. "I mean, just because you're going back, that isn't the end."

"Right," she said. Tears glistened in her eyes and spilled down her cheeks. "Right."

So she left in the morning, driving her rented car, refusing to let me take her to Missoula because she hated airport partings. I stood in the front lot and waved to her, and then her car went around the driveway curve into the woods, and she was gone.

In the afternoon Karyn gave Pam Shriver a good tussle in the women's exhibition, and then the tournament concluded with Lendl beating Cash in three sets, 2–6, 6–2, 6–4. Lynette Jordan showed up, bubbling over with the news that she now had a job with the Denver *Post*. We got the crowds out of there and things settled down to an almost eerie quiet in the evening, and while Avery Whitney and some of his helpers counted the money, I had a visit with Ted and Karyn.

Karyn announced her plans to take Ted away at the end of the week.

Ted looked up, momentarily interested, but lapsed at once. "I can't allow that. I have to look for a buyer for this place."

"There isn't going to be a buyer," Karyn replied calmly. "Brad is going to run it while we're gone, and Mr. Whitney is going to be the manager."

"There's no money. All the debts and lawsuits—"

"*They* don't want to give up, Ted. Why should you? Just be quiet. Assuming the criminal charges will be dismissed, we'll leave

Friday. We'll have some fun and then you can come back ready to take charge again."

Miserable, he twisted his hands together. "You have to get back to the pro circuit. You don't have time for this."

"Be quiet, Ted," Karyn repeated.

"I'm no good for anybody—"

"Ted. Be quiet."

"Just because the tournament was a success—"

"Ted. Be *quiet*."

He looked up at her. Her expression combined good humor and her tremendous, stubborn determination, and a shiningly transparent love.

Slowly he grinned. "Yes, ma'am."

Cleanup crews began to get our grounds back in order. The bleachers started coming down under a swarm of laborers. Our real estate man showed us three purchase contracts on condominium units. We got sued by a plumbing company that said we owed them four thousand dollars.

Ivan Lendl stayed over a day. We played golf. He lost a ball in the woods on Number 8. I got lucky and took him for four dollars.